Praise for *Standoff*

"Bradley has done it again with her unique brand of mystery and intrigue, penning another gripping tale of greed and betrayal, as well as redemption and hope. Brimming with action, romance, and page-turning thrills, *Standoff* will hook readers. What a fantastic start to a brand-new series!"

Elizabeth Goddard, award-winning author of the Uncommon Justice series

"An explosive start to a brand-new series by Patricia Bradley that suspense lovers won't want to miss. Full of family secrets, a mysterious old flame, and murder."

Lisa Harris, bestselling author of the Nikki Boyd series

"With a plot as twisting as the villain's schemes, Patricia Bradley's *Standoff* spins a tale that will keep the reader racing through the pages and wondering 'Who is the killer?' until the thrilling conclusion."

Lynn H. Blackburn, author of the Dive Team Investigations series

"Patricia Bradley's latest release, *Standoff*, is an action-packed Christian suspense novel. Patricia Bradley is an amazing romantic suspense writer. The whole novel was well-written and engaging from beginning to end."

Urban Lit Magazine

"My first ever Bradley book, and I very much enjoyed it! I really wish that I could give it more than 5 stars. Her style of writing is astounding! I'm a fan for life."

Interviews & Reviews

"*Standoff* is an engaging and suspenseful read that you won't be able to put down! If you love romantic suspense, this one definitely needs to be on your to-read list!"

Bookworm Banquet

"Patricia Bradley knocks it … tall-
ment of her new series! Tv … and
suspense galore keep reade … ntil
the very last page."

…d-Life

Books by Patricia Bradley

Logan Point Series

Shadows of the Past

A Promise to Protect

Gone Without a Trace

Silence in the Dark

Memphis Cold Case Novels

Justice Delayed

Justice Buried

Justice Betrayed

Justice Delivered

Natchez Trace Park Rangers

Standoff

Obsession

NATCHEZ TRACE 2 PARK RANGERS

OBSESSION

PATRICIA BRADLEY

Revell
a division of Baker Publishing Group
Grand Rapids, Michigan

Published by Revell
a division of Baker Publishing Group
PO Box 6287, Grand Rapids, MI 49516-6287
www.revellbooks.com

Printed in the United States of America

Library of Congress Cataloging-in-Publication Data
Names: Bradley, Patricia, 1945- author.
Title: Obsession / Patricia Bradley.
Description: Grand Rapids, Michigan : Revell, a division of Baker Publishing Group, [2021] | Series: Natchez Trace Park Rangers
Identifiers: LCCN 2020018614 | ISBN 9780800735746 (paperback) | ISBN 9780800739621 (hardcover)
Subjects: GSAFD: Suspense fiction. | Mystery fiction. | Christian fiction.
Classification: LCC PS3602.R34275 O28 2021 | DDC 813/.6—dc23

LC record available at https://lccn.loc.gov/2020018614

21 22 23 24 25 26 27 7 6 5 4 3 2 1

To Jesus, my Lord and Savior,
who walks with me
on the writing journey.

1

The January warm spell had definitely ended in South Mississippi. Emma Winters zipped her National Park Service jacket against the biting north wind as she hiked the quarter mile from the gate to the Mount Locust Visitor Center on the Natchez Trace. A hike that wouldn't have been necessary if she hadn't forgotten the gate key. Or the folder she needed to finish a report due by midnight.

Forgetting things wasn't like her, but her mother's resistance to tracking down her brother had Emma off-center. Her cell phone broke the silence, and she checked her caller ID. She wasn't sure she was ready for her mother's reaction to the email she'd sent and let two more rings go by. In fact, she was tempted to not answer her mother's call at all because she just didn't want to hear her objections. But just before it went to voicemail, Emma punched the answer button. "Hello," she said, forcing a cheery note in her voice.

"Oh, good, I caught you," her mother said. "I received the flyer you emailed."

"And? What did you think?"

"Honey, I think you'll get a lot of nutcases if you send it out. Like you did before when you offered money for information on Ryan."

"But someone might know some—"

"Your brother's choices in life are his. I hate to see you throw good money after bad."

"It's my money," she muttered. As each year passed, finding her twin brother pressed deeper into her heart, but she should have known her mother would kick up about the flyer. If she knew the whole story . . .

"What are you doing? You're breaking up."

"Walking to my office."

"You're . . . Mount Locust . . . night?"

"Mom, we have a bad connection," she said. "I'll call you when I get home."

Emma ended the call and shrugged off the sense of failure that seeped into every fiber of her body whenever she thought of Ryan. But it wasn't so easily shrugged off. She glanced toward the sky just as a pale sliver of moon broke through the clouds, giving off enough light to cast eerie shadows on the ground.

A shiver ran over her body. Maybe next time she would ask someone to come with her. Or bring a gun. Not likely. She'd never desired to be a law enforcement ranger and was quite satisfied being on the interpretive side of the National Park Service.

In spite of that, the hair on the back of her neck rose as she approached the stone and wood building. *Come on. Don't get all spooked.* She worked here, and Mount Locust was as familiar as the backyard where she'd grown up. And it wasn't like being here after dark was something new. From November until the days got longer, she locked up every day in the dark. Besides, she'd never been afraid of the dark. Even so, she scanned the area, trying to shake the sense she wasn't alone.

Nothing moved as she scanned the grounds, her gaze stopping at the lighted maintenance building a quarter mile away and visible through the bare trees before moving to the tractor shed a few yards away. Probably should check on the ground penetrating radar machine that had arrived earlier today. Tomorrow she was supposed to begin the preliminary mapping of the historic quarters and the adjoining cemetery.

She'd left word for the new district law enforcement ranger on the Natchez Trace to have someone swing by every few hours to check for trespassers. Now would be a good time for a ranger to arrive . . . as long as it wasn't Samuel Ryker. Emma hadn't seen her once-upon-a-time fiancé since he returned to Natchez and had avoided talking directly to him on the call for assistance. But eventually she would have to face him, and she might as well make peace with it.

Something rustled to her right. Emma froze with her hand on the doorknob. She turned just as a bottle rolled from the open passageway separating the office from the restrooms.

"Who's there?" She tried for commanding, but the tremor in her voice destroyed the effect.

A bedraggled gray-and-white tabby walked around the corner and sat down, its doleful stare almost as pitiful as its meow. Emma released the breath caught in her chest and leaned against the door. "Where did you come from?"

The cat couldn't be over three or four months old. It stretched and then rubbed against her leg, and Emma stooped to pick it up. She could count the poor thing's ribs. With it still in her arms, she turned and unlocked the door. There was half of a roast beef sandwich in the mini refrigerator she'd recently purchased so she could eat at her desk when she worked alone at the visitor center. Maybe the cat could eat the meat.

As she bent to retrieve the beef, Emma spotted the file she'd come for. Beside it, the landline blinked with a message. She would feed the cat first, then listen to the voicemail. Emma shredded the meat and set it on the floor. The cat sniffed the food, then tore into it, making little growling noises as it ate. When it finished, the cat sat down and looked up at Emma as if to say, "Where's the rest?"

"That's all I have," she said. Funny how having another living thing with her made the place seem less scary. "I'll bring you something in the morning—how about that?" she asked and punched the play button on the phone. "Or maybe I'll take you home with me tonight."

The cat wound around her ankles as a voice that belonged on the radio echoed in the empty room.

"Emma, where are you? You're not answering your cell phone. Give me a call before you begin your excavation."

She groaned. Corey Chandler would be the death of her. Not the attorney exactly, but his client, whoever that might be. Corey wouldn't tell who objected to the excavation of the slave quarters and the survey of the cemetery. Emma straightened her shoulders. It would take more than a phone call to stop the project. Besides, it wasn't like she was going to dig up the cemetery. That was the purpose of the GPR machine—to locate and determine once and for all the number of graves there.

Conflicting reports had abounded for years that bodies had been missed in the research project conducted in 2000, and that bothered Emma. Her goal was to find every grave and make sure each person received the dignity and recognition that had eluded them in life.

It was hard to understand why anyone objected to the research project anyway, but she didn't have time to worry about Corey's client tonight. "Come on, Suzy," she said, deciding the tabby was female, and then grabbed the folder and stuffed it in her backpack.

Suzy shot out the door, and Emma followed suit, locking it behind her. A screeching sound jerked her attention to her right, and she fisted her hands. Another gust of wind whistled through the trees, followed by the screeching sound again, and she identified the source. A branch scraping against the window on the side of the building. Adrenaline left as fast as it had come.

What was wrong with her tonight? If Brooke Danvers were here, she would have a ball teasing Emma. But Emma was the first to admit she wasn't as brave as her best friend. A tree frog seemed to agree as he serenaded her with his song and then was joined with a chorus of other males, each one vying to outdo the other. Poor things were singing for nothing. The last two weeks of warm weather had them confused and singing to the female frogs who were not in the mood to answer them in the middle of January.

Another sound overrode the frogs, and Emma cocked her head toward it. Someone was operating machinery. Had the maintenance supervisor come back after supper and started some of the road equipment? She doubted it, since the noise appeared to come from the inn area, not the tractor shed or the maintenance building.

Maybe it was those kids she'd run off earlier. Just before closing time, she'd caught three teenage boys pulling up the flags she'd staked out where the slave cabins used to be. Had they come back and hot-wired one of the backhoes?

"Stay here," she said, as if the cat would. After she set the backpack beside the door, she flipped on her flashlight and walked up the brick path that led to the inn, which was really just a four-room log cabin with a dogtrot in the middle for ventilation in the summer. If it was the teenagers, this time she would get names and call the parents.

Instead of remaining behind, Suzy followed her to the deserted log structure, and they climbed the steps together. Emma walked through the dogtrot to the back porch and cocked her ear again. The sound had quit. She swept the light toward the maintenance building. The equipment looked untouched. Then she flashed the light against the trees, revealing only stark trunks and bare limbs except for the occasional live oak.

Wait. On the other side of the trees in the slave cemetery, the light revealed a yellow backhoe. Yep. Had to be those kids, since the maintenance supervisor wouldn't have moved the equipment. While she wasn't afraid of the teenagers, there was such a thing as common sense, so she checked her cell phone for service. One bar and it looked iffy.

She would try 911 anyway and let whomever the dispatcher sent deal with the boys. Preferably anyone but Sam.

When the operator answered, Emma could only make out a couple of words. She identified herself and asked for a patrol ranger to come to Mount Locust, hoping the operator understood the call.

When the operator didn't respond, she checked her phone again. The call had dropped. She'd have to walk either to her office or the visitor center for better reception.

A rifle report split the night air as Emma hopped off the porch. She froze as a bullet splintered the wooden post where she'd just stood. Then she dove for the ground and scrambled under the house. Her heart stuttered in her chest as another report sent a bullet kicking up dirt a few yards from her hiding place.

Why was someone trying to kill her?

Like that mattered at this moment. She had to move or be trapped in the crawl space under the house. Frantically she looked for the cat. If it had any sense at all, it had high-tailed it back to the visitor center.

Emma scanned the area, looking for a way to escape. She couldn't go back the way she'd come—it was too open—but there was ground cover from the side of the house to the edge of the woods only thirty feet away. Emma belly-crawled to the nearest tree, scraping her hand on a rock.

A dry twig snapped to her left.

Emma hoisted the rock and flung it away from her before she darted in the opposite direction toward the tractor shed. Another shot rang out, and the bullet embedded in a nearby tree.

With her heart exploding in her chest, she ducked under a live oak limb that dipped down to the ground and pressed against the huge trunk. Her lungs screamed for air. Heavy footsteps stomped through the dead leaves, and she pressed closer to the trunk, biting back a cry as the bark gouged her back.

A faint siren reached her ears. The 911 operator had understood her!

The footsteps halted. The shooter had heard it as well. But where was he? She dared not peer around the tree and remained absolutely still, surprised that he couldn't hear the pounding of her heart. Seconds later, footsteps retreated toward the service road. Then a motor roared to life, and the car sped away.

Emma's knees buckled, and she braced against the tree, her fingers shaking as she dialed 911 again.

2

Sam Ryker wheeled the Ford Interceptor off the Trace into the Mount Locust entrance. His heart had almost stopped when the 911 operator contacted him. If anything had happened to Emma . . .

His headlights flashed across an older-model Toyota pickup parked in front of the locked gate to the visitor center. He recognized the truck that had been her brother's back in the day. Emma must have walked from the gate to the building, but why? Surely she had a key to the gate. He turned right on the road that led to the well-lit maintenance building and beyond it, the tractor shed. Behind him, his field ranger, Clayton Bradshaw, made the same turn.

Sam's radio crackled to life.

"Ranger Winters indicated the suspect is escaping on Chamberlain Road," the dispatcher said.

Sam released the breath trapped in his chest. If Emma had called in the report, at least the suspect didn't have her. "You want to take that, Clayton?" he asked, speaking into his radio. "I'll check on Emma and then provide backup."

"Roger," Clayton said. Seconds later his junior officer's SUV reversed direction and sped toward the other side of the entrance.

Since Emma would not be happy to see him, he probably

should have gone after the car and let Clayton handle Emma. And he would have, but Clayton was more familiar with the roads around Mount Locust.

Sam scanned the woods, catching the beam of a flashlight. He scrambled out of the Interceptor and flipped the strap off his service semiautomatic. A figure ran toward him, but he couldn't make out whether it was male or female. "Halt! And drop your light!"

"Sam, it's me! Don't shoot!"

Emma. He would know her voice anywhere, even after ten years. "Anyone with you?"

Still running, she dropped the beam of the flashlight to the ground. "I'm alone."

The crack in Emma's voice raised his worry level. She'd never been afraid of anything, and if she was scared, something bad had happened. Sam holstered his gun as she barreled into his chest. Automatically, he wrapped his arms around her, feeling her body tremble. "Are you hurt?"

Emma shook her head. "H-he missed when he shot at me."

His arms tightened around her. "Someone fired at you?" No wonder she was shaking.

She pulled away from his embrace.

"Uh, sorry." She wrapped her arms around her waist. "I shouldn't have crashed into you like that."

"No problem."

Her stiff, boardlike stance conveyed how uncomfortable she was. That made two of them. Sam made a conscious effort to relax. Even though they worked different sides of the National Park Service, with Emma working as an interpretive ranger at Mount Locust and him the district law enforcement ranger, they would run into each other fairly often. No need to make it harder than it had to be. "Why'd you leave your truck at the gate?"

"I forgot the key to the lock."

Sam had never known Emma to be forgetful. The overhead

lights barely reached the area, but they were strong enough for her full lips and heart-shaped face to capture his attention. He gulped. Staring at her had been the wrong thing to do and only reminded him of what he'd lost.

In spite of that, he couldn't look away. Were her eyes as green as he remembered? *Don't go there.* The low lighting didn't allow him to see that anyway. As if she'd read his thoughts, Emma dropped her gaze to the ground, her arms still wrapped across her body as if to ward him off. "What were you doing here this late? And by yourself?"

Her head snapped up. "Excuse me? Don't use that tone of voice with me. And I hardly think 9:00 p.m. qualifies as late."

"If someone was shooting at you, you could've been killed!" He swept his hand around the area. "This place is deserted at night. You of all people should know the Trace isn't always safe after dark."

"Who do you think closes up every night? And there's no *if*—someone fired at me!"

So much for hoping they could avoid fireworks. Little Miss Independent hadn't changed one whit, still packed with dynamite in her five-foot-three frame. Sam raked his fingers through his hair as another SUV with flashing blue lights pulled into Mount Locust then turned on the same road Clayton had taken. Sam caught the logo on the side of the door when it rounded the curve. He spoke into his mic. "Clayton, you have an Adams County deputy on your tail for backup. I'm staying here with Ranger Winters."

"Roger that," Clayton said.

Sam turned to the woman he'd planned to marry at one time. "Tell me what happened."

She stared at him briefly, hurt in her eyes, then she toed her sandal in the dirt, unearthing a rock. "I'm not sure. After dinner I realized I'd left a report here and came back to retrieve it."

Which explained why she wasn't in uniform. "So, you forgot the gate key and walked to the visitor center."

"Yes. Then as I was locking up, I heard a backhoe. Thought it might be the maintenance supervisor or even the teenagers that had been messing around earlier."

He listened as she filled him in about the teenage boys she'd caught around the slave cemetery and then the shots fired. He doubted the boys would have shot at her.

"The bullet plowed into the post where I'd been standing," Emma said.

"And you didn't see anyone?"

She shook her head. "But I think it was a man."

"Why's that?"

"The way he tromped through the woods. I think it was just one person, and it sounded like someone heavier than the boys who were here earlier."

He rubbed his forehead. "Explain to me why you decided to investigate this noise? Most people would have called 911 and let us handle it."

Tension crackled between them as her eyes narrowed. Emma opened her mouth and then closed it. He thought she might explode, but instead she blew out a hard breath.

"Like I said, I thought it was the maintenance supervisor at first," she said, her voice in control mode, enunciating each word. "Then I thought it might be the teenagers, and I figured I could handle them since we'd talked earlier. Besides, it's not like I don't know this place inside and out. I could walk every path around here blindfolded."

He bet that was true. "Sorry, I didn't mean to insult you."

"Well, you did."

He needed to start over, instill a little confidence between them. "Are you up to walking to the inn? Maybe we can find that bullet."

Emma eyed him suspiciously. "Won't that contaminate the crime scene?"

"We'll go the long way around, through the gate to the visitor center, and then up to the inn." That way they wouldn't disturb anything in the wooded area between the tractor shed and the slave cemetery. "And could we start over? We seem to have gotten off to a rough start."

When she didn't shoot him down immediately, he stuck out his hand. "Hello, I'm District Ranger Samuel Ryker, and I apologize for being heavy-handed. I understand you've had a little problem here tonight, Ranger Winters."

Her mouth twitched. "I'd say it was more than a 'little' problem."

"Right."

Indecision played on her face, and then she took his hand, gripping it firmly. He hadn't expected the electricity that her touch brought. "Thank you, Ranger Winters, for being willing to start over."

"We can *try* starting over," she said dryly. "And you can call me Emma."

"Probably should stay with Ranger Winters for now," he said, swallowing a smile.

She saluted. "Why would anyone mess with the equipment, anyway, Mr. District Ranger?"

"They may have been trying to steal it."

She shook her head. "I don't think so. The vehicle I heard leaving didn't have a trailer attached to it."

"Good point. Why don't we check out the inn?"

They walked the gravel road in silence, their past hovering overhead like a storm cloud pregnant with water. Sam wasn't one to avoid a problem, especially with someone he would come in contact with on a regular basis. "Have you heard from Ryan?" he asked, breaking the quiet.

A small gasp came from Emma, and she stumbled. Sam grabbed for her, but she brushed his hand away. "I don't need your help." She lifted her chin. "And no, I haven't heard from my brother since the night you left him on his own."

Her accusation hit him like a 9mm slug. Bad question and even worse answer. How could one night have changed so many lives? He'd hoped her twin brother had been in contact with the family.

But he wasn't apologizing. Not again. His apology hadn't done any good ten years ago when Emma broke their engagement, and he doubted it'd do any good now. Not that Sam had anything to apologize for. Ryan had been a grown man, responsible for his own choices. But if what almost everyone believed at the time he disappeared was true, it shouldn't surprise Sam that Emma's brother hadn't contacted anyone.

"I know what you're thinking," she said. "But he didn't kill that girl."

3

Before Sam could respond, another siren drew his attention toward the road. A vehicle approached on the Trace from the north, lights flashing and siren blaring. It turned into Mount Locust and pulled up to the gate where they stood. He shaded his eyes against the glare from the headlights.

The driver doused his lights, and after killing the engine, a man climbed out of the vehicle. He was glad to see the Adams County sheriff. Sam's first order of business after he took over the district office had been to introduce himself to the Purple Heart recipient and first African American to be elected sheriff in Adams County since Reconstruction. Rawlings hitched his belt and then strode toward them. When he was close enough, Sam extended his hand. "Good to see you again, Sheriff, although I'm a little surprised."

The sheriff's hand gripped his. "I wasn't far away when I heard the call and thought you might need help. And just call me Nate. Still getting used to being called Sheriff."

Sam nodded. Rawlings, who was a good ten years older than Sam's thirty-one, had won the November election but had taken office only two weeks ago, moving from chief deputy to the top job. "Thanks for sending a deputy to back up Clayton."

"No problem." Nate's gaze slid to Emma and he smiled. "You okay?"

"Better than I was," she said with a shiver.

"Fill me in." He made no comment until she finished explaining what had happened. "Do you often come here after dark?"

"It's dark when I lock up," she said, her voice testy.

Nate palmed his hands. "Whoa!"

"I'm sorry," she said, making a face. "I didn't mean to snap, but I'm used to it being dark when I leave, so I didn't think anything about returning to pick up a file I needed."

Nate dipped his head. "I understand. So, unless someone was following you, they wouldn't have expected you to be here."

"No one followed me—I would have seen their headlights in my rearview mirror."

"Then it sounds like you may have interrupted something," the sheriff said.

"I think so too." Sam nodded toward the inn. "Ranger Winters here says one of the bullets splintered the post on the porch at the inn. We were taking the long way around so we wouldn't contaminate the crime scene. Want to join us?"

Nate's expression was noncommittal as he raised his hat and smoothed his short-cropped hair. "We don't have adequate light, but I don't see any harm in doing a preliminary look-see. Who knows, if they were operating the backhoe, they may have been burying a body."

The three of them walked past the visitor center, up the pathway, and then climbed the steps to the Mount Locust Inn. The restored four-room cabin was a favorite for modern-day visitors on the Trace, but it was hard for Sam to imagine the early 1800s when fifteen or twenty travelers might stop overnight at the inn and sleep on the front porch or the ground.

"This is where I was standing when someone fired at me," Emma said after they walked through the dogtrot to the back porch. Sam used his phone app to shine a light up and down the post she pointed to, stopping where the wood was splintered.

"The backhoe is over there." Emma flipped on her flashlight and pointed it toward the trees.

"Stay here with Emma. I'll check out the backhoe," Nate said as he unhooked his flashlight and set out for the machine.

"You didn't see anyone?" Sam asked.

"No," Emma said. "I only heard whoever it was."

A few minutes later, Nate returned. "It looks like someone was digging a hole when you interrupted them, but I didn't find evidence of anything they were burying."

Like a body. "Do you want to rig up lights and search the area?" Sam asked.

"No. I have to justify any overtime pay for my crime scene techs, and this doesn't warrant it," he said. "The evidence isn't going anywhere, so we'll wait until daylight. Otherwise we might blunder around here and destroy something. I'll get one of my deputies to secure the premises." The sheriff pressed the button on his mic. "Where are you, Trey?"

"On my way to Mount Locust."

Out of the corner of his eye, Sam could see Emma stiffen and jerk her head toward the Trace.

"You okay?" he asked quietly as the sheriff talked with his deputy.

She nodded curtly.

"Trey is on his way," Nate said, turning back to them. "And if you're ready, we'll head back to the gate."

"My field ranger can help with guarding the scene as well," Sam said, keeping an eye on Emma as she drummed her fingers against her leg, a sure sign she was nervous, at least it had been ten years ago.

Another transmission came in, and Nate stopped while they continued on. Sam turned to her. "Do you have a problem with Carter? Other than him being Sheriff Carter's son?"

"I never held who his father was against him. Trey has always taken up for Ryan." Her fingers stilled. "He might not be glad to see me, though. We dated a while back, and he's not happy just being friends."

"You dated Trey?" He'd figured Emma had left a string of broken hearts through the years, but he never dreamed the deputy would've been one of them. "I'm sure his dad wasn't too happy about that."

"I doubt he ever knew. Our former sheriff has Alzheimer's."

"I didn't know," Sam said. "Any particular reason for the breakup?"

"That isn't any of your business."

"It's my business if there's bad blood between the two of you."

"It's nothing like that. Between my job and finishing up my master's degree, I haven't had time for dating." She shrugged one shoulder. "I'm usually better at breaking off a relationship, anyway."

They had reached the low brick building that housed the visitor center, and she glanced past him toward her pickup. "I'm tired. I think I'll pick up my backpack and head on home."

"Not a good idea," he said. "Since I can't leave yet."

"I don't know what your leaving has to do with me."

He counted to ten to keep from snapping at her. "Now you sound like one of the heroines in a horror movie."

Emma frowned. "I don't know what you're talking about."

"You know, a serial killer is on the loose and the woman hears a noise in her basement and decides to check it out. The audience is yelling, 'Don't go!' as she creeps down the stairs . . ."

She rolled her eyes. "You're being ridiculous. There's no serial killer, and I'm not going down in a basement. Just going home."

He stared at her, not believing she didn't get it. "Someone just shot at you. We don't know if you were the target or just in the wrong place, but either way, you shouldn't be on the road alone."

"As far as I know, I don't have any enemies, so there's no reason for me to be the target. Someone was probably just trying to scare me so they could finish whatever they were doing."

"Indulge me. I shouldn't be much longer," he said.

Indecision played on her face. "Okay," she said. "But I'll wait in my truck."

A small but grudging victory. Emma was as exasperating now as she'd been years ago. But he had to hand it to her—she was gutsy. A lot of women would have folded after being shot at.

Emma was halfway to the gate when another SUV pulled into Mount Locust and a deputy climbed out and walked toward her. Had to be Trey Carter. He frowned as the chief deputy stopped to talk with Emma, then a minute later he turned and marched away.

"I see Trey made it," Nate said as he rejoined Sam. "Where is Emma going?"

"Her truck. She's waiting for me to follow her home."

"Good deal. I was afraid she would want to leave by herself."

They both turned as the chief deputy sauntered toward them. Back in high school, Trey had thought highly of himself, and judging by his swagger, he still did.

The deputy removed the toothpick hanging from his mouth and nodded to Sam. "I heard you'd taken the district ranger job," he said. "Came here all the way from Wyoming. Don't know that I would've traded that gig for Natchez."

"To each his own." Sam wasn't answering Trey's implied question of why. "Congratulations on making chief deputy."

For the briefest second, the muscle in Trey's jaw twitched, then he tipped his head. "Thanks. I expect to learn a lot working with the sheriff."

From the newspaper accounts Sam had read, Trey had come in a distant second in the November election. Sam turned to Nate. "What time in the morning do you want to meet here?"

"Eight too early?"

"Perfect," he replied. "I better catch up with Emma, or she'll leave me behind."

"You got that right," Trey said, narrowing his eyes as he looked past Sam to Emma's truck.

She was right—the chief deputy wasn't happy just being friends.

4

Sam Ryker. Emma's face burned at the way she'd run to him and wrapped her arms around his waist. It'd only been a gut reaction to being shot at. *Yeah, right. Keep telling yourself that.* She leaned her head back on the headrest. Did she really want to think about the only man she regretted breaking up with?

Thinking about Sam was better than letting the events of the last hour run through her mind in an endless loop. He did look good and had filled out from the beanpole he'd been back in high school and college. Yet there wasn't an ounce of fat around his waist.

Sam wasn't pretty-boy handsome like Trey Carter. More rugged with his square jaw and intense brown eyes. *Don't go there.* But it was hard not to. If her brother hadn't disappeared, she and Sam probably would have been married by now and had a couple of kids running around.

But no, Ryan had deserted her, and so had Sam, because that's what men did. *Really?* Okay. She'd been the one to return Sam's ring, but only to preempt him. And maybe she should have given him his ring in person instead of handing it over to his sister, but Emma had been furious with Sam for leaving Ryan at the Hideaway after he'd promised to stay with her brother. If she'd known he wasn't going to keep his promise, she would have stayed, even though the stress of Ryan's drinking had triggered a migraine.

Liar. That's not why you gave his ring back. Emma jerked her attention to where the three men stood. "Come on, Sam," she muttered, shoving thoughts of him away, but they bounced right back.

Ranger Winters. That's what he'd called her. She crossed her arms. He acted as though they had no history at all. Emma sat up abruptly and glanced toward the gate again to see if Sam was coming yet.

He had not moved. Why did she even need anyone to follow her home? Because Sam and Nate thought she was the shooter's target . . . or she had an enemy. That option was impossible. She wasn't the kind of woman who had enemies. Not even Trey. Breaking up with him had been a little messy . . . okay, so a lot messy. Even so, Trey would never shoot at her.

She shouldn't have dated him in the first place, not with him being Sheriff Carter's son, but he'd challenged her to not lump him in with his dad. She always was a sucker for a challenge. It'd been a big mistake.

Emma drummed her fingers on the steering wheel, wanting to get away from Mount Locust before Trey made another appearance. His "Hey, sweetheart" still irked her. She was not his sweetheart. Although the deputy's attention had been flattering—what woman wouldn't love being wooed by a six-two, broad-shouldered Adonis with abs of steel?

And at first, their relationship had been good, but it turned out he was more like his dad than he thought. It hadn't taken Trey long to change, and he gradually chipped away at everything about her—her clothes were too dull, she didn't wear enough makeup, and even her taste for classical music was boring. But when he griped about her being friends with Clayton Bradshaw, one of the law enforcement rangers on the Trace, she'd had enough. Clayton was like a brother.

Headlights flashed in the window, startling her. She hadn't seen Sam walk to his SUV. He pulled parallel with their driver's sides facing, and Emma lowered her window. "Are you ready?"

"Yes, ma'am."

Her conscience pinged. She wasn't usually this cranky with someone trying to help her, even though she didn't need his help. But maybe it was time to play nice. "Thanks for taking your time to escort me home," she said.

"Not a problem."

There was that distant edge to his voice again, but what did she expect? That he would just forget the past? She glanced toward the other vehicles. "I thought Trey was guarding Mount Locust tonight," she said as both SUVs pulled past them.

"Nate called in two other deputies. Something about Trey needing to check on his dad."

She nodded and turned the ignition key. The former sheriff was in an Alzheimer's unit in an assisted living facility. "Then I guess we're ready. Do you need my address, in case we get separated?"

"That's right. You probably don't live at home any longer."

"No. I'm renting an apartment in one of the older homes not far from downtown." She gave him the address.

"Want to give me your cell number as well?"

"Sure." Two seconds after she rattled it off, her phone rang.

"Now you have mine," he said. "I'll follow you."

Short and sweet. Short, anyway. Emma shifted into first gear and pulled out onto the Trace. Twenty minutes later she parked under a streetlight in front of the early 1900s converted home. After grabbing her backpack with the report, she climbed out of her truck. Sam had parked behind her and waited on the sidewalk. "You didn't have to get out," she said.

"It'd be kind of hard to check out your apartment if I don't," he said and turned toward the two-story house. "Nice. I've always loved these old houses."

She glanced toward the house. "I like it, and renting suits me. That way I can pick up and leave if I want to without having to get rid of a house. And you don't have to check out my place."

"Humor me," he said and guided her toward the steps to the door.

Emma tried the front door that opened into a common area, but the automatic lock had already kicked in. She fished her key out of her backpack.

"Is this door always locked?" he asked as she turned the key and pushed the door open.

"No, but both this door and the back door are set to lock from 6:00 p.m. until 6:00 a.m. Something that I usually forget."

"I think you should talk to your landlord about having it locked 24/7."

Probably wouldn't be a bad idea. "I'll bring it up at our next tenants' meeting."

She followed Sam inside the large two-story house that had been converted into five apartments, three upstairs and two downstairs. A hallway ran the length of the building, and they climbed the staircase on the right side. Once inside her apartment, she followed behind him as he checked out the rooms. "I told you there was no one here," she said when he finished. "But thanks for checking."

"No problem." He stopped at the front door. "By the way, what was going on at Mount Locust with Trey? Is he always that grouchy?"

"Did he say something?"

"Wasn't what he said, but how he said it."

"He didn't take our breakup well."

"I got that," he said. "Do you think he's the one who shot at you?"

"No . . . He wouldn't have known I would be at Mount Locust tonight. I didn't even know I would be until I didn't have this," she said, holding up the folder. "And that report is still waiting on me."

"Don't worry, I'm going. What time do you plan to leave in the morning?"

"I'm always at work by eight, but you don't have to escort me. I need to run by Walmart and get cat—" She slapped her forehead. "I can't believe I forgot the cat!"

He looked confused. "What are you talking about?"

"There was a stray cat at the visitor center, and I meant to bring it home." Maybe she should go back after it.

"How long has it been there?"

"I don't know. Tonight was the first time it came around. I gave it some beef from a leftover sandwich."

"It should be okay until morning, then," he said.

She started to argue with him, but did she want to make another trip to Mount Locust tonight? The cat might not even still be around. "I'll want to leave by seven fifteen at the latest," she said.

"I'll be here at seven ten." With a tip of his head, he walked out the door. Almost immediately, her doorbell rang. She opened the door.

"Yes?"

"I didn't hear you dead-bolt the lock."

"Sorry. I would have before I went to bed."

"Do you mind dead-bolting it now?"

"Yes, *Dad*."

His face flushed. "I want you to be safe."

She palmed her hands. "And I appreciate it. I'll lock the door as soon as I shut it."

Which she did and then folded her arms across her chest as his footsteps clumped down the stairs. Emma didn't remember Sam being so bossy. Or maybe overprotective was a better word. Bossy would fit Trey better. Not that he would ever admit to the description. Trey simply never thought he was wrong.

5

A quick glance at the clock told him it was near midnight. His fingers trembled as he laid the nine gerbera daisies on the table. Arranging flowers calmed him like nothing else. He definitely needed calming tonight.

Refocus. This arrangement was special. He'd chosen daisies because they were a symbol of purity and innocence. Nine because it was the number of forever love. Other than his mother, he'd only ever given three women this particular bouquet.

He arranged and rearranged the white flowers and still was not quite satisfied with the bouquet. Perhaps a different vase. After rummaging through his cabinets, he found the perfect container—an antique pitcher that had belonged to his mother. As the flower arrangement came together, he thought about the last daisies he'd given someone.

Kimberly Fisher.

He clenched his fist, and a bitter scent stung his nose. The delicate daisy lay crushed in his hand, ruined. No! He had to have nine white daisies for Emma. Unlike Kimberly, she would understand his message, that she would be his, now and forever. Grabbing his shears, he hurried to the greenhouse.

People who thought they knew him would be surprised to learn he was an avid plantsman, but he was close to so few people he needn't worry anyone would discover his secret. With a flip of the switch, light flooded a small room filled with seven different species of daisies. His passion, fueled by his mother's love of the flower. She'd been such a gentle soul. Innocent. Pure. Not once in the years since her death had he failed to take nine daisies to the cemetery on her birthday. He'd loved his mother and despised his father who still lived. It was his fault she was dead.

"The woman you marry must be like the daisy," his mother had always told him. "Pure and innocent."

He snipped a perfectly shaped gerbera. Emma wasn't like the others. But what if she turned him down? He brushed that thought aside. She loved him. He could tell by the way she smiled at him. The way her gaze lingered in his when they talked and the desire that burned in those eyes that were the color of emeralds. And then there were the messages she sent him on her Facebook page. Secret messages he decoded, telling him how much she loved him, and how scared that made her. Poor Emma . . . too afraid of her own emotions to stay with any man long. Except him. He understood her. Understood her fear. Understood she couldn't acknowledge her love for him just yet.

One day she would, though.

You believed that of the others.

But he hadn't met the others on his mother's birthday.

Five thirty a.m. came much too early after a restless night, and Emma hit the alarm off button. Why had she told Sam seven fifteen? Oh yeah, cat food. The cat was one reason she hadn't slept well. If she hadn't been worrying about it, she'd been trying to figure out who had shot at her. Maybe she would just lay here for a minute . . .

Her backup 6:00 a.m. alarm jerked her awake, and she stumbled out of bed. Should have gotten up the first time. An hour and ten minutes didn't give her enough time for her usual run. After a quick bowl of cereal and a shower, she threw on her uniform and rushed out the door, almost stumbling over a white ceramic pitcher with gerbera daisies.

She gasped and glanced both ways, but the long hallway that separated her apartment and the one across from hers was empty. Who could have sent her favorite flower and why? Kneeling, she plucked the card that had her name printed in block letters.

Her fingers trembled as she opened it. *Life is short. Enjoy each day.* No signature, and the words were hand-printed like her name. A shiver rippled through Emma as she stared at the flowers, unsure what to do. No one had ever sent her daisies before. Trey had sent roses once, but he'd signed the card.

She glanced down the hallway at the other two apartments on the second floor; the one across the hall mirrored hers, the other was an efficiency at the end. Just then the door across the hall opened, and her neighbor Gregory Hart stepped out, dressed for his job at City Hall. "Good morning," he said, barely pausing as he strode to the stairs. "Nice flowers."

She had to look up to meet his gaze. Greg was a couple of years older than Emma, and at times she'd felt vibes that he had more than a passing interest in her.

"You didn't happen to see who delivered them, did you?"

"No." He shifted his briefcase to his other hand. His neck turned a blotchy red, but he was so shy the redness happened almost every time she spoke to him. "But I do know they weren't there when I came back from my run at six."

At least that narrowed the timeline. "Maybe I should call the sheriff."

"I don't understand." His brows lowered into a frown. "You want to call the law because someone sent you flowers? It's probably a secret admirer—someone who's too shy to let you know."

Emma didn't realize she'd said that out loud. "I'm probably overreacting."

"I think you are." The redness crept from his neck to his face. "You are very pretty, after all. Just enjoy them." He gave her a timid smile before checking his watch. "Well . . . have a good day," he said and hurried down the stairs.

That was the most conversation she'd had with Gregory since he'd moved in five months ago, and he definitely thought she was overreacting. But what if the person who sent the flowers was the one who shot at her last night?

Not wanting to add her fingerprints to the vase, she grabbed a drying cloth from the kitchen and gingerly carried the flowers inside, the pungent scent tickling her nose. It probably meant nothing, but she would tell Sam about the flowers when he came to follow her to Mount Locust. And maybe she'd knock on the door to the one-bedroom apartment at the end of the hall. No. Not a good idea. The young woman who lived there—Taylor something or other—usually didn't get home until the wee hours of the morning. Maybe Emma could catch her this evening.

She grabbed the backpack she used as a purse again and hurried downstairs. The daisies remained on her mind as she waited for Sam by her truck, but she wasn't going to let the unexpected gift take away her excitement over working with the ground penetrating radar machine today. She'd texted the operator not to come until after lunch. Surely Sam and the sheriff would be finished with their investigation by then. She just hoped no one disturbed the flag grid she'd spent half of yesterday setting up.

Emma checked her watch and scanned the street. Where was Sam? Late as usual . . . a little fact she'd forgotten. Some of their biggest arguments before they broke up had been over his tardiness. Back then, Sam seemed to have no concept of time. She'd hoped he had gotten better about it.

In five minutes, she was leaving for Mount Locust with or without him. Her cell phone vibrated in her pocket, and she yanked it out, glancing at the ID. "You're late. Where are you?"

"Half a mile away, so wait for me," Sam said and then he added, "Please."

At least he recognized that he'd barked out the command and sort of made it a request. If she hadn't wanted to show him the flowers, she probably would have left already. As soon as he arrived, he motioned her on.

She waved him down. "You need to see something," she said after he lowered his window. "Park in front of my truck."

Her heart hitched when Sam strode toward her. He'd left his bulky jacket in the SUV, and she tried not to notice how buff he was, like a running back, lean and muscular. Being in close contact with him might be very difficult.

"For your information, I'm rarely ever late now," he said. "But Jace woke up with a fever. Jenny had an early morning parent-teacher meeting, and he's too young to be home by himself, so I had to stay until Mom could get there."

"It's okay. Are you staying with your sister?" Jenny and her ten-year-old son, Jace, had recently attended Sunday night services with Sam's mother at the same church Emma attended. Which meant Sam would probably go there as well now that he was back in Natchez. Or not. After the cool reception his sister had given Emma the few times they'd crossed paths at church, Jenny might try a different church. Emma would hate to be the reason why.

"Yes." He tilted his head. "You wanted me to see something?" Sam was using his cool, professional voice again.

"Someone left flowers outside my apartment door. Gerbera daisies."

"Who were they from?"

"Well, if I knew, don't you think I would have said?"

Sam's stomach tightened. Emma used sarcasm when she was nervous. He needed to cut her some slack while keeping his distance. Otherwise, being around her was going to get very difficult. "Sorry. Of course you would have. Are these the first flowers you've received from an anonymous admirer?"

"Well, yes." She lifted her shoulder in a tiny shrug. "I'm not exactly the type to receive flowers from men I don't know. Haven't gotten too many from the ones I do know."

He didn't know why not. There was no denying she was pretty, leaning more toward the all-American look with her red hair and handful of freckles sprinkled across her cheeks. And when her emerald eyes weren't pinning him against the wall, they reminded him of the lush greens of summer. He stiffened and took a step back. If he wasn't careful, she'd slide right under the wall he'd built.

"There was a card with no name on it," she said. "Just a sort of message that creeped me out."

Focus. "What did it say?"

"*Life is short. Enjoy each day.*"

The skin on Sam's neck prickled. He hadn't paid much attention to the neighborhood, and he turned and scanned the area. One house was for sale on the street that dead-ended into the one Emma lived on, but there was no activity around it. Several of the larger houses had been turned into apartments with little access to parking, and cars lined both sides of the street. But nothing looked amiss. "This may be confirmation that you have a stalker."

Color drained from her face. "Don't say that. Maybe the shooting and the flowers are just a coincidence."

"You don't really believe that, do you?" He tried to ignore the way the desperation in her voice tugged at his heart.

"Then he may get more than he bargained for," she said, fisting her hands on her hips.

That sounded like the old Emma. How could someone be so strong in the face of danger yet so fragile when it came to relationships? He nodded toward the house. "Show me the flowers and card."

Sam followed her inside and up the stairs, the fresh, cottony scent he remembered so well trailing behind Emma. Bittersweet memories best left behind.

"They were right here," she said, pointing at the floor in front of her door.

"You didn't touch the vase, did you?"

Emma pulled a key from her backpack and unlocked the door. "Of course not. I watch enough cop shows on TV to know better than that. I used a dish towel when I moved them."

He resisted pointing out that the towel could have smudged any fingerprints when she lifted the vase. The vase of daisies sat on the middle of her island. Sam glanced around, not surprised that Emma had left her apartment so tidy. She'd always been a neat freak. He brought his attention back to the flowers. "How many people know daisies are your favorite flower?"

"You remembered?" Surprise laced her voice.

That and so much more. He waited for her answer.

"I don't know—anyone who knows me well."

Sam counted the flowers. "Nine is an odd number to send someone. Any significance to that?"

"As far as I know, not with daisies," she said.

He shot her a question with his eyes.

"Trey sent me nine roses once, and he made sure I knew that nine was the number for eternal love. I figured the florist told him." She shivered. "Maybe my secret admirer doesn't know that. And maybe it only applies to roses."

Sam was pretty sure whoever sent the daisies knew the meaning of nine flowers, and if he knew what her favorite flower was, it would have the same meaning as roses. Lead settled in his stomach. "And you don't have a clue who sent them?"

"I wish I did."

"Could Trey . . . ?"

"I doubt it. He never sent daisies when we were together—always roses, even though he knew gerberas were my favorite. He said daisies made him sneeze."

"But you two aren't dating now so he wouldn't be around them. Did he always send nine?"

"No. Just that last time, after I broke it off with him. I told him if he'd wanted to impress me, he should've sent the kind of flowers I liked."

It was too obvious for Trey to be their culprit, but then, maybe he was going for obvious. Sam unhooked his cell phone and dialed the sheriff. When he answered, Sam explained about the flowers. "I doubt there are any prints, but I'm dusting for them anyway, so we'll be late," he said. "We should arrive at Mount Locust within the hour."

Once he disconnected, he hooked the phone back on his belt and turned to Emma. "I'll be right back with my fingerprint kit."

He retrieved the kit from his SUV and hurried back inside to find Emma drumming her fingers on the counter. "Are there any security cameras set up in or around the apartment?" he asked.

She blew out a breath. "No. There are only four tenants, three upstairs and one down, and she's gone to visit her daughter, plus the owner, who is out of town as well. We talked about it at our last get-together, but nothing came of it. We should have bought one ourselves after our landlord refused. She's older and doesn't want to spend any more money than she has to."

"How about someone else in the neighborhood?"

"Not that I know of, and their camera wouldn't be pointed toward this apartment, anyway. I don't know any of my neighbors very well either," she said. "Maybe it's like Greg said and the flowers are harmless."

"Who's Greg?"

"He lives in the apartment across the hall. Nice guy."

"What did he say?"

Her face colored. "That I was pretty and it was probably just someone too shy to give them to me in person."

That was possible. In fact, he'd like to think it was probable. Still, he wanted to check for prints. He removed the flowers from the vase and handed them to Emma, observing her stiff body. She hadn't been this tense last night. "So, how are your parents?"

She frowned, then her shoulders relaxed slightly. "Good as they can be. Since you left, Dad became chief nursing officer at Merit, and Mom's in Jackson. She's an assistant district attorney and thinking about running for the top position when the DA retires." Emma put the flowers in another vase and then sat across from him at the island. "I know what you're doing—trying to make everything normal."

He grinned at her and continued dusting the vase.

"They divorced, you know."

"Yeah, I'd heard that, and I'm sorry."

"When Ryan left, they had different opinions on how it should be handled. Then the strain of Ryan being accused of murder was too much." She picked at a hangnail. "I think Dad would take Mom back in a minute, but that would mean he'd have to move to Jackson, and that's the last thing he wants to do."

His mother had kept him updated on Emma's family, and he could see her dad not wanting to leave Natchez, just like he could see her mom not wanting to give up her career in Jackson. Even as a teenager, he'd seen the two had been as different as oil and water. Jack was laid-back, and Dina a classic type A overachiever and a workaholic.

He picked up the dark powder and bent over the vase, lightly twirling the side of the camel-hair brush over the surface. "Any chance they might get back together?"

"For a long time, I thought they would if I could find Ryan and bring him home. Looking back, I can see their marriage was shaky years before Ryan disappeared, but I believe that was the tipping point."

She fell silent for a minute, and Sam looked up.

"You're pretty good at that," she said.

"There's an art to it," he said, pausing with the brush in his hand, "but I've had a lot of practice."

She nodded and a few seconds later drummed her fingers on the counter again.

"This shouldn't take much longer."

Abruptly the drumming stopped. "Sorry. I'm not the most patient person."

"No kidding." He glanced her way, sending his heart into overdrive. No matter how hard he fought it, she still stirred his heart.

She hopped off the stool and grabbed a glass, filling it with water. "How about your mom? I see her at church, but we don't talk," she said from across the room. The shakiness in her voice told him he had an effect on her as well.

"She's busy with Jace when she's not at the newspaper." His mom was a copyeditor for the *Natchez Democrat*. "He's the light of her life."

"I can understand that. I've seen him at church, and he's a sweetheart." Emma took a sip of water. "I didn't see her last Sunday night."

"She was busy." Helping his deadbeat dad.

"How about your dad?"

His mouth twitched. "What about him?"

"How is he? He helped me find this apartment. My dad says he's a really good real estate agent."

"I wouldn't know. Haven't seen him in a while." He didn't want to hear anything about him either. Sam straightened up and put the brush away. "Is there anyone else in the picture other than Trey?"

She gulped a sip of water, and when he continued to wait for an answer, she shrugged. "No. I take it there weren't any prints?"

"Nope, no prints," he said and tilted his head. "What happened with you and Trey?"

Her cell phone rang, and she quickly answered it. After a few words, she moved the phone away from her ear. "It's my volunteer. When do you think we'll be leaving?"

"Next five minutes," he replied.

She relayed the information and pocketed her phone. "I'm ready whenever you are."

In other words, don't ask her about any wannabe boyfriends. Or maybe she just wanted to get away from him.

"What's up with you after we finish our investigation this morning?" he asked as they walked down the stairs.

"I'm expecting someone from Jackson to operate the GPR machine when Nate finishes his investigation."

"What're you using ground penetrating radar on?" He hurried and held the door open for her in time to see her face light up.

"I'm surprised you know what the acronym stands for."

"I've used the machine on a case or two when we were looking for buried bodies."

"Oh." Emma made two syllables of the word as her full lips formed a perfect circle. "I've been assigned the task of exploring the area where the slave cabins were. And checking the two cemeteries again for more graves. It was supposed to have been done last summer, but the excessive rain canceled the operation."

"I helped with the one conducted twenty years ago," he said.

Suddenly Emma's foot caught on the threshold and she stumbled. "Ah!" she cried.

Sam caught her before her knees hit the porch floor. "You okay?"

"Yes. Thank you." She pulled her arm away. "I hate being so clumsy."

"It happens to all of us," he said and held her arm, guiding her down the porch steps.

"Me more than others," she muttered. "You worked on the Southern Miss project?"

"Yes. I was in the National Park Service Youth Program. Worked as a gofer for the anthropology students when they excavated the site of the cabins and surveyed the cemetery. They even let me use one of the steel probes to locate a burial spot," he said.

"I didn't know that. The research I read said they found forty-three graves in the slave cemetery, but from the oral history I've researched, I believe there are more. I want to find them, make sure no one is overlooked."

She stopped by her truck, color highlighting her cheeks.

"You're excited about this," he said.

"You bet." A self-conscious smile tugged at her lips. "I finally get to put my American history and anthropology classes to good use."

"Sounds like it'll be interesting. Would you like help? Like when I'm not patrolling?" What was he saying? Had he lost his mind? Sam needed to put distance between them, not manufacture a reason to be around Emma.

"You'd do that?"

He couldn't think of a way to backtrack. "I don't want you at Mount Locust alone, at least not until we know more about the shooting and now the flowers."

"I'll take any help I can get."

He opened her truck door. "I have an appointment at Rocky Springs later this morning and will have to leave around eleven," he said. Something he could comfortably do since Nate would still be on site investigating the shooting. "I'll be back by one or two to help."

"Thanks. You do know it'll be hard work," she said dryly.

"Evidently you don't think I'm up to it."

"I didn't say that."

"But that's what you meant. I'll help this afternoon, and since tomorrow is Saturday and I'm off duty, I'll help again."

"You're on," she said and slid behind the wheel of her pickup. "See you this afternoon."

"Actually, you'll probably see me all morning. The investigation, remember?"

Emma's face turned somber. "Oh yeah, that."

He glanced over the white pickup. "Is this Ryan's old—"

"It was my dad's," she said sharply and pushed in the clutch as she turned the key. "Ryan just drove it until he got the Mustang."

"You've taken good care of it." He seemed to put his foot in his mouth every time he turned around. She pulled away from the curb while he hurried to his SUV. He hadn't planned to offer his services and was just as surprised as she was when the words came out of his mouth. But it was his responsibility to guard the Trace and anyone on it who might be in danger. And Emma definitely needed someone to watch over her.

Although it would be extremely difficult for them to see through his darkly tinted side windows, he ducked down as the two vehicles passed his parked car.

What was the ranger doing at her apartment? And why was he following her? Jealousy stabbed his heart, and he quickly brushed it away. When Sam Ryker had retrieved a box from his SUV, he'd used binoculars to see what it was. A fingerprint kit. She must have told him about the flowers, but didn't she understand they were from him?

He removed the windshield sun screen and cranked the car. Emma hadn't posted her message to him on Facebook yet. That was unlike her. Maybe it was because of the ranger . . . he certainly seemed familiar with her, holding her arm, helping her down the steps. Was the ranger going to be a problem? That bore thinking about.

He shifted his thoughts back to Emma and the flowers. Did she get the meaning of the nine daisies? *Forever mine.*

He remembered when they'd bumped into each other, the way her hand had lingered on his arm even as she talked about being friends. She was testing him. Her smile sent a different message, one that said she loved him but they couldn't be together just yet. He was willing to wait.

For a while.

After waiting outside Walmart for Emma to pick up a bag of cat food, Sam followed her to the Trace, then through the gate to the visitor center at Mount Locust. Once she got out, he circled back toward the maintenance building and parked beside the sheriff's SUV. Nate Rawlings walked toward him from the woods. "What've you found?" Sam asked.

"Someone hot-wired the backhoe, and the hole is bigger than I thought it was," Nate said. "I'll show you."

Sam followed him through the woods and saw the yellow backhoe long before they reached it. Beside it was a mound of dirt. He stopped at the edge of a hole. His chest tightened. A few feet deeper, and it could pass for a shallow grave. "Did your techs find any prints?"

"No, not even any footprints. Found a scrap of newspaper, though. He must have laid paper on the floor of the backhoe. Trey just got here and is digging a slug out of the post at the inn."

"Reckon what the intruder was digging for?"

"Good question. One of my deputies is bringing a metal detector to go over the ground. Thought I'd ask Emma to use that fancy machine to see what's beneath the ground. But it's not likely anything of value is buried here."

"Do you think the intruder found what he was looking for?"

"Hoping that GPR machine will tell us."

Sam stared at the hole. No one trespassed at a federal park in the dark and hot-wired a piece of equipment to dig a hole this size for nothing. Or fired at someone coming to investigate. He followed Nate to the Mount Locust Inn, where they found Trey working at the back of the cabin. The chief deputy acknowledged him with a nod as he inserted a laser rod in the bullet hole.

"Find anything?" Nate asked.

"Just got started." Trey nailed a string beside the rod. "How's Emma today?"

"Fine until she received a bouquet of daisies this morning," Sam said, watching for a reaction.

"You mean I have competition?" the chief deputy said. "Who were they from?"

"The person didn't leave his name on the card," Sam said. "Thought they might be from you."

"It wasn't me. I would have signed my name if I'd sprung for flowers. Do you suppose it had anything to do with this?" He jerked his head toward the post.

Sam shrugged. "At this point, I don't have enough information to tell."

Trey let the string drop and stepped off the porch. "It should be easy enough to track down the sender. Whoever sent them must have ordered them from a florist since daisies don't grow around here this time of year."

"True, and I'll be checking that out." Sam had to admit Trey's reaction didn't fit a guilty person, but maybe he was a good actor—he certainly had a ready answer about the daisies.

8

Several cars were already parked in the visitor center parking lot, including a couple of Adams County deputy vehicles, when Emma pulled into Mount Locust. After realizing she would be late, she'd contacted Guy Armstrong, the head of maintenance, and asked him to unlock the gate.

Emma parked and scanned the grounds for the gray-and-white tabby that had showed up last night. It was probably hiding out from all the activity buzzing around the visitor center. When she entered the building, her volunteer was circling a Trace map for a visitor. Sheila was helping out this winter while Emma worked on the mapping project.

"I'm sorry, the Mount Locust Inn is off-limits today, but be sure to stop here," Sheila said, pointing to the Sunken Trace. "It's twenty-six miles up the road."

After the tourist left, she turned to Emma. "What's going on? Nobody will tell me anything."

That was a first. Sheila could usually worm information out of a scarecrow. "We had a little disturbance here last night." Emma set the bag of food on the counter. "Have you seen a cat around here?"

"Cat? No," she said. "Must have been more than a little disturbance. Half the sheriff's department is here. And since I'm having to turn visitors away, it would help if I could tell them why."

"I'm afraid it might frighten them instead. Someone shot at me last night when I came back to Mount Locust for a file."

"You're kidding." The volunteer's voice dropped. "Who was it?"

"It was too dark to see. I just hope whoever it was doesn't come back." Emma poured the dry food in the bowl she'd bought.

"Do you think it was someone messing with that machine that came yesterday?"

"No, the intruder was fooling around with one of the backhoes."

"You think someone was trying to steal it?"

"I don't know. We didn't want to destroy evidence, so we didn't look around last night. I'm going now to check on the GPR machine and see if the sheriff has discovered anything." She stopped at the door. "If I'm still with the sheriff when the GPR operator arrives, send him on up the hill."

After Emma shut the door, she rattled the bowl of dry food.

"Come here, kitty," she crooned, setting the bowl against the wall on the back side of the building. Almost immediately, the tabby rounded the far corner and made a beeline for her. Emma's relief surprised her.

"There you are," she said as the cat wound around her ankles. She didn't want to forget to take the little thing home at the end of the day, but hopefully tonight no one would be shooting at her. She knelt and stroked the cat's back. "You're not very old. And we have to get you fattened up, but right now I have work to do," she said and set out for the inn, leaving Suzy to her eating.

The sun felt good in the fifty-degree weather as she walked to the inn. Maybe they would have a return of warmer weather. Voices came from the back side of the cabin, and she climbed the steps and walked through the dogtrot to the back porch, where she caught sight of Trey.

Rats. She'd hoped he would not be here. Emma was tired of repeating that she only wanted to be friends. Just as she started to backpedal, he looked up.

"Emma," he said with a nod.

"Did you find the bullet?" she asked.

"Yes. Judging from the position, even if you'd been standing on the porch, it would have missed you. Way too high."

Trey was being extremely professional. She saw the reason why when Nate Rawlings stepped around the corner of the house with Sam and two more deputies. She recognized the older one. Martha Cooper was the first female hired by the Adams County Sheriff's Department and had to be getting close to retirement age. Emma didn't recognize the freckle-faced redhead holding a metal detector. "Good morning, Martha," she said and nodded. "Sheriff."

"Morning." He nodded toward the deputy with red hair. "I don't think you've met Chris Wilson. He's from Vicksburg and is our unofficial photographer-slash-deputy."

She exchanged nods with the young deputy and then turned back to the sheriff. "Have you discovered anything?"

"Nothing new, just the hole by the backhoe. Do you know why anyone would be digging around the slave cemetery?"

That had puzzled her last night. "No. Any type of excavation here at Mount Locust is strictly forbidden."

"That's what I thought," Nate said. "I'd like you to take me through what happened again, this time showing me your movements."

His request wasn't unexpected, and Emma had been rehearsing the events in her mind. While the sheriff opened the recorder app on his smartphone, she glanced at Sam, and the memory of his arms wrapping around her last night rocked her heart. Why was she torturing herself this way? Shuttering her thoughts, Emma focused on Nate and took him through her actions, ending with jumping off the porch.

"Then I crawled to the woods there," she said, and walked the path she'd taken. Scuffled leaves helped retrace her steps as the men followed.

"This is where I hid," she said when they reached the live oak with limbs that dipped down to the ground. A curtain of moss swayed in the light northerly breeze.

"He wasn't trying to be quiet," she said, remembering the heavy footsteps. "He fired at me again, and there should be a bullet in one of these trees. Then I heard the sirens. That's when he took off."

"Do you think it could have been more than one person?"

She thought a minute. "There was really no way I could tell."

The sheriff shut off the recorder and motioned to Chris, who was holding the metal detector. "Let's see if we can find that bullet."

He raised it, sweeping up and down the nearby tree trunks. When it went from silent to full sound midway up the trunk of a basswood tree, he stopped. "Should be here."

After a brief search, Sam found the bullet embedded a good eighteen inches higher than Emma's five-foot-three height.

"Either your shooter was a bad shot or he didn't mean to hit you," Sam said. "This is twice he fired over your head."

"So he was just trying to scare me?" If so, he'd done a good job.

"Or scare you off." Nate ran his hand over his short hair. "Get a trajectory on the bullet," he said to Martha.

"Trey's still using the laser kit," she replied.

"Budget cuts." The sheriff spat the words out. "Don't see how the county expects us to do our job without the proper tools." He turned to Sam. "Don't suppose you have one?"

Sam shook his head. "We have the same problem. I don't even have one trajectory kit."

The sheriff shook his head. "Might as well see what Trey's found. Tie a ribbon around the tree, and then see if you can find any cartridges with the metal detector."

Martha and Chris stayed behind while Emma, Sam, and Nate trekked back to the inn, where Trey was finishing up his work. Her gaze followed the white line that stretched from the post to a tree two hundred feet away.

"You find where he stood when he fired the shot?" the sheriff asked Trey.

"Yep, and according to the laser and this cord, he was about my height." Trey jerked his head toward the bare white oak tree where he'd attached the string. "There's a marker on the ground where the leaves are disturbed. The cord hits me about shoulder high when I stand by the marker."

"Good work."

He held out a piece of metal. "Got this out of the post. Looks like a .22 long rifle."

"Does that mean he used a rifle?" she asked.

For the first time, Trey's eyes met hers, his expression going from unreadable to concerned.

"Not necessarily. There are semi-automatic pistols that fire .22 longs, but I'd say this time a rifle was used." Trey rolled his shoulders and turned to the sheriff. "If you don't need me, I'm heading back to the jail."

"Good work, Trey, but I need the trajectory for another bullet before you leave." The sheriff pointed in the direction they'd just come from. "The bullet is in a tree east of the live oak. It has a ribbon around it."

Trey glanced at Emma, his brown eyes soft. "I'm glad he didn't hit you," he said.

"Thanks. Me too." She hugged her arms to her waist. Trey could be caring, and he wasn't really a bad guy, but she just didn't see a future for them.

His eyes narrowed. "We'll catch whoever did it, I promise you that."

Sometimes Trey even surprised her. As he walked toward the live oak, Emma caught sight of a man approaching them. "I think this is my GPR operator," she said. If it was, he was early.

Nate turned toward the man. "Good. I'd like him to run the machine over the pit. See if he can tell if anything is buried there."

She met the older man at the front steps of the inn. "Randy Gibson?"

"That'd be me," the lanky Gibson replied.

"I'm glad you didn't get my message about waiting until later," she said.

"I did, but I was already on my way. What's going on?"

Emma explained the situation. "Before we get started on my project, the sheriff wants you to explore the site where the intruder was digging when I interrupted him."

"I can do that. I assume my machine arrived."

"Yes. It's chained to a steel post at the tractor shed over there."

She pointed him in the right direction and then handed him the key to the lock. While he went after the machine, Emma joined the sheriff and Sam at the backhoe, where Chris was photographing the hole the intruder had dug. It was about a hundred feet from the only marker in the cemetery, but not near any of the flags that marked the slave graves. Turning, she took in the split-rail fence that had been knocked down to get the machine in place.

"What do you suppose the intruder was digging for?" she asked.

"Good question," Nate said.

Emma looked around. "Did the metal detector alert to anything?"

"A couple of bottle caps," Sam replied. "Probably your teenagers drinking beer."

Once boards were placed over the pit, Randy started the GPR machine, which resembled an oversized lawnmower with a screen attached to the handle. He slowly worked his way across the site and repeated the action two more times. "Do you have a plot diagram of the cemetery?"

She had grabbed the folder for the project earlier and leafed through it. "Here," she said, handing him a map from the archeological project. "This is from the University of Southern

Mississippi research project in 2000. The flags you see correspond to the graves they recorded."

Ground penetrating radar hadn't been available to the students who conducted the cemetery survey. Instead, steel probes had been used to identify the randomly scattered graves. Randy ran the machine over the grave nearest them, then returned to the pit and repeated the process.

"Definitely something here." Randy turned the paper so that the arrow pointing north lined up. After studying it, he checked his screen. "According to this paper, there shouldn't be anything buried here, but take a look at this."

Sam and Emma and Nate crowded next to him. "What do you have?" Sam asked.

"Let me bring up both screens," Randy said. "The bottom screen shows the burial plot from over there," he said, pointing about fifty feet away. "The top screen is where the pit is—let's call it Section A. See these? They're called anomalies." He pointed out rounded lines on the screen. "This is the known grave. Compare it to Section A."

"It looks the same," Emma said.

"Yes, but look at the difference in depth," he replied. "According to the screen, whatever is in Section A is only buried a little over four feet deep. That's much shallower than the six feet for the older grave."

Emma examined the squiggly lines on the screens. A chill chased over her. What if someone had recently buried a body? And what if they had returned last night to move it? She tried to think if anyone had gone missing recently.

Ryan.

No. It'd been ten years, and she refused to believe her brother was dead. She looked up. "Maybe it's from the Civil War time and a landowner buried their gold or silver here."

"Not impossible," Randy said. "But wouldn't it have been found in 2000?"

9

Can you tell how long ago the ground was disturbed?" Sam asked, staring at the screen on the GPR machine. He'd like to believe gold or silver was buried in the pit, but he had a bad feeling about the site.

"I'd say there were a lot of years between the slave graves and this one."

"Can you tell if there's a body in it?" Nate asked.

"Afraid not, but the disturbance matches the size of the graves," he said. "It'll take excavating to know for sure what's down there."

"Something we'll start this afternoon," Nate said.

Randy nodded. "I have an appointment in Jackson later this afternoon, but you have the equipment assigned to you for a week." He turned to Emma. "Would you like me to show you how to operate it?"

"That would be great," Emma said. "But how will we know when we reach the bottom?"

"You'll have to keep checking the screen. When you reach compacted ground, it will look like this." He pointed to the fairly straight lines below the pit.

Sam listened in as Randy explained how to operate the GPR machine. When he finished, Randy handed Emma a sheet of paper. "These are step-by-step instructions if you forget, but if you need to, give me a call," he said.

"Thanks." Emma studied the sheet of paper as Randy walked away.

Nate turned to Sam. "Do you think we need to get a court order since this is National Park Service property?"

Sam rubbed the back of his neck. The only other time he'd had to excavate on park service land was when a dog had dug up a human bone, making a court order unnecessary. But this wasn't as cut and dried. "What do you think?" he asked, glancing at Emma.

She looked up from the instruction sheet. "Since someone hot-wired the backhoe and excavated this area, I believe my superintendent will view it as a crime scene and give the go-ahead. Nate, do you want to check? Or do you want me to do it?"

"Since it's your site and your supervisor, why don't you," he said.

While Emma walked a short distance away until she was out of the trees and made the phone call, Sam brought up the flowers again.

"And she doesn't have a clue who they're from?" Nate asked.

Sam shook his head. "There're no security cameras unless a neighbor has one, and even then, I doubt it'd capture anything at the apartment building."

"Flowers. And a message with no name." Nate rubbed his jaw. "My suspicious nature makes me think the shooting could be connected to her receiving flowers—the shooter pointing out that she can't hide from him?"

A real possibility. "That makes sense."

"I heard you talking to Trey about it. If he'd sent the flowers, he would've wanted credit." The sheriff checked his watch. "I'm leaving for the jail shortly. I'll follow up with him on this."

Sam looked up as Emma came closer. "The superintendent agreed that it sounded like there was enough evidence to warrant a thorough investigation without a court order," she said.

Nate blew out a breath. “Good. I hate getting court orders. Especially with Judge Tate out of town. The only other judge available gives me a hard time.”

“Getting a court order would have been easy compared to going through a 106 compliance review,” she said. “Believe me, you don’t want to do that.”

From Nate’s mystified expression, Emma had lost him at the 106 compliance review part. “This is a historic site and that means you would be dealing with the historical society,” Sam said. “There would be paperwork involved and a committee who would rule on whether you could dig here.”

“Then I’m doubly blessed,” Nate replied. “As soon as we can get someone to operate the backhoe, we’ll get started.”

Emma cleared her throat. “Um, the superintendent also suggested I should be part of the excavation. She wants me to sift for artifacts in every scoop of dirt shoveled out of the ground.”

Nate crossed his arms over his broad chest. “I’m assuming we can pile the dirt up and don’t have to wait for you to sift it, right?”

“That’ll work,” Emma replied. “We’ll only want to use the backhoe for probably another twelve inches, then we’ll use shovels and finally trowels and a brush.”

Sam bit back a smile at the excitement in Emma’s voice. She was itching to take part in discovering what was buried, and it was hard not to catch her enthusiasm. Hopefully she wouldn’t find a body.

Sam checked his watch. Eleven fifteen. Part of him was relieved that it was time to leave for Port Gibson and the noon meeting with his Ridgeland counterpart. He was getting a little too comfortable being around Emma. It surprised him when another part of him wished he could cancel the meeting and stay on at Mount Locust. Not good.

“See you later,” he said and double-timed it to his SUV, leaving Emma as she surveyed the rest of the cemetery with the GPR machine. He gunned the vehicle out of the parking lot and turned left on the Trace while he calculated the twenty-five miles to Port Gibson against the fifty-mile-an-hour speed limit. Barely enough time, but he set the cruise control on fifty.

Sam made it with minutes to spare, and the meeting with District Ranger Evan McCall went well. Their districts overlapped up around Jackson, and McCall had wanted a face-to-face to work out a schedule for patrolling the area. With Brooke Danvers still at the trial in Jackson and then off tomorrow, Sam was short-staffed, and McCall agreed to take on the bulk of patrolling over the weekend.

When he arrived back at Mount Locust, it was nearly three thirty. The pile of loamy soil deposited beside the hole had grown and the backhoe had been moved a few yards from the site. Someone had erected a tent over the pit, where two NPS maintenance men were shoveling dirt out. A familiar scent tickled his nose. Sassafras. There were several of the trees nearby, and they must have cut into a root. Emma had shed her jacket in the sixty-degree weather and leaned over a contraption made from PVC pipe.

With her unaware of his presence, he took the opportunity to observe her. Her petite frame filled out the ranger uniform very nicely. She'd put her coppery curls up in a ponytail and looked like a teenager. Unexpectedly she looked up and caught him admiring her.

"What's that?" he asked, pointing to the PVC pipe.

She straightened up, stretching her back. "It's a shaker screen for sifting dirt. I invested in it after I took archeology classes and had to lug a wooden one to the different sites. Plus, it's perfect for my height—I don't have to bend over as far. Still backbreaking, though." Emma turned to the men. "Hold up a second and let me check the depth."

She stuck a yardstick in the hole. The depth was thirty-two inches, and she nodded to them. "Let's get the next six inches, and after that you're free to leave. I'll excavate the rest."

"I don't remember you taking archeology," Sam said.

Her face flushed, and he didn't think it was from the heat. "My last year. Took a forensic one, as well."

Sam was impressed. He nodded at the mound of dirt. "You've been busy, but sifting it will take forever."

"Can't be helped."

He nodded that he understood. "Is Nate back?"

"Yes, but I think he walked over to the inn, or maybe the visitor center."

It would be dark in another two hours, and at the rate Emma was sifting, she would barely make a dent in the pile. Besides that, the investigation was in his backyard, and he needed to be a part of it. "How about if I help?"

"In those clothes?" She eyed him. "I know you said you wanted to help, but neither of us considered how dirty you would get. You'd never get the stains out or your shoes clean again. But I appreciate your offer."

"I think I can fix that. Do you have a key for the maintenance building so I can change?"

"You have work clothes?" she asked.

"Yep." Sam always carried sneakers and a pair of jeans and a T-shirt in his SUV in case he wanted to change out of his uniform.

She fished a ring of keys from her pocket and handed it to him. "It's the skinny one."

"Thanks! Be right back."

He jogged the quarter mile to his SUV, grabbed his clothes, and unlocked the maintenance building. There was an office on either end of the building with a kitchen and bathroom in the middle. The office to his left evidently belonged to the maintenance supervisor—while it was neat, it had none of Emma's personality in it. A quick look at the other office confirmed his hunch—the oak desk had a photo of Emma with her parents, a cheery flower arrangement sat on the bookcase, and several photos of Mount Locust adorned the walls.

He closed the bathroom door behind him and changed into

the jeans and short-sleeved shirt, ruefully realizing a shirt with longer sleeves would have been warmer than the close-fitting T-shirt that hugged his abs. It would have to do since it was the only extra shirt he had.

His heart quickened as he remembered the brief flash of appreciation in Emma's eyes when he offered to help. *Don't go there.* She would only break his heart again.

10

What do you want me to do?" Sam asked.

Heat washed over Emma, and it had nothing to do with the temperature. "Um, uh, I don't think there's room for you in the pit, so . . . you want to sift for a while?" She pulled her gaze from his sculpted pecs and pointed to another shaker screen a few yards away. "I can show you how."

While the two maintenance men continued with their excavation of the pit, Emma unfolded the screen, positioned it near hers, and shoveled dirt in it. "Just rock it back and forth, like I'm doing. Then use your hand to knock what's left through the holes." Reaching in her backpack, she pulled out an extra pair of gloves. "These will help protect your hands."

They worked in silence as Sam got the hang of rocking the screen back and forth. "What do you do when the soil is wet?" he asked.

"Pour water through it," she said with a grin. "Usually by hooking up a water hose. It's really messy, though." He glanced at the dirt on his gloves and shoes and raised an eyebrow. She laughed. "Yep, messier than that."

"If you say so." Sam rocked the tray again, and a clump of dirt broke apart, revealing something black embedded in the clod.

"Hold on," she said, picking it up. "Oh, wow!"

"What is it?"

Her heart kicked into high gear as he stood behind her, peering over her shoulder. Momentarily she enjoyed the warmth his nearness brought. He reached for the clod, and their arms accidentally touched, sending an electrical jolt through her.

Sam brushed the dirt away from the object. "An arrowhead! I've never found one that small."

She drew in a shaky breath and stepped out of his shadow, breaking the connection. "It's a bird point. Looks like it's made from obsidian." She frowned. "But I don't understand how it got buried this deep . . . unless it fell in when the hole was originally dug."

"How did it get to Natchez? There isn't any obsidian around here."

"Probably traded from tribes either from Ohio or even out West," she said, looking up. Big mistake.

Emma did not know what was going on with her. True, she'd loved Sam back before . . . reality set in. Before he let her down. If Sam had done what he'd promised, all their lives would have been so different. *Get real, girl.* It was her fault Ryan had deserted her.

Her jaw clenched. If only she could stop the memories of her last words to her brother. It didn't matter that Ryan had been the one who made bad choices, that he was the one who didn't know when to quit drinking. Her words to him must have been the tipping point. *Think of something else.* Emma shifted toward Sam. He turned, and his smoking gaze turned her knees to water.

"We better get back to work," she said, jerking her attention away from Sam's scrutiny and the brown eyes she'd gotten lost in. "But first, let me snap a photo of your arrowhead and put it on Facebook and Instagram."

"You do that much? Post on social media?"

"Sure. It's great publicity for the Trace and Mount Locust. I usually do a couple a day."

Once she had the photos posted, Emma went back to work, very aware of his presence as they sifted the dirt in silence. Just as the sun dropped below the tree line, one of the men said, "It's quitting time, and I think we've dug as deep as you wanted us to."

Emma wasn't ready to quit. Just a little deeper and they might discover what was buried here. She grabbed the stick and measured the hole. A little over three feet. It was time to use the trowels. "Thanks, guys. I'll take it from here."

As the other two men walked away, Sam said, "I'm going to change."

After they all left, she busied herself picking out the hand tools she would need and hoped that Sam left with the men. Instead, he returned a few minutes later, dressed in his green-and-gray uniform.

"You ready to leave?"

"You don't have to stay," Emma said. "I need to get everything set up for tomorrow, and I'm fine closing up alone—I do it every night." Still not looking at him, she picked up a hand trowel and set it with the other tools.

He stilled her hands, his touch searing her heart. "You are not staying here by yourself."

His voice brooked no argument, sending a wave of anger through her. She probably should quit for the day, but Emma didn't like Sam assuming she would leave when he said so.

Emma jerked her hands away and stepped back, tripping over one of the tent poles. Sam grabbed for her as she tumbled into the hole and landed on her outstretched hand. Sharp pain shot through her wrist. She was barely aware when Sam jumped down next to her. In seconds he scooped her up and set her on the edge of the hole.

"Are you okay?" he asked gruffly.

As much as she wanted to say yes, the knot that popped up on her hand would give her away. That and the wincing every time she moved her fingers. "I think I've broken something."

"Let me see." He gently examined her wrist. "Can you move your fingers?"

She tried and gasped. "Not without pain."

"Yeah, you've probably broken something. I'm taking you to the hospital."

"No! I'll ice it when I get home."

"Emma . . ."

"I don't have time to go to the hospital. I need to wrap things up here." She pulled her hand away from his. Bad mistake, as pain shot through her wrist. She hugged her hand to her chest, with pain now throbbing with each heartbeat, making her nauseous. "Or maybe not. What time is it?"

He checked his watch. "Almost five. I can take you to the ER and your dad could meet us there."

"No, don't call him." Friday night was when her dad got together with several of his buddies to unwind, something he desperately needed by the end of the week. She wasn't taking him away from that because of her clumsiness. "Take me to the sports clinic. They should still be open."

His eyes narrowed as he studied her. Finally, he nodded. "Do you have any ice at the visitor center?"

She tried to think. "No, but there may be some in the kitchen at the maintenance building."

"Do you want me to carry you?"

In spite of how she hurt, Emma laughed. "It's my wrist, not my leg," she said.

"Right. Still . . ."

"Thank you, but I can walk to the office."

A few painful minutes later, she fished the key from her backpack with her good hand, and he unlocked the door to the building. Gently, he guided her to a chair in the kitchen area. "You sit here."

A few minutes later, he placed ice wrapped in a towel around her wrist. "Think you can hold it in place?"

"Yes." The ice gave cooling relief.

"Then if you're ready . . ."

"Give me time to collect myself."

"Five minutes, and we need to leave. Otherwise, we might get to the clinic too late," Sam said and nodded toward her office. "Do you use your office much?"

He was trying to take her mind off the pain. "If I have a volunteer at the visitor center, I come over here and write reports."

He walked around the kitchen, studying the different photos taken at stops along the Natchez Trace. "Good shots," he said, and then he cocked his head. "How's the pain?"

In other words, was she ready to go to the clinic? "Better."

"Good." He held the door open for her. "We'll take my SUV."

Emma hadn't even considered that she couldn't drive. Sam walked her to his vehicle and steadied Emma while she climbed in. It dawned on her that there would be a lot of things she couldn't do.

Twenty minutes later, Sam held the door open at the Cole Orthopedic Clinic and then filled out her paperwork since she couldn't use her right hand. "Aw, man," she said. "I just realized all the paperwork this little accident will take. And with my left hand, no less." She was in trouble for sure, since anything written with her left hand was illegible.

"I can help you."

"It's okay, I—"

"Ms. Winters, come on back," a nurse said.

"I can go with you, if you'd like."

Emma hesitated. His presence was comforting, and at least five patients had been called ahead of her. No telling how long she'd be stuck waiting in one of the little cubicles by herself. Why did things have to be so hard? And why did her heart want him to stay? Her head knew better.

"Seriously," he said. "I feel partly responsible for this happening, anyway." Guilt or compassion, she didn't know which, filled his brown eyes.

"Okay. Thank you."

After an X-ray, which the technician refused to give her any information on, they were put in a small room to wait.

"I called Nate and told him what happened," Sam said. "He's sending a deputy to guard the site."

"Good." She shook her head as she thought of everything that needed to be done. This accident couldn't have happened at a worse time. "Hopefully, I'll be back to the site in the morning."

"You're kidding, right?"

"Nope. If no bones are broken, there's no reason I can't return to work."

After staring at her like she'd lost her mind, he walked around the small room, glancing at the diplomas on the walls. "Do you know this Dr. Cole?"

"Sure. You do too. Gordon Cole . . . graduated a couple of years ahead of us. Ryan's friend, even though Ryan was younger."

Sam snapped his fingers. "Oh yeah, Doc Cole's son, Gordy. He was at the Hideaway with—" His Adam's apple bobbed as he swallowed hard. "Sorry. You don't need to deal with that tonight."

No, she didn't.

"So, Gordy became a doctor?"

"Yep. I think he's going by Gordon now. He pretty well runs this place now that Doc Cole has semiretired." Everyone knew Doc Cole, especially if they had a sports injury.

"He's been here since med school?"

"No, he joined his dad in the clinic last year after practicing several years in Jackson. He's a good surgeon—did Dad's knee replacement," she said as a light tap sounded on the door before it opened, and Dr. Cole walked in.

"Emma, what have you done to yourself?" he asked.

"Hopefully only sprained my wrist." Given the pain, she doubted it was that simple.

He tipped his head toward Sam. "Been a while," he said.

"I've just moved back to Natchez."

"I'm sure Emma told you I haven't been back long." He typed into the computer, and like magic, her X-rays appeared on the flat-panel screen hanging on the wall. "Well," he said, "it looks like you may have dodged a bullet."

She startled. It was almost like he knew someone had shot at her. *Relax*. It was a common phrase. "My wrist is just sprained?"

"It definitely is that, but . . ." He used his pen to point out one of the bones in her hand. "This may be a tiny break, but nothing we need to cast." He gently examined her hand, and she flinched when he squeezed the side of her wrist. "Ice it at least four times a day to keep down the swelling. How did you do it, anyway?"

"It was Sam's fault. We were at Mount Locust and arguing about quitting time and there was this hole . . ." She shrugged.

His eyes narrowed. "Sam pushed you?"

She laughed. "That didn't come out quite right. We were arguing about quitting time, and I stepped back into the hole."

He opened a drawer and took out a compression wrap. "You're excavating at the site? I thought I read in the newspaper you were only mapping out the slave cabins and cemetery."

"That was the original plan, but something came up that changed everything." She didn't plan to tell him what. "It will be okay if I drive, won't it?"

"Before you answer that," Sam said, "you might need to know she drives a stick shift."

Surprise crossed the doctor's face. "Not many of those around."

"It's my dad's old truck," she said.

"The old '97 Tacoma Ryan used to drive in high school?" he asked.

Her throat tightened. She hadn't expected him to remember it. "Yeah. After Ryan got the Mustang, Dad gave the truck to me."

Gordon wrapped the compression bandage around her wrist and hand. "I'm going to leave your fingers partially free, but it would be better if you didn't drive until the swelling goes down, regardless of whether it's a stick shift or automatic," he said.

She frowned. "But—"

"Let me put it this way—if you'd injured your foot like this,

I would tell you no weight bearing on it if you want to avoid surgery. Same thing here." He gently pressed the Velcro end to the bandage. "Have you heard from your brother?"

Why did everyone want to bring up Ryan tonight? "No. It's like he just dropped off the face of the earth." Ryan and Gordon had been really close before her brother took off. "Have you heard from him?"

"No," the doctor said. "But I've always understood why he didn't come back, not that I believe he killed that girl."

"He might think he'd be railroaded," Sam said.

"Like before," Emma said. "Sheriff Carter tended to jump to conclusions and then defend them even if he was proven wrong."

Anger burned in her chest at the former sheriff. She'd never understood why he'd fixated on Ryan being Mary Jo's killer, unless Carter had gone off half-cocked and then was unwilling to fix his mistake. "How long will this take to heal?"

"A month, if you rest it. Longer if you don't."

"Does that mean I can't drive for a month?"

"I think driving will be okay after ten days. I'll know for sure when you come back."

She wanted to roll her eyes. "Thanks for nothing, Doc."

"That's Dr. Cole to you," he said, then grinned. "Doc is my dad. Just call me Gordon. Or Dr. Gordon like the kids do."

She sighed. "When do you want me to come back?"

He cocked his head to the side. "This is Friday . . . I'll have the receptionist make you an appointment for next Friday. Unless it gives you trouble—then get yourself back here."

"Looks like you'll need me to drive you back and forth from Mount Locust for a few days," Sam said.

Just what she needed—more time around him. And he didn't sound all that happy about it either.

11

Darkness and cold met them as they left the clinic. Sam held the door open for Emma, then hurried to open the car door, thankful she didn't have a bad fracture. The sight of her falling into the open pit had cost him at least two years of his life.

"I can get the door," Emma said.

"And my mama would skin me alive if I let you," he replied. Once he had her settled, he walked around and climbed in on the other side. "Are you hungry?"

"I could probably eat," she said.

"How about a plate of catfish at Jug Head's?"

Her eyes lit up. "I haven't eaten there in ages."

"Good. It'll give us a chance to talk about your plans for the next few days," he said. "And maybe we can figure out how we're going to get through them without taking each other's heads off."

Or not, considering the way her lips pressed together in a firm line.

While the restaurant wasn't far from the clinic, stop-and-go traffic flowing across the Mississippi River to and from Vidalia, Louisiana, slowed them. Sam's stomach rumbled as he turned into a white gravel drive and searched for a parking spot in front of the quaint plank building. "Pretty busy," he said. "Want to try somewhere else?"

"It's Friday—all the restaurants will be busy."

"Right." A car pulled from its spot and Sam grabbed the parking space. He hurried around to Emma's door and helped her out.

He guided her as they walked the zigzag ramp to the door, where the tantalizing aroma of fried food met them.

"I'll gain five pounds just breathing the air," Emma muttered.

He agreed. There was no better fried catfish in Natchez. Or hush puppies. Or onion rings. The recipes at Jug Head's had been handed down from one generation to the next since the early fifties.

"Y'all come on in and find a seat," the waitress called from behind the counter.

Sam glanced around for a table. Very little had changed about the family-style restaurant since he'd left, including the red-checkered tablecloths and a packed house.

"Over there in the corner," he said, placing his hand on the small of Emma's back, steering her to the right. Once he had her stomach filled, he hoped to talk about more than her schedule. Whether he liked it or not, their past needed to be dealt with. If nothing else, they needed to make peace with it.

"Hello, Emma." The greeting came from a table on the left.

Emma paused, and Sam almost bumped into her. He didn't recognize the speaker, a man with blond hair and pale blue eyes who was dressed in what looked like a tailor-made suit, but Sam did recognize the man's interest in Emma.

"Corey, I didn't see you," Emma said.

"I noticed you when you stepped inside the door. What's wrong with your hand?"

"It's all his fault," she said, glancing at her bandaged wrist and chuckling. When Corey's eyes widened, she added, "Not really. I sprained it—nothing major. Do you two know each other?"

"Afraid not," Sam said.

At the same time, the other man said, "Sam Ryker? Correct?"

Sam frowned. He didn't remember meeting this Corey.

"Didn't I see in the paper that you were the top ranger for this district on the Natchez Trace?"

That explained it. He'd forgotten the write-up a reporter had done on him.

"Let me introduce you properly," she said. "Sam Ryker, Corey Chandler. Corey is an attorney."

Sam held out his hand. "New to Natchez?"

"I've been here three years." He seemed reluctant to shift his attention away from Emma long enough to accept Sam's hand. "Nice to meet any friend of Emma's."

He had expected Chandler's grip to be wimpy, but instead it was firm. No calluses, though, like his own hands.

"Corey's been trying to stop the project at Mount Locust from going forward."

That didn't sound like much of a friend, but Sam kept his mouth shut.

"Not me, Emma. One of my clients."

"Is there any difference?" she asked, patting him on the arm.

"Definitely. I don't enjoy crossing swords with you," he said. "Since it's so crowded here, would you two like to join me? I'm almost finished and then you'd have the table to yourselves."

Emma hesitated and glanced at Sam.

"I see a table in the corner," he said. "But thanks for your offer. Nice to meet you."

"Sure." The attorney pinned him with steely eyes. "I hope you enjoy your meal."

They moved on to the corner table, and Sam held out the chair that faced away from Corey for Emma. "He likes you."

"Corey?" She frowned. "He's a friend, that's all."

"I think he'd like it to be more." He glanced past her to the table where Corey was on his cell phone. Not only had the attorney's eyes spelled out more than friendship toward Emma, they let Sam know Corey didn't like him.

"You're crazy. Corey has never indicated any interest in me at all—not even to grab a cup of coffee with him." She rubbed her arm. "Thanks. Now I'll be uncomfortable around him."

"Maybe it's just my imagination." He glanced over the menu as the waitress arrived. Norma Jean was stitched on the pocket over her heart. The name rang a bell, and he studied the woman's lined face. Unless he was mistaken, Norma Jean was working here the last time he'd visited Jug Head's, over ten years ago.

"What'll it be, folks?"

Sam glanced at Emma. "Know what you want?"

"Small catfish filet dinner," she said.

"And your drink?"

"If your coffee is as good as it used to be, I'll take that."

"If you like it strong, we brew some of the best coffee in Natchez," Norma Jean said and turned to Sam.

"What she's having sounds good to me." He handed the waitress the menus back. "But make mine the large-size order of fish."

The waitress stopped at Corey's table as he laid his phone down and glanced up at her. Sam couldn't hear him, but from the way she laughed, he must have said something funny. He did see the wink the attorney gave her. Maybe he was wrong, and Corey wasn't interested in Emma. Maybe that was just his way.

Sam looked back at Emma. "How's your hand?"

"Throbbing, but not as bad since I took the Tylenol." She leaned back as the waitress set two cups of coffee on the table.

"Thank you," Sam said, then turned his attention back to Emma. "You're not going to try to work tomorrow, are you?"

"No trying to it. I'll be there at eight, like always. I want to see what's buried."

"And just how do you propose to get there?"

"I'm taking you up on your offer to pick me up," she said, grinning. "You did offer, didn't you?"

"So I did." His heart thudded in his chest when she caught his gaze and held it. A strand of hair had come loose from the ponytail, and he wanted to brush it behind her ear. His thoughts must have shown on his face because she quickly looked away. "There's something else we need to do," he said softly.

Wariness crept into her face.

"We're going to be spending a lot of time together, so we need to talk about the past and deal with it."

Before she could answer, Corey walked to their table. "Why didn't you tell me the project was on hold?" he asked. "And that someone took shots at you last night?"

Emma gaped at him. "How did you find out?"

"You know better than to ask me that," he said, still not smiling. "Is it true?"

Irritation flashed across Emma's face. "Which part? Oh, never mind. Yes, I was shot at last night, and no, the project isn't on hold. I'll still be mapping out everything as soon as we settle the issue of what was buried in the slave cemetery in the last few years."

"I understand you found a body?"

"Where did you hear that?" Sam asked. The only people who knew something might be buried there knew to keep it under wraps.

"You know Natchez. Word travels pretty quick."

"There's been no body found," Emma said.

"Then what have you discovered?"

"We don't know," she said before Sam could intervene. "And if I did, I couldn't tell you."

Even though she said the words with a smile, her voice brooked no argument. He should've known Emma could handle the attorney.

"But you are digging around in the slave cemetery?"

"Like you can't tell me who your client is, I can't talk about this," Emma said, raising an eyebrow. "I can tell you it's out of my hands. If you have any questions, ask my district supervisor or Sheriff Rawlings."

"Really? So, you did find a body."

"Didn't say that," she replied. "The GPR machine didn't give us an indication of what was in the ground. Could be buried treasure."

"Don't even joke about that," Sam said. He could just see the site being overrun with treasure hunters.

Emma winced. "Sorry." She turned to Corey. "Please don't repeat that."

"Don't worry. But I would appreciate knowing what you find."

"Maybe, if you'll tell me who your client is," she said.

He gave her a crooked grin. "I'll be in touch."

"Why do you suppose the client doesn't want the project to go forward?" Sam asked when Corey returned to his table. He also noted even though the attorney had told them he was almost finished with his meal, he was in no hurry to leave.

"He won't say, but I suspect whoever it is fears I'll disturb the graves. He doesn't understand the new equipment, and that using the GPR machine will be like taking an X-ray of the ground. I won't have to dig."

Just then Norma Jean arrived with their food. "Y'all enjoy," she said and refreshed Emma's cup. "How'd you like the coffee?"

"It's delicious."

"Told you so." She laid the bill on the table.

They both reached for it, but Sam beat Emma to it. "My treat," he said. But his mind was still on Corey's client. Could that be who attacked Emma last night?

12

It seemed odd to be sitting across from Sam like the last ten years had never happened. Except his remark about dealing with their past had filled her with dread. Emma didn't want to discuss anything personal with Sam Ryker.

"You never said how we were going to get my truck home from Mount Locust."

"I didn't, did I," Sam said, looking up from his plate of golden fried fish and onion rings. His dark eyes gave nothing away. "Are you going to eat?" he asked and bit into an onion ring.

She picked up her fork with her left hand. This should be interesting.

After Sam took a bite of the fish, his eyes widened. "Wow! I'd forgotten how good their food is."

Just when she thought he was going to ignore the question about her truck, he said, "I thought we had that settled. You heard the doctor. I'll get Clayton to help me get it to your apartment tomorrow. Okay?"

"Good." She gingerly picked up a slice of lemon with her left hand and managed to get it between her finger and thumb. She squeezed it over her fish, shooting juice on Sam's cheek.

"Oh no!" Emma dropped the wedge on her plate and grabbed a napkin, dabbing at his face. Wrong move, as her heart leapt into her throat. "That didn't get in your eye, did it?"

"No damage done," he said softly and took the napkin from her fingers.

Electricity arced between them. Once again it was as though ten years had not passed. *Stop it.* Her track record with men was terrible. No need to make it worse by even thinking about starting up a relationship with Sam again.

"What just happened is a good reason for you not to drive," he said. "You're not very handy with your left hand."

No. Ryan had been the lefty.

"Let's eat," he said, "and then we'll talk."

"About . . . ?"

"I don't want to be Captain Obvious here, but I think we have unfinished business, and we might as well address it."

"Do we have to talk about it now?"

"No, but we need to clear the air so we don't feel like we're tiptoeing around our past. How would you like to take a walk downtown after dinner? I don't think it'll be too cold."

"I meant do we have to talk about this at all tonight?" Realizing she had unresolved feelings for Sam scared her.

"Look, we're going to be thrown together until the case is solved, and that might stir up old feelings. We both know giving in to those feelings would not be a good idea. We have too much baggage, but I would like for us to work together as friends, at least."

She looked down at her food. His words about baggage stung, but he was right. They would be working together, and it would be better if their past didn't hang over them. Emma simply didn't know how to do relationships. Never had, or she wouldn't have ruined the one between her and Sam.

"Hey. Where'd you go?"

She looked up into his warm brown eyes. "I'm sorry. Got lost there for a minute."

Maybe it was time to stop wallowing in the angst from her teenage years, especially since Emma couldn't deny the undercurrent of emotions between them. She brushed the thought away. It wasn't like Sam would ever trust her with his heart again. Ryan stood between them. "Look—"

"I'm sorry I said anything—this isn't the time or place," he said. "I'll take you home if you'd like."

She stared at the filets on her plate. He'd paid hard-earned money for their meal, and her conscience wouldn't let it go to waste. "No, catfish needs to be eaten hot."

Emma picked at her food, managing the onion rings and hush puppies well enough with her left hand. After forking a piece of catfish and immediately dropping it on the table, she gave up and used her fingers.

The waitress approached to refill their drinks. "You want a to-go box, hon?" she asked, eyeing Emma's half-eaten food.

She shook her head. As much as she loved fried catfish, she didn't love it warmed over. But then she remembered the cat at the visitor center. The cat she'd forgotten again. "Oh, wait, I believe I do."

A few minutes later, Emma stood near the door as Sam waited behind Corey at the cash register, stepping back as a customer entered the restaurant. Trey. Her heart plummeted. Why did she keep running into him?

"Emma," he said and glanced at her wrist. "What happened to your hand?"

"Sprained it, maybe broke a bone."

"How?"

"She's telling everyone it's my fault," Sam said as he and Corey joined them.

"I only said that twice," she said. "And only because I'm tired of everyone telling me how clumsy I am, but blaming it on you wasn't the answer." Even if he was partially responsible. If he hadn't stilled her hands, she wouldn't have jerked away.

"I hope it heals quickly," Corey said.

Sam agreed and turned to Trey. "Are you guarding the site at Mount Locust?"

"Till one, then someone else will take over. I stopped by here to get a couple of burgers to-go for later."

"Good choice."

"Hey, Trey," the cashier called. "Your order is ready."

"Coming. Be sure to add coffee to the order." He nodded. "Hopefully it'll be a quiet night, but then I'll need caffeine to stay awake."

Sam held the door for her and then silently walked her to the car. When he opened her car door without saying anything, her insecurity kicked in. Either he'd gotten upset about something or she was misreading his body language. When the silence continued as they drove to her apartment, she said, "Cat got your tongue?"

His head jerked toward her. "What?"

"You haven't said a word since we left the restaurant. Did I do something?"

Confusion crossed his face. "Why would you think that?"

"Forget I said anything."

"Was that a trick question?" he asked.

Men. Emma couldn't believe she had to explain it to him, but men just didn't get it. "You were so quiet I thought you were angry about something."

"No. Just trying to figure out how to keep you safe when you probably won't listen to me."

"I really don't think I'm in danger," she said.

"That's what I mean."

"I think last night's shooting was a one-time thing to scare me away so the intruder could finish whatever they came to do."

"I'd rather you be safe than sorry." Sam glanced in his rearview mirror, then turned off the main street.

"Where are you going?" she asked. "This isn't the way to my apartment."

"I know. Just making sure no one is following us."

Emma looked over her shoulder. Theirs was the only car on the street, but that didn't ease the tightness that suddenly gripped her chest. "You really think the man who fired at me might try again, don't you?"

"It's entirely possible."

He was using his keep-your-distance voice again. She sucked in a breath of air. If she had to be around him, and she did until she could drive again, Emma did not want to feel like she was walking a tightrope all the time.

"Maybe we do need to clear the air," she said when he parked in front of the house. "Want to come up for a cup of coffee? I brew a really good cup of joe, even better than Jug Head's."

Emma's face warmed as Sam's eyes questioned her. "Are you sure?"

No, she wasn't sure, but confronting the problem was better than this uneasiness. "Yes."

"Sorry if I came across wrong, but I'd hoped to get you home earlier. When we came out of Jug Head's, it hit me how easily someone could attack you again with it being so dark."

That made her feel slightly better, except for the being attacked part. Sam came around to her side of the car and opened her door. "Thank you," she said and climbed out of the car, but he didn't seem to hear her.

A frown creased his brow as he glanced up and down the street.

"What's wrong?"

"I don't know. Something seems off."

A shiver raced down her spine, and she followed his gaze down the tree-lined avenue. Spanish moss floated like ghosts in the light wind. Her sharpened senses caught the scent of burning wood—probably from the Johnsons' house. A dog barked two doors down. Normal things. So why was the hair raised on her arms?

With the overhead streetlight out, darkness hid his form as he pressed against the giant oak in the yard. The tree limb forked at just the right height to rest the rifle he'd assembled and afforded him an unobstructed view of Emma's apartment building at the end of the block.

He'd parked on the next street over and carried his black case to the vacant house with a for-sale sign in the yard. This street dead-ended into the one Emma lived on. Even though there wasn't much traffic in the area, he'd only ever come here once in the daytime and that was this morning. At night with his dark clothing he could blend with the shadows, and the overgrown shrubs afforded him privacy from any neighbors who might look out their windows.

A light wind brought the scent of burning wood and a memory of being cold and his mother struggling to lift a log his father hadn't split. His father. His jaw clenched just thinking about him.

The whine of tires jerked his attention back to Emma's street. Not them. They should have been here by now.

Waiting was always the hard part. While he waited, he pointed the powerful nightscope to a second-floor window. Emma's bedroom window. It was up to him to protect her.

Another vehicle approached the apartment building, and his pulse quickened. An SUV with the National Park Service logo on the door pulled to the front of the apartment house, and Sam Ryker climbed out of the driver's side. Emma waited in the vehicle until he walked around and opened her car door. He held his breath as Ryker made her sit in the car while he scanned the area. Even though his black clothing blended in with the shadows, he couldn't keep from shrinking back. He lined them up in the crosshairs of the nightscope as they hurried up the steps.

"Let's get you inside," Sam said and guided her with his hand on the small of her back.

"I have to get the key out for the front door." Emma fumbled in her purse and pulled the key out, only to drop it. As they both stooped to retrieve it, she heard a faint *pop*, and the wood above them splintered.

She froze. It was last night happening all over again. Except this time, she'd put Sam in jeopardy.

"Go!" Sam covered her with his body as he pulled his gun.

There was nowhere to go. The door was locked, and she wasn't about to rise up and unlock it. Emma crawled to the other side of the porch and held her breath, waiting for another shot to fire. When it didn't happen, she searched for Sam. He was hunkered down behind the column on the porch with his cell phone in one hand, gun in the other.

"Do you think he's gone?" she whispered.

"I don't know. I called 911 and then the sheriff."

As the adrenaline rush subsided, questions crowded her mind. What was going on? Why was someone trying to kill her?

13

The Natchez police arrived first, followed by Nate, and Sam helped them secure the area.

"Any sign of your attacker?" Nate asked.

"I never saw him. It's like he was a ghost." Sam nodded toward the huge live oaks that lined the street. "He could've hidden anywhere. The doorframe is so splintered I can't even tell the direction the bullet came from."

The dry wood had fragmented into a hundred pieces and would have to be put back together like a jigsaw puzzle. Nate shined a light on the frame, then used his knife to dig the bullet out. He held it up. The bullet had mushroomed on impact.

"It looks bigger than the bullet from last night," Sam said. A text beeped in, and he checked his phone. Clayton.

Do you know if Trey is coming?

He hasn't arrived? I saw him less than an hour ago and he was on his way to the site.

He's not here yet.

Sam turned to the sheriff. "Have you heard from Trey? He hasn't arrived at the site yet."

"Sorry, I meant to tell you he had to run by the nursing home to check on his dad."

"How is Carter?" he asked as he texted his ranger the information.

"The Alzheimer's is getting worse. Half the time he doesn't even know Trey, and when he does, he's abusive."

"It's a terrible disease," Sam said. He'd seen it take brilliant people down.

Nate agreed with him and then said, "Fill me in, starting with when you left Mount Locust."

Sam started with the visit to the walk-in clinic and ended with their drive from the restaurant. Nate rubbed the back of his neck. "Did you notice anyone following you?"

"No, and I checked. We didn't have a tail. I figure whoever fired the rifle—and it definitely was a rifle—was waiting for her to come home."

"Show me exactly where each of you were standing when it happened," Nate said.

Sam retraced their steps in his mind. "I was here." He pointed to the left of the door. "Emma was in front, ready to unlock it. If we both hadn't tried to catch her key when she dropped it . . ." Each time he thought about how close Emma had come to being hit, his stomach churned.

Nate frowned. "So, you weren't right behind her?"

Sam shook his head. "I was standing a little to her left."

The door opened from the left and he'd stood almost in front of the doorframe. His breath caught in his chest as he stared at the bullet hole that was level with his eyesight. If he hadn't bent over to catch the key . . . "The shooter was aiming at me?"

"That or he was a bad shot."

"We keep saying *he*, but there's nothing that keeps the shooter from being a woman," Sam said. He scratched his chin. "But why me? I haven't been back in Natchez long enough to make enemies."

"Good question."

Nate had to be wrong, at least about Sam being the target. "Maybe the shooter was just trying to scare her again," he said.

"From what?" Before Sam could answer, both men's attention shifted as a car turned into the drive and one of the Natchez officers stopped it. The officer questioned the driver and then allowed the man to proceed to the back of the house.

"If that's one of Emma's neighbors, I'd like to question him," Sam said. A hallway ran the length of the house. "I bet he'll come in the back way."

"I'll stay here in case he comes around front."

Sam was waiting when a man who had the lean look of a runner came in the back door. His eyes widened when he saw Sam. "Who are you? And what's going on? That policeman wouldn't tell me anything."

"Ranger Sam Ryker. And you are . . . ?"

"Gregory Hart." He shifted the case he carried to his other hand. "I live here. Why are all these policemen here?"

Hart looked to be in his early forties and stood a couple of inches taller than Sam's six-one. "There was a shooting tonight."

The man blanched. "Here? In this neighborhood? You must be mistaken." He looked past Sam as Nate joined them. "Sheriff? I'm surprised to see you here."

"Greg." Nate nodded. "No reason for me not to be here." Then he turned to Sam. "He works at City Hall."

"You don't normally deal with city matters. Why this one?"

For a second, Sam thought Nate would ignore the man, then he said, "It's connected to a county investigation. Have you seen any suspicious people hanging around the neighborhood?"

Greg frowned. "Does this have anything to do with the flowers Emma received this morning?"

"You know about those?" Nate asked.

"I was leaving for work when she discovered them in front of her door. Is Emma the one who was shot at?" He directed his question to Nate.

"Maybe. Did you see who left the flowers?"

"Like I told her, I didn't see anyone. If our landlord had installed the surveillance system as we requested . . ." Greg's eyes widened. "Wait. You do think the flowers are connected to the shooting."

"Could be," Nate said.

"Sheriff, that's crazy. Emma's an attractive woman, and she probably gets flowers from guys all the time."

"Sounds like they could've been from you," Sam said as he studied the case in Greg's hand. It was definitely large enough for a disassembled rifle.

Red crept into his face. "They weren't. If you two will excuse me, I haven't eaten dinner yet." He nodded to the case. "Symphony practice went longer than usual."

"Greg plays trumpet in the symphony orchestra," Nate said.

Sam nodded. "If you see anyone suspicious hanging around this area, give us a call."

"I will. I'd hate to see anything happen to Emma. Good night, gentlemen." Greg walked to the steps.

Sam waited until the man ascended the stairs and his door clicked shut. "What do you think?"

"He's not the type to go around shooting at people—it takes a certain amount of passion to kill someone. The only thing Gregory Hart has ever been passionate about is himself and his music," Nate said. "Besides, my wife plays violin in the symphony, and they've been practicing every evening for the past week for the Valentine's Day concert, so he couldn't have been at Mount Locust. And if you were the target, well, let's just say I don't think he would be shooting at you since he doesn't even know you."

"Ask your wife if he was at practice." Sam wasn't so quick to dismiss him as their suspect. "I'd have loved to have seen inside that case."

"And he would have been highly insulted if you'd asked. It wouldn't be worth the animosity—you might need something from City Hall one day."

"You're saying he'd hold a grudge?"

"Like an elephant," Nate said with a chuckle. "Where's Emma?"

"Upstairs with one of the city detectives. He's taking her statement."

"I have a few questions for her as well, but before I talk to her, I want to run something by you. We just received two license plate readers. Haven't tried them out yet, but with Pete Nelson's approval, I want to set up the cameras in front of Emma's apartment."

Sam was familiar with the ALPR devices that recorded the license plates of cars that passed by. "I didn't realize Adams County had anything like that."

"We just got them, thanks to a federal grant," Nate said. "Hers will be our test case."

"Maybe that will help us catch her stalker," Sam said as he followed the sheriff up the stairs to Emma's apartment.

She opened the door before Nate had a chance to respond. Relief showed in her eyes when she saw the sheriff.

"Come on in."

"How's your hand?" Nate asked.

"Hurting."

"I'm sorry." Nate turned to the Natchez police officer and held out his hand.

"You planning on taking over the case?" the detective asked as he shook hands with the sheriff.

"No, sir. I'm only trying to figure out how it connects to a case at Mount Locust. Are you in charge here?"

While Emma was focused on the two men as they talked, Sam checked her out. She'd regained her color, and trouper that she was, she showed no sign of the fear she must have felt when the bullet plowed into the doorframe. She turned, and he looked away, but not before she caught him watching her.

"I'm going to make an ice pack for my hand," she said, color rising in her face.

Sam nodded and turned his attention back to the detective. He extended his hand. "Sam Ryker," he said. "Friend of Emma's and the Southern District law enforcement ranger on the Trace."

The two men shook hands. "Jonathan Rogers, sergeant with Natchez PD. No reason we can't work together on this, right?"

"None whatsoever," Nate replied. "In fact, I want to discuss putting two ALPR cameras out front."

"You have license plate readers? I've been trying to get the chief to purchase one for the past six months."

"I'll get them to your chief tomorrow." The two men discussed the best place to locate the cameras, and when they finished, Rogers slipped his notepad in his jacket. "I'm done here and need to check on my men. Keep me informed."

As the detective closed the door behind him, a text alerted on Sam's phone, and he glanced at it. His sister, Jenny.

Where are you?

In town. Whatcha need?

Jace wants a milkshake.

I'm tied up right now. How is Jace?

He purposely didn't mention Emma's name since Jenny had been less than sympathetic when he told her about the attack last night. Talk about holding grudges. Jenny was still upset at the way Emma had dumped him.

Better. Call me when you can.

Sam texted her a thumbs-up. Jace needed a positive male role model, and helping out with his nephew had been one reason for accepting the district ranger position after Jenny's deadbeat husband took off. He looked up from his phone when Nate nudged him. "I'm sorry. Text from my sister. What were you saying?"

"Just making sure you're driving Emma back and forth to Mount Locust."

"And anywhere else she needs to go," Sam added. "She's a ranger, and one of the shootings happened on NPS property. Emma will be my top priority until this person is caught."

"Good. I asked Chief Nelson to station an officer at the apartment," Nate said, "but he doesn't have the manpower. He did agree to have his night-shift officers drive by more often."

Pete Nelson had been the third law enforcement official Sam had sought out after his arrival, and from what he'd seen of the man, he seemed to be the sort who would do what he said. "I think Emma will be safe here in the apartment, and I'll check out the area before I pick her up."

"Sounds good," Nate said. He turned to Emma as she approached with a bag of ice on her wrist. "See you tomorrow."

"You okay?" Sam asked after the sheriff left.

Her eyes narrowed. "What I am is mad. Why would anyone target me?"

"You might not be the target," he said. "But if you are, I'm beginning to believe your attacker is a terrible shot."

"What?"

"This is the third time he's shot at you and missed, if he was shooting at you." Sam explained what he and Nate had discovered.

"You think you could have been the target?"

"It's possible."

She tipped her head to one side. "I don't buy that. You're too new to the area."

"I can't discount it altogether," Sam said. "Any chance I can get that cup of coffee we talked about earlier?"

14

Emma laid the ice pack on the counter while she made a pot of coffee. "You still like it black?" she asked from the kitchen area. When he answered in the affirmative, she smiled. "Good. You really don't want to ruin my coffee with any additives."

"That good, huh?"

"I make just about the best coffee in town. Sit down and I'll bring it to you." At least her attempt to lighten the mood didn't fall too flat. And she did make good coffee, buying Kona coffee beans and grinding them herself.

When the coffee finished brewing, she poured Sam's cup and took it to him before returning for her own. He'd taken the leather recliner, leaving her either the gold paisley chair or the blue-and-white sofa. The extra-strength Tylenol she'd taken earlier had dulled the pain in her wrist, and she was starting to get the hang of using her left hand. The pill had done nothing to calm her nerves, though. Her insides twitched like a jumping bean.

"You okay?" he asked.

The gleam of concern in his eyes touched her. Maybe getting shot at again had broken the barrier between them. "As good as anyone could be after getting fired at two nights in a row."

"You're tough," he said.

"I assume the two shootings are connected."

"Maybe. Probably," he corrected.

"Which is it?"

"It's not impossible that there are two different shooters, but until we have more evidence, I really can't hazard a guess."

How did she get in this kind of mess? When she couldn't think of anything else to ask him, Emma took a sip of her coffee. Even though she'd asked him up to discuss their past, now that the time was here, she wasn't ready. Maybe if she poked food at him . . . "I have some chocolate chip cookies, if you'd like one."

"No, your coffee is good enough without anything." His brown eyes twinkled. "But when did you start liking chocolate chip cookies?"

He remembered a lot more about her than she would've ever dreamed. "I haven't. I keep them for other people."

They both fell silent, and Emma felt like the man in a downstairs apartment waiting for the other shoe to drop. Finally she couldn't stand it any longer. "Look—"

"I think—"

There was a pause, then they both laughed at having spoken at the same time.

"You first," she said.

"No, ladies first."

She took a fortifying breath. "There seems to be a lot of tension between us, and I don't know how to change it. Being around you is like walking on eggshells. One minute I'm convinced you'd like to be a hundred miles from me, and the next, I think maybe we can be friends."

He stared into his coffee without answering. When he looked up, there was hesitancy in his eyes. "There's something I'd like to know."

"What?"

"I never understood why you broke off our relationship."

That made two of them. It'd seemed her only choice at the time, but she wasn't proud of that time in her life. "I was so angry at Ryan for deserting me, the family. He wasn't here to blame, but you were."

"But you had started pulling away even before Ryan left."

"I don't remember it that way," she said. "You were the one pulling away."

Sam stiffened. "What are you talking about? I had just asked you to marry me."

No . . . He *had been* pulling away—just like her high school boyfriend who dumped her for someone else.

That had been the last time she'd been humiliated because of a relationship. At her first doubt, she ended it before the other person could. Emma raised her gaze, and the pain in Sam's eyes almost undid her. What if she'd been wrong about him all these years?

"But you let me go without a fight," she said, her voice low. "I thought it was what you wanted."

He set his cup down and moved from the recliner to the sofa beside her and took her hand. "I thought *you* wanted out."

She'd probably given that impression. "It wasn't just that I thought you were pulling away. I was so hurt when Ryan deserted us, and I took it out on you." She couldn't think with him so close, his fingers covering her left hand. Emma swallowed hard and pulled from his grasp, immediately missing the strength his touch conveyed. Her wrist throbbed again, and she held her hand to her chest, above her heart.

"Hurting again?"

"A little." Not nearly as much as her heart. "I'm sorry for the things I said when he went missing."

Sam was quiet for a minute. "I really wish you could accept that whatever happened that night wasn't my fault and it wasn't your fault either."

He hadn't heard the words she'd hurled at Ryan. "I wish my head could believe you about my part."

"I understand—I really do. Ryan was my best friend, and in the beginning, I blamed myself after he disappeared."

She bit her lip. "You had no choice, not with your sister stuck on the side of Highway 61 with a flat tire. Ryan was too old for a babysitter, and your sister needed help."

His face flushed. "There's—"

"You don't owe me any explanation. I know you hated what happened." Even now she could remember the sadness in his eyes when he learned Ryan hadn't come home.

"I . . ." He bit his lip. "That doesn't mean I don't feel really bad about it."

"I know you do. I just wish I knew where he is and why he's never contacted us." She ached all over and rubbed the back of her neck. "His disappearance split our family apart. It was too much for Mom and Dad's marriage, and it caused a huge rift between Mom and me. She'll barely discuss Ryan with me anymore."

"What do you mean?"

Emma stretched the tight muscles in her neck. If she wasn't careful, she'd get a migraine. She raised her head. "You know Ryan's history. The marijuana. Drinking. It's no wonder he and my parents didn't get along. Dad was a little more lenient—Mom always said he enabled Ryan. They were always fighting about him."

"Yeah," Sam said. "I remember those days. I was even part of the problem for a while."

"But you quit." She frowned. "Did you ever even use marijuana?"

"No. And I stopped drinking when our coach gave us an ultimatum—alcohol or football. I chose football—"

"And my brother chose drinking." She blew out a breath. "Maybe if I hadn't been the favorite, it would have made a difference in him."

"I don't think your parents consciously made you their favorite."

"He thought they did, especially Mom. Said she always believed me over him. According to Ryan, I was Little Miss Perfect in her eyes."

"Well, you were the 'good' kid. You didn't give them any trouble."

"I didn't want any of Mom's tough love." A dull throbbing started on the side of her head, and Emma pulled the ponytail holder off, letting her hair fall free. "Mom thought I was as bad as Dad about enabling him, covering for him when he messed up."

"What I remember is you pushing him to stop drinking and finish his degree," Sam said gently.

"Evidently I didn't push him hard enough." But it seemed the harder she pushed, the more he drank. "If I could just find him and know he's all right."

Sam was quiet for a minute. "Do you think he could be dead?"

"No!" She refused to even consider that scenario. "Even as kids we always felt each other's pain, and if he'd died, I would know it."

"Okay, tell me what you've done to find him."

"That's just it. Nothing other than badger Sheriff Carter for as long as he was sheriff to send out inquiries, but I don't think he ever sent the first one." Every time she thought about Carter, her blood pressure rose. "All we had was what the sheriff told us—that he'd run away. Carter said he'd tracked him to Memphis through a credit card purchase at a liquor store and that the Memphis police had found his Mustang stripped in South Memphis. That's where the trail ended."

"Do you have Sheriff Carter's report?"

"No, but last year, I asked Trey about it and the night Ryan disappeared."

"What did he say?"

"He kept putting me off."

Sam cocked his head. "When did you and Trey start dating?"

She gave him a wry shrug. "Right after I asked about Ryan. He offered to discuss it over coffee, and then we dated a few months. We were never serious. At least I wasn't, especially after he became so controlling."

Sam lifted an eyebrow. "Controlling?"

"He didn't like my clothes or my lack of makeup . . . that sort of thing."

"Did he remember anything significant about the night Ryan left?"

"Not really, other than they'd left him at the Hideaway right after you went to help your sister. Trey said Ryan had gotten obnoxious."

"He wasn't a crying-in-your-beer type of drinker." Sam stood and paced in front of the closed blinds. "I've gone over that night so many times in my head. Gordy was drinking pretty heavily too, but he tended to just get quieter. Trey was pretty well sober when I left," he said, "and Mary Jo was arriving with someone."

"Are you sure? I never heard that," she said.

"I couldn't swear to it, but there's a hazy memory of a guy . . . let me think about it."

"That would be awesome," she said, her pulse increasing. "I was always led to believe Ryan was the last person known to see her. You weren't questioned?"

"Sheriff Carter questioned me once, but then I went back to school in Arizona."

She couldn't believe Sheriff Carter had only interviewed Sam once. "The sheriff never would give my parents a copy of the investigation report. My thinking now is he either bungled the investigation . . . or was covering up something. I tried to get a copy of the report after Carter retired four years ago, but the new sheriff just blew me off. He didn't last long, and I thought when Nate was elected, I'd get the report. But when I asked him about it a week ago, he said it was missing."

"What do you mean?"

She shrugged. "Nate looked for the file, but it wasn't there, and with Sheriff Carter's Alzheimer's, we can't ask him where it is. Trey claims he knows nothing about the report or the case."

"Do you believe him?"

"I do about the report," she said. "Trey was still in college at Ole Miss when all of this happened—it was four or five years later that he went to work for his dad. And Nate has no reason to reopen the case unless something new surfaces." Like her brother returning to Natchez.

Sam picked up his coffee cup. "Would you like more?"

"I better not. I'm already wired."

He walked to her kitchen and refilled his cup, then stood at the island. After a minute, he turned around. "I wish someone like a private investigator had conducted a second investigation."

"That would be nice."

Sam tilted his head. "Do you know if there was any type of physical evidence linking Ryan to Mary Jo's death?"

"No." Emma bit her lip. She never thought the day would come that she could calmly discuss Ryan with Sam. "Sheriff Carter always claimed my brother was only a person of interest, but that was enough for everyone to believe Ryan killed her, especially since he'd taken off for no telling where."

"Do you think he did it?"

"No," she said, almost too quickly. Emma pinched the bridge of her nose. But on her worst days, she wondered if it was possible.

15

"You're tired," Sam said and checked his watch. Eleven thirty? Seemed like it should be much later. He drained his coffee and rinsed his cup, then found Emma's and rinsed it. "I better head out. What time do you want to leave for Mount Locust in the morning?"

"Seven thirty would be good since I don't have to get cat food. I want to get started back on excavating that hole."

"I'll help you."

"Really?" She seemed relieved.

"Until we catch this guy, you're my main concern," he said with a smile. "Really. Brooke will be back, and while she's off tomorrow, she would be available if anything came up. Clayton too."

Emma frowned. "I wonder why she didn't call me?"

He'd gotten a text from Brooke while they were waiting for the Natchez officers to arrive. "The trial ended late, and she was probably tired."

She stood, uncertainty crossing her face. "Um . . . I think maybe I should give you a key to my apartment in case you ever need to get into the building after six."

He nodded slowly. "That's probably a good idea."

"I'll be right back."

Less than a minute later she returned with a key and handed it to him. He put it on his key ring. "Hope I never need to use it."

"Me too," she said and walked him to the door. "And thanks for everything."

"You're welcome. In the morning, I'll come to your apartment door to get you after I check out the neighborhood." Sam didn't know why, but something inside him had shifted.

Soberly, Emma saluted. "Yes, sir."

His breath caught in his chest at the desire that swept through him to take her in his arms and kiss her. Emma's pupils widened. The air between them crackled with electricity. Her full lips were parted slightly, and he wanted to trace his thumb down her jawline. Abruptly, Sam stepped back. Was he crazy? She'd broken his heart once. He'd be stupid to give her the chance to do it again.

"Do you think we could start fresh from tonight?" she asked, her voice hesitant.

Even as he told himself to say no, he nodded. "I think I'd like that."

He had to come clean with Emma. Tomorrow he would find a way to tell her. Sam surprised himself by bending over and kissing the top of her head. "See you tomorrow."

He should have told her the truth about the night Ryan left. The thought dogged him all the way down the stairs, and halfway down, he almost turned around and returned to her door. Almost. She was tired. And in pain. There would be a better time.

The Natchez police had finished their work, and Sam paused at the top of the porch steps, scanning the area. He didn't sense being watched like he had earlier, but then, he didn't figure their assailant had hung around. His cell phone rang, and he unhooked it from his belt. Jenny.

"I'm on my way," Sam said by way of answering. "What kind of milkshake does he want?"

"None." Her tone was curt. "He's asleep."

It was late—of course he was asleep. Sam had missed another

night of saying good night to Jace. When the weather was good, they liked to look out the window over the boy's bed for a special end-of-the-day moment to see what phase the moon was in.

"Look, I'm sorry, but I couldn't come earlier. There was a shooting."

"You're not hurt, are you?"

"No, but I could have been."

"Thank goodness," she said, her relief evident. "Jace was awake a few minutes ago, asking for a drink of water. He may not have fallen back asleep yet."

"Be there in five."

Before he could end the call, his sister added, "Sam . . . I'm sorry for being so snarky about Emma this morning before you left, but I'd hate to see you get mixed up with her again."

Jenny had practically idolized Emma before the breakup and had taken her rejection personally. Another reason to keep his distance from the lovely park ranger. "Don't worry, Sis. Not happening," he said, ignoring the memory of wanting to kiss Emma.

Sam hooked his phone on his belt and hurried to his SUV. It was important to catch Jace before he went to sleep, and he let his speed creep above the limit in the short distance to his sister's small house.

He'd been in love with Emma since high school, and it had been torture watching her flit from one boy to another. Then the first year at the junior college they both attended had been his turn, and he'd been surprised when they became a steady item even after he went away to college in Arizona on a full scholarship.

A couple of buddies who had been Emma's castoffs warned him not to get serious about her. He should have listened. Instead, he asked her to marry him when he came home for the summer and she accepted. He'd given her a ring and was about to chuck the rest of his Arizona scholarship to attend Mississippi State with her and Ryan. At least she broke the engagement before that happened.

He thought he'd gotten over her, but being around her had reopened old feelings. And old fears. Presently, only three people knew the truth about what happened between him and Ryan the night he disappeared. Ryan, Jenny, and Sam.

He'd even had a perfect opening at one point tonight when he could have told her what really happened. How he and Ryan had gotten into a fight in the parking lot when her brother wouldn't leave the tavern. Sam had already been on his way home when Jenny called, needing his help. Emma and everyone else assumed he'd left Ryan because of his sister's trouble, and he'd let them believe it.

While it wasn't a lie, neither was it the whole truth, and he wasn't proud of that. But then Emma had hurt him so deeply when she broke up with him that he didn't see any point in correcting her impression.

Sam slowed in front of his sister's small house and turned into the drive. He really needed to get a place of his own. Maybe even next door. He'd noticed their neighbors had moved out over the weekend, and he'd meant to call the owner this morning to see if the house was available. Tomorrow he'd make the time.

He glanced up at the crescent moon before he inserted his key in the lock, hoping Jace would be awake. The key turned much too easily. Jenny had left the door unlocked again. She was sitting on the sofa folding clothes when he walked into the den. Her hair was pulled back into a ponytail. She and Emma had that in common, if nothing else—the ponytail part, not the color. Jenny's was blonde but Emma's fiery curls matched his mood. "How many times have I told you to keep the doors locked, especially the front door?"

"You don't have to take my head off," she said. "I forgot. Okay?"

He raked his fingers through his hair. "I just want you and Jace to be safe. Natchez isn't like it was when we were kids."

She palmed her hands. "I'll try to remember. Where were you when I called?"

Sam hesitated. If he told her, she'd be on his case again, but he was tired of avoiding the subject. "Emma Winters's apartment," he said. "I'm going to check on Jace."

Sam walked to his nephew's bedroom and sighed when the ten-year-old was asleep. He really had meant to get home in time to check out the moon with him. His heart swelled at the sight of the sleeping boy. Jace was smaller than most ten-year-olds and still had an angelic face at times. That almost made him laugh out loud. Jace would not like Sam thinking he looked angelic.

The boy's eyes fluttered open. "Sam, you're here," he said sleepily.

Sam had refused to be called Uncle Sam. "Yep, buddy, I'm home. Are you feeling better?"

"Uh-huh. Is it too late to look for the moon?"

"Let's see." He crossed the room and pulled the curtain aside as Jace scrambled to his knees on the bed. The thin white arc hung overhead against a black night. "Do you remember what we call this phase?"

"It's a crescent moon."

"Good. Now, is it waxing or waning?"

Jace held out his hand facing the moon and made a *C* with his thumb and forefinger. The moon fit neatly in the curve. "It's waxing, right?"

"Yeah. What does that mean?"

"It'll be a full moon in a couple of weeks," Jace said, looking around at him.

"Good, you remembered. I'm proud of you." Words he never heard from his own father.

"Thanks for waking me up."

"I didn't mean to, but I'm glad too. Now, let's get you tucked in before your mama skins me alive."

Jace wrinkled his face into a frown. "I'm too big to be tucked in."

"Maybe just this one time?"

Grudgingly Jace settled down in the bed, and Sam tucked the Dutch Boy quilt his mom had made under the boy's chin. "Good night, sleep tight, buddy."

"And don't let the bedbugs bite," Jace said with a giggle.

"See you in the morning." Sam ruffled his hair and walked back to the living room. "You have a good kid there," he said to his sister.

"Yeah. His dad is missing out on a lot."

He studied his sister. She'd lost weight since the divorce, and fatigue in her slim face intensified the gauntness. "Are you sleeping okay?"

Her answer was a shrug as she stood. "As well as ever."

Jenny picked up the folded towels and crossed the room. Tonight the limp she'd had since childhood was more pronounced. Another regret filled him with guilt. Standing all day in a classroom couldn't be good for her, but teaching kindergarteners wasn't a sit-down job. "Anything I can do to help?" he asked.

"You can put these away." She handed him the towels. "And go see Dad."

He flinched, her words hammering him. "Not happening," he said, and took the towels to the linen closet. When he returned from the bathroom, she was waiting for him with arms crossed.

"Why not?"

"How can you ask after the way he treated Mom . . . and us?"

"He's changed, Sam. Big-time. He owns a real estate brokerage firm now, and he's helping Mom out with her bills. Me too when I need it."

"If he hadn't been the way he was, you wouldn't be worried about money in the first place. You would've found a decent sort to marry instead of—"

"And I wouldn't have Jace, would I?"

She had him there, but when she started to say something else, he held up his hand. "I don't want to talk about dear old Dad tonight. Or ever."

"All right already. But he's a good man now." Like always, Jenny had to get in the last word. She tilted her head. "Why were you at Emma Winters's apartment?"

This subject was no better. "Someone took a shot at her last night, and I've been assigned to make sure she gets back and forth to Mount Locust safely."

"Why you?"

"She's a ranger. The shooting happened on park service land. And—"

"Wait. When you called you said there'd been a shooting—was that different than the shooting last night?"

"Yes."

"Two nights in a row?" Her eyes widened. "I'm assuming she wasn't hit last night, but how about tonight?"

"No. We'd both stooped to pick up the key she dropped, and the bullet crashed into the doorframe."

"You could've been hit. You need to hand her off to someone else."

"I wasn't, and I'm not. Right now she's my responsibility," he said.

"Why were you so late getting her home?"

"We'd stopped to get something to eat after getting her hand wrapped at the clinic."

"Wait. You took her out to eat?" She shook her head. "I can't believe you've forgiven Emma Winters for the way she treated you."

"I forgave her a long time ago. Doesn't mean I'm opening my heart to her again." He didn't understand why Jenny had it in for Emma the way she did. Well, he did, but it'd been ten years since Emma had given his ring back.

"Whatever. Tell me what happened."

"We're both too tired to talk about this, and I need to check in with Clayton."

"What does Clayton have to do with anything?"

"He's guarding Mount Locust with Trey Carter."

Jenny wouldn't let up until he explained, peppering him with questions, and he briefly ran over the details of what had happened at the inn.

"Do you think there's a body buried where you're excavating?"

"I hope not," he said, taking his phone out.

"Why else would anyone be so anxious to remove whatever is there?"

He dialed Clayton. "Maybe it's buried treasure." The call went to Clayton's voicemail.

"And they left it untouched all this time?"

"Maybe." He dialed Clayton's number again and got the same results. It wasn't for lack of service because it didn't go straight to voicemail. More likely he just wasn't answering, and that wasn't like Clayton. His stomach knotted, and he tried to force calm through his body as he hooked his phone on his belt. "I need to drive out to Mount Locust."

"Why? It's late."

"Clayton's not answering."

"Is there even reception there?" she asked.

He nodded and tried again. Still no answer.

"Didn't you say Trey was with him? Try him."

"Sometimes you have really good ideas," he said with a grin.

But Trey didn't answer either. "I'll be back as soon as I can. Lock the door behind me."

She rolled her eyes but followed him to the door, and he heard it click after he closed it. On the way to the Trace, he called Nate. "Have you heard from Trey?"

"No. What's up?"

"Neither he nor Clayton are answering their phones. I'm on my way to make sure everything's okay."

16

Emma hugged her arms around her waist after Sam left. The electricity between them was still there, reminding her that he'd been her only true love. So why had she ruined it? Not an easy question to answer, especially when she had a throbbing wrist to deal with.

Raising her wrist eased the pain slightly while Emma rummaged in her backpack for the bottle of Tylenol. She found it and stared at the childproof cap that had to be pushed down and turned to open. With one hand. Her left one. Two attempts later, she thought about a hammer. No. She would not let a bottle cap best her. After trapping the bottle against her body, she managed to get the top off and took two pills. Now to ice her wrist again until the Tylenol took effect.

As she sat in her recliner with an ice pack on her hand, thoughts of Sam returned. He'd appointed himself her guardian, which was so like him. It wasn't going to be easy to be around him and not lose her heart to him again. If she hadn't already.

Emma had to ignore her feelings for Sam. They could never surmount the past, and she doubted he wanted to after the way she'd taken her anger out on him after Ryan left. That, coupled with her belief that he was losing interest in her, had pushed her to give his ring back. And then he'd left for Arizona without even trying to work it out.

Looking back, Emma couldn't blame him if she was honest with herself. Even if he'd tried, which he hadn't, she would've been too stubborn to admit being wrong. She was seriously messed up ten years ago, and it had affected more than her relationship with Sam. The one with her mother needed mending as well.

Not that either of them had ever acknowledged a problem existed. Instead, they'd just drifted apart after every discussion they had about Ryan ended in an argument. When was the last time she and her mother had a meaningful discussion that went deeper than the weather?

She thought about calling her, but making amends with her mother needed to be done in person. That way Emma could gauge her reactions. She fished her cell phone from her back pocket.

"Hey Siri, call my mom," Emma said before she could change her mind about setting up a time they could get together. On the sixth ring, she was almost ready to hang up when her mom answered.

"Emma? Why are you calling so late? Is something wrong?"

Her mom's attorney voice came through on the other end, a businesslike voice that served her well with the cases she tried. Not so much between the two of them. "No," Emma said, wincing when she checked the clock on the wall. "I didn't realize it was so late. I just wanted to see how you're doing, and maybe set up a time to drop by your condo."

"That would be wonderful," she said warmly. "And I'm fine, keeping busy with this latest case, but it's coming together. The defendant is considering a plea deal, and we might not have to go to court."

Her mom, the workaholic. She thought about not wanting to quit at Mount Locust earlier. Must be where she got it. Perhaps they were more alike than she realized.

"How are you?"

"I've—I'm okay." Emma had almost said she'd been better, like when she didn't have someone shooting at her, but that would open up a thousand questions she didn't want to answer tonight.

"Oh, and I, ah . . ." her mother said. "I've been thinking about that flyer."

Here it comes. Emma tensed up for what was sure to follow. "And?"

"It might not hurt to post it on social media," she said softly.

Emma was stunned. "Did you just say—"

"Yes. Don't sound so surprised. Just because I didn't fall apart when Ryan left doesn't mean I don't want to find him. I wouldn't have hired a private investigator if that had been the case."

"*What?*" She sat down hard on the sofa. Surely she hadn't heard her mother right. "When did you hire a private investigator?"

"Right after I moved to Jackson—about six months after Ryan left. Why?"

"Why didn't I know about it?"

Her mother fell quiet.

"Are you still there?"

"Yes. I'm here. We didn't tell you at first because we didn't want you to get your hopes up, and when the investigator didn't find Ryan, you were doing so much better emotionally that your dad and I decided not to say anything about it."

"So, Dad knew too." It wasn't a question. "Do you still have the investigator's report?"

"Yes. Why?"

"I'd like to see it." Her mind hadn't quite recovered from learning her mom had hired a PI.

"I can save you the trouble—there isn't much to it," she said.

"Do you remember if the report had a copy of Sheriff Carter's case file?"

"It's been ten years . . . but yes, I think there was one. Why the sudden push to find Ryan? First with the flyer and now wanting to see the investigator's report. Have you learned something you're not telling me?"

"No," she said quickly. "And I . . . I don't know why."

"Hmm."

Her mother's favorite way of showing she wasn't buying her answer. It wasn't even a word, but it got her point across. Emma tried to formulate a different answer. Was it because Sam was back? No. She'd had Ryan on her mind before this week.

"I think because next month it'll be ten years . . . on our birthday," Emma said. "I read somewhere that cold case units get more inquiries around anniversaries and birthdays of their missing loved ones than any other time." It was the best she could come up with and at least partially true. Ten years was a long time to go without seeing her twin.

The silence on the other end of the line drew out. "I'll have to find the report. When do you want it?" Her mother's voice sounded almost defeated.

"How about I drive up to Jackson after I get off work tomorrow? We could have dinner together, call it my birthday celebration." She glanced at her bandaged hand. "Oh, wait. I'll have to find someone to drive me."

"Why?"

"I broke a bone in my hand." Emma explained to her mom what had happened.

"You've started on the Mount Locust project?"

"Something like that. Let me call around and see if I can get someone to run me up there tomorrow night," Emma said. "I'll let you know first thing in the morning."

Once again there was silence, then her mother said, "I'm sorry I haven't exactly been there for you on your birthday, but you understand why, don't you?"

"It's not easy for me either," she said.

"I know, honey. I'll wait to hear from you before I make reservations."

"I'll make it happen someway." Emma would have to take a change of clothes to work. Her mom favored high-end restaurants and would frown if she showed up in a park service uniform. Seconds after she disconnected, her phone rang. Her friend Brooke Danvers. Emma punched the accept button. "Hey," she said. "When did you get home?"

"About half an hour ago," Brooke said. "How's your hand?"

"Hurting, but I'll survive. How did you find out?"

"Sam told me."

Emma should have known. "How'd the trial go?" Her friend had arrested two teens on the Trace for driving a stolen car. Not a big case, but time-consuming since one of the teens was the son of a wealthy businessman, and his high-dollar attorney was dragging out the case.

"About like you'd expect—he got off with community service."

"Maybe he'll learn something."

"You always were the optimist." They both laughed, and Brooke said, "What's going on at Mount Locust? Sam told me just enough about your accident to whet my interest before he had to hang up."

Emma glanced at her bandaged hand. Maybe Brooke could take her to Jackson and even back and forth to work. "It's a long story. What are you doing tomorrow?"

"Luke's back in town, and we have a date tomorrow night."

Her heart sank. There went asking Brooke to take her to Jackson. That only left Sam. "How about during the day?"

"Why?"

"Thought you might like to do a little digging."

"At Mount Locust? I'd love to, but I have a hair appointment at ten, and no way can I cancel—you know how hard it is to get in with Miranda, and besides, Luke is picking me up at four." She paused. "What's this all about?"

"Nothing." Just like nothing was working out like Emma wanted. It looked like it would be her and Sam tomorrow.

"I don't believe you. Spill it."

"With my hand wrapped, I'm not supposed to drive. Don't

give it another thought. Sam will take me." She hoped. Emma balanced the phone between her chin and shoulder. "Are you working Sunday?"

"Yeah."

"Would you mind giving me a ride to Mount Locust? And then picking me up after five?"

"Sure, but why do I think there's more to this story than you're telling?"

Emma sighed. "It's a little awkward being around Sam after the way I broke up with him."

"Don't you think you should work that out? With him back in Natchez and working as a ranger, you'll be running into him all the time."

"Yeah, but we still have too much bad history between us."

"Only if you let it. It's really your choice," Brooke said.

"It's not that simple. I don't think he'd ever trust me not to hurt him again, and while I no longer blame him for Ryan taking off . . ." She sighed. "It's like I said, awkward."

"Your brother wasn't Sam's responsibility."

"I know that." He was Emma's.

"Or yours," Brooke added. "You've got to let go of this guilt you're carrying around."

"I don't feel—"

"Yes, you do. It shows up as anger, because that's easier to deal with. Have you ever thought about seeing a therapist?"

"I don't need a therapist," Emma said. "Are you getting your hair trimmed?"

"Go stick your head in the sand if you want to," Brooke said. "And yes, I'm getting my hair cut."

She valued her friend's advice, but this time she was wrong. All Emma needed to do was find her brother and everything else would fall into place.

Sam tried Clayton one last time before he hit the Trace. It wasn't like his second-in-command not to answer his cell phone. Eighteen minutes later, he turned off at the Mount Locust exit and drove to the tractor shed. A light shone where they'd been digging earlier, but Sam didn't see the tent. Or either man, even though Clayton's and Trey's SUVs were there.

Frowning, he parked beside Clayton's vehicle and grabbed his flashlight, powering it up before he stepped out of his SUV. Sam cocked his ear. Quiet. Too quiet, with not even the singing of tree frogs he'd heard last night.

Sam unsnapped his holster and pulled his Sig 320 as he hurried to the site. Halfway there, his gut twisted when the light beam flashed on a body, propped against a tree. Clayton. With his heart knocking out of his chest, Sam knelt and felt the park ranger's wrist. Relief was immediate. The ranger's pulse was steady and strong, a good sign, but puzzling. It was like he'd sat down and gone to sleep.

He stood and scanned the area. Where was Trey? When he didn't see him, Sam walked toward the dig, calling the deputy's name. Silence answered him. A few minutes later, the sight of the backhoe once again at the dig site stopped him. Who had moved it back to the pit? When he and Emma had left earlier, the backhoe was a good twenty yards from the dig.

Sam noted the upright position of the bucket and then turned as headlights flashed from the Trace. Seconds later he recognized Nate's Tahoe as he parked beside the other vehicles. Sam took out his cell phone and punched in 911 as he walked to meet the sheriff. When the dispatcher answered, he gave his location and asked for two ambulances. He didn't have a good feeling about Trey.

"What's going on?" Nate asked when they met up.

"Not sure. The backhoe is at the dig site again, and I found Clayton passed out. He seems to be breathing okay, just not conscious," he said. "Can't find Trey anywhere, so I called for ambulances as a precaution. I was on my way to look for him when you pulled in."

"Let's see if we can find him." They trekked through the woods to the excavation site. The tent lay toppled, and the backhoe lights were aimed at the pit. But no sign of the deputy. Sam peered into the shadowy pit and flashed his light around the bottom. A trowel lay in one corner, and he was pretty sure Emma hadn't left it there. The hole looked deeper than earlier too. He found the measuring stick. The pit had been three feet deep when they left, and now the depth measured a little over four feet. "Whatever was buried here is probably gone," he said.

Nate nodded. "Let's find Trey. I'll take from here to the visitor center, and you can cover north of the site."

Sam had walked almost to Chamberlain Road when he heard Nate yell.

"Over here!"

He jogged to where the sheriff was helping his deputy to sit up. Trey groaned and held his hand to the back of his head.

"What happened?" Nate was asking him.

"I don't know. I fell asleep, and when I woke up, I heard someone at the site."

"What do you mean, you fell asleep?"

Trey ran a hand over his face. "I know it sounds crazy, but that's what happened."

"Go over everything you did from the time you arrived," Nate said.

"It's all still kind of fuzzy." Trey took a shaky breath. "I stopped off to visit my dad and then came straight here. First thing Clayton and I did was to secure the area. Everything looked normal so we returned to the SUVs to eat the hamburgers I'd gotten at Jug Head's." Trey rolled his shoulders and grimaced, then he continued. "He'd brought donuts, and about ten we ate them and drank coffee. It was after that when we decided to walk the perimeter—Clayton took one side and I took the other. And that's the last thing I remember until I woke up and heard the backhoe running."

"Did you get a look at the person running the backhoe?" Sam asked.

Trey shook his head and winced. "I was disoriented and everything was blurry. The lights from the backhoe made it hard to see anyone. They went out, and I heard someone running away, so I followed. Then there was this pain in my head, and everything went black."

Nate was quiet for a minute. "You were evidently drugged and then knocked out. But how were you drugged?"

"I don't know. Nothing like this has ever happened to me before." Trey rested his head in his hand. "Is Clayton okay?"

"Knocked out, like you," the sheriff said.

"The coffee," Sam said. "Did Clayton drink any of it?"

"We both did."

"Was it possible someone tampered with it?"

Trey raised his head and winced. "I don't see how."

"Did you keep the thermos with you until you ate?"

Trey frowned. "No. I left it in the SUV with the burgers."

"Did you lock your vehicle?"

The deputy studied on Sam's question. "I almost always do, although I can't swear I did tonight. But the Tahoe was always in my line of sight."

Sam turned and looked toward the maintenance area. True,

the vehicles were visible, but partly in the shadows. If Trey left the Tahoe unlocked, someone could have gotten in on the passenger side without being seen. The dome light wouldn't have come on either since all police vehicles came from the factory with the light disabled. "How about at the nursing home? Did you leave your vehicle unlocked?"

"No . . . Maybe . . . I was just going to be there a minute."

"Okay. That's two opportunities for someone to slip drugs in your thermos."

"But how would anyone have known I had coffee?"

"Could have seen you when you bought it," Nate said. "But then again, it's not exactly a secret that you drink a lot of coffee. Do you remember anything else?"

Before he could answer, a groan from Clayton drew Sam's attention, and he hurried to where the ranger struggled to stand.

"What happened?" he mumbled.

"I don't know. Just sit there until the ambulance arrives," Sam said. "Do you remember if Trey's coffee tasted funny?"

He scrubbed his face. "I don't remember anything unusual. But drinking the coffee is the last thing I do remember."

"Where's the thermos?" Sam asked as Trey and the sheriff approached. A few miles out, the wail of sirens announced the arrival of the ambulances.

"It's in my SUV," Trey said. "At least that's where I left it."

They all turned as the ambulances turned off the Trace and drove to the maintenance area. "Let's get you two checked out." Sam helped Clayton while Nate assisted Trey.

While paramedics looked over the two men, Nate retrieved the thermos from Trey's vehicle. "There's about half a cup left in the bottom, and I'll get it tested."

Sam walked with him to the excavation site, where they were careful to not disturb anything. "What could be buried here that's so important someone would knock out two officers to get? He took a big chance of getting caught."

"Two things come to mind. Skeletal remains or some type of treasure, and I don't think it's treasure." Nate opened an app on his phone. "This afternoon, I pulled all the missing persons reports for the past fifteen years. There've been twenty, but fifteen have follow-up reports that showed the person was found—most of them teens who returned home. Three were found dead of natural causes when they wandered away from their homes in the dead of winter, and two have no resolution. I figure we just haven't found the bodies yet. Emma's brother is one of the two."

Emma was so certain Ryan was still alive. Sam wasn't so sure. It wasn't the first time he'd considered the possibility since the GPR machine had located the disturbed soil. Especially since the woman Ryan had been accused of killing was found not too far from Mount Locust. "Do we want to wait until morning to look for evidence?" Sam asked. "Or do you want to process the scene now?"

"Morning. Like last night, there's too big a chance of destroying evidence. I'll assign two deputies to guard the site and make sure they don't drink any coffee that's been out of their sight. And I'll have another deputy make regular drive-bys," Nate said, taking out his phone.

While Nate contacted his deputies, Sam edged closer to the pit and shined his light along the bottom. *Wait.* "Look at this," he said to Nate.

The sheriff hooked his phone on his belt and peered into the hole. "Is that a shoe print?"

"Looks like one to me," Sam said. "We may have gotten lucky."

"I'll get a tech out here to cast it ASAP, but processing the rest of the crime scene can wait until morning."

Sam checked his watch. Almost one thirty. Too late to call Emma and tell her about the new developments. He hadn't asked her if she'd considered they might be excavating a grave, but maybe he needed to prepare her . . . just in case.

18

Emma looked out her window. No sign of Sam. She checked her watch. He was five minutes late already. She'd seriously considered renting a vehicle with an automatic transmission until she remembered that if she drove after being advised by a doctor not to and had an accident, her insurance wouldn't pay.

She picked up her phone, scrolled to Sam's name, and punched it. He answered on the first ring.

"I'm turning on your street now. Give me a minute to look around."

"What's your excuse this time?"

"Afraid I don't have one."

She laughed. "At least you're honest. Ring me when I can come down."

Shaking her head, Emma slid her phone in her back pocket. People like Sam just didn't have any concept of time. They always thought they could crowd one more thing into their schedule. She moved from the window and grabbed the clothes she planned to wear after work just as her cell phone rang again. Jack Winters showed on her caller ID.

"Dad, is something wrong?" Emma suppressed a groan. She sounded just like her mother.

He chuckled. "Does there have to be something wrong for a man to call his daughter?"

His upbeat baritone calmed her nerves. "No, but I can't remember the last time you called me at seven thirty on a Saturday morning."

"I wouldn't have if you'd called me last night."

She stared at her bandaged hand. "Dr. Cole phoned you."

"No, I ran into Corey Chandler. He said he saw you at Jug Head's. How is your hand this morning?"

"Okay. It hardly even hurts." Unless she forgot and tried to use it. Or let it dangle.

"How about if I stop by and check it out later today?"

"You don't get enough nursing on the job?" she teased.

"I rarely get to take care of anyone now."

Emma had been a little surprised when her dad moved into the administrative side of nursing. "Thank you for your offer, but I'm leaving for Mount Locust any minute now."

"How are you getting there?"

"Sam Ryker is picking me up."

"I'd heard he was back in town. How is he?"

Her parents had always liked Sam and, unlike her, had never blamed him for Ryan's disappearance. "Fine. He's taken over the district ranger position on the Trace from Natchez to Jackson."

"Good. About time he came home. Is tonight a good time for me to drop by?"

She hesitated. "I'm having dinner with Mom tonight if I can get someone to take me to Jackson."

"I can take you."

That would just be weird, but it was an option. "I can't ask you to do that. Sam will take me."

"Let me know," he said. "But I would like to see you."

"How about dropping by tomorrow after I get off work? I'll find something around here to make for supper."

"Tomorrow night sounds good, but let me bring the food—I've had your cooking," he said, chuckling.

"That's even better." A text popped up on her phone, and she glanced at it. "Sam's here. I have to go," she said.

"Tell him I said hello."

"I will. And I'll let you know if he can't drive me up to Jackson." Emma disconnected and hurried down the stairs. Her heart missed a beat when she opened the door and Sam was standing there in his green-and-gray uniform. Before she could erase the thought, she was struck by his quiet strength and how handsome he was. Her heart fluttered again as admiration reflected in his dark eyes, then he tipped his head.

"It's all clear," he said.

All clear of what? Reality jerked her out of her fog. She couldn't believe she'd forgotten even for a nanosecond that someone was stalking her. "Oh, good. Thank you for checking."

He guided her with his hand as they descended the steps, and she breathed deeply, enjoying the crisp air as the sun peeked over the trees. It should be a beautiful January day. "My dad said to tell you hi."

"How is he? And what are the clothes for?"

"He's fine. As for the clothes—I have plans after work that might include you."

"Oh?" he asked with a raised eyebrow.

"Mom wants me to come for dinner, and since I can't drive myself—"

"It's not a problem. I'll drop you off and pick you up."

"Really? You sure you don't mind spending your evening ferrying me back and forth to my mom's in the Fondren District?"

"It will actually fit in with my plans." Sam opened the passenger door. "I need to touch base with Chief Ranger Cordell, and if he's good with it, I'll meet with him after I drop you off."

Emma eyed him as she climbed into the SUV. "You really expect me to believe your chief ranger is going to meet with you on a Saturday night?"

Red crept up his neck. "We'll see, but he's been bugging me to have a face-to-face. He even suggested a weekend."

Sam closed her door, and a sense of being watched crept over her. She scanned the neighborhood. Everything looked normal. Emma turned toward Sam as he slid behind the wheel. "You're not going to believe this, but Mom hired a PI to look for Ryan."

"Really? When?"

"Right after she moved to Jackson. When she told me that last night, I was so shocked I had to sit down. She's going to give me the investigator's report tonight."

"That's really good. We're going to need it." He pulled away from the curb and pointed his SUV toward the Trace.

Emma shot a sharp glance at him. "What's going on? You're . . ." She searched for the right word. "It's like something's wrong and you're not telling me."

Sam didn't answer, and he gripped the steering wheel like it was a lifeline.

"Has something happened?"

He took a deep breath and briefly glanced her way. "There was another incident at Mount Locust last night."

"Incident? What do you mean?" She swayed against the seat belt as he turned onto the Trace. "Was someone else shot at?"

"No, but someone spiked Trey's thermos of coffee, and he and Clayton were incapacitated after they drank it."

"You're kidding. Do you know what was in it?"

"Some type of benzodiazepine. Nate has a friend in Jackson who runs a private lab, and he sent a small amount of the coffee to him. We won't get the official report back for at least a week."

Her grandmother had used a benzodiazepine sometimes for anxiety. Once she'd used too much and was out cold when Emma found her. "That stuff will knock you out. Are they okay?"

"Yeah. But Trey also got a blow to his head when he woke up too soon."

Her mind whirled. This didn't make sense. "Start at the beginning."

She listened as he explained. When he finished, Emma said, "And you're certain they unearthed more of the site?"

"The pit was only a little over three feet deep yesterday, right?" When she nodded, he said, "The hole now measures four feet."

Emma didn't know what to think. Other than that someone really wanted whatever was buried there. She pushed away the dark thought that wormed its way into her mind, but it wouldn't stay gone. "What do you think this person is looking for?"

Sam's lips pressed together in a thin line. "For someone to go to this much trouble and risk going to jail, if I were a betting man, I'd bet on a body. Especially since the GPR machine indicated the original hole was the same length and width as the graves."

She processed his words. This time the fear she'd kept at bay threatened to crush her.

"It's not Ryan," she said, her voice breaking. Even saying the words stabbed her heart.

"I didn't say it was, but you may need to prepare yourself for someone's skeletal remains."

19

Emma stared out the window as the trees passed by in a blur. Mount Locust was just ahead. "What if the person recovered whatever was buried?" she asked. "If he did, we'll never know what was there."

"I hope he didn't have time to remove everything. First Trey woke up, and then I arrived, but we should know soon enough. Nate's crime scene techs should be there processing the scene."

"Does that mean I can't finish the dig?"

"Depends on whether they're through. I found a shoe print in the bottom of the pit, and they cast it last night," he said.

Emma sat up straight. One problem after another, but nothing was stopping her from finding the truth. Could all of this be happening because someone didn't want her exploring the Mount Locust site? Or was it something more sinister? Did it have anything to do with Ryan's disappearance or Mary Jo Selby's murder? She needed that PI's report.

"I see Nate's already here," Sam said and turned off the Trace.

She glanced toward the maintenance area. Several cars and SUVs were parked there, including one with the sheriff's department logo on it. "Let me out, and I'll unlock the gate and walk to the visitor center," she said. Saturday was one of their busier days, and Emma needed to unlock the door for the volunteer.

"I can drop you in the parking lot."

"That's silly. I can use the time to let my mom know I'm coming tonight. Besides, it's only a quarter of a mile, and I need the exercise. I didn't get in my normal run yesterday or today. And don't see it happening tomorrow either."

He nodded. "As you wish."

She shot him a quick glance, and he appeared as surprised as she felt. Whatever made him think of *The Princess Bride*? She'd discovered the movie on VHS tape when she was sixteen, and Ryan and Sam had teased her mercilessly when they learned she'd worn the tape out.

Emma tried to think of a quote from the movie that would fit as a response, but nothing came to mind, so she rolled her eyes instead. He laughed out loud and then seemed to catch himself and turned somber.

"I'll see you in a few minutes," she said and grabbed her backpack.

With the lively bagpipe music from *The Princess Bride* running through her head, her feet wanted to dance as she hurried to the visitor center. For a few minutes, it had been like old times with Sam. Just before she reached the building, she called her mom and confirmed she would be there by seven thirty. When she disconnected, the gray tabby bounded around the corner of the building.

"Are you hungry, Suzy?" Emma chuckled, wondering what she'd do if the cat answered. It followed her in when she pushed open the door and stood by the bowl Emma had put behind the desk. If it weren't for raccoons, she would feed Suzy outside. "Okay. Give me a second."

She texted her volunteer and told her the visitor center was open, then picked up the bag of cat food, almost dropping it as she tried to navigate the bag with her left hand. Using that hand was getting old fast.

While she waited for Suzy to finish eating, she received a text from Sheila that she was approaching the turnoff. Good. Suzy finished her dry food, and Emma shooed her out the door.

While the cat seemed to be making it okay at the visitor center, if she didn't take her home, Emma would have to drive to Mount Locust to feed the kitten on her days off. Either way, the little thing would be by herself a couple of days a week. Mentally she added a cat carrier to the list of things she needed to get if she took the cat home with her. That way she could bring her back and forth.

Still feeling the lighthearted music in her heart, Emma paused while the cat wound herself around her legs. She'd better enjoy this moment of calm. No telling what the rest of the day might bring.

Emma waited until Sheila parked her vehicle, and then with a wave she walked to the back of the inn, where orange flags marked the location of the slave cabins. Passing them, she followed the path to the cemetery and wound her way to the investigation site, careful not to step inside the markers that indicated where someone was buried. She glanced at the small concrete post to her right. Handmade markers were long gone, and it was her dream to have more than a wooden sign naming those who were laid to rest in the slave cemetery.

She wanted individual markers, even though she had no idea who was buried where. DNA could give the world those answers, but that would mean excavating the graves. Judging from Corey's client, that was not going to happen. And part of her could understand not wanting the graves disturbed, especially by someone who didn't have a relative buried here. At the very least, she wanted to make sure every person buried here was accounted for.

If someone had been buried in the pit, she wanted them identified and closure brought to that family as well. It was her fervent prayer that she hadn't been excavating a burial site. Emma cocked her head toward the cemetery as angry voices reached her. What was going on?

20

While Emma checked in at the visitor center, Sam drove to the maintenance area and parked next to Nate's SUV. After grabbing a flashlight and his camera along with a box with gel lifters, he climbed out of the Interceptor, eyeing the white Lexus in the parking lot. He hadn't been back in Natchez long enough to know who drove luxury cars, but he doubted anything good could come from the car being there.

As he approached the site, he noticed the tent was once again over the pit, and it looked like Nate's crime scene crew hadn't arrived. Good. He'd wanted to search for prints on the backhoe before they went over it. But for now, the heated argument between Corey Chandler and Nate caught his attention. So that's who the Lexus belonged to.

"You are desecrating the cemetery, and my client will not stand for this. He's prepared to take you to court to stop this." Red splotches dotted Corey's face as he waved a paper.

"And I say this is a crime scene," Nate said, standing almost toe-to-toe with the attorney.

Evidently Corey's client had learned they'd been digging at Mount Locust. Sam would love to know how Corey, and his client as well, got their information.

"You better dig all you want today, because I'm seeing the judge later this afternoon," Corey said.

"We're pretty well through digging, aren't we?" Sam asked.

Turning, Corey stepped out of Nate's space. "What are you doing here, Ryker?"

"My job, and bringing Emma to work."

The attorney looked beyond Sam. "Where is she?"

"At the visitor center. Why does your client want to stop the study? And who is it?"

"That's privileged, and he doesn't want to stop the study, but he'd like to see a person of color conducting it. Most of all, he doesn't want anyone digging around the cemetery. It's sacred ground, and Emma promised that wouldn't happen."

Nate folded his arms across his chest. "Evidently you're not listening to me. Emma didn't dig this. An unknown subject dug the hole you're looking at. We're just investigating whatever was buried here."

"And Emma told you that last night at Jug Head's," Sam said.

Corey's mouth twitched. "That's true, but I had no idea a *backhoe* was involved. That's not quite the same thing as excavating with a shovel."

"You're still not listening. We did not dig this hole." Sam clamped his mouth shut and counted to ten. The man was unreasonable. He tried again. "And even if we did, according to the diagram from the previous project, there was no grave at this particular spot."

"And ground penetrating radar indicated the soil has been disturbed since that study, so something was buried here," Nate said. "Something important enough that a person risked jail time to retrieve it."

"How do you know it's not gone?"

"It probably is, but they could have left something behind. This is now a search and recovery for evidence." Sam turned to Nate. "Right?"

The sheriff nodded. "And the park service director in Natchez asked that Emma conduct the dig in order to preserve any artifacts."

"Do you have the diagram?" Corey asked.

"I have it," Emma said, emerging from the back side of the cemetery. All three of them turned toward her.

"Good, you're here. How's your hand?" Corey asked, his voice suddenly warm.

She waved off his concern. "It's fine. What's the problem? I heard you clear on the other side of the cemetery."

The attorney frowned. "You assured me you weren't going to dig up the cemetery."

Confusion crossed her face. "We're not digging it up. We're trying to discover what was here." She glanced at Nate as if to ask how much she should tell.

The sheriff's jaw shot out. "It's like I said. A crime was committed here Thursday night, and then again last night. I'm investigating it. Emma is here to look out for the interests of the park service."

"The diagram, please." Corey held his hand out.

Emma took it from her backpack, but she didn't give it to him, unfolding the paper instead. "As you can see, I've marked the graves with orange flags according to this diagram." The attorney looked over her shoulder as Emma pointed out each grave and a corresponding flag.

"There is no grave shown at this spot, yet the GPR reading showed disturbed layers of soil just like the graves, only shallower." Emma looked up at Corey. "We have to find out what was here."

Corey stared at the map, then shifted his gaze to the sheriff. "What did you mean when you said a crime was committed again last night?"

"The person returned last night," Nate said grimly. "And used the backhoe to dig the hole deeper."

"Why didn't you post guards?" the attorney asked.

"We did, two of them." Nate kicked at a dirt clod. "Whoever robbed the grave doctored their thermos of coffee, knocked them out."

Corey turned to Emma. "It sounds dangerous for you to be here."

Sam wondered what the attorney would say if he knew someone had fired at them last night at Emma's apartment, but she spoke before he had the chance to speak.

She swept her hand toward the men around her. "These men are packing heat, so I'm fine. But I do need to get to work. Are you going to forget about talking to the judge since we won't be doing any more excavation other than scraping away a few layers?"

Corey shifted his attention from Emma to the hole. "I'll hold off until the investigation is finished, but my client is adamant about any of the graves being disturbed." Corey slipped the paper in an inside pocket of his suit just as an alarm went off on his watch, and he tapped it.

"I have an appointment back in Natchez," he said and turned to face Emma. "But you and I need to sit down and discuss this survey you're conducting."

"We will when you tell me who this client of yours is."

"I've told you before, his name is confidential. I will tell you he thinks it should be conducted by someone with a personal stake in the cemetery."

Understanding dawned on Sam. Corey Chandler must represent a descendant of the slaves who were buried at Mount Locust.

"Does he think I won't do a good job? I want to make sure all the burial sites have been found. And by excavating the cabin area, I'll discover what the lives of the people who lived in the cabins were like." She stopped to catch her breath. "And I would be happy to work with him, if that's what he wants."

Corey palmed his hand. "I'll pass that along. Could we please sit down over dinner and discuss this? And not at Jug Head's . . . maybe at the Guest House downtown? Strictly business, of course."

Why would Corey need to discuss the matter with Emma over dinner at a ritzy restaurant? His stomach soured as she actually seemed to be considering the offer.

"Call me either tomorrow or Tuesday, and we'll set up something," she said.

Sam's hands curled into tight fists. Surely he wasn't jealous of the attorney. His body said otherwise, and he quickly forced himself to relax. Emma was free to date anyone she wanted—Sam had no claims on her. The man wasn't even Emma's type, although Sam was certain his earlier assessment that the attorney was interested in Emma was correct.

Could Corey be her stalker? Not if her stalker and the person who operated the backhoe Thursday night were the same person. His hands hadn't been callused enough for someone who worked a backhoe. Sam wondered if the man had ever gotten his hands dirty, much less dug up a grave.

Corey patted Emma's shoulder. "I personally believe you would do a great job here, and for what it's worth, I'll pass that along to my client."

Silence fell on the others as the attorney turned and walked to his Lexus. Once he'd backed up and pointed the car toward the Trace, Emma broke the silence.

"Are we ready to get to work?"

"You're not going to meet him for dinner, are you?" Sam asked.

She tilted her head. "I may. You don't have a problem with that, do you?"

So Emma was interested in Corey. Not what Sam expected. "What if he's your stalker?"

"Corey Chandler? Not in a million years."

Sam wasn't so certain. And not because he didn't care for the attorney or because he had success written all over him.

"What are you carrying?" Emma asked.

"Gel lifters."

"For . . . ?" Nate asked.

He turned to the sheriff. "I want to see if I can find any latent footprints on the backhoe floor."

"Don't you think he put newspaper down again?"

"Maybe, but I thought I'd check. Any objections?"

At first Sam thought Nate was going to insist he wait for the crime scene techs, then he nodded. "My team was called to a homicide first thing this morning on the other side of the county. You know how to use the gel sheets?" he asked, nodding at the box.

"Yeah. And I have my camera to document anything I find. And a box to store any prints I make. It'll hold two sheets, and I have more boxes in the SUV if I need them."

"Are you telling me you can lift shoe prints off something like the floor of the backhoe?" Emma asked.

"It's not the best place, but yeah, I can get a partial. You can watch if you'd like, unless you need to get to work on the pit."

She glanced at the pit and then back at him. "How long will it take?"

"Not long."

"This I've got to see. And I can't do anything until Chris gets here with the camera, anyway." She turned to Nate. "Is he with the crime scene techs?"

"Yes, but he radioed he was on his way. I'll check to make sure," he said and walked toward his vehicle.

Sam pulled on a pair of latex gloves before he dusted the handle on the cab. It was clean, but he hadn't expected any fingerprints because he figured the man probably wore gloves.

He opened the cab door. His heart sank. The gray plastic mat covering the backhoe floor looked clean. Holding his flashlight at a low angle, he looked for prints. Nada.

Probably wouldn't be anything on the step either. And it had a pattern in the steel. Not a good place to find prints. Holding the flashlight so that the light cut across the step at a ten-degree angle, he caught his breath. There were several prints, but one stood out. "Do you see it?"

She squatted even with the step. "Shoe prints! How did you do that?"

"Ever had the sun come in through a window at a low angle and expose all your dust? Same principle. The clearest one should be the last one made. Hold the light, and I'll get photos."

She took the flashlight and shined it where he pointed.

"Can you hold the light at a lower angle?" When the print became visible, he said, "Right there."

Sam laid a numbered chip beside the footprint and photographed it, then photographed it with a ruler to show the scale. After peeling the back off the quick-gel sheet, he carefully pressed it against the footprint and used the heel of his hand to smooth the sheet against the step.

"How long do you have to let it set?" Emma asked.

"This should be long enough." He peeled the gel sheet off and shined his flashlight against it. Perfect. "It doesn't look like the same shoe print we found in the pit," he said.

"Do you think there were two of them digging last night?"

"Maybe. I'd wondered if there might be an accomplice, but it's possible the print belongs to a maintenance worker." Sam doubted that scenario. The print wasn't overlaid with any of the other prints. "Whoever was here Thursday night didn't leave prints anywhere. I'm thinking he didn't have time to be as careful last night."

21

There were thousands of acres of untamed woodlands up and down the Mississippi River, and out of those thousands he'd found the perfect plot of ground, three thousand acres complete with a modern cabin that a rich client of his had built and grown tired of. It even had a powerful generator—the cabin was so isolated, the local power company had yet to run lines to the property.

He turned off the gravel road and wound back through the trees to the cabin nestled on a bluff on the banks of the Mississippi. At the bottom of the bluff was a small inlet with a boathouse and an inboard motorboat. In his mind's eye, he could see Emma helping him clear the trees, giving them an incredible view of the sun setting every evening.

Their life would be perfect. They could even take the boat out on the Mississippi occasionally.

Once inside the cabin, he viewed the furniture with satisfaction. He'd picked up on the colors and designs she liked on her Pinterest page. He ran his hand lightly over the butter-soft leather sofa. It and its twin had set him back almost five grand. It had strained his budget, but they were so perfect for the glass-walled addition to the cabin.

The builder had inquired as to why he wanted all the windows to be bulletproof. Deer hunters, he'd told him, but the truth was, using bulletproof glass ensured one could not get into or out of the cabin through the windows. He realized it would take a few days for Emma to adjust to living here, but eventually, she would be happy to call the cabin home.

He made a trip back to his pickup and tugged an oversized bag from the back. He couldn't believe how their tastes matched so perfectly. Emma would be pleased when she saw the goose-down comforter for their bed. He'd seen this exact one on her Pinterest board.

He arranged the comforter and pillow shams on the bed. His last purchases before he brought Emma here. Warmth spread through his chest. If everything went like he planned, by this time next week, Emma would be in her new home.

Ryker will try to stop you.

Ryker. It was becoming clear he had to do something about the ranger.

22

When the crime scene techs arrived, Emma walked to the tent where Nate stood.

"Find anything?" the sheriff asked.

"Sam found a shoe print on the step."

"Really?"

"But that's all I found," Sam said as he joined them, holding a shoebox under his arm.

The sheriff looked inside the box where Sam had placed the gel sheet. "It doesn't look like the same shoe that was in the pit."

"That's what I thought." Sam pulled off the latex gloves.

"I meant to ask earlier," Emma said, turning to the sheriff. "How's Trey?"

"I'm fine." The voice came from behind her.

Emma whirled around. She hadn't heard the chief deputy drive into the parking lot, much less walk up on her. "You scared me."

"Sorry," he said, not sounding at all sorry. "Doc says I had a slight concussion, and to just take it a little bit easier today."

"Where have you been?" Nate asked. "I tried to reach you earlier when I needed you to take charge of the homicide investigation."

"Sorry, had my phone turned off, and then I overslept. Do you want me to check on them now?"

While Nate gave Trey directions to the location of the other crime scene, Emma ducked under the tent and walked to the edge of the pit. A light breeze from the south brought an earthy scent from the pit. When Nate called Sam over, she couldn't help but notice he didn't seem too happy to see Trey either. Surely he wasn't jealous of her ex-boyfriend. At least not like he was of Corey. Emma brushed that thought away as soon as it popped into her head. She had no idea if that were true.

She turned and almost bumped into Trey. Emma shivered, and it wasn't from the fifty-degree weather. "I'm sorry. Did you need something?" she asked.

"I'm leaving to go on patrol, and I just wanted to tell you again that I'm sorry about all this trouble you're having."

"Oh." Sincerity rang in his voice this time, surprising her. "Thank you."

"I want you to know, I've never believed Ryan killed Mary Jo Selby."

Trey sounded so sure. "Why did your dad make it sound like he had?"

"That was my dad, not me, and he could be wrong sometimes. Not that he would admit it." He ducked his head. "And while I'm at it, I'm sorry about some of the arguments we had and how I tried to make you into someone you're not. Especially since it was me who needed changing."

She looked askance at him. "Who *are* you and what did you do with the real Trey Carter?"

His face turned red. "I'm trying to turn over a new leaf."

"What brought this on?"

"I'm trying to deal with some of my anger issues. And if you could find it in your heart to forgive me . . ." He let the request dangle, then he smiled. "And maybe give me a second chance? Unless you have something going on with Sam."

She didn't know what to do with this turn of events. It was easier to lump Trey in the bad-guy category than to think of him in a new light. "I forgave you months ago," she said. "But as for dating again, I'm not dating anyone for a while."

He stiffened and glanced toward Sam. "Doesn't look that way to me, but if you change your mind, you know where to find me," he said.

"Uh, sure. Thanks." Time would tell if Trey had made a real commitment to changing or if he was conning her again. After he left, Emma gathered the tools she needed in the pit.

Nate and Sam approached, and the sheriff eyed her hand. "Do you think you can work with your wrist wrapped like that?"

"I'll use my left hand for most of it, and I brought a bread wrapper to put over the bandage to keep it clean." She glanced toward the tent over the pit. "Can I start digging?"

"Yep. Everyone's finished." Nate cocked his head. "But could Corey Chandler have actually stopped us?"

"I don't know, but he certainly could have delayed us."

Nate made a face. "Then I need to stop by and see Judge Thorpe sometime today to make sure he understands this is a crime scene just in case Corey changes his mind." Then the sheriff nodded toward Chris and his 35mm camera. "He'll be staying with you today and will maintain the chain of evidence should you find anything."

"If you're shorthanded," Sam said, "I can document everything."

"I'm not that shorthanded. In the unlikely event we find evidence to make an arrest, it'll be important that I used my deputy to maintain a clear chain for court—it'll be one less link to account for," Nate said. "I would like to use a forensic anthropologist instead of Emma, but then we'd have to delay the investigation since Southern Miss can't send anyone for two weeks."

Sam turned to Emma. "I can help you," he said. "You can start at one end, and I'll take the other. It'll take half the time that way."

His presence in the pit would distract her. "Uh, let me explore a little first. The area is kind of small for both of us, especially right now. I promise, if I have trouble with my hand, you can take my place, and I'll direct you. Right now, you can be my surgical nurse."

"What do you mean?"

She grinned. "When I call for a tool, you can hand it to me."

"You mean I can be your gofer," he said dryly.

"I thought nurse sounded nicer." Emma slipped the plastic wrapper over her hand. The easy banter they sometimes slipped into reminded her of times past, times she missed. After wrapping rubber bands around her forearm to secure the plastic, she grabbed a handful of orange flags to mark her work area and hopped down into the pit, where the earthy scent was much stronger. Emma frowned when her feet sank into loose dirt.

"There's a loose layer of dirt here," she said.

Sam peered into the pit. "Our thief probably scattered dirt to cover up any impression left in the ground."

"Let's just hope he didn't have time to pack the dirt, and I can find an impression of what he was trying to hide. Let me stake a grid, and then you can hand me the mason trowel and a bucket."

Once she marked the first area she planned to work, Emma looked up at Sam, who held a trowel in each hand, one flat, the other beveled.

"Which one?"

"The flat one." Over the years, Emma had found the pointed, flat-bladed trowel usually used in bricklaying was the best tool for scraping loose soil away. "And hand me one of the brushes."

She set to work, scraping away a thin layer of dirt and depositing it in a bucket. Half an hour later, she straightened up and peeled her jacket off. Working with only one hand was difficult. She called Chris over. "I'm back to the hard ground in this section. Do you want to photograph the area?"

He moved in to take photos with a zoom lens, and Emma stepped out of his way. When he finished, she went back to work.

If there was an indentation, the loose dirt would have filled it in, which made a brush the best tool to use. She swept the section carefully, her pulse increasing when two narrow trenches appeared. She'd done enough archeological work to know she was looking at impressions of a tibia and fibula.

Emma stared at the shallow trenches, heaviness settling in her chest. It was one thing to think she was working on a grave site, and quite another to actually see evidence of it. "Okay, gentlemen, I do believe we have leg bone impressions here," she said grimly and continued to brush dirt away.

"Are you sure?" Sam asked.

"Unfortunately, yes. Help me out so Chris can photograph it."

While he took pictures, she grabbed a bottle of water from the cooler the sheriff had provided. Her hope that this wasn't a grave was gone, and given the extensive work completed twenty years ago, it didn't belong to a slave. Which meant the body had been buried in the intervening years.

23

While Chris finished photographing the impressions, Emma elevated her throbbing right hand above her heart as she tapped the trowel against her leg.

"You want me to dig a while?" Sam asked.

"No. I want to see this through."

"But it's evident your hand is bothering you."

She wasn't about to admit it throbbed like a toothache. "It could be worse."

"I think you should let me take over for a little while at least."

"Tell you what," she said as Chris climbed out of the pit. "Let me work another hour, and then you can give me a break."

He reluctantly agreed, and she eased down into the pit again. After studying the indentations, Emma shifted her work area closer to the wall. If what she'd found were leg bones, what followed was the foot. Perhaps the grave robber had overlooked some of the smaller bones or even a phalange from a toe.

Time slipped away as she focused on scraping away the dirt, one layer at a time. Emma ignored pain coming from her back and down her leg until it was impossible. Just one more scrape and she would hand it over to Sam for a while.

Her breath caught when the trowel uncovered a speck of something light. Using the brush, she carefully swept away dirt. "Hand me one of those dental picks," she said.

"What've you found?" Sam asked, handing her the tool.

"Not sure. Give me a second." Gently, she used the pick to remove the dirt around a perfectly preserved bone. The middle phalange of a toe bone if the memory from her A&P class served her correctly. Their thief had overlooked it in his haste. How many small bones had he left behind? Leaving it undisturbed, she climbed out of the pit with Sam's help and waited for Chris to photograph her find.

"Nate picked up sandwiches," Sam said. "You want to stop for lunch while Chris finishes?"

She didn't want to, but just as she started to shake her head, her stomach growled. "Sure."

A few minutes later, Chris grabbed a sandwich and reported in to Nate, leaving Sam and Emma alone. They ate in silence until their sandwiches were almost gone, then she said, "I wonder what he did with the other bones?"

"I'm thinking the river," Sam replied.

"Makes sense." It made her sick to think that whoever had been buried here had been gathered up like garbage and dumped into the river. If that was what happened, they would never find the rest of the bones. Neither of them spoke the question that lay heavy on Emma's mind. She did not want to speculate who the body belonged to, but she was pretty sure Sam would think it was Ryan.

As if reading her mind, he asked, "Would you be willing to compare your DNA to the DNA they find in the bone?" When she hesitated, he added, "It would be one way to rule Ryan out."

"It is not my brother!" As soon as the words were past her lips, Emma pressed her hand to her mouth. She must really be tired to snap at him like that. None of this was his fault. She dropped her shoulders and sighed. "Of course I will, if nothing more than to prove it isn't Ryan. But we have to finish excavating the site first. Maybe we'll find something that will identify the remains." And point them away from Ryan.

"Would a billfold still be intact if the body had been buried in the past twenty years?"

At least he didn't say ten years. "Possibly. But don't you think our thief would have seen a billfold and taken it with him?"

"Yeah," he said reluctantly.

Emma finished the rest of her sandwich in silence as a nagging thought kept intruding. What if it were Ryan's bones? She'd never let herself dwell on the possibility he was dead, always finding a reason why he hadn't contacted them. The main one being he was afraid of being framed for Mary Jo's murder. Was she ready to deal with that possibility? But she and her twin had been so close. She'd been told they'd even had their own language as babies . . . wouldn't she have known if her brother was dead?

Regardless of whether it was Ryan or not, the person's family deserved closure. And justice. She slipped two Tylenol from her pocket and downed them before Sam noticed. If he thought she was in pain, he'd insist on taking over, and Emma wanted to finish the job she'd started. She wadded up the sandwich wrapping. "Ready?"

"Sure. But let me dig a while."

"Not yet." When he started to object, she added, "Please."

"Your hand is bound to be hurting."

"Nothing I can't handle."

"Why is this so important for you to do?"

She didn't know, just that it was. "After someone tried to run me off Thursday night, I have a personal stake in this." Then she shrugged. "Or maybe it's because I'm stubborn."

He laughed with her. "I'll go with the second."

Emma grabbed the brush and a dental pick. Once back in the pit, she scraped layer after layer of dirt, looking for more small bones. Forty minutes into her promised hour, none had materialized.

If the person had been buried with their shoes on, could the shoes still be intact? If they were leather, possibly. Had the thief dropped the phalange when he moved the body? If so, the bone would have been on top of the ground, not buried. She looked at the bone again. Was it possible their thief pressed it into the dirt when he was trying to cover up the other indentations? So many questions and so few answers.

A shadow crossed where she worked, and Emma sat back on her heels and looked up. Nate had joined them.

"How's it coming?"

"Okay. I'm thinking about moving my search toward the other end of the pit, where the skull should be."

"Makes sense," Nate said.

Sam picked up a trowel. "I keep trying to convince her to let me help."

"You'll get your clothes dirty."

"I can change."

Nate scratched his chin. "Looks to me like there's room for both of you if you're working at different ends. It would cut our time in half, so let's try it."

She'd been able to block Sam from her mind with him standing on the ground above her. If he was in the pit, it would be impossible to be unaware of his presence, but it didn't look like she had much choice.

Emma quickly moved her tools to the other end of the grave while Sam went to change. When he returned, he dropped down into the hole. His musky aftershave brought the memory of how electricity had arced between them last night. She hadn't admitted it to herself then, but she was disappointed he hadn't kissed her.

She shook the thoughts off and concentrated on the dirt she scraped away. Emma had thought she'd removed all the loose dirt earlier, but she'd been wrong. The dirt she was scraping now wasn't compact and dense, at least not like the other end. She went a little deeper with her trowel, then repeated the action. Maybe she should move over a little and go to work closer to the top of the wall. Her heart stilled when she hit solid ground, and she quickly exchanged the trowel for a brush.

Even though the person had gone to a lot of trouble to pack the dirt here, it didn't have the solid feel from years of not being disturbed, and after she'd swept it a few times, a sunken impression appeared. "I think I have something," she said and sat back on her heels again. A strand of hair fell across her eyes, and she blew it back.

Sam peered over her shoulder. "I think you've found where the skull was."

Emma's stomach bottomed out, and she almost lost the sandwich she'd eaten. Finding where the skull had lain hit her ten times harder than finding the toe bone. Blinking away tears that burned her eyes, she went to work again, looking for anything that would help identify their victim.

24

The church was tastefully decorated. Candles flickered on either side of the altar where he counted the seconds for "Ave Maria" to segue into Mendelssohn's "Wedding March." He couldn't wait to get his first glimpse of Emma in the beautiful princess-style dress he'd picked out. Mother sat on the second row, and he glanced over, giving her a wink. For once he'd made the gentle soul proud.

His mother was thinking how lucky he was that Emma said yes. Emmy, as he'd taken to calling her, would make the perfect daughter-in-law. Slowly his mother's head turned toward the back of the church. Emmy must be at the door.

Why was his mother frowning? And why was the prelude going on too long? He exchanged worried glances with his mother as she faded from his sight. *No! Don't leave.*

Frantically he searched past rows and rows of guests to the back of the church. The wedding march should have started by now. Where was Emma? She should be walking down the aisle. A deathly silence filled the church, and he closed his eyes.

She wasn't coming.

And it was all Sam Ryker's fault.

When he opened his eyes again, there were no guests, no church, and he sat in his car.

Ryker was just like Dad. Always ruining everything he touched.

Look at Emma's hand. If it weren't for Ryker, she wouldn't have hurt it.

He had to protect Emma from Sam. He pretended to be all nice and concerned on the outside, but when they were alone, Sam Ryker was just nasty. A womanizer. Emotionally abusive. Just like his dad. He'd heard Ryker make fun of Emma, put her down. Oh sure, he'd pretended he was joking.

Ryker wanted Emma. He could see it in his eyes. But the ranger would break her heart.

And he wasn't going to let that happen. She belonged to him. Or she wouldn't belong to anyone.

25

Finding the impression the skull made in the ground had knocked Emma's feet out from under her. She stared down at where she'd been cleaning. Seeing it drove home in a way the toe bone hadn't that a person had been murdered and buried here.

"You okay?" Sam asked.

He'd climbed out of the pit, and she looked up. "Yeah," she said. Emma turned back to the bucket of dirt she'd accumulated and lifted it up to him. "It's just that . . ." She closed her eyes and shuddered. "All of a sudden, what we're doing here is too real."

He knelt and held out his hand. "Why don't you take a break?" he asked gently.

No, she needed to get this job done so that whoever was buried here could have justice.

Almost as if he'd read her mind, he said, "A short break won't stop the progress. And it'll give you the energy to finish." When she still hesitated, Sam said, "I know how you feel—pretty sure it's the same thing I feel whenever I investigate the murder of a John Doe. You want to discover the victim's identity so you can give the family closure."

Maybe a break would be a good idea. Then she could go back to work refreshed. "Have you investigated many John Doe cases?" she asked once he'd lifted her out of the pit.

"Enough."

She dusted her knees off and looked back at the hole that was the length and width of a grave. "How do you keep doing it? I never want to do this again."

"I won't say you get used to it, because you never do," he said. "But you learn to distance yourself, kind of like a medical examiner."

Medical examiner. Emma couldn't do that job either. "Where did Nate go?"

"To his SUV. He lost reception and wanted to touch base with the office on his radio."

She looked over the two mounds of dirt. The smaller pile they'd taken out today wouldn't have to be sifted, but the one dug with the backhoe had to be processed once they excavated the pit. She would be sifting it weeks from now.

"Whoever removed the skeleton didn't have much time last night," Sam said, uncapping a bottle of water before handing it to her. "He's bound to have left something behind other than a small bone and a shoe print."

She tilted the bottle up and took a welcomed sip. "Any news about the kind of shoe it was?"

"A Nike."

That only eliminated about half the population of Adams County. "How long do you think the intruder was here?"

"Trey and Clayton were put out of commission sometime between ten and eleven," he said. "I arrived a little after midnight and the intruder was gone, but I got the feeling he hadn't been gone long."

"That's two hours at most." Once again she looked at the fresh dirt piled beside the pit. "Of course, he wouldn't have been trying to preserve the site, and he used the backhoe to dig down another foot."

"He might have even scooped the remains up with the backhoe."

Her fingers itched to get back to work, but first she checked her watch. Four o'clock. It would take two hours to drive to her mom's, leaving an hour before she needed to change. Emma set the timer on her watch for sixty minutes and gingerly climbed down into the pit again. She didn't understand why she hurt all over. It'd only been her hand that had been injured. Of course, she'd hit the bottom of the pit pretty hard, jarring her. Couldn't let Sam know how badly her hand hurt. If he knew, he'd want her to stop, fearful that she would further injure her hand. But she couldn't stop. Something drove her to discover who had been buried in the grave.

Sam jumped down into the pit with her. Time passed quickly as they scraped layer after layer away and dumped the dirt in buckets. A chill settled over the area as the sun hung low in the sky. She scraped over the ground again and met resistance. "I think I have something here."

"What is it?"

"I don't know. Something hard, though." She looked around for a dental pick, but she must have taken it out of the pit. "Do you have a pick?"

"Hold on a sec."

Once she had the tool, she used it to scrape at the object and caught her breath when a red stone appeared. "It looks like a ruby." Excitement buzzed in her chest.

Sam leaned over her shoulder as she brushed away more dirt and then used the dental pick to remove dirt from around the object. It wasn't long before a whole stone appeared, obviously the top of a ring. This time they both caught their breath as a university name came into view.

No.

Her hand shook. It wasn't a ruby but a garnet with Mississippi State University engraved around it and the year 1878—the year the university was founded. The ring was identical to a smaller one in her jewelry box that she'd received in the spring of her junior year, just like Ryan had. He'd worn his ring the night of their birthday dinner. Her heart pounded in her chest. It couldn't be his.

"Chris needs to photograph this," Sam said.

She straightened and looked for the photographer. He was by the backhoe with Nate, who had returned. Sam yelled for him to come over.

"Can I help you get out?" Sam asked as the photographer ambled toward them.

Emma couldn't move. The ring couldn't be Ryan's. She wouldn't let it be.

Sam hopped out of the pit and knelt down to give her a hand up. "Emma?"

She pulled her gaze away from the ring, looking up into his sad brown eyes. He thought it was her brother's. Tears she refused to shed burned her eyelids. A heavy weight pressed on her chest.

"Take my hand," he said softly.

Her mind numb, she let him help her out and waited for Chris to take his photographs. She was simply tired. That was the reason she couldn't form a coherent thought. Emma hugged her arms to her waist, her mind totally blank. She should be preparing herself for the possibility that the ring belonged to her brother, but she couldn't wrap her mind around the thought. Sam put his arm around her shoulders and drew her to his side.

"It's not Ryan's," she said angrily.

He didn't answer, just squeezed her shoulders. Which was an answer in itself. Once Chris had his photos, Sam hopped back into the pit before Emma could and lifted the ring from the ground, knocking out the dirt caught in the middle. "It's densely packed," he said.

"That means it's probably been there since the body was buried," she said.

Once he held it in his hands, she could see the graduating year on the sides. 2012. The year she graduated. Sam used his phone flashlight to examine the inside. Color drained from his face, and he wouldn't look at her.

"It's Ryan's, isn't it?" Emma said, her voice barely above a whisper.

Sam didn't look at her. "The initials are RTW."

Upon seeing that ring, she'd known in her bones who it belonged to. Just like she should have known that something had happened to her brother. She couldn't hurt any worse if someone had slammed their fist in her stomach.

26

Sam had wanted the initials to be anyone's but Ryan's. Or for the year to be other than 2012. If Ryan Thomas Winters had not disappeared, he would have been in the class graduating from Mississippi State University that year along with Emma. Sam climbed out of the grave and handed the ring to her, pointing out the engraving.

"It's possible it's not his," he said, "but—"

She swayed and dropped the ring as her knees buckled. Sam caught her before she hit the ground. Swinging her up in his arms, he carried her up the walk to the back of the Mount Locust Inn. She came to before he reached the back porch and pulled away from him.

"I'm okay now. You can set me down."

"You're not going anywhere, and be still. I don't want to drop you."

Sam felt her stiffen in his arms, but he kept walking. He couldn't believe how light she was, but her tough manner always made him forget how tiny she was. And if she struggled again, he feared he would lose her. "Just relax. We're almost there."

Emma huffed a breath, but then she relaxed. He didn't realize she was crying until he felt her shoulders shaking.

"It's going to be okay," he murmured. That seemed to make it worse as she buried her face in his chest.

When they reached the inn, he set her on the porch steps.

"I'm sorry," she said, wiping tears from her face with the back of her hand. "I don't know what happened."

"It's been a hard day," Sam said gently and handed her a clean handkerchief from his back pocket. This produced more tears from Emma. He didn't know what to do. Everything he said or did made it worse. Awkwardly, he patted her shoulder and looked helplessly at Nate, who had brought up the rear.

"Th-thanks," Emma said and pressed the handkerchief against her eyes. When her tears subsided, she blew her nose and leaned against the post.

"Try this." The sheriff uncapped a bottle of water and handed it to her.

Once she downed half the water, she shook her head as if trying to clear it.

"Before you lock in to this being your brother, we need to do a DNA analysis of the bone you found," Nate said. He fished the ring from his pocket. "And check with the university about the initials."

"Unless there's another RTW who graduated in 2012, it's Ryan's." She pressed her lips together and shook her head. "Not much chance of that, is there?"

"I'll check Monday." Although Sam felt pretty sure the ring belonged to her brother, it would be easy enough to do the research and faster than waiting for DNA results.

"I kept telling myself he was alive," she said, her voice cracking. "That I'd know it, no, that I'd *feel* it, if he'd died."

"I did the same thing," Sam said. "I kept picturing him in Alaska. It's where he always wanted to go."

"Why did someone kill him?" Emma took a shaky breath and released it. "He wouldn't hurt anyone."

Nate tapped his fingers against his leg. "I figure it has to do with that girl's death. Mary Jo Selby."

"I never believed he killed her," she said.

"Someone wants everyone to think he did." Sam glanced toward the grave. "Whoever killed her even drove his car to Memphis to make it look as if he'd left the area."

"That way no one was looking for the real killer," Nate said.

"How did the killer get home from Memphis?" Sam asked.

"Could've taken the bus—"

"Or rented a car," Sam said, finishing the sheriff's sentence.

Emma took a deep breath and released it. Color had not yet returned to her face, making the dark circles under her eyes even darker. Weariness shadowed her.

She pressed her fingers to her temples, then she raised her head, tears glistening in her eyes again. "My parents . . . I have to break the news to them."

Sam took her hand. "I'll help you tell them."

"I don't think you should tell them until the DNA results are back," Nate said. "We'll keep what we've found under wraps until then."

Relief showed in her eyes. "Yes. We want to make sure it was Ryan who was buried here. Where do I take the DNA test?"

"I have a kit down at my office," Nate said. "You want to drop by in the morning?"

While Nate and Emma set a time, the sun slipped behind the tree line, taking any warmth that had been in the air with it. Sam checked his watch. After five. It was too late to check with the university or the ring company today. What was he thinking? It was Saturday. An alarm on Emma's phone went off.

"It's my reminder to get dressed, but I don't know . . . maybe I should cancel . . ." Then she shook her head. "No. We need that private investigator's report now more than ever."

"What kind of report are you talking about?" the sheriff asked.

"Emma talked with her mom last night, and Dina had hired a private investigator to find Ryan not long after he went missing. She still has the investigator's report, and there might be a copy of Sheriff Carter's report in it."

"I'd like to see that," Nate said. He turned to Emma. "Are you up to getting it? Otherwise, I can contact your mom."

"No, don't do that. It would make her suspicious." She squared her shoulders and turned to Sam. "Give me ten minutes to grab my clothes and get dressed."

"I'll change as soon as you finish."

While Emma went to change, Nate said, "I'll take a closer look at Sheriff Carter's files. It isn't an active case, and there's no reason for his report not to be there. Maybe I just overlooked it," he said. "Files don't just get up and walk off on their own."

27

Emma's fingers trembled as she tied a silver-and-black scarf around her neck. She dreaded the closure that would come if the grave held her brother's remains. That wasn't the kind of closure she'd hoped for. In fact, she wanted to pray the remains belonged to someone other than Ryan because if they were his, her hopes of finding him were destroyed.

She wouldn't think about it now. There was still a possibility the ring didn't belong to her brother and her DNA wouldn't match the bone she'd found. Mentally Emma shifted gears. Focused on making it past this dinner with her mom and getting the private investigator's report. Or maybe not. Maybe she'd think about riding to Jackson with her good-looking escort. Not a good choice either.

She tugged the sparkly black sweater, trying to stretch it a little. Giving up, Emma slipped on dressy jeans and the high-heeled boots that would give a little height to her short frame. Not her regular look, and all purchased by her mom in hopes of improving Emma's wardrobe. Thank goodness she didn't have to walk through the woods in the boots.

Frowning, Emma removed the scarf and retied it, letting the ends dangle. That was a little better. She should have known to try on the new sweater, but maybe the scarf would help cover that it was a little snug. Too late now to do anything about it since she hadn't brought anything else to wear.

She peered in the faded mirror. Maybe a little powder and the tinted moisturizer for her lips to complete the look. Her mother would expect Emma to look her best when they went out. She'd just returned her lipstick to her backpack when her cell phone rang. Her mom? She wasted no time answering.

"Since I haven't heard differently, I assume you're coming," her mother said, bypassing normal pleasantries.

"Yes. I'm about to leave Mount Locust now."

"Meet me at the house, and we'll go to Ricco's from there."

"Great. See you there. Still at seven?" Silence was the only answer Emma received. Her mom had hung up. Dina Winters had been in full attorney mode.

Emma took a small black clutch from her backpack and slipped the cell phone inside. If she was wrong and it was seven thirty, all it would cost her was thirty minutes of time. That was much better than being late. She sighed. It was going to be a long night, made longer by keeping Ryan's probable death a secret.

Sam was waiting at his SUV when she locked the door to the building. Standing a little straighter, she carefully walked toward him. The look of approval in his eyes warmed her heart, even as she tried not to turn her ankles in the boots.

"You clean up well," he said softly.

She punched him on the shoulder. "Thanks. I think. Wait, how did you get changed?" she asked, noticing he was in his ranger uniform. "I didn't hear you inside."

"I slipped inside one of the sheds," he said. "And I was just teasing about you cleaning up well. You always look good."

Now she was really flustered. Maybe he was being nice because . . . She blocked the thought and gave him her mom's address.

"You said she lives in the Fondren District?" Sam asked.

"In a small gated community there. The address is in my phone's GPS if you want me to activate it," she replied.

"Maybe when we get to Jackson," he said and opened the passenger door. "Sorry it's the official vehicle, but my pickup is at Jenny's."

"This is fine. You're only taking me to Mom's." Emma fastened her seat belt. It wasn't like he would be valet parking at the expensive restaurant. Not that it would bother Emma, but she wasn't sure about her mom—she was such a stickler for appearances. Emma wanted to keep the two apart, anyway. She wasn't up to being interrogated by her mom about her relationship with Sam. Or her non-relationship.

There was little traffic on the Trace, and they rode in silence with the events of the afternoon hanging between them. Her thoughts kept returning to her brother, and she fished a tissue from her bag and dabbed her eyes.

"I can't get Ryan off my mind either." Sam's voice was husky.

"It's like it's not real." Her mind hadn't completely accepted that her brother was dead. Just thinking about it made it hard to breathe. Could she even get through this dinner with her mother?

"I keep thinking, if I had stayed with Ryan . . ."

"Don't do that to yourself," she said. "It wasn't like you had a choice."

"Maybe I did."

She knew what he was referencing. Words Emma had thrown at Sam. "I had no right to blame you," she said. "And it was unreasonable for me to suggest you could have called a tow truck for Jenny. I know you didn't have the money for that."

Sam flinched and gripped the steering wheel until his knuckles turned white.

His dad had left the family when Sam was a teenager, and what he made working as a seasonal ranger on summer break from college went to help his mom pay her bills. Anything left over went to pay for the things his scholarship to the university in Arizona didn't cover.

Their dates had been whatever free activities they could find.

Not that she minded. A smile touched her heart as she remembered some of their dates. Free concerts in the park. Fishing in a local lake. Picnics, and since her brother and Sam were best friends, when Ryan was sober, he sometimes accompanied them. She sighed. Emma had some good memories of her twin brother. "How long do you think it'll take to hear back about the DNA results?"

"Depends. Nate and I talked about it, and he plans to take two swabs and send one to a company he sent the coffee sample to—those results should be available in two to three days. The other swab will go to the lab the state uses, and how long it takes will depend on how backed up they are."

"What about this Rapid DNA machine I've read about?"

"None here yet." Sam turned off the Trace onto I-20. "You can turn on the GPS anytime."

Emma opened her app and tapped on her mom's address. A very British accent directed them to exit onto I-55 north. She remembered Nate talking about how strapped his department was for funds. "I didn't realize the county had money to conduct two tests."

His face colored. "I told him I'd pay for one of them."

Her heart warmed. "I can't let you do that. I'll pay for it."

"No, you won't. It's already taken care of, and it wasn't much money, anyway."

She ducked her head. Somehow she would make it up to him. "If Nate sends the tests in on Monday, do you think we'll hear something by the end of the week?"

"I hope so."

Emma had to live a whole week without total certainty the grave they'd found belonged to Ryan.

28

Emma stared down at her hands. She'd shredded the tissue, leaving little pieces of it on her dressy jeans. "Rats," she muttered and used her hand to smooth them away.

"What's wrong?"

"I have tissue lint all over my jeans." Tears sprang to her eyes. The closer they got to her mother's place, the more dread she felt. What if she let something slip about Ryan?

"Try one of the latex gloves in my console," he said. "They work pretty good to get lint off my clothes."

Emma grabbed a glove and tried to wiggle it over her left hand, huffing a breath when she couldn't get the glove on.

"Hey, what's bothering you?"

"Nothing."

"Doesn't sound like nothing to me."

"I can't get the glove on, and I'm tired of trying to do everything with my left hand, and . . . I can't get Ryan off my mind."

"I'm sorry. I'll help you get the glove on when we stop, and we can talk about your brother, if you'd like."

Emma didn't want to discuss Ryan. She wanted to quit thinking about him, but she heard herself ask, "If it wasn't my brother buried in the grave, how did his ring get there? If it is him, who killed him? And how about Mary Jo? She was found three miles away, and her killer hadn't tried to bury her body." She caught her breath and turned to Sam. "What if Ryan killed her and lost his ring when he dug the grave?"

"But he didn't bury her. Coon hunters found her body."

"Maybe they found her before . . ."

"Then whose body was buried at Mount Locust?"

Emma leaned back against the seat. "I've thought about this until my brain is mush."

"We'll get it figured out," Sam said. "I don't believe he killed anyone, and I'm pretty sure it was his body buried in the grave, which I think the DNA test will confirm."

Her left hand curled into a fist as a flash of anger burned in her chest. "Then I want to track down whoever killed him and make him pay," she said. "And I will if it's the last thing I ever do."

"Absolutely not!" He held his hand up. "You are staying out of the investigation. This person is dangerous and you are not trained."

He was not locking her out. "You're saying you don't want the private investigator's report?"

Silence filled the cab. "Emma, you could get hurt, or worse."

The report was the only leverage she had over him, and she wasn't above using it. "If I'm with you all the time, I don't see how you're going to investigate without me," she said with a satisfied grin.

Evidently he had no answer, and she slipped a sidelong glance at him. The muscle in his jaw worked furiously. "I trust you to keep me safe," she said. "Do you have a bottle of water? I'd like to take something for my hand before we get there."

"Afraid not, but I can pull off at the next fuel station."

He seemed to be glad to get off the subject of Ryan. While he went inside for the water, she used the wadded glove over her jeans, surprised at how well it worked. When he returned, she took out her pill bottle and downed two pills, wishing she'd taken them earlier.

"What are we waiting for?" she asked when Sam didn't put the SUV into gear.

"Are you going to be all right seeing your mom and not telling her about Ryan?"

Instead of answering, Emma put the pill bottle in the small purse.

"Well?"

"I'll have to be." She zipped the bag shut, then looked up to find him studying her. "It won't be easy, though. Since Ryan disappeared, I feel like I'm walking on eggshells when I'm around Mom."

"But you two were always so close."

"A lot of things changed after that night." She rubbed the top of her bandaged hand. "Mom was so unemotional through it all. And she practically agreed with Sheriff Carter that Ryan could have killed Mary Jo since the two of them had an on-again, off-again relationship, and Mary Jo knew how to push Ryan's buttons."

"Your mom actually said she thought Ryan killed Mary Jo?"

Emma stilled her hand. "Not in those words. But Mom always called a spade a spade. I think she was prepared for the worst."

"She and your dad had been through a lot with Ryan."

"Yeah, and she sees everything as black or white."

His forehead wrinkled in a frown. "But she hired a private investigator to find him."

"I've been thinking about that. Mom's a lawyer . . . what if she wanted to find him and bring him back to defend himself? She would have stood by him, but she also wanted to get rid of the cloud hanging over him."

"Have you talked to her about the way you feel?"

"Are you kidding? Did you forget I'm the kid who never rocked the boat? I'm not sure how to approach her about it, anyway. My mother isn't the kind of person you disagree with. I learned that when I was a kid." She checked her watch. "Uh, we need to go or I'll be late."

Sam pulled out into traffic. "Have you talked to your dad about this?"

"No. He's coming to supper tomorrow night. Maybe I'll talk to him then."

A few minutes later they pulled up to the gated entrance. "Nice place," Sam said. "I always liked this area of Jackson."

"Me too, especially Fondren after 5."

"What's that?"

"Block parties—first Thursday night of the month from April to October. It's a blast," she said and gave him the code to get in. "And it'll be the same coming out."

He parked in front of her mom's condo. "Want me to come in with you?"

"Not tonight. I don't know what kind of mood Mom is in since I've asked for the investigator's report. I'd hate for you to walk into a hornet's nest." Or for her mom to quiz him about his intentions.

"Gotcha." He put the SUV in park and hopped out to come around and get her door.

"Thanks. I'll call you from the restaurant and let you know when I'm ready to leave. You know where Ricco's is, don't you?"

"Yes."

When she reached her mom's door and looked back, he still stood at her side of the car, and she waved. It would invite too many questions if her mother knew that Sam had brought her, so Emma waited until he drove away before she took a deep breath and rang the doorbell. And waited. She'd lifted her hand to ring it again when her mom opened the door.

"Good, you're on time," she said, checking her watch.

"I figured you had reservations, and I didn't want to be late," she said.

"Come in while I grab my purse and cell phone." She paused at the hallway. "How is your hand?"

"Healing, I hope." She closed the front door behind her as her mother disappeared down the hall. When she returned, Emma said, "You look good."

Why couldn't she have inherited her mom's height? With her looks and five-ten frame, she could have easily been a model. Maybe she'd gotten her mother's youthful genes, though. More than once they'd been mistaken for sisters, which made her mom feel good. Emma not so much.

"Thank you. You look nice as well, but are you certain you're not in pain?" her mom asked.

"Yes. I took something on the way."

"Then why are you frowning?"

"Sorry. I have a lot going on." Emma felt like she was on the witness stand, and with an imaginary brush, she swept away her thoughts and used the same brush to mentally smooth her countenance. She spied a large envelope on the kitchen table as she followed her mom to the back door. "Is this the private investigator's report?"

"Yes. I can't believe I almost forgot." Her mom pushed a strand of blonde hair behind her ear. "It's not much of a report."

Emma swallowed hard. "Why did you do it? Hire the detective?"

A sadness that mirrored Emma's heart briefly flashed in her mother's face. "That should be obvious. He's my son, and he was missing."

"But you thought he was guilty of killing Mary Jo." Had she actually said that?

The color left her mother's face. "Whatever made you think that?"

Emma's heart hammered in her chest. She'd faced wild boars that hadn't made her knees knock like answering her mother's questions. She swallowed hard. "You said you weren't surprised that Carter accused him—"

"That's a long way from believing he killed Mary Jo, Emma."

Her face grew hot under her mother's scrutiny.

"Is that why you pulled away?" When Emma didn't respond, her mother said, "Why didn't you say something years ago?"

"That's easier said than done. I've never been able to win an argument with you."

"There would have been no argument. Given the circumstances and your brother's past history with drugs and alcohol, I understood why Carter named Ryan as a person of interest."

The cloud that had hung over her for ten years lifted. Her mom didn't believe Ryan killed Mary Jo. They should have had this conversation years ago, and it was Emma's fault they hadn't. She'd projected her own guilt over Ryan leaving onto her mother because it was easier than admitting the hateful words she spewed at her brother may have been the catalyst that sent him running.

"If that's settled, shall we go?" Without waiting for an answer, her mother opened the back door. "You didn't say how you got here."

Emma followed her out into the garage. They went from one fire to another. "A friend dropped me off and will pick me up at the restaurant after we eat."

"You could have invited her."

Emma thought fast. "I didn't want to share you tonight." That wasn't a lie and kept her from having to say it wasn't a "her."

Her mother's face softened. "That's sweet of you. I hope we can do this more often, perhaps even include your dad."

"Dad?" She couldn't keep the surprise from her voice.

"Why not?" Her mom glanced at her and chuckled. "We're only divorced, Emma. Not enemies."

"I know that, but . . ." Emma needed to close her mouth before she said something else she would later wish she hadn't. "Do you two get together often?"

"About once a month, but before you start getting ideas, your dad and I are not getting back together. It just wouldn't work. My career is in Jackson, and he'll never leave Natchez."

While she'd come to terms with her parents' divorce, a part of her still wished they could get back together. Wasn't that almost every child's dream for divorced parents, even an adult child?

29

Sam pulled up to Ricco's and texted Emma he was there. A few minutes later, she emerged from the restaurant and hurried to his SUV.

"Thanks," she said as she climbed into the passenger seat and laid an envelope on the console. She sounded relieved.

"How'd it go?"

"It started off rocky, but it got better."

"How so?"

"We actually talked, and I asked her if she thought Ryan killed Mary Jo."

"That had to have been hard." Emma had never been an in-your-face person, and even as a teenager, she never bucked her parents. "I assume she convinced you she didn't."

When an answer wasn't forthcoming, he glanced at her. Emma had a faraway look on her face. "Actually, yes," she said with a sigh. "I'm so far out of the loop. I just found out my parents are getting together once a month for dinner."

"Any chance of them getting back together?"

"Mom says not, and she's probably right. They are both so different, and they want different things out of life. They seem to get along better since the divorce than when I was growing up."

He hoped that wasn't true of his parents. After they were on I-55, he asked, "The Trace or Highway 61?"

"How about the Trace? That way we can swing by and check on the dig site at Mount Locust."

"Good idea," he said. Clayton was off tonight, leaving only one deputy at the site.

"Just watch for deer." Emma picked up the envelope and clicked on the reading light on the passenger side.

"Is that the private investigator's report?"

"Yeah, and Mom was right. There's not much in it."

"Who was the investigator?"

She pulled out the sheets. "Harry Bell signed it."

Sam frowned. "The name sounds familiar."

"It says at the bottom of the page he's a former FBI agent."

The name and a face clicked. Harry "Bulldog" Bell. "He taught a class at Glynco, Georgia, when I went through the academy there." He exited off onto I-20 west, then a few miles later took the Trace exit. "I wonder if your mother lost part of the report?"

"Why do you ask that?"

"Harry Bell was a good agent and an excellent teacher. I can't see him doing a half-baked investigation . . . or report."

"Really?" she said. "But it wouldn't be like my mother to lose something like that."

While Emma sifted through the papers, he turned on the overhead light. "See if it looks like anything's missing."

She was quiet except for the turning of pages for a minute. Then she looked up. "The pages aren't numbered, but what's at the bottom of some of the pages doesn't line up with what's at the top of the next page. And the sheriff's file on Ryan that Mom said was included isn't here."

"See if there's a number to call Bell."

"There are two—looks like an office number and one for a cell."

"While we're still in Jackson and have cell coverage, do you want to call him and find out if he had included Carter's file?"

Before she could answer him, her cell rang. "It's Dad," she said. After she answered, Emma told him she was with Sam.

"Put us on speaker," he overheard her dad say. "I'd like to say hi."

After Sam and her dad exchanged pleasantries, he asked, "How did your evening with your mom go?"

"Okay . . . well, better than okay."

"Good. Did you get the private investigator's report?"

"How did you know—"

"Dina told me. I think she wanted to warn me you might ask me about it."

"Have you seen it?" Sam asked.

There was hesitation on the line, then he said, "I have."

Beside him, Emma caught her breath. "Can you remember what was in the report?" she asked.

He heard Jack take in a deep breath, and Sam exchanged glances with Emma. Her expression mirrored his feelings. Maybe they shouldn't have asked.

"Dad, I'm sorry. I wasn't thinking, hitting you with that question out of the blue."

Jack cleared his throat. "No, it's okay. It's just that your brother has been on my mind a lot recently."

"Mine too," Emma replied.

"Do you remember whether Sheriff Carter's file on Ryan was in the investigator's report?" Sam asked.

"I don't remember the exact details, Sam, but I do remember seeing a copy of the sheriff's report, along with his opinion that Ryan killed Mary Jo Selby. That's about where I quit reading. Why do you two want to know?"

Sam nodded for Emma to answer the question.

"Just wondering," she said. "Sam has offered to help me look into the case again."

He gave her a thumbs-up. That was generic enough without fibbing.

"Do you have a copy of the investigator's report?" Emma asked.

"No. Your mother never offered to share a copy, and I didn't ask for one," he said. "I assume she gave you her copy."

"Yes. She gave me what she had, but some of it seems to be missing."

"I wouldn't know anything about that," her dad said with finality in his voice. "Are we still on for tomorrow night, say around sixish? I thought I might pick up steaks and grill them at your place. You're welcome to come, Sam."

Sam wasn't sure Emma wanted him there tomorrow night and shot her a questioning look. She nodded. "Thanks, Mr. Winters. I'll see you then," he said.

They both said goodbye, and Sam's lips quirked up as she slipped her phone in the small black bag she carried. First time he'd seen her with anything but her backpack since he returned to Natchez. When she'd walked out of the maintenance building in those boots and with her copper-colored hair falling loosely about her shoulders, he'd almost lost his breath. The skinny jeans and black sweater didn't help his breathing any either.

"Do you want to contact Harry Bell," Emma asked, "or do you want me to?"

"You better. You have a legal right to the report whereas if I get involved, we might need a court order."

She checked her watch. "It's nine. Do you think it's too late to call him?"

"Why don't you text the cell number and see if he responds, but let me pull over since we'll be out of cell range a few miles from here." Sam turned into a pullout while she texted a message. Almost immediately she received an answering text.

"He said it was okay to call him." Emma punched in Bell's number, and when he answered, she identified herself and said, "Mr. Bell, I have a copy of your report on my brother, Ryan Winters," she said. "But there seems to be missing pages. Could you email me a new copy of your report?"

Bell cleared his throat. "You say you're Dina Winters's daughter?"

"Yes, sir. Like I said, I'm looking at my mom's copy right now."

He paused. "I'd like to call your mother and get permission to share it. After that, we can FaceTime, if you'd like."

"Sure."

Sam tapped the steering wheel while they waited. Five minutes later, Emma's cell rang the distinctive FaceTime ring and she answered, turning the phone slightly for Sam to see as well.

Harry Bell had changed little since Sam sat under his teaching. Maybe lost a little more hair on top, but his wizened face didn't look any older than it had eight years ago.

"Who's that with you?" Bell asked.

"My friend Sam Ryker."

"That name is familiar."

"We met at the academy at Glynco. I was one of your students."

"Oh yeah. I remember you."

Emma turned the phone so it showed her image again.

"You favor your mother, Miss Winters. Now what's this about missing pages in the report?"

Sam listened while she explained the discrepancies they'd found. "My mom said there'd been a copy of Sheriff Carter's file on the Mary Jo Selby death among the documents."

"Let me think. Ten years ago I wasn't doing digital files, so I only have a hard copy and it's at the office."

They waited for him to continue.

"Yes, come to think of it, I did get a copy of that file from the Adams County sheriff."

"It's not in your report now. Would you email me another copy, including the sheriff's file?"

"You haven't heard from your brother?"

"No . . . Can we speak confidentially?" she asked.

"Most certainly."

"We think he may be d-dead . . ." Emma collected herself and continued. "We found evidence he may have been buried at Mount Locust all these years."

Bell's mouth turned down. "I'm so sorry," he said, shaking his head. "I was hoping for a different outcome."

"So were we," Sam said.

The older man sighed. "That explains why I never found him." Then he rubbed his jaw. "I don't understand why you want my report if you believe you've found his remains."

"Sheriff Carter's file on the case is missing from the sheriff's department's records," Sam replied.

"Oh." He made at least two syllables out of the word. "That's interesting."

He figured Bell would think it was. Sam would love his help in this. The man hadn't earned the nickname Bulldog for nothing.

"I only have the sheriff's preliminary report, not the outcome." The PI rubbed his jaw. "If your brother was buried at Mount Locust, how did his car get to Memphis?"

"We discussed that with the current sheriff, Nate Rawlings. Whoever killed him must have driven it up there to make it look like he'd left the Natchez area. He, and we're assuming it's a male, either rode the bus back to Natchez, or he could have rented a car."

"Or he had a partner."

The words hung in the car. Sam hadn't considered two people might be involved. That put a new spin on the case. "I'm planning to canvass the car rentals in Memphis to see if their records go that far back."

"That would be a miracle," Bell said. "I'll go to the office after church tomorrow and scan the report and email a copy to you. And if there's anything else I can do to help, just let me know."

"We will," Sam said, and Emma disconnected. Her face held so much hope, making his stomach clench. There were so many possibilities. And ten years had passed. He feared finding any kind of trail, much less a paper trail, would be next to impossible.

30

He had kept two cars between him and Sam's SUV all the way from Mount Locust to a house in Jackson that belonged to Dina Winters. Emma was a good daughter, spending time with her mother, but he would expect no less from her. And now he was following them back to Natchez.

It had thrown him off when Sam pulled into the pullout. But it was dark and he'd driven to the next historical marker and waited for them in his pickup. Twenty minutes later, the ranger's SUV passed by, and when the taillights disappeared around a curve, he fell in behind them again.

Emma would have asked him to take her to Jackson, he knew that, but she didn't want to cause people to whisper about them. *What about Sam and Emma? Won't people whisper about them?* He brushed the thought away. They were both rangers. Everyone would assume they were working together on something.

Besides, Emma wasn't interested in Ryker. She didn't send him Facebook posts every day and never looked at the ranger the way she looked at him. He plucked a box from the console and flipped the top open. A two-carat diamond sparkled under the lighted dash. She would be so pleased when he gave it to her.

What if he'd accidentally shot her last night? He'd been aiming at Ryker, but he shuddered at how close it had come to Emma. Pain stabbed his head as the beginning of a migraine started.

Maybe he'd go home instead of following them to Emma's apartment.

No. Not knowing whether Ryker would attempt to kiss her when he took her to the door would torment him. Not that she would let him, but the ranger might force himself on her. And then he could save her.

The headache intensified as mile after mile passed. They approached Mount Locust, and the SUV ahead of him slowed and swung into the entrance. He could do nothing but drive on by. Maybe Ryker would simply make a loop and reenter the Trace, so he slowed. When the car lights didn't reappear, he swore. Only one thing to do. Drive to his spot near Emma's apartment and wait. He should even have time to stop and get a coffee. Maybe that would get rid of the headache.

Forty-five minutes later, he'd almost finished the coffee when the ranger's SUV pulled in front of the apartment house, and Ryker escorted Emma to the front door. Wait. He was going in.

He held his breath as her living room light came on, providing him with a front-row seat. The ranger crossed out of his line of sight while Emma stayed in front of the window. Then he returned and—

No!

It was like watching an accident about to happen and just as impossible to take his gaze away from as Sam took Emma in his arms. He gripped the Styrofoam cup, crushing it.

31

Emma sat on her sofa in the dark, her third cup of coffee in her hands as her clock chimed six times. Sam had checked out her apartment when he dropped her off around eleven last night, and then hugged her and left. A platonic hug. Why had she wished it'd been more?

She pinched the bridge of her nose. Sleep had been fitful, and when the clock rolled over to 4:00 a.m., she'd given up and climbed out of bed. What little shut-eye she'd gotten had been marred with dreams of walking the woods around Mount Locust, calling Ryan's name. She sipped her coffee, now bitter and lukewarm. Regret tasted just as bitter, especially when it was laced with anger.

Emma set the cup on the table and leaned her head back. If she could just get a catnap . . . She jerked her head up. A board in the hallway outside her door creaked as though protesting someone's weight. Maybe it was her neighbor Greg on his way to his morning run. She checked her watch. She'd dozed for forty-five minutes. Then she frowned. Greg never ran this early on Sunday, not before the sun rose.

Emma cocked her head, listening for more sounds. It'd probably been her imagination. She needed more coffee. After Emma poured another cup, she popped it into the microwave for thirty seconds. Halfway back to the sofa, she froze. A card had been shoved under her door. She jerked the door open, pulling the envelope with it. Dr. Gordon Cole whirled around, his eyes wide. "Emma?"

Was that guilt on his face? Had he left the note? And the flowers? "Gordy? I mean Gordon." He stared at her, and amusement crossed his face. She looked down at her Minnie Mouse pajamas. "Ah, did you see anyone else in the hallway?"

"No."

The answer came almost too quickly. "What are you doing here?"

Red crept into his face. "I, ah . . ." He stared at his feet.

The door to the efficiency apartment at the end of the hallway opened, and her neighbor stepped out. "Gordon?" Taylor said, a look of puzzlement on her face. "I heard voices, but I thought you'd left."

Realization dawned. So the doc and her neighbor were an "item." Emma had heard Gordon had gotten married right out of college, and hadn't realized he'd divorced until he returned to Natchez last year, single and looking. While he didn't interest her, Gordon Cole was a hunk, in a California sort of way, tanned, blond haired, and blue eyed.

While Emma didn't know Taylor that well, the girl was barely out of college and at least a decade younger than the doc. *None of my business.* If she made Gordy happy, what did age matter?

The doctor's face had turned crimson now. "I stopped to listen to a voicemail and answer a text," he said, answering Taylor.

Who would be texting him this time of the morning?

Almost as if he read her mind, he said, "We've been to the casino, and I forgot to turn on my phone until just a minute ago. One of my patients has been admitted to the ER. That's where I'm headed." He nodded at Emma, then turned to Taylor. "See you tonight."

Taylor's answer was a smile that lit up her face. Emma waved and shut the door after she used her foot to nudge the card into her living room. If it was a threat, she didn't want to get her prints on the envelope and grabbed her tongs from the kitchen and a rubber glove for her left hand.

After she pulled on the glove, she picked up the envelope with the tongs. The seal was barely stuck, and she used her fingernail to flip it open. Gingerly she lifted the folded paper out, again by the corner, and a drawing fell out.

A dead rat caught in a trap. The illustration took her breath. Across the bottom in bold black lettering were the words "***Beware the rat.***" She carefully laid the card on her coffee table. Then she took out her phone and dialed Sam.

"It's early," he said by way of answering. "I can't be late yet."

"Didn't I tell you Brooke was picking me up?"

"No. What's wrong? You sound funny."

"There's . . ." She gulped a breath. "It's a drawing of a dead rat. I just got it. Somebody stuck it under my door."

"I'll be there in ten minutes."

He hung up and Emma stared at her phone. She should call Nate. Her fingers shook as she punched the sheriff's cell phone number. "Rawlings," he said.

"I received another threat this morning."

"I'll be there ASAP," Nate said.

Emma had barely changed into her gray-and-green uniform when her doorbell rang, and she hurried to answer it. She really needed a peephole. "Who's there?"

"It's me," Sam said.

Emma let him in. He hadn't shaved, so the clean fragrance that sent her heart soaring had to be his soap. It made her want to feel his arms wrapped around her.

"Where's the card?" he asked.

"On the table. There's a pair of kitchen gloves beside it."

Before he looked at the card, Sam hugged her. "I'm sorry this is happening. I'll install a security camera outside your door tomorrow. I should have already put it up."

The tears that sprang to her eyes surprised her. Emma thought she had a grip on this. "Why would anyone send me a drawing of a dead rat with that caption?"

"I don't know, but I intend to find out." Sam studied the drawing. "How is this person getting into your building?"

"Do you think he might have a key?" she asked.

"Could be. How many people have keys to the entrance doors?"

"There's no way to know. I gave Dad one, but most people I buzz in if they visit after six."

"This puts a different slant on the matter. Whoever—"

"Wait," she said as her doorbell rang. "Hold that thought. That may be Nate."

She opened the door and told the sheriff to come in and then followed him back into the living room. "Would you two like coffee?"

"I haven't had my two cups yet, so yes. Black, please," Nate said, and Sam shook his head.

While she put on a fresh pot of coffee, the sheriff set a briefcase on the table and examined the card. "What do you suppose this means?"

Sam folded his arms across his chest. "We have someone obsessed with Emma. He probably knows we went to Jackson together last night. It confirms, to me at least, that the shots fired Friday night were meant for me. Evidently, I'm the rat. It's his way of warning her not to trust me."

"How about Thursday night?" Nate asked and slipped the card and envelope into an evidence bag.

"Yeah," Emma said from the kitchen.

"I think you caught someone digging and he was trying to scare you off."

"Do you think it's the same person?"

"Could be," Sam said. "But more than likely the shooting at Mount Locust is tied to Ryan's death."

"You think we're dealing with two different people." Nate

rubbed his jaw. "Makes sense, because the shooting Thursday night was definitely aimed at Emma. Anyone in love with her wouldn't be taking potshots at her."

"I said obsessed because I don't think this person knows what love is," Sam said. "Of course, he probably thinks he's in love, and quite possibly believes she returns his feelings."

The final gurgle from the coffeepot let her know it was finished, and she escaped to the kitchen. After pouring Nate a cup, she took it to him and then refilled her own cup, hoping more caffeine would clear the fog in her brain. She simply couldn't comprehend that someone was obsessed with her and was willing to kill because of it. "You really think the person was firing at you Friday night?"

"If I hadn't stooped to catch your keys, the bullet would have nailed me, not you. If I'm right, your stalker believes I pose a threat to his relationship with you."

Cold chills shivered down her back. She'd only halfway embraced the idea someone was stalking her, but now, there was no question. But who could it be? Wouldn't it have to be someone she knew or at least came in contact with? That would encompass a lot of suspects. Emma gulped a sip of coffee and winced as the hot liquid burned her mouth and throat.

When she could speak again, she asked, "If someone were obsessed with me, wouldn't he make himself known?" When neither man answered, she said, "It wasn't a rhetorical question."

Sam rubbed his jaw. "It depends. He may not be ready to let you know how he feels. Or he thinks you already know, and you return his feelings."

"He could be like John Hinckley Jr., the guy who shot a president because he was in love with Jodie Foster," Nate said. "He was obsessed with her, and she didn't have a clue he existed for years."

"Then he would have to be crazy, right? And I don't know anyone who is that mentally off balance. I think we need to come up with a different scenario, because I don't buy your theory that it's two different shooters. That would be some coincidence."

"But not impossible," Nate said. "Either way, you weren't supposed to be at Mount Locust. Like Sam, I think you surprised the intruder, and he fired at you as a ploy to distract you so he could get away."

Emma pondered that. She hadn't driven into the visitor center parking lot that night, so there would not have been any headlights announcing her arrival. He must have heard her when she climbed the steps to the inn. And the bullet that plowed into the post *was* way over her head. She set her empty cup down. "This is just so hard to take in."

"You can't think of anyone who might think they're in love with you?" Sam asked, pacing her living room. "Like Trey? Or someone else you've dated?"

"I've stayed friends with most of my exes," Emma said wryly. "Even went to some of their weddings." When Sam shot a curious glance at her, she lifted her hands. "What can I say? I'm usually good at breaking up and staying friends. As for Trey, I just have a hard time believing he'd shoot at me . . . or you."

"I don't think it's my deputy either," Nate said. "Except, if he is still asking you out and you're saying no, he is the type to become obsessed about winning you over."

She frowned, remembering his apology yesterday. "I just don't buy it being him. Besides, he told me he'd turned over a new leaf."

32

After the sheriff entered Emma's apartment building, he jogged down the street, then crossed over to her side and came back toward the apartment. Keeping his head ducked, he stopped beside the rear tire of Ryker's SUV and pretended to tie his shoes but instead planted a GPS tracker in the wheel well.

Then he jogged to the corner and back to his car. The ranger had been in her apartment for over an hour now, but at least they weren't alone. But what could she be talking to him and the sheriff about for this long? He hadn't expected her to call anyone when he shoved the card under her door. He only wanted her to be aware Ryker wasn't to be trusted.

Were they talking about the card he left? Surely not. He needed a way to know what was going on in her apartment. Maybe a bug. Yes! That's what he would do. He should have ordered one when he bought the tracker, but the local discount store had them. A quick check of his watch indicated there was time to pick one up before he had to be somewhere. Maybe he'd get two.

Still he hesitated to leave, wanting to see if Emma left with Ryker.

Maybe he'd stay just a few minutes longer.

33

Emma rolled her shoulders. Her body felt as though she'd pulled an all-nighter, and she needed more caffeine if she was going to work today. It'd been hard enough to think one person was trying to kill her. Now the thought of being in the crosshairs of two different people was almost more than she could take.

Nate checked his watch. "The morning briefing is in twenty minutes, so let's discuss this later at Mount Locust." He opened the briefcase he'd brought in. "I have the two DNA kits. Thought as long as I was here, we could get this taken care of."

Her heart stuttered. She hadn't expected him to bring the tests to her. When Nate handed her the paper-encased cotton swabs, Emma hesitated, then took them and peeled back the paper on one. "How do I do this?"

"Just swab the inside of your cheek," Nate said.

She did as he instructed and handed the stick to him. Then she repeated the process with the other stick.

"I'll send a deputy with one sample to Jackson today, and get the other one off tomorrow, and ask both labs to put a rush on it. If we're lucky, we should get the results from Jackson back by the middle of the week."

Once Nate left, Emma rubbed her forehead with her left fingers.

She was surprised when Sam pulled her to him, and she laid her head on his chest as his arms wrapped around her.

"You look like you could use a hug," he said softly.

Oh, brother, did she need one.

"I'm sorry you're having to go through this."

"Thanks." His steady heartbeat calmed her, and his arms around her made her feel safe, but she had things to do. Yet she didn't pull away.

He tilted her face up until she was looking into brown eyes that were warm with compassion. She'd been such a fool years ago.

"It's going to be okay," he said, tucking a strand of hair behind her ear.

"It's good to know you have my back." His touch sent shivers through her. Surely he felt the electricity between them when they were together. She held her breath, feeling his every heartbeat as he searched her face, his gaze going from questioning to awareness.

His touch sent shock waves through her as he cupped her chin and traced his thumb along her jaw. Emma's head told her to run, but her heart held her in his embrace. Barely able to breathe, she slipped her arms around his waist. He kissed her lightly on the tip of her nose, and she leaned into him. Sam bent his head and lowered his lips to hers, kissing her softly.

Emma melted into his embrace, returning his kiss with a passion that came from the depth of her heart. Never before had she felt the way she did at this moment, not even when he'd professed his love and gave her a ring all those years ago.

Slowly he released her. "Wow," he said softly.

"Yeah, wow." She laid her head against his chest.

"I didn't know that was going to happen," he murmured against the top of her head.

"Are you sorry?"

"Oh no. How about you?"

Emma raised her head. "No, but does it complicate things?"

He chuckled. "For my part, it was already complicated."

"So you were fighting it, whatever *it* is, too."

"You might say that."

She looked into eyes that made her feel safe and loved. She wanted him to kiss her again, but if he did, they might not leave. Evidently, he felt the same way, as he sighed and released her.

"I better leave now."

"Yeah." She moved toward the door with him. "And Brooke will be here soon."

"Aren't you forgetting something?"

She stared blankly at him. *My backpack.* Heat burned her face. "I'm a little distracted."

"That makes two of us," he said softly, then asked, "Did you get the file from Bell?"

"No," Emma replied. "He won't send it until after church."

"Are you sure you don't want me to drive you to Mount Locust instead of Brooke? I'm going there anyway. In fact, we could leave now."

Emma considered his question. She definitely wanted to spend more time with him after that kiss and wished she hadn't asked Brooke to swing by and pick her up. "Okay, but let me text Brooke and tell her you're taking me." Once that was done, she asked, "Have you said anything to her about the ring and that maybe the grave belonged to Ryan?"

He shook his head. "I haven't seen her, and that's something I don't want to talk about over the phone."

"If I see her first, is it okay for us to discuss it?"

"I don't see why not. She'll be helping with the investigation anyway."

Brooke texted back a thumbs-up and that she would stop by Mount Locust sometime during the day. Emma poured coffee into her insulated cup and grabbed a breakfast bar.

"Have you eaten?" she asked, and when he said no, she tossed him a breakfast bar as well. "That should hold you until lunch. Coffee?"

"Yes, ma'am, if you have a Styrofoam cup with a lid," he said.

"I have another insulated tumbler."

"That'll work."

She poured what was left of the coffee into another tumbler. "I'm ready."

Emma handed him the coffee, and his fingers brushed hers, bringing back the memory of their embrace. What if he regretted it?

"You okay?"

"Yeah. How about you?" Hesitantly, Emma lifted her head and sought his eyes. She had to know how he felt. Her heart soared when his smile made it all the way to his brown eyes. "I mean, do you regret kissing me?"

"I was a little surprised, but I would never regret it."

"What do we do now?"

Sam laughed out loud. "We go to Mount Locust and finish the work there, and we come back to your house and have dinner with your dad."

Just like a man to put it all into perspective.

"We need to take whatever this is slowly," he added and took her arm as they walked down the stairs.

Part of her disagreed and wanted to go full steam ahead. But he was right. She definitely didn't want to rush things and have a repeat of ten years ago.

He stopped at the front door of the house. "Let me check out the street."

Sam did make her feel protected. When he returned, he said, "It's all clear and one of Nate's deputies just made a pass by so we ought to be good to go."

He'd pulled into the drive and hurried her to the waiting SUV. She almost stopped as she felt someone watching her. It had to be her imagination. Sam had scoped the area out and would surely have seen if someone were hiding. Emma scanned the street. Two vehicles were waiting to turn left on her street, a dark sedan and a light-colored pickup.

The driver in the dark sedan blew his horn and the pickup lurched forward, the sun glinting off the windshield. The sedan driver gunned his motor as he made the turn and blew past the pickup. She shook her head. People were so impatient.

34

He glanced up at Emma's window, hoping to see her, but the blinds were pulled. His mind drifted to the cabin he had for her. He couldn't wait to take her there. It was the perfect place where they could be happy, and no one would bother them. Soon. He would take her there very soon.

His attention jerked back to the apartment as Ryker stepped out on the front porch. The ranger was leaving. He watched him as he scoped out the neighborhood.

Suddenly a patrol car in his rearview mirror caught his attention, and he froze. He'd hung around too long. With his heart in his throat he ducked down in the seat, and as soon as the sound of the car's motor faded, he raised up. Time for him to leave in case the patrol car made another loop. Except he wanted a glimpse of Emma. No. He needed to leave and quickly started his truck and pulled out of the parking space.

At the stop sign, he was about to turn when Emma emerged from the two-story house with Ryker on her heels. Fire exploded in his chest as the ranger placed his arm around her waist. Ryker shouldn't be touching her that way. He gripped the steering wheel, and his jaw clenched so tight it hurt. He was almost as angry as he'd been last night.

A horn blew behind him, and he jumped. Both Emma and Ryker glanced toward the street, and he hastily made a left turn, away from town. It took a mile for his heart to calm down again. That had been close. At least they didn't appear to recognize him, but what if Ryker made note of his pickup? Stupid driver behind him. He'd almost flipped him off when the idiot sped around him, but with drivers being the way they were nowadays, it might have caused an altercation. And that would have drawn Ryker's attention.

His chest tightened at how Ryker just couldn't keep his hands off Emma. She'd tried to move away from him, he'd seen her, but Ryker maintained a firm hand on her. He narrowed his eyes. The ranger had to go.

35

Once Emma was inside the SUV, Sam relaxed but not completely. A door would not stop a bullet.

"Do you think life will ever be normal again?" Emma asked.

"We're going to catch this guy," he said. "What're your plans for the day?"

"You're trying to distract me."

"Maybe. Did it work?"

She smiled. "A little. I plan to finish the excavation, then maybe use the GPR machine around the cabin area. And I'm looking forward to Dad's steaks. You still coming?"

"Absolutely, and I'll bring dessert. That okay?"

"What? Are you baking a cake?" Her eyes twinkled.

"No," he said. "But I could. Mom and my grandmother who lived with us made sure I knew how to cook for myself before I went off to college."

"They were wise women."

"Who taught you to cook?"

"Granny, Mom's mother." Her voice broke. "I'm afraid it didn't take very well. I still manage to burn water."

Sam kept one hand on the steering wheel and squeezed her fingers with the other. "I hate I didn't get back for her funeral."

"You'd think after six months, I would be past it."

"You can't rush grief," Sam said softly. "And she was one special lady."

"Independent too. Never did get her to move out of that neighborhood."

"She was generous with her love, I remember that," he said.

"I hope I'm like her whenever I get married and have children."

"You will be. Why don't you lean your seat back and rest until we get to Mount Locust?"

"I might do that. This not sleeping is getting to me."

The silence that filled the SUV as Sam drove through the light Sunday morning traffic in Natchez allowed his mind to second-guess what had happened at her apartment. Emma had looked so forlorn after taking the DNA test, he'd tried to comfort her. When he took her in his arms, he hadn't meant to kiss her. At least not consciously. That she returned his kiss the way she did blew him away.

Sam drummed his fingers on the steering wheel. Now he had to worry how she would react when he told her what happened the night Ryan disappeared. He should have taken it slower, explained exactly what had happened, before today. If he told her now, it would destroy her confidence in him.

Besides, there wasn't enough time between Natchez and Mount Locust to deal with the fallout. But what if he waited too long and someone else told her? There was only one person who could. His sister, and she wouldn't do that to him.

Tomorrow. He would tell her tomorrow when he installed the doorbell camera. That would give plenty of time to explain without someone interrupting. And time to repair any damage the truth caused.

Having that settled in his mind lightened his mood. Once they were on a straight stretch of the Trace, he took his eyes off the road long enough to glance at Emma. Even with the dark circles shadowing her eyes, she was beautiful. Like last night, she wore her hair down, her natural curls framing her face. She opened her eyes and caught him staring. Busted.

"You need to watch the road."

"No traffic and no curves," he said and put a smile in his voice.

She returned the seat to the upright position. "Next you'll be saying, 'Look, Ma, no hands.'"

"Who? Me? You know me better than that." He loved that she could joke when her heart was breaking. All the reasons he'd fallen in love with Emma in the first place flooded him. She was smart, and caring, and—

He swallowed hard. And now maybe they had another chance at love.

A car approached from the north, and Sam directed his attention back to the road. But his mind wandered into the future. One with Emma.

"How come you . . . uh . . . never married?" she asked.

Their thoughts must be running the same path. He lifted his shoulder in a dismissive shrug. "Been too busy."

"You're kidding."

"No. When would I have had time? I finished college in three and a half years, attended a federal law enforcement training, and went to work full-time for the park service out in Arizona and worked my way up the ladder." It was easier to eat, drink, and sleep being a ranger than to invest time in a relationship that would probably go nowhere. "And now I'm back in Natchez."

"Why did it take you so long to come home?"

"I don't know. Coming home was hard. Part of me wanted to—the part that helps with Jace, but—"

"Because of your dad?"

Not a subject he wanted to discuss.

"I saw him not long ago, and of course I saw quite a bit of him when I was looking for an apartment. He's really knowledgeable about real estate around here," Emma said. "But he looks bad."

He clamped his jaw, feeling the muscle jump. "I wouldn't know since I've made it a point to avoid him."

Sam checked his speed limit. He was crowding sixty and slowed back to the speed limit. "How about you? Why haven't you married?"

Turnabout was fair play, and the blush that crept into her face indicated it wasn't a subject she wanted to discuss either. "I've been busy too."

His mouth twitched. "You're kidding," he said, using Emma's own words against her.

"It's different for me. With your looks, I'm surprised you don't have women beating a path to Natchez."

"So, you think I'm handsome?"

"I, ah . . . it's the uniform."

"Hmm."

Her face was beet red now.

Her cell phone dinged, and she grabbed it. "It's an email from Harry Bell." A few seconds later she groaned. "He decided to swing by his office on the way to church, but now he's having trouble scanning the report to his email. He's going to wait until his secretary arrives tomorrow so she can send the report."

"Email him back and see if he can copy it. If he can, Brooke can pick it up this afternoon. She'll be up that way."

Emma quickly responded, and it wasn't long before there was an answer. "He said that will work. He'll meet her at the office."

They passed the one-mile marker to Mount Locust, and he slowed to turn in. "I'll text Brooke his number and the directions, and they can work out the logistics."

"Good," she said as they turned into the entrance. "Just drop me off at the gate so I can feed Suzy and leave a note on the door for visitors telling them I'll be at the slave cemetery."

"I'll take you to the parking lot. How are you going to feed her on the days you're off?"

"I plan to take her home tonight. Otherwise I'll have to drive back out here tomorrow to feed her." Emma glanced at him and caught him smiling. "What?" she asked.

"Just thinking about when we were kids and you used to take in all the stray animals. Drove your mom crazy."

"You remember that?"

"I remember a lot about you," he said, brushing a strand of coppery hair from her face.

She leaned into his touch. Behind them, a horn blew and he dropped his hand and looked in his rearview mirror. Nate. A second later the sheriff tapped on Emma's window.

"Give me the key, and I'll open the gate," Nate said.

From the expression on Nate's face, Sam was in for some ribbing from the sheriff.

36

Emma zipped her uniform jacket against the cold wind that had come up. The day had passed quickly, and with the sun setting, temperatures would soon dip into the low forties. She hadn't meant to work past four thirty, but it had taken longer to excavate the last few inches of the pit than she'd expected.

"Ready?" Sam asked as he placed the last board over the hole.

She nodded and started the GPR machine, slowly pushing it across the planks, all the while watching the screen. "I believe we've hit rock bottom," she said when the screen showed smooth lines. Emma rolled the machine onto the grass and let Sam view the image as well.

"I think you're right," he agreed, his voice flat.

Emma knew how he felt. She'd hoped they would find more evidence too, but whoever took the skeletal remains had left only a small bone and the class ring behind.

"If you're ready, I'll take you home," Sam said.

"Did Brooke say when she would get here?" she asked. Brooke had texted Sam earlier that it was taking longer to get the report than she'd expected.

"She hoped to be here by now. Let me check and see where she is," he said. When she didn't answer, he said, "I'll contact her on the radio when we get to the SUV."

There was nothing more to do at the site, and she nodded. "Thanks for staying."

"No problem. What time did your dad say he was coming?"

Emma caught her breath and then groaned. "Around six. I totally forgot."

"Then we better get a move on. I'll drop you off and then go home and change and come back."

That sounded like a plan. "Dad has a key, and I'll text him to go on in if he gets there before I do," she said.

Sam pushed the GPR machine as they walked toward the tractor shed. After he secured it, the north wind sent them hurrying to his vehicle. "I won't complain about the heat this summer," Emma said as he held the door open for her.

"Yes, you will, or at least about the humidity," he said, laughing. Once he slid behind the wheel, he radioed Brooke.

"Sorry, but I'm still forty minutes out," she said. "There's no need for you to hang around at Mount Locust. I can bring the report by Emma's apartment on my way home."

"That'll work," Sam said, looking over at her. "Or do you have a problem with that?"

"Dad will be there."

"He doesn't have to know what Brooke is dropping off, but I think it's a mistake not to let him look it over. He might remember something that could help with the investigation."

Something inside her resisted. What if one of them let slip that they'd found the ring?

"Besides, he already knows we're getting the report," Sam said gently.

Dad would probably ask about it, anyway. "I just don't want him to know it may have been Ryan's body in the grave. Not until we know for certain."

"I don't either," Sam said. "Are you still taking the little cat home with you?"

Emma had forgotten she'd planned to do that. She scanned the area, looking for the gray tabby. "I don't see her," she said.

"Maybe she's at the visitor center."

"I'll check before I lock the gate." If she wasn't around, Emma didn't have time to hunt for her. She had decided to return to Mount Locust for a few hours tomorrow anyway, so feeding Suzy wouldn't be a problem. But she did want to get the cat checked out by a veterinarian while she was off.

Sam pulled into the empty parking lot, and Emma checked around the restrooms for Suzy. No cat. She turned to leave when a plaintive meow came from behind the building.

"Come here, kitty," she called and walked through the open passage. Suzy sauntered toward her, and Emma scooped her up. "I don't have a carrier, so you have to ride in my lap, okay?"

Emma wasn't certain how this would work out. Maybe she could wrap Suzy in her jacket until she got home. She wished she'd picked up a carrier. And a litter box. And litter. She'd have to go to the store after her dad left.

"You found her," Sam said. He was waiting by the passenger door when she approached with the kitten in her arms.

"Would you hold her a minute while I take off my jacket to wrap around her?"

"No need. I have an old shirt in the back we can use."

Once Emma was settled in the passenger seat, Sam placed the T-shirt across her lap and wrapped the cat in it. "That way she won't scratch you if she gets scared."

At first Suzy tried to escape, but as Emma crooned to her, she settled down. It wasn't long before purring sounded in the SUV. "Think you can take me to the store after Dad leaves? I need to buy a few things for her."

"Why don't I pick up what you need before I come to dinner?"

Emma gladly agreed, and it wasn't long before they pulled in front of her apartment building. "There's Dad's car," she said, pointing to a white Toyota. "He's here already."

Sam helped her get the cat upstairs and unlocked her door. "Be back in an hour, max," he said.

She shut the door and set Suzy down. A faint scent she didn't recognize tickled her nose. Her dad must be using a new cologne.

"Dad?" she called, but there was no answer. The hair on the nape of her neck raised. Maybe that wasn't her dad's white Camry on the street.

37

He jogged to his car, his heart pounding in his chest. That had been close. He'd checked the GPS reading on the tracker on Ryker's SUV, and from what he'd seen, the ranger's vehicle had still been at Mount Locust. That would have given him plenty of time to plant the listening devices, but he'd barely hidden the first one in her bookcase, when a key turned in the front door. He'd fled out the back and down the stairs, surprised he hadn't gotten caught.

His heart had almost returned to normal by the time he reached his car on the next street over. Once safely in the driver's seat, he opened his glove compartment and stashed the lock picks he'd used to gain entry to her apartment.

It couldn't have been Emma who unlocked the door. There was no way they could've made it home that fast. So who was it? Who had a key to her house? Using his phone, he dialed the number for the SIM card, activating the listening device. Soon he heard someone whistling and dishes rattling.

"Now where would Emma put her seasonings?" It was an older male voice. Jack Winters, maybe? "Ah, here they are . . ." More sounds, this time paper rustling, then the sound of a door opening and closing.

He disconnected from the call. No need to run the battery down on the bug, not when he wanted the battery to last until he took Emma to the cabin. He glanced in his rearview mirror. Emma and Ryker shouldn't pass by where he was parked, but there was no need to take a chance of being seen. He started his truck and pulled away from the curb.

While he'd wanted two listening devices in her apartment, he'd have to be satisfied with one. It would be too much to hope that the stars would line up again like they had this evening with all her apartment neighbors away.

He hated that he had to resort to planting the bug, but he'd had no choice. She should have told Ryker to leave her alone, but that wasn't her way. Emma was like him, too kind for her own good. That's what made their relationship so perfect. He'd even decided it was wrong to kill Ryker unless he did something horrible. Emma loved *him*, not the ranger. Unless the listening device confirmed that the ranger was a threat to Emma or that he was pushing her into a relationship, he would let him live.

Ryker would never have her. Emma Winters was destined to be his. And soon.

And that meant he had to stock the cabin. His heart raced at the thought of showing her what he'd created for her. A quick glance at the back seat confirmed the framed photograph was still there. It was his favorite of all he'd taken of Emma, and she would be so surprised. And pleased. He had the perfect place for it in their love nest. He would take it to the cabin tomorrow.

38

She called again, and her dad didn't answer. Maybe Sam should have checked her apartment this time. Movement on her balcony caught Emma's eye just as she spied the white butcher paper on the counter, and she released the breath she'd been holding. The tension in her shoulders eased as well. Her dad always bought his steaks at a little shop in town where the butcher wrapped them in white paper. Then she saw him bent over the grill.

Emma hated how all this stalking made her paranoid. Suzy rubbed against her leg, and she knelt beside the kitten. "It's okay. This is your new home," she said, smoothing her left hand down the cat's bony back. "We need to get you fattened up." She filled a bowl with water and set it on the floor.

"You stay here," Emma said to the cat as she crossed to the back door and stepped out on her balcony, flipping on the outside light. The balcony was one perk she really enjoyed about the apartment. She could relax out here and come and go on the stairs leading down to the back parking lot—if she ever parked back there. Her dad looked up from the grill.

"Hey, honey. Didn't know you were home yet," he said, closing the lid.

Even in his midfifties, Jack Winters had very little gray in his hair, just a little around his temples. Wearing jeans that covered his rich brown cowboy boots and a pullover under his denim jacket, he looked nothing like the hospital executive he was, or even the nurse he used to be. Put a cowboy hat on him, and he looked ready to round up a few head of cattle.

"And you really shouldn't leave that back door unlocked."

Emma's gaze shot to the door. She couldn't have left it unlocked. She always double-checked to make sure everything was secured before she left. But had she this morning? It'd been hectic with Sam and Nate both here, and then the DNA test . . .

"I'll make sure it doesn't happen again," she said.

"How's your hand?"

She glanced at her bandaged right hand. "It doesn't hurt as much . . . I wonder if I can take this bulky wrap off?"

"We'll see. I'll check it in a bit."

"Thanks," she said. "Sam will be here soon, so I'm going in to take a shower and change."

Her dad eyed the dirt on her knees and scuffed toes of her boots. "What have you been doing?"

"Nothing major. Just excavating a bit at Mount Locust," she said, keeping her tone casual.

"The slave cemetery?"

"No. Corey Chandler has a client who doesn't want us to bother the cemetery. I'm trying to work something out there." Then before he could ask more about the dig, she added, "His client doesn't seem to mind if I explore where the cabins were located, so I'll start there next."

"That should be interesting, but aren't you off tomorrow?"

"I'm volunteering a few hours," she said.

"This project must be important to you."

If he only knew. "It is, and I only have the GPR machine a week."

"I'm off Thursday. I might drop by."

"Good. Be back in a bit." She stopped at the door. "Oh, I brought home a gray tabby that's been hanging around the visitor center—don't let her out."

"I'll try not to," he said. "Are you keeping her?"

"Until I can find her a good home," Emma said.

Her dad opened his mouth, then shut it and shook his head. Just like he used to do when she was a kid and found a stray kitten. When Emma stepped back inside the kitchen, Suzy sat at the door with a look that was plainly unhappy. Emma laughed. She'd forgotten how much cats disliked being on the other side of a closed door. "Sorry." She grabbed a bread wrapper to keep her hand dry and hurried to the bedroom with Suzy close behind.

After she showered, Emma chose a burgundy sweater and a pair of jeans to slip into. She loved to wear red, and burgundy was the best shade for her copper-colored hair. Suzy hopped up on her dressing table, another gift from her mother, along with the makeup and bottles of lotions and nail polish. Sitting in front of her mirror, she loosened her hair and brushed it out, letting it fall softly around her face. Maybe she'd wear it this way tonight instead of pulling it up in a ponytail again.

She wasn't wearing it down because she'd seen the admiration in Sam's eyes last night when she'd stepped out of the maintenance building. It was easier to manage. Yeah, right. Who was she kidding? After a quick brush of powder to her face, Emma dabbed on lipstick, something she could easily do with her left hand. The doorbell rang and she hurried to the living room with the cat trailing behind her just as her dad let Brooke into the apartment.

"Long time, no see," her dad said.

"I know. You're looking good, Mr. Winters," Brooke said, slipping her backpack off her shoulders and setting it on the floor.

"How many times have I told you to call me Jack? You make me feel old."

"Sorry. I'll try to do better." She turned to Emma and fanned herself with her left hand. "Don't you think it's a little warm in here?" she asked and wiggled her fingers.

Emma gasped when she saw the ring. "Shut the front door! Luke proposed! And you're just now telling me!"

"Yep." Brooke's grin spread across her face. "I had to see your face when I told you."

Emma grabbed Brooke's hand and inspected the ring. The diamond was an emerald cut surrounded by smaller diamonds. "It's beautiful. But why were you working today? You should have been out celebrating!"

"Luke was just in for yesterday, but he'll be back next weekend and we'll celebrate then."

"Have you set a date?"

"Not yet. I know five months isn't much time to plan a wedding, but I want to be a June bride," she said and shook her head. "It hasn't sunk in yet that I will soon be Mrs. Luke Fereday. You'll be my maid of honor, won't you?"

"You know I will." She couldn't believe her best friend was getting married.

The kitten meowed loudly as she rubbed against Brooke's leg. "Were we not paying enough attention to you?" she asked and picked her up. "Where did she come from?"

"She just showed up at the visitor center," Emma said. "She sure likes you. I think you need to take her home with you."

Brooke set the tabby on the floor. "I can't have pets at my apartment. Will they allow that here?" she asked.

"I don't know yet." Emma didn't think she remembered a clause against pets in her lease. She would have to find out.

"Good luck." Brooke took a folder from her backpack and handed it to Emma. "This is the report Sam wanted."

"I'll give it to him." Emma laid it on the bookcase.

"Why don't you stay for dinner?" her dad asked. "There's plenty. It's steak . . ."

"Sounds good," Brooke said. "But I promised Mom I'd meet her at King's Tavern for one of their flatbreads to celebrate. Maybe a rain check?"

"Next time I grill steaks, I'll make sure Emma calls you," he replied.

Brooke turned to Emma. "See you tomorrow?"

She walked with her to the door. "I probably won't get to Mount Locust until afternoon. I need to take Suzy to the vet, and then I have a few other errands to run."

"I'll check after lunch and see where you are." Brooke's cell phone rang, and her face lit up. "It's Luke. See you later."

"Tell him I said congratulations!" Emma called after her.

She hummed as she took out her not-every-day china. It wasn't anything fancy, just plain stoneware, but at least it wasn't chipped. Then she made a quick salad.

"Putting out your good stuff, huh?" her dad said.

"It's not every day you grill steaks for me," she said, slipping her arm around him and squeezing his waist.

"Or that Sam Ryker comes to dinner . . ."

"Don't go there."

"He's one of the good guys, Em," he said, using his pet name for her. When she didn't comment, he nodded toward her bookcase. "Is that the private investigator report you were talking about last night?"

Instead of answering, she pulled out her better silverware. Why couldn't he be like some of the people she knew who didn't remember anything that happened yesterday? Not only did he never forget anything, he was very good at putting two and two together. "It is," she said reluctantly.

"I would like to read it after dinner," he said. Her face must have shown alarm, because he added, "Your mom called this morning and told me she was going to hire another private investigator, but I'd like to see what Bell said first."

"Why did you hire the PI in the first place? And why did you wait six months?"

"Sheriff Carter asked us to wait until he finished his investigation. He said he was actively searching for Ryan, but we finally decided he wasn't doing anything. She and I discussed it, and since she was with the district attorney's office in Jackson, I told her to take the initiative and use their resources."

Carter. Just thinking about the man clenched her stomach. *Relax*. Every time she thought she'd put aside her anger at the former sheriff, it reared its ugly head again. The man had Alzheimer's. *Let it go. Focus on the fact that my parents didn't ignore Ryan after all.*

"Mom didn't say anything about hiring another investigator last night," Emma said as she set water glasses around the table.

"I think your visit triggered the decision," he said. "Which is fortunate."

"What do you mean?"

"Em, years ago I reconciled myself to the probability that Ryan isn't with us any longer, but your mom refused to consider it until now."

Maybe Sam was right that her dad needed to know what they'd discovered. But not before Sam arrived. "Sam thinks you should read the report, and he wants to ask you what you remember from that time, but I discouraged it. Guess he was right, but could we not talk about it before dinner?"

"Do you think Sam will be here soon?" he asked just as the doorbell rang.

"That should be him now."

39

He sat up as something caught his ear. What was this report they were talking about? Hopefully not something else to worry about. He hadn't planned on coming back to Emma's tonight, until he'd heard that Ryker was returning. After that, he'd wanted to be where he could watch what went on.

He'd parked a block away on the street that ended in front of Emma's apartment, far enough away that Ryker wouldn't notice him. Using binoculars, he trained them on the apartment front door as Emma's friend came out on the porch with a phone glued to her ear. She glanced down the street. His stomach dipped when Ryker pulled in front of the apartment.

His grasp tightened on the binoculars as the two talked, then Ryker embraced Emma's friend, taking her in his arms as she wrapped her arms around his neck. He clenched his jaw so hard it sent pain through his head. Suddenly he was spiraling back to the day he and his mother interrupted his father's little tryst with *her* best friend. His mother's face as she realized what they'd stumbled on was imprinted on his brain. If only he hadn't gotten sick that day at school and his mother hadn't had to bring him home early . . .

The memories tumbled through his mind one after another. How he'd frozen every time his parents fought. How his father's ridicule and caustic words belittled his mother and pierced her to the core. Words that sent her straight to the happy pills she'd tried again and again to wean herself from. But that wasn't what killed her. His father had. And then he'd had the nerve to cry at her funeral. He'd wanted to kill him. Still did.

Pressure built in his chest until he thought it would explode. He narrowed his eyes. Sam Ryker was just like his dad, handsome and smooth-talking. Neither of them seemed to be able to keep their hands away from women.

It was obvious Ryker wanted Emma for himself. But she wouldn't fall for his looks and charm. She was his, not Ryker's, and he'd do whatever it took to keep her.

He would not let Emma be hurt like his mother.

40

Sam set the box of litter and cat pan on the floor. It'd been a struggle to get the cat items and a white bakery box filled with brownies up the stairs without dropping anything. He raised his hand to ring the bell again when Emma opened the door.

"Thank you," she said and took the bakery box he handed her.

"You sound surprised. I told you I would bring dessert." He responded to Jack Winters's greeting by waving. "I borrowed a carrier from Jenny to make it easier to take your cat to the vet tomorrow. I'll get it later."

"Tell me how much all of this is, and I'll get your money," she said as Sam set the box of litter inside the door.

"Consider this my gift to your new pet," he said. "I didn't know how much cat food you had at your apartment, so I picked up a few cans—it's in the white bag. And a couple of bowls for food and water." He looked around. "Where do you want the litter pan?"

"The laundry room," she said and put the brownies on the island. "But I'll take care of it."

"I don't think so." She was so independent, he ought to let her, except he was afraid she might hurt her hand when she tried to fill the litter box. "You'll need help, so why not let me do it in the first place?"

"While you two argue," her dad said, "I'll put on the steaks. I know how Emma likes hers, how about you, Sam?"

"Medium, a little pink showing."

While Jack stepped outside, Sam followed her to the laundry room and set up the cat's litter station.

Emma sighed. "I keep forgetting what I can't do—that would have taken both hands," she said. "I was wrong and you were right."

"That wasn't too hard to admit, was it?" he teased.

"What do you think?"

They both laughed, and once they'd introduced the cat to her bathroom, they returned to the living room. "By the way, you just missed Brooke," she said.

"I caught her before she drove off," he said.

"It's so exciting," Emma said with a sigh.

He grinned. "When she came out of the house, she was on the phone with Luke, and he'd just told her he's being assigned to the Jackson area for the next year. She was pretty ecstatic," he said, remembering how his field ranger had thrown her arms around him.

"And you're just now telling me?"

"Sorry, but I think we've been busy with your cat," he said, but she wasn't listening to him and instead had a faraway look in her eyes.

"Brooke's planning a June wedding, you know," she said softly.

"That would be great, as long as she doesn't quit on me." While Brooke was still finding her way as a law enforcement ranger, she gave 110 percent to her job. "And now that her court case is over, I'm counting on her to help with the investigation at Mount Locust."

Emma's smile faded, and she walked to her bookcase, where she picked up a large tan envelope and handed it to him. "Bell's report, and Dad wants to read it too."

"Have you told him . . . ?"

"No. Maybe after we eat. He's gone to too much trouble with

the steaks to ruin his appetite," she said and added, "How about we don't even discuss the report until later?"

Sam agreed, although he'd like to get a look at it now. "Why don't you check on your dad?"

"You mean keep him occupied while you read it?"

"Do you mind?"

"No."

After Emma closed the back door behind her, Sam opened the envelope. There were newspaper clippings and two files. He removed the clip from Bell's file and held his breath as he scanned it and then scanned Sheriff Carter's report, seeing a brief paragraph detailing Carter's interview with Sam. Tension eased from his body. There was nothing in the files about Sam and Ryan's fight. He hadn't really thought there would be since no one had seen it.

There was no mention of a date being with Mary Jo at the Hideaway, but Sam had a hazy memory of a man hovering in the background with her. If only he would emerge from the shadows. Why hadn't he come forward when Mary Jo's death hit the newspapers? Had he killed Mary Jo and then Ryan and let Ryan take the rap for it?

Sam switched back to the private investigator's file, which was basically a rehash of Sheriff Carter's report except for a copy of the report the Memphis Police Department had filed on Ryan's abandoned car. He tapped the papers. The former sheriff made no mention of his son or Gordon Cole being at the tavern that night. While only a scant two pages, his summary on the second page left little doubt that he believed Ryan killed the girl.

Questions dogged Sam. It puzzled him that Sheriff Carter had spent so little time and effort looking for Ryan. And why hadn't he mentioned Trey and Gordon? They had come home for the weekend from Ole Miss and were some of the last people to see Mary Jo and Ryan. The back door opened, and he shoved the papers back into the envelope as Emma and Jack came into the kitchen.

"Wash up," Emma said. "We'll be ready to eat in five minutes."

Forty-five minutes later, Sam pushed back from the table. "That was the best steak I've had in a long time," he said. He didn't know when he'd enjoyed a meal more, and it wasn't just the food. Conversation had flowed freely, with Jack Winters cracking jokes, keeping them laughing. Even Emma had loosened up.

"It was good," she chimed in. "And thank you both for cutting my meat."

"Glad you enjoyed them." Jack made a bowing motion. "I rarely grill just for myself, and worried that I might have lost my touch."

While Emma was making coffee to go with Sam's brownies, Jack asked what brought him back to Natchez.

"My family. Mostly my ten-year-old nephew. His father checked out and—"

"You're stepping up to the plate," Jack said. "That's what I remember most about you. Always taking on other people's responsibilities. I never understood why you didn't come back after college."

Sam shifted in his chair.

"I'm sorry, I didn't mean to be nosy," Jack said.

"It's okay. It's just that Natchez holds no fond memories for me. Mostly it reminds me of my failures," he said, giving Jack a wry smile. "Once I left for Northern Arizona University, it was easier to keep going in a different direction. Making the decision to come back, even to help my nephew, was hard. Getting the promotion to district ranger helped, though."

"I'm glad you're back," Jack said. "Did you play football in college?"

"I didn't have time."

"That's a shame. I still remember the state playoffs and that pass you threw in the last seconds of Game 4."

"Game 4 isn't the one most people remember," Sam said. No.

Most people remembered the last game and the fumble he made when he got sacked that lost the championship. His dad had made it a point to let him know what a loser he was. Not that his dad ever needed an excuse to criticize him or remind him of his failures. Like being responsible for his sister almost losing her life and ending up with a limp.

"Well, it's the one I remember. Thank you, honey," Jack said, accepting the cup Emma handed him.

"Sam brought the brownies." She turned to him. "Coffee?"

"I'll get it."

As they enjoyed dessert, the conversation veered to Jack's job as chief nursing officer at Merit Hospital. Once the coffee was gone and talk had dwindled, Emma picked up Sam's plate.

"I'll do this," he said. "And you can let your dad look at your hand."

He cleared the table and stacked the dishes beside the dishwasher while Jack and Emma moved to the sofa, where Jack unwrapped the bandage around her hand.

"Is there anything I can wear besides this clunky wrap?" she asked, flexing her fingers.

"Maybe. I talked to Gordon, and he approved this," Jack said, taking a box from the supplies he'd brought in. "But only if you promise not to pick up anything. Or drive."

She narrowed her eyes. "When can I drive?"

"Didn't Gordon tell you ten days?" Sam said from the kitchen.

"Don't pay any attention to him," Emma said.

"It depends on what the X-rays show when you go back to see Gordon," her dad said. He removed a brace from the box and put it on her hand.

"That's much better," Emma said. "At least I can wiggle my fingers."

"Just remember what I said about lifting," her dad said, then he turned to Sam. "Emma said you received the private investigator's report. Mind if I look at it?"

Sam handed him the envelope. "Let's move to the table where we can spread out."

Once they were seated around the table again, Sam removed the two reports. For the next few minutes, the only sound in the room was that of pages turning. While they read the reports, he scanned the newspaper clippings. Mary Jo's body had been found at the bottom of a cliff at Loess Bluff by coon hunters, and the articles left no question that everyone suspected Ryan of the murder. Sam took out his phone and googled the distance from Loess Bluff to Mount Locust. Three miles. Interesting.

The next article was an interview with Sheriff Carter where he was quoted saying that it appeared the Selby girl was running from someone and they struggled and she fell, hitting her head. Then he went on to point out that Ryan Winters, a person of interest, had gone missing. Carter might as well have put out a Be On the Look Out alert. Sam looked up as Jack laid the report on the table.

"I didn't remember Bell's report being this thorough," Jack said. "Do you have Sheriff Carter's file on Ryan's disappearance?"

Sam handed him the sheriff's report. Jack grew very quiet as he read the report and then handed it to Emma. "Looks like he didn't go to much trouble looking for Ryan," he said. "There's no mention that he even put his information into NamUS."

Emma's dad must have been conducting his own research to know about the National Missing and Unidentified Persons System. "I'm not certain NamUS was that well known when Ryan went missing," Sam said. "And from what I've learned since I've returned to Natchez, Carter was lazy."

"It always looked to me like he *wanted* to pin Mary Jo Selby's murder on Ryan. My question is why?" The older man stared at the reports spread out on the table. Sam could almost see his thoughts churning, then Jack raised his head. "But before we get into that, I'm getting the feeling you're not telling me something. So, let's hear it."

This was the very thing Emma had feared. She glanced at Sam. He looked as though he wanted to be anywhere other than her living room.

"We all knew Ryan," Sam said. "He wasn't capable of killing anyone, and especially not Mary Jo."

"You're not answering my question." Her dad tilted his head. "But maybe you did. You said 'knew' Ryan, as in past tense." He looked from Sam to his daughter. "He's dead, isn't he?"

She should have known her dad would figure it out. "We don't know for sure," Emma said. "The dig at Mount Locust. We believe a body was buried there."

Her dad crossed his arms over his chest. "You've been digging there for three days. Either a body was there or it wasn't."

"Originally we weren't sure," Sam said, "and then someone stole whatever had been in the ground."

"You're kidding."

"I wish," Emma said. "We continued the excavation and found one bone. The thief must have dropped it when he carted off the rest of the body."

"Was that all you found?"

"We uncovered a . . ." She swallowed. "A ring . . ."

Sam finished the sentence for her. "A man's 2012 Mississippi State class ring."

Color drained from her dad's face. "You think it was Ryan's."

"It looks like it, but it hasn't been confirmed officially yet," Emma said, her voice breaking. "RTW was engraved on the inside. And I gave Sheriff Rawlings a DNA sample today to compare to the DNA in the bone we found."

"I plan to check with the university and the ring company tomorrow," Sam added.

"There won't be two people with those initials graduating from State in 2012." Her dad leaned back, his body sagging in the chair. "I've known all along this day would come."

Emma rubbed her forehead. What if it wasn't Ryan? Was it wrong to destroy her dad's hope that his son was still alive? Would this be yet another regret she'd have to live with? "Maybe we shouldn't have told you."

"No. You did right," he said.

"I feel so responsible," Emma said.

"Why? Your brother made his own choices." A frown creased his brow. "You haven't been blaming yourself, have you?"

"No. Yes . . ." She slumped in the chair. If only she hadn't told him . . . "I don't know. If I'd just stayed with him that night . . ."

"You did nothing wrong. You had a migraine and had no way of knowing what was going to happen after you left."

She couldn't bring herself to look at him.

"Emma, honey, don't tell me you've lived with guilt all these years."

She looked up at him, and something must have shown in her face.

He groaned. "I should have realized you felt that way. Honey, you have to put this behind you and move forward."

"How?"

Her dad was quiet a minute. "The way I did."

"You felt guilty?" she asked. "Why?"

"For the same reason—I kept thinking if I'd gone with you after we left the restaurant, he'd still be here."

Ryan's disappearance had affected each one of them. "How do you deal with it?"

"I've accepted that I can't change history—just like you can't unscramble eggs. And I've come to understand that the choice to not go with you two that night wasn't the wrong choice. I had to work the next day. You and Ryan were twenty-one, old enough to fly on your own." He stood and took his cup to the coffeepot. Once he filled his cup, he turned back to them. "And lastly, I took it to God and came to realize that he was big enough to carry it. But it didn't happen overnight."

How she envied the peace in her dad's face and in his voice.

"I've tried to tell Emma that," Sam said. He'd been quiet until now.

She turned to him. "How about you? You said you were still struggling with your decision to leave the Hideaway."

"You felt responsible for my son?" her dad asked. "Why?"

"I'm afraid that's my fault." Heat flushed Emma's face. Sam might not have felt that responsibility if she hadn't pushed it on him. "I should never have asked you to stay with Ryan. And I shouldn't have gotten angry when you made the choice to help your sister."

Sam pinched the bridge of his nose. Then he took a deep breath. "As long as we're confessing—"

"Look, I think we've beaten this rug long enough," her dad said. "We need to switch gears and start looking for whoever killed Ryan, if that was his body buried at Mount Locust. And if it's not, then we need to track him down wherever he is, once and for all."

Her dad was right, but first she wanted to make sure Sam understood none of this was his fault. She turned to face him, her heart hurting at the sadness his eyes bore. "You did nothing wrong that night. I was wrong to make you think you did."

A look crossed his face she couldn't read.

"I wouldn't say that," he said softly and squeezed her hand.

"Are we good now?"

"I hope so."

His touch was like an electric current racing up her arm. Would it be too much to hope they might have a future? She marshaled her thoughts back to the reports and found Sheriff Carter's thin file. "It says here that witnesses saw Mary Jo and Ryan together at the tavern and that they left together. But the only witness Carter names is the owner of the Hideaway." She looked up. "Who are the others?"

"I don't know," Sam said. "I've never seen such a sloppy job in an investigation and don't know how he got away with it."

"He made Ryan the handy scapegoat." Her dad picked up the sheriff's report. "Do you think Carter could have killed Ryan?"

"If he did, we'll never find out now. I've heard he can't even remember who his son is half the time," Emma said.

"Since Trey was one of the last people to see Mary Jo alive, maybe that's why the sheriff accused Ryan of killing her," her dad said. "He was protecting his son."

"Why were Trey and Gordon even in Natchez that weekend?" Sam asked. "It wasn't spring break or anything."

"That was Ryan's doing," Emma said. "He got them to skip class on Friday and drive down for our twenty-first birthday celebration—those two were always looking for a reason to party, Gordon especially."

Sam nodded thoughtfully. "Wasn't Carter running for re-election that year?"

"Yes, and it was a hotly contested race," her dad said. "I think he won by a narrow victory. If his son had been accused of murder, he probably would have lost the election."

"And by pointing the finger at Ryan, it looked like Carter had solved the crime," Sam said. "It wasn't his fault Ryan had disappeared—although we know why now. I wonder if the FBI investigated the crime since it happened on park service land?"

"I don't remember hearing anything about the FBI." Her dad

rubbed the back of his neck. "Didn't the Selbys have two daughters?"

She searched through her hazy memories of Mary Jo. They'd gone to school together since junior high when the family moved to Natchez, and while she and Mary Jo hadn't been close friends, they'd known each other and were in the same church youth group. "I have my school yearbooks . . . if she has a sister, maybe she's in one of them."

Emma hurried to her bedroom and dug into her cedar chest for her yearbooks, quickly realizing she'd have to have help. Just as she opened her mouth to call for her dad, Sam appeared at the door.

"Need help?"

"You know I do," she muttered and stepped aside so he could get the annuals.

She followed him back to the living room, and each of them took a yearbook. Emma started with her tenth-grade one while her dad and Sam took other years. Right away she found Mary Jo's photo not too far from hers. The girl had had the *it* factor. Cheerleader, class president, voted most beautiful in their sophomore class.

"There are no Selbys here other than Mary Jo," Sam said and put his annual aside. He took out the newspaper clippings while Emma picked up another annual. After a few minutes, he said, "Mary Jo's obituary lists the sister as Sandra Wyatt. It doesn't give her age, but she was already married by the time Mary Jo died."

Emma set her annual aside and peered over his shoulder at the obituary. "I wonder if she has a Facebook page?"

Sam quickly connected to the social media site. "I don't find anything."

"I wonder if she or her parents still live in Natchez? I'd like to talk to them," Emma said.

"Good idea." Her dad stood. "But we can't tonight, and I have an early morning meeting."

Weariness radiated off him like heat. She'd not seen her dad so tired in a long time. "I wish we didn't have to deal with this again."

"I know, sweetheart. And since we don't know anything for sure yet, we don't want to tell your mom."

"My thoughts too." She stood and hugged him. "Thanks for dinner."

"Anytime." He turned and shook hands with Sam. "Can I count on you to watch out for my girl here?"

"Yes, sir," Sam replied, his face somber.

She hated that her dad was worried about her. Thank goodness he didn't know about someone shooting at her. A chill raced down her spine. Was someone shooting at her because she was getting too close to discovering what had happened to Mary Jo?

42

He pressed his phone close to his ear. Jack Winters had left, and Ryker and Emma had moved away from the living room, making it difficult to hear them. If only he'd had time to place the other bug in her kitchen. Twice he'd about had a heart attack when someone fumbled around the bookcase.

One thing for sure, Ryker hadn't told Emma how he'd hugged her friend. Confirmed Ryker was trying to hide it from her. And he didn't tell her that he'd had a fight with her brother at the tavern. That was something he could put in his arsenal and use against Ryker.

They had discussed Mary Jo's sister, Sandra. That was a problem he hadn't anticipated. Did she remember him? They'd met only that once and briefly at that, but had Mary Jo talked about him? He didn't want to kill Sandra—he wasn't a monster. He hadn't meant to kill Mary Jo. Ryan, yes, but not that sweet girl.

But in the end, she hadn't been so sweet. Screaming those horrible names at him because he'd shot Ryan. He hadn't meant to kill her, but she shouldn't have run from him.

He stiffened. Emma was crying. What had Ryker done to her? He pressed his lips tight. This could not go on. This week, maybe tomorrow, he would do *something* to make sure Sam Ryker would never hurt Emma again.

43

After Jack left, Sam's thoughts whirled as he helped Emma put the dishes into the dishwasher. Mentally he made a list in order of priority, starting with talking to the owner of the Hideaway, but first he had to get his name.

"I saw your dad the other day," Emma said.

Sam stopped with a plate halfway to the bottom rack. He hadn't seen that coming. "So?"

She ducked her head. "Nothing. Forget I said anything."

He heard the tears in her voice and quickly set the plate down. "What's going on?"

"Really, I shouldn't have mentioned him."

"I'll agree with that." He used his knuckle to raise her head. Tears glistened in her eyes. "But something else is going on. What is it?" Tears leaked onto her cheek, and he brushed them away. "Is it Ryan?"

"No. Maybe."

He pulled her to his chest. "I'm sorry this is happening. You deserve better than this. Ryan deserved better. We're going to get his killer."

"I keep thinking if I could just talk to my brother again, there is so much I would tell him, but most of all that I loved him. I'll never be able to do that." She pulled away from him, and for a few minutes they were silent as she washed and he dried. "I've heard your dad has become a Christian."

Sure, he has. To be a believer one had to admit they were wrong and ask God for forgiveness. People like his dad never admitted they'd committed any wrong. "I don't want to talk about him," he said.

With a sigh, she nodded and finished loading the dishwasher in silence. "There's something I should have already told you."

"If it's about him, I don't want to hear it."

"He has cancer," she said.

Sam absorbed the information. "I hate to hear anyone has cancer, but it doesn't change the way I feel or what he did."

"I get that, but there's something else you need to know before it happens." She took a breath. "I've heard your mom is going to let him come home so she can take care of him."

"Mom would never do that."

"She told her Sunday school class that's what she planned to do. Her class is going to help with meals."

The betrayal almost knocked his legs out from under him. He clenched his jaw so tight pain radiated down his neck. Sam made a point of checking his watch. "It's getting late, and I better go home."

"Don't hold on to your anger, Sam. It'll only hurt you."

She hadn't lived with his father. She hadn't been called stupid and irresponsible. She hadn't borne the welts on her back from his father's leather belt. "I have a few things I need to do tonight. Do you know what time you want to take the cat to the vet tomorrow?"

His face burned under her scrutiny. "Whenever I can get an appointment."

"I'll call you in the morning," he said.

"Don't you have to work?"

"I'm taking the morning off. Brooke can handle the day shift by herself."

A few minutes later, Sam sat in his SUV staring up at her windows. Emma meant well, but she didn't understand. He took out his phone and sent her a text.

Sorry for the way I acted. Make it up to you tomorrow.

He held his breath, waiting for her reply.

That's okay. I shouldn't have tried to push you into something you didn't want to do. See you tomorrow. xoxo

Feeling better, he started his SUV. It wasn't that late, and he had time enough to check out the Hideaway. Once he checked Google for the name of the owner, he drove to the sports bar out on Highway 61 that featured wide-screen TVs and dancing. Judging by the packed parking lot, business was good. Once Sam was inside the building, he paused to let his eyes adjust to the dim light. He doubted his lungs would adjust to the cigarette smoke. Sam ambled to the bar and nodded to the bartender wiping the counter.

"What'll it be?" he asked, tossing the cloth on a counter behind him.

"Is Charlie Shaw in?" Sam asked.

The bartender looked him up and down. "You a cop? 'Cause we don't serve minors in here."

"Nope." Sam was glad he wasn't wearing his uniform and gun.

"What do you want with Mr. Shaw?"

"I knew him when I lived here a few years back, and now that I'm home again, thought I'd touch base."

"Then you should have recognized him when you came in."

Sam shot the bartender a puzzled look, and the man nodded toward the door. Sam turned. A couple danced to slow music on the floor, but beyond them a short, squat man with an almost nonexistent neck sat at the first table inside the building. Sam didn't remember the owner resembling a bullfrog. "Didn't say I knew him well," he said. "And he's put on a little weight since I last saw him."

"You could say that."

"Thanks." Sam made his way through the crowd to Charlie Shaw's table. "Mr. Shaw?" he said.

The man removed an unlit stogie from his mouth. "Depends on who's asking."

"Sam Ryker." He held his hand out, and the bar owner ignored him. "Mind if I sit down a minute?"

"It's a free country, but unless you're buying something, I don't have time to chew the fat," he said as a petite waitress appeared.

"You have fountain drinks?"

"Yes, sir," she said.

"A Coke, then."

"That all?"

"Yep."

Shaw eyed him suspiciously as Sam took the chair opposite him. "You a cop?"

"Not exactly."

"Now, either you are or you ain't. Which is it?" Shaw asked and stuck the cigar back in his mouth.

"I'm a ranger for the Natchez Trace Park Service."

"Same thing. What do you want?"

"I'd like to ask you a few questions about something that happened ten years ago."

Shaw appeared to work that over in his mind. "Go on."

"Mary Jo Selby and Ryan Winters. Those names ring a bell?"

He chewed on the cigar. "The Winters guy was accused of killing the Selby girl."

Sam nodded. "And they were here at your establishment the night she died. Do you remember that?"

"Yep."

"Why is that?"

"Carter almost shut me down over that."

"Care to talk about it?"

"Not much to talk about."

"Could you tell me what you remember?"

"My memory is kind of fuzzy. You know how it is with old folks. Of course, I've heard green stuff helps memory."

Sam had maybe a hundred dollars on him. A hundred dollars he wouldn't be reimbursed for if he gave it to the bar owner, but if it got him answers, it would be worth it. "Do you suppose a hundred greenbacks would help your memory?"

Shaw leaned forward. "I think it might indeed."

Sam took five twenties from his billfold and laid them on the table. Shaw reached for the bills. "Not yet," Sam said, pulling the money closer to him. "Let's hear what you remember first, and I'll decide if it's worth the money."

Shaw sat back against his chair. "Mary Jo came here often, sometimes with somebody, sometimes by herself, but she always left with a man. That night was no exception, except she left with three men that night."

"Three?" Carter's report only mentioned one—Ryan.

The older man nodded. "I'll tell you the same thing I told Sheriff Carter. She left with that Winters guy and Doc Cole's boy . . . and the sheriff's son. Funny thing is, I never heard anything about her leaving with anyone but the Winters kid."

And that was the only person mentioned in Carter's report. "Do you know if there was an FBI investigation?"

"If there was, nobody from the FBI came around here."

First thing in the morning, Sam would check with the FBI office in Jackson and see if an agent had investigated Mary Jo's death. "Carter's report mentioned a witness who saw Mary Jo leave with Ryan Winters. Do you know who that witness might be?"

"Carter fabricated the story he wanted told, and I always figured the sheriff made the witness up."

"Why didn't you tell someone that Carter wasn't telling the whole truth?"

"Didn't want no deputy sitting a quarter of a mile from my establishment pulling my customers over and giving them a hard time." Shaw leaned back in his chair, his arms barely reaching across his belly. "One week of that and my business would have tanked."

"Is that what he threatened you with?"

The cigar bobbed up and down as Shaw chewed on it. "Let's just say he laid the scenario out for me. Besides, he'd already tried and convicted that Winters kid of the crime. Sure was handy that the kid never was heard from again."

"You think the sheriff could have killed him? Or covered up for the murderer?"

The music slid into another slow dance song. "I never said that, but I'm sure the sheriff and his son were real happy Winters never showed his face around here again."

It didn't take a genius to know the sheriff hadn't wanted Trey involved in the investigation. "Did Mary Jo come with anyone that night?"

A look that could have passed for sadness on anyone else crossed Shaw's face. "That gal was a pretty little thing," he said. "Shame that she died like that." Then he seemed to remember Sam's question. "You were asking if she came with anybody?"

"Yes."

"I've given this a lot of thought. She did come with someone, but don't ask me who 'cause I couldn't tell you if my life depended on it. Never saw him before or after, but she was right friendly with him when they first came in. Then those four college boys came in, and Mary Jo and her date had a spat, and she left him high and dry, started flirting with the Winters kid. The guy she came with just disappeared. Figured he must've left right after their little fight."

Sam had been one of the four. "Could you describe the boyfriend?"

"Are you kidding? Like you said, it's been ten years. I can't remember what my sainted sister looks like, and she's just been gone five."

The music slid into a loud, fast dance song that made his head hurt. Sam took out a business card and wrote his cell number on the back. "If you remember anything else, doesn't matter how insignificant, give me a call."

He stood and held out the hundred dollars. Shaw looked at it, then shook his head. "Keep your money, son. Just find out who killed that girl."

Sam hadn't even attempted to kiss her goodbye last night. Relationships were hard. Maybe too hard. Even so, Emma's heart kicked up a notch at the thought of seeing him later today.

Emma slipped a sweater over her head, glad she didn't have to button a shirt today. Until the accident, she'd had no idea how difficult it was to use only her nondominant hand to complete the simplest tasks.

A quick glance at the floor-length mirror assured her the sweater was long enough to come to a respectable length over her leggings. With her left hand, she pulled her curls away from her face and snapped them in a barrette. At least she was getting better at that. The gray tabby wound around her legs, and she scooped the wiggly kitty up.

"I look like an elf, Suzy," she said as the cat jumped back to the floor. Or a kid. Her mother would be aghast if she saw her. Too bad Emma hadn't considered the effect before she went to the trouble of pulling the leggings on.

The clothes would do for a visit to the vet. In the living room, she opened the door to the small carrier Sam had brought up before he left last night, and Suzy circled it, then investigated inside. Good, it shouldn't be a problem getting her in it.

Emma googled the closest veterinarian office and dialed the number shown. When the receptionist answered, she gave Emma an appointment for nine forty-five. The phone rang just as she ended the call, and she almost dropped the phone. *Corey?* "Hello?"

"Just in case your caller ID didn't work, this is Corey Chandler," he said. "I trust that you're well."

The warmth in his voice was like a hug. "I'm fine."

"I'm calling to see if we can get together and discuss the project at Mount Locust."

Emma winced. She'd totally forgotten he'd said they needed to get together. "I'm pretty busy all day . . ."

"I was thinking more along the lines of dinner at the Guest House this evening, say sixish? And if not tonight, maybe tomorrow night?"

While she didn't have anything planned for tonight, Sam's comment about Corey's interest in her popped into her mind, making her hesitate. She liked him fine—for a friend—and didn't want to lead him on. But then again, Sam could be completely wrong. Emma had certainly never noticed any interest. At least she hadn't until he brought it up.

"Tonight will be fine," she said, deciding she might as well get it over with. Maybe while they ate dinner, she could get him to reveal the person who was trying to stop the project. At the very least, she could plead her case and show him her passion for the work.

"Great. I'll pick you up at five forty-five?"

"Looking forward to it." Emma disconnected. Somehow she didn't think Sam would be happy about this dinner, but she had little time to think about telling him when her phone rang again, this time Sam.

"Good morning," she said.

"My, you're chipper this morning," he said.

"Probably from not having to button a shirt," she said with a laugh. "Or worry about cooking tonight."

"Oh? Why's that?"

"Corey just invited me to dinner at the Guest House."

"And you said yes?"

"I did. I would like to resolve the issue of surveying the cabins and cemetery."

"Want me to tag along?"

"I, ah, don't think he invited you."

"Well, just be careful. We still don't know who's stalking you."

"I should be safe enough with Corey Chandler—he *is* an attorney."

"So was Ted Bundy."

"No, I don't think Bundy ever earned a law degree," she said. "Have you checked on the ring?"

"I did, and both the university and the ring company said they would get back to me," he said. "I also talked to the FBI office in Jackson. They didn't investigate Mary Jo's death."

"Why not?"

"They rarely get involved in a local murder unless there's a compelling reason, and Carter convinced them he had it under control," he said. "What time are you taking your cat to the vet?"

"Nine forty-five, but why don't I take an Uber and free you up?"

"There's no need for that. I took the morning off so I could take you. I don't think it's a good idea for you to be out and about by yourself until we catch whoever is stalking you."

"You can't go everywhere with me. Besides, so far he hasn't attacked me during the day."

"Doesn't mean he won't. I'll pick you up at nine thirty."

"Yes, sir." Emma was relieved she didn't have to arrange for different transportation. An Uber might not like having a cat for a passenger.

At ten thirty, the vet visit was behind them, and the vet had confirmed that Suzy was indeed a female and about three months old. When they returned to the apartment, Sam installed a new doorbell that included a camera. "Now you should be able to see and record anyone who rings your doorbell."

"Thank you." She hesitated, then asked, "Are we going to interview the Selbys today?"

"I am, but you're not."

"Why not? I have a vested interest in this."

He crossed his arms. "You're not in law enforcement."

"But I have a stake in this."

"If the Selbys believe your brother killed their daughter, they may refuse to talk if you're with me."

Emma considered that and tried to recall how much contact she'd had with Mary Jo's parents. The only time she'd met them was at their daughter's funeral, and she doubted they even noticed her. "Maybe they won't remember me, and if you don't tell them my last name . . ."

"That would be lying."

"No, it would be misdirection. Cops do it all the time on TV."

"Come on, Emma, this isn't some TV show. They'll know who you are anyway—you and Mary Jo were in the same class."

"But Mary Jo and I never hung out together—she was part of the 'in' crowd, and I wasn't, and I played volleyball and she played basketball. She was a cheerleader and played in the band, and I did neither—we didn't interact that much . . ." Sam was not leaving her out of the visit to the Selbys. Emma fisted her good hand on her hip. "With or without you, I'm going to talk to the Selbys," she said and walked to the hallway.

"Where are you going?"

She lifted her chin. "To change into my uniform."

When he tried to stare her down, she refused to look away. Finally, he palmed his hands. "Okay. But it's just this one time. After this, you'll leave the investigating to me."

Emma didn't know about that. She let the comment slide and hurried to her bedroom, where she struggled out of the leggings and into her uniform. The brace made buttoning the shirt almost impossible. Gritting her teeth, she ripped the brace off and buttoned her shirt, the movement sending pain up her arm. Why didn't they use snaps instead of buttons? Once she was dressed, she returned to the living room and held out the wrist contraption. "Would you mind?"

Without commenting, he leaned in close and wrapped it around her hand. His nearness and the heady scent of his aftershave sent her heart into overdrive.

"I just don't want you getting hurt," he said softly as he attached the Velcro.

"I'll be with you," she said. "Besides, how could talking to an older couple be dangerous?"

45

Sam tested the snugness of the splint, his fingers lingering on hers. When he looked up, the warmth in her green eyes caught him by surprise. Desire to wrap Emma in his arms blindsided him. How quickly things changed. He'd gone from swearing to never give her the power to hurt him again to practically handing his heart over with a red bow tied around it. She pulled her hand away, breaking the spell.

"Thank you," she said. "Have you contacted the Selbys?"

"Actually, I thought it'd be better to drop in without letting them know we're coming." He didn't like letting Emma tag along, but if he didn't, there was no doubt in his mind she would investigate on her own. At least this way, he had some control. "But first, you have to promise you won't nose around in this investigation on your own." When she hesitated, he said, "The deal is off, then."

She held up her left hand. "Okay, I won't investigate on my own."

"Is that a promise?" Emma always kept her promises.

"Yes," she grumbled.

"If you're ready, then . . ."

She picked Suzy up and hugged her. "I'll be back, and I don't want my curtains shredded while I'm gone. Got it?"

He smiled. "Are we talking to animals now?"

"*We* aren't talking to anyone. I am. And I don't get any flack back from her."

"Yes, ma'am."

He opened her door just as her neighbor unlocked his. Sam tried to place the name.

"Good morning, Greg," Emma said.

Sam remembered now. Gregory Hart.

"Good morning." He eyed the two of them. "Isn't this your day off?"

Emma glanced down at her uniform. "It was, but you know how it is."

"Yeah. Your time is never your own. Well, have a good day," he said and disappeared into his apartment.

Okay, Hart knew when Emma worked and when she didn't. Interesting. "Does he always keep up with you?"

"I wasn't even aware he knew my days off, although it wouldn't be hard to figure out."

She started down the stairs and he said, "Let me go first."

"What? So you can stop my fall?"

"Something like that." Once they were on the ground floor, he said, "Wait here."

Sam stepped out on the porch, scanned the area, and then checked the street in front of the apartment, noting that the Natchez PD hadn't installed the license plate readers yet. He would call Nate and see if the readers had been delivered to the police department. Then he scanned the neighborhood again, and everything looked normal. He stepped back inside and said, "All clear."

The Selbys lived just outside of Natchez, and a few minutes later they drove to Highway 61 and turned south.

"Are you sure you shouldn't call them and make sure they're home?" Emma asked. Her tone made it evident she didn't think just dropping in was a good idea.

"Trust me, I've done this before."

"I hope they know something that will help us."

"I keep telling you there's no 'us.'" He stopped at a traffic light, and while he waited for the light to change, he glanced at her. "Why do I get the feeling you want to find Ryan's killer by yourself?"

"Are you kidding? We let the authorities handle it for ten years and we're just now finding his body."

"You don't trust me or Nate to solve this?"

"I do, but I want to help." She turned toward the side window. "Do you ever wish you could go back and change something that happened when you were a kid?"

"All the time," he said, thinking about when his sister chased a ball in front of a car because he wasn't watching her. A horn tapped behind him, and he glanced at the light and quickly gunned the motor. "What would you change?"

She picked at her thumbnail. "I wouldn't let Ryan take the blame for me when I dented Mom's car."

"What do you mean?"

Emma sighed. "I knew as a little girl that there was a certain structure in our family. Everyone had their place, and mine was that of being the good kid. The one with the good grades, the one who always obeyed. Ryan on the other hand was the athlete, but he was rebellious and usually the one in trouble.

"One day when we were fifteen, I took Mom's car without asking and backed into a pole. We'd just gotten our permits and weren't supposed to be driving without an adult in the car. When she discovered the dented bumper, she automatically blamed Ryan. I remember the hurt in his eyes, but he didn't rat me out when I didn't own up to taking the car. I didn't want to lose my place as the good kid. The favorite."

"You really thought you were the favorite?"

"I'm afraid I did," she said sheepishly. "Soon after was when Ryan broke his leg and got hooked on pain meds. I've often wondered if I'd told the truth, would it have made a difference in the choices Ryan made? Would his life have been different?"

"You don't know—"

She held up her hand. "Don't. I know you mean well, but I

can't change the way I feel. And now that I know Ryan's gone, I have to get justice for him."

Sam wished he could tell Emma the remains in the grave hadn't been Ryan's, but the odds were 99 to 1 that it was his body. "I'm not going to tell you I know exactly how you feel, but I know how guilt feels. My sister wouldn't be limping today if I'd watched her like I was supposed to the day she got hit by a car."

"That wasn't your fault. You were what? Ten?"

"Eight, but the age doesn't matter. She was damaged for life. Do your parents know that it was you who dented the car?"

Emma sighed. "No, and I surely don't want to tell them now."

"Try it. When I feel really guilty, I try to remember what Mom told me. That even if I should have been watching Jenny, that was the past. It's over and done and can't be changed. Jenny has forgiven me, and I'm sure if Ryan were here, he'd forgive you for letting him take the blame."

"You really believe that?" Hope was in her voice.

Most days he did, but sometimes watching Jenny struggle with her bad leg hurt him to his core. And truth be known, he'd gone into law enforcement looking for something big to redeem himself and prove his dad wrong—that he was good for something. But working for the park service hadn't brought him the acceptance he needed. He wasn't sure what would. Maybe like Emma, it was finding Ryan and Mary Jo's killer.

She brushed her hand across her cheek. "Thanks."

He took his eyes off the road briefly. Her eyes were wet, breaking his heart.

"You're telling me I need to forgive myself."

"That's exactly what I'm saying."

"I don't see that happening, but thanks for letting me get it off my chest," she said as his phone rang.

Sam started to ignore it until Balfour Ring Company showed up on his dashboard screen.

Sam had pulled off the highway to answer the phone, and Emma stared out the car window at the curtain of Spanish moss hanging from a large live oak tree. Her breathing slowed as she listened to Sam's end of the conversation with the ring company.

"Yes," he said, then listened to whoever was on the other end of the call. "I see. Well, thank you for letting me know."

He ended the call but made no attempt to resume their trip to the Selbys, and her stomach took a nosedive.

His phone rang again. "I have to catch this."

She nodded. Why couldn't he let it go to voicemail? He knew she was waiting to hear what he'd learned.

"Ryker," he said.

She strained to hear what was being said on the other end of the call, but Sam's side was all she could hear.

"Really." He was quiet again, then his shoulders slumped. "Okay. Thanks for letting me know. I'll tell Emma."

"What will you tell me?" she asked after he hooked the phone on his belt.

Sam stared through the windshield, not answering.

"Sam . . ."

He licked his lips. "The first call was from the ring company. Their research showed only one ring was shipped to Mississippi

State in 2012 with the initials RTW. It was made for Ryan Thomas Winters."

"Maybe someone stole it." She knew better, but right now she was looking for any lifeline she could find. Emma would almost rather believe Ryan had dropped it digging the grave. At least that way her brother would still be alive.

Silence. He cleared his throat, then he turned to her and the answer was written in his face. "The last call was from Nate. Turns out the private testing company has the integrated microfluidic system . . ."

"And? Spit it out, Sam!"

"It's a Rapid DNA testing machine. The DNA in the toe bone was a match to yours."

Cold shot through her body, leaving her head swimming and her muscles useless. She sank against the seat.

"It's not official and won't be until the state results come in," Sam said. "But . . . it was Ryan's body in the grave."

His voice penetrated the murkiness filling her head. No matter how many times she'd prepared herself, it wasn't enough. Her brother was dead. Her mouth was so dry, she couldn't swallow.

"I'm sorry, Emma," he said. "Do you want me to take you somewhere? Maybe to see your dad? We can talk to the Selbys later—they're not expecting us."

Ryan is dead. And his murderer had gotten away with it for ten years. Emma sucked in a life-giving breath and willed steel into her backbone. "No. We have to find out who killed Ryan, and we have to start somewhere."

She turned her gaze to Sam. The pain in her heart was reflected in his eyes. He was hurting too. Emma rubbed her good hand across her face. "Give me a minute to pull it together, and then let's go talk to Mary Jo's parents."

He reached to the back floorboard and pulled out a bottle of water and uncapped it. "Here," he said, handing it to her.

She took a long draw. The water wet her dry mouth but almost made her throw up. It was one thing to think her brother might be dead and another to know it for a fact. "Who could have killed him?" she whispered.

"I don't know," he said. "But I promise you I'll do everything in my power to get justice for him."

"Do you think it's the same person who killed Mary Jo?"

Sam didn't answer right away. "I think she's the key," he said. "I haven't told you, but I talked to the owner of the Hideaway last night. Charlie Shaw."

She bolted upright. "What did he say? Did Mary Jo leave with Ryan?"

Emma listened as Sam filled her in on what he'd learned from Shaw. "Let me get this straight. Mary Jo came with one person and left with Ryan and Trey and Gordy?"

"Yes."

She was having a hard time wrapping her mind around the information. "This doesn't make sense. Why weren't Trey and Gordy in Sheriff Carter's report?"

"I have a theory." He rubbed the steering wheel.

"Are you going to tell me what it is or do I have to drag it out of you?"

"I can't let you get involved in this any deeper, now that it's definitely a murder investigation," he said.

"Fine," she snapped. "Take me home."

He turned and pinned her with a frown. "What are you going to do?"

"What I do doesn't concern you." Emma calculated the time it would take to get an Uber to take her to Mount Locust for her truck. Two hours at the most and then she would drive to the Selbys without Sam.

"I'm not going anywhere until you promise you'll let me handle this."

She folded her arms across her chest. "I'm not promising you anything. You might be able to lock me out of the official case, but you can't stop me from asking questions."

"Come on—"

"Don't *come on* me. Ryan was my brother, and I intend to find out who killed him. I'd rather do it with your help, but either way, I will get some answers."

"And get yourself hurt, or killed," he said.

"That's why I'd rather work with you. I figure you'll try to keep me safe." She pointed her finger at him. "But if you shut me out, I'll find a way around you."

Sam gripped the steering wheel and stared out the windshield, his jaw clenched and the muscle in his cheek working. Gradually his jaw relaxed and the muscle calmed. "If I let you tag along this time," he said, turning to face her, "will you then leave the solving of this case to Nate and me?"

She took a shaky breath. She'd won the battle, but not the war. "I promise I won't do anything without running it by you. Now, let's go talk to the Selbys."

47

Emma and Ryker were going to see Mary Jo's father. He checked his watch. The conversation he'd listened to took place twenty minutes ago. They were probably already at Selby's house. He cursed the situation that kept him from tuning in to their live conversation. But his job required certain obligations, and until he went off the grid, he had to fulfill them.

Ryker wouldn't learn much at the Selbys', and he tried to let that information calm him. The mother had died, and Mary Jo had always complained that the old man never paid any attention to her.

The sister. What if they talked to her?

When he and Mary Jo dated, she lived with the Wyatt woman, and he'd met her briefly when he arrived early for a date with a bouquet of daisies in his hand. What if the sister remembered him . . . or mentioned the flowers?

His name had not come up in the first investigation, and it couldn't come up now. Maybe he needed to pay another visit to the nursing home. Make sure he had no worries there. In his last visit, he could see that the dementia had advanced significantly, and if the new sheriff, or even Ryker, interviewed him, they would quickly discount anything he might say.

Stay on target. Right now, Sandra Wyatt was his concern. He couldn't take the chance of her identifying him. He grabbed his keys and picked up the .22 caliber rifle. No. He laid it back down and grabbed the pistol.

48

Letting Emma tag along wasn't a good idea, but for Sam it was safer than her going out on her own. Something he had no doubt she would do. At least this way he had a little control. GPS directed him to turn left off the highway and then again a mile later. Maybe the Selbys wouldn't be home. Then he could come back later by himself. When he reached the address he'd programmed into the map, a car sat in the drive.

"Oh, good," Emma said. "It looks like someone's here."

She didn't wait for him to come around to the door but scrambled out and met him in front of the SUV. Sam rang the doorbell. The man who opened the door looked much older than the sixty-five Sam's research had indicated George Selby would be. Sallow and thin, he gave the impression that time and circumstances had taken their toll on him.

"Can I help you?" the older man said.

"Are you Mr. Selby?" Sam asked.

He pushed black horn-rimmed glasses up on his nose and ran his gaze up and down Sam, stopping briefly at his gun. "Who's asking?"

"Sam Ryker. I'm a law enforcement ranger with the US Natchez Trace Park Service."

Selby blanched when Sam mentioned the Trace. "What do you want?" he asked, his attention moving to Emma.

"I'd like to ask a few questions about your daughter Mary Jo," Sam said, softening his voice.

The man seemed to shrink another inch. "Guess there's no need to stand out there in the cold," he said and stepped back.

They followed him inside to the living room, where a single lamp beside a worn leather recliner broke the darkened gloom. Newspapers lay strewn about, making Sam wonder where Mrs. Selby was.

"Sit wherever you can find a spot," Mr. Selby said and sank into the old recliner.

Sam sat on the sofa across from Selby while Emma moved clothes from the only other chair and sat on the edge. "Your wife, is she here?" Sam asked.

The old man shook his head. "Passed a month ago."

Beside him Emma gave a small gasp. Sam was just as surprised. His research hadn't shown that Jane Selby had died. "I'm sorry," he said.

"She's better off now. At least she's with Mary Jo and knows what happened. I wish I was with her." Selby turned to Emma. "And you are . . . ?"

"Emma," she said. "And I'm so sorry about your wife."

He nodded and blinked away the wetness in his eyes before turning his attention back to Sam. "What is it that you want?"

"New information has come to light, and your daughter's case is being reopened," Sam said.

Selby gaped at him, then closed his mouth. "Have they found the Winters kid?"

Sam noticed Emma flinch. This was going to be difficult in more than one way. "Something like that."

"Where'd you find him? Alaska? That's where Sheriff Carter thought he ran off to."

"We found him buried at Mount Locust," Emma said, her voice tight. "And he'd probably been there all this time."

Selby turned to her, his eyes rounded. "I . . . I don't understand." A range of emotions crossed his face, and he shook his head as if to clear it. "But . . . Carter said the Winters boy killed

Mary Jo. Why would he be dead . . . unless he didn't murder my daughter?"

"We're almost certain he didn't kill her," Sam said. "We figure the same person is responsible for both of their deaths. Can you answer a few questions for me?"

"I don't know much. Could I call my daughter and get her to come over here?"

"Sure. Does she live nearby?"

"Next house up the road." He picked up the receiver to an old push-button phone, and after he explained that someone wanted to talk to her about Mary Jo, he frowned. "I'll see." He turned to Sam. "Sandra wants to talk to you."

Sam took the phone and identified himself as Emma carried on a conversation with Mr. Selby.

"Dad said you're there about Mary Jo," Sandra said. "What exactly do you want?"

He moved as far as the landline would allow him. "Last night I talked with Charlie Shaw, and—"

"Please don't mention his name or the Hideaway to Dad. It really gets him down. He can't handle that Mary Jo went to a place like that."

"I'll do my best," Sam said, lowering his voice. He would move to another room except the phone was attached to a cord. "Shaw said she was with a date at the beginning of the night. Do you know who that might have been?"

"Before I answer any of your questions, I want to know why you're investigating her death again. Sheriff Carter all but assured my parents that Ryan Winters killed my sister."

Sam explained what they'd discovered.

"Oh no. His poor family," she said. "I taught Ryan in the tenth grade and never quite believed Sheriff Carter's accusation."

"What do you mean, you taught Ryan?"

"I taught English at Natchez High School for fifteen years—until I took a leave of absence last year to take care of Mom. Of course, when Mary Jo attended Natchez High, she didn't want anyone to know we were sisters."

Mrs. Wyatt. He remembered her now. Tall and willowy with blonde hair. "Do you know who your sister might have gone on a date with the night she was killed?" Sam asked again.

"No. Mary Jo fell in with the wrong crowd at college, got involved in drinking and partying. I don't think she ever got into drugs, though. And as for the men in her life, she never brought any of them around . . ."

Suddenly she fell silent.

"Wait . . . let me think." Silence filled the air briefly. "There was this one guy . . . I met him a couple of weeks before . . ." Her voice dropped, and she took a breath. "He came to the house to pick her up, and he had flowers . . . Look, you need to see her journal. It might have his name in it. I'll be right there."

"What kind of flowers?" Sam asked, but she'd already hung up. He replaced the receiver and turned to Emma and Mr. Selby. "She'll be here in a few minutes."

"Good. I was just telling the ranger here that I let Mary Jo down by not being home more," the older man said. "I was working twelve-hour shifts at the local bottling company and didn't see her much. Jane—that's my wife—said I needed to be firmer with her. Sandra was complaining about her coming and going all hours of the night."

"She wasn't staying with you at the time of her death?" Sam asked.

"No, we'd had another one of our arguments, and Mary Jo was staying with Sandra until she could get enough money to go back to Southern Miss." He shook his head. "Seems like once she got grown, argue is all we did. Anyway, she'd come home to save money. Mary Jo was always good about money. What she wasn't so good about was boundaries."

"What do you mean?" Sam asked.

"Mary Jo came and went as she pleased at Sandra's, like it

was her own house. She thought nothing of coming in at three in the morning, waking her older sister up, and I'm afraid that's my fault."

"How so?"

"After my wife had so much trouble carrying Sandra, we never expected to have another child, so twelve years later, Mary Jo came as quite a surprise. When she was a little girl, she could wind me around her little finger like a rubber band." Mr. Selby's eyes got a faraway look in them, then he wiped his eyes. "Anyway, Sandra was complaining to my wife, and she wanted me to talk to Mary Jo . . . and I never got around to it."

"I remember Mary Jo from school," Emma said. "She was very popular."

He took another look at Emma. "You look a little familiar. Were you friends with my daughter?"

"We were in several classes together," she said.

Suddenly red flooded his face. "Oh, my goodness. I haven't even offered you two refreshments. My wife would be horrified. There's drinks in the refrigerator, or I can make a pot of coffee." He stood and started toward the kitchen.

"Nothing for me," Sam said quickly.

"Or me," Emma added.

George Selby turned around. "You sure?" When they both nodded, he said, "Be sure to tell Sandra I offered. She's as bad as her mama was about things like that."

Sam checked his watch. It'd been ten minutes since he talked to Selby's daughter. "Did you say she lived next door?"

"Her house is about a quarter of a mile—don't take long to walk the path." A crease appeared between his brows. "But she shoulda been here by now."

Unease crept into Sam's mind. "Why don't I go check on her?"

"Take the path from the back of my house to hers. It's a shortcut. Go right down the hall and out the back door, and you'll probably meet her."

Sam nodded and hurried out the back. Right away he saw the trail that curved out of sight, but no Sandra.

He jogged down the path, and just beyond the curve, a body lay slumped on the ground, facedown. Sam rushed to her side. Blood spread from a bullet wound in her back, and he jerked out his phone, dialing 911. When the operator answered, he identified himself. "I need an ambulance at . . ." What address had he put into the GPS? He couldn't remember. "Look up the 911 address for George Selby on Lake Drive. I'm outside at the back of the property."

Sam knelt and pressed against the side of her neck. Nothing. Gently, he turned Sandra over. No exit wound. He pressed two fingers against the inside of her wrist. His heart jumped. Was that a pulse?

Someone screamed his name.

49

"I can't imagine what's taking Sandra so long." Mr. Selby glanced toward the back of the house, then turned back to Emma. "You ever had a feeling you should remember something but you're not sure what it is?"

"Absolutely." Sam had been gone for a few minutes, and the older man had been staring into space. She wondered why he'd fallen silent. Emma glanced around the ranch-style house that looked as though it hadn't been updated in twenty years, and noticed a potted peace lily blooming in the corner. "What a beautiful plant," she said. "I have one but I can't ever get it to bloom."

Mr. Selby snapped his fingers. "That's it! There was this guy who sent flowers to Mary Jo's funeral." He swallowed hard. "At least Sandra thought it was a guy—there weren't no card, but Sandra remembered someone giving her the same kind a couple of weeks before."

"Flowers?" It couldn't be. "What kind?"

He scratched his head. "Daisies—them fancy kind. You can ask Sandra about them when she gets here."

Emma's breath stilled in her chest. Mary Jo had received daisies? That couldn't be a coincidence.

Mr. Selby stood. "I'm going to make us a pot of coffee."

"Really, I don't want any coffee," Emma said. She wanted to know more about the flowers. And where was Sam?

"Well, I do, and Sandra will want some, and maybe you'll drink a cup once I get it made," he said and walked toward the hall.

"Wait, and I'll help you."

"No, you sit right there. Won't take me a minute to get it started. Sandra bought me a newfangled coffeepot. All I have to do is push a button and it grinds the coffee and then brews it."

Sounds of Mr. Selby opening a cabinet reached Emma as she picked at the Velcro on the brace. "Are you sure I can't help you?" she called.

"No, I'm—who are you?" Mr. Selby demanded, his voice loud. "No—"

Thwock.

Emma's breath froze in her chest. She'd heard that sound before. Friday night.

A crash came from the kitchen, and she jumped up.

Run!

Her feet wouldn't move. She couldn't leave Mr. Selby. She crept to the hall and listened. Silence. Did the intruder know she was here? If she called 911, he would hear her. But Adams County had recently gotten the text-to-911 capability, and Emma pulled out her phone and quickly shot off an emergency text.

Intruder. 3544 Lake Road. Shots fired. Possible gsw.

Footsteps, then a screen door slammed. She tried to swallow, but her mouth was too dry. When she didn't hear another sound, she eased down the hallway.

Pausing just outside the kitchen, she cocked her head, listening. The jackhammering of her heart overrode any other sound until a low groan raked her ears and she became aware of sirens approaching. How could they have gotten here so fast?

"Help . . . please . . ." His voice sounded so weak.

Mr. Selby. She scrambled around the corner and screamed for Sam.

The older man lay face up on the floor. Emma's head buzzed at the sight of blood staining the front of his shirt. She pressed her lips together and knelt beside his body. So much blood. She needed to staunch it. Emma frantically scanned the room.

A towel hung from a hook by the door. She grabbed it and pressed it against his chest. Blood quickly saturated it, staining her hands. The room swirled. She could not pass out.

"Police! Put your hands in the air!"

"He'll bleed out if I do!"

Nate Rawlings pushed into the kitchen. "Emma? What happened?"

"How'd you get here so fast?"

"This case has been bugging me, and I was on my way to talk to George Selby when the call came in. Where's Sam?"

"He went to check on Mr. Selby's daughter." Relief made Emma's arms like noodles. "Is the ambulance here?" she asked.

"First responders just got here, but they're looking for someone outside."

"Maybe something happened to the daughter."

Nate turned to his deputy. "Give them the okay to enter and see if you can find another victim!" He dropped to his knees beside her. "Man, he looks bad. Let me take over. See if you can find another towel."

She stood and jerked open drawers until she found dish towels and grabbed a handful.

Nate pressed the towels against the man's chest. Blood quickly soaked through, making her stomach heave. He was going to die. "I should have come to the kitchen with him."

"This isn't your fault, Emma," Nate said. "And you might have been shot too."

Before she could respond, paramedics burst into the room and immediately took over for Nate. He hustled her out of their way. Now that the immediate danger was over, the shakes took over and she hugged her arms to her waist.

"We can't do any more here. Let's find Sam," the sheriff said.

She nodded, then followed him out the door. "D-do you th-think he'll live?"

"I don't know. He's lost a lot of blood," Nate said, glancing at her. "You don't look too good. Do you need to sit down?"

Emma hugged her body tighter and forced air into her lungs. "I'll be okay. It's j-just I've n-never seen anyone sh-shot before."

"What happened?"

The buzzing in her head had stopped, and she sucked in another deep breath. Her galloping heart slowed, and strength returned to her legs. "I wish I knew," she said, glancing back at the house. "Sam had gone to see why Mr. Selby's daughter hadn't arrived. After he left, Mr. Selby went to make coffee. Someone came into the kitchen and shot him."

"Did you see who it was?"

"No, and they never spoke a word."

Nate hugged her. "Are you okay to stay here while I check on the daughter?"

She did not want to be by herself. "I'll go with you."

"Did you learn anything from Mr. Selby before he was shot?" he asked as they hurried down the path.

Emma's mind blanked. "I can't remember one word of our conversation. Maybe in a few minutes," she said as they rounded a curve. A second set of paramedics was bent over a woman, and Sam stood to the side.

"How is she?" she asked when they reached him.

"Not good," Sam said. "She had a pulse, but it was weak."

"Is that Mary Jo's sister?" Nate asked.

"Yeah."

Emma turned toward the victim and gasped. "Sandra Selby is Mrs. Wyatt from high school?" she asked, pressing her hand against her chest. What little equilibrium she'd gained vanished. Her legs buckled and she sank into the dead grass along the path, unable to take her eyes off the paramedics as they worked on Mrs. Wyatt. For the life of her, she couldn't think of her as Sandra.

"You know her?" Nate asked. He pulled a pair of latex gloves over his hands.

"Yes, but I didn't know she was Mary Jo's sister."

"How about you, Sam?"

"She told me on the phone who she was and that she had taught Ryan at the high school. Before that, I never made the connection between Sandra Selby and Mrs. Wyatt." Sam didn't seem to be able to turn from the scene either. "She was bringing Mary Jo's journal to show me."

"Maybe it's here." The sheriff picked up a coat the paramedics had removed from Sandra and felt the pockets. When he finished going through it, Nate shook his head. "Nothing in the coat."

"Her shooter must have taken it."

"Sheriff!" Nate turned as one of his deputies jogged toward them from the Selby house. "There's been a four-car pileup on 61. Shut the highway down and three casualties so far."

Nate winced. "I need to go."

After the sheriff left, Sam helped Emma up from the ground. As he walked toward the paramedics, she dusted her pants off and glanced around at her surroundings. The path between the two houses looked well used. On one side, trees bordered the path, and on the other was a chain-link fence with a vine covering most of it. She caught her breath. The warmer weather a week ago had fooled the vine into blooming, and yellow jasmine peeked out from the green foliage.

Flowers!

"Sam!"

He whirled around. "What's wrong?"

"Mary Jo received daisies, just like I did."

He hurried back to her. "What do you mean?"

"After you left, Mr. Selby remembered that a bouquet of daisies was sent to the funeral home. There wasn't a card."

"Maybe this is the break we need." He rubbed his jaw. "When I get back to town, I'll check the florists and then enter what information I have on Mary Jo's murder into an information sharing system. If there are any similar cases, they'll pop up."

"You think whoever killed Mary Jo killed someone else?"

"It's possible. I want to talk to the paramedics, and then we'll leave."

He walked to where the medics were loading Sandra onto a gurney. Emma couldn't hear their words, but she imagined he was asking her condition.

How many people would die before they caught this person?

50

Adrenaline pumped through his body as he jogged through the woods, dodging low-hanging limbs. His truck was half a mile away, parked at an abandoned old barn he'd found years ago when he spied on Mary Jo. He heard sirens and looked over his shoulder to make sure no one chased him. He was good, but then a thin limb slapped him and anger spewed out of him.

He hated Sam Ryker. The ranger had forced him to kill. Why couldn't he leave the investigation like it was? Ryan was dead and that couldn't be changed, so why not let him take the blame for Mary Jo's death?

Ryan *was* to blame. If it hadn't been for him, Mary Jo would be with him now.

No. Mary Jo wasn't right for you. She never would have made the perfect wife. Not like Emma.

Emma. He was doing all this for her. So they could be together.

His truck came into sight, and he slowed to a walk. He had plenty of time to get in and drive away before anyone came looking. Everyone was too busy taking care of the chaos he'd left behind.

He opened the truck door and tossed the black journal on the passenger seat. Sandra Wyatt had been carrying it, presumably to hand over to Ryker, but the ranger would never see it. Within seconds, he pulled out of the gravel drive and turned toward the highway.

Once he was miles away from the area, he pulled over and opened the journal. *Mary Jo Selby. 2011.* Good thing he took it. No telling what Mary Jo had written about him.

But his and Mary Jo's secret was safe now.

51

It was three thirty when Sam escorted Emma to her apartment and walked through to make sure it was safe.

"You want a sandwich?" she asked. "I know you're not hungry, but . . ."

"That sounds good." Neither of them had eaten lunch, and hungry or not, they needed to eat.

"What are your plans for the rest of the afternoon?" Emma asked as she took meat from the refrigerator.

"I'd like to stay here, but I need to pick up my computer and find a quiet place to upload everything in Mary Jo Selby's file into the Regional Information Sharing System, including the daisies." Especially the daisies. "But I don't want to leave you alone, so while you're making our sandwiches, I'll phone Brooke to come and guard the apartment building until I can return."

"Thanks. I wonder if that's necessary." Emma palmed her hand. "Don't get me wrong. I know we're dealing with a dangerous person, but he could have killed me at the Selbys, and he didn't."

She had a point. "Maybe so, but I'd feel better if you had someone here."

A quick call to Brooke revealed she was up near Jackson, and so was Clayton, so they were out. His next call was to Pete Nelson.

"I have three officers out with the flu and I'm short-staffed," the chief said after Sam explained the situation. "The best I can do is have an officer drive by every hour."

That beat nothing. "I appreciate that. Have you received the license plate readers?"

"A deputy just dropped them off this afternoon. They should be installed by tomorrow," Nelson said.

"Why don't I pick them up and hang them myself? I've installed the cameras before." Anything to get them in place.

"That would be great."

Sam ended the call and dialed Nate. "Do you have a deputy you can spare? I don't want to leave Emma unprotected, and the Natchez PD are short-staffed and Brooke is two hours away."

Nate was silent for a second, then he said, "Let me call one of the constables. I'll get right back to you."

They had almost finished eating when Nate called and Sam put the call on speaker. "Jay Blackwell is on his way to her apartment."

"I know him," Emma said. "He goes to my church."

Sam thanked Nate and hung up. "I'll wait until he gets here," he said.

"This regional sharing system. Once you enter the data, what kind of information will you get?"

"The program will tell me if any part of the information fits other murders in this region. If I don't get a hit, I'll enter the file into the national database."

"So you really don't think Mary Jo's murder was an isolated case?"

Sam lifted his shoulder slightly. "I don't know, but after learning she received daisies from an unknown admirer, I have to wonder. Daisies aren't your typical flower to send to someone you love."

Emma shivered and rubbed her arm just as Sam's phone rang. It was the constable and he was parked out front. After Sam disconnected, he turned to Emma. He shouldn't have made that comment to her about the daisies. "Are you okay?"

"I'll be fine. Go. You have work to do." She tucked a strand of hair behind her ear. "And if I'm going to my dinner with Corey, I need to get ready."

Sam caught himself before he reacted. And it was not a jealous reaction. *Then what was it?* The question was in his mind before he could blink. He'd checked Corey Chandler out and discovered the man was a respectable attorney and involved in several worthwhile charities. In fact, he seemed perfect. Maybe that was Sam's problem with the man. No one was perfect.

"You sure you're up to it?"

"No, but it'll be better than sitting here, dwelling on what happened this afternoon."

Sam agreed but wished it were him she was going out with. "Do you think Corey will tell you his client's name?"

"That's my whole purpose in agreeing to the meeting."

"Please be careful around him. You don't know him that well."

"He's a respected member of the bar, so I figure I'll be perfectly safe," she said, smiling. "Besides, I can take care of myself."

The image of Sandra Wyatt's bloody body lying on the path ambushed him. If that happened to Emma . . . "I know you can, but whoever killed Mary Jo and attacked her family is smart, and that makes him dangerous."

His caution drained the levity from her face, and Sam pulled her into his arms, feeling her body tremble. "I didn't mean to frighten you, but . . ." He looked down into her emerald eyes, and his world tilted.

"I know," she whispered.

"I have to go catch a killer." He'd rather stay with her, hold her in his arms.

"And I have to get a shower." She kissed him lightly on the cheek. "Stay safe."

"That goes double for you."

Sam waited until Emma locked the dead bolt after him, then he descended the stairs, his heart light. At the bottom of the steps his lightheartedness crashed as his conscience whispered in his ear. *You didn't tell her your secret.*

He almost turned to go back and tell her the truth about the night her brother died. No. She was probably halfway to the shower already. He had no excuse for not already telling Emma that he'd lied to her, but in his wildest dreams he never thought he would let himself fall in love with her again. Besides, there hadn't been an opportune time to tell her. *Really?*

Maybe now was the time Sam would have to trust God that the right time would come up and she would forgive him. At least he still believed in miracles. He pushed through the front door onto the porch. A late-model Impala with a constable emblem on the door sat parked in front of the apartment. Sam hurried over. The man who climbed out of the car had a couple of inches on Sam and his handshake was firm.

"I'm Jay Blackwell," the constable said. "And I'm happy to help out. Emma is one special lady."

Sam agreed. "She'll be leaving around six, and I'd appreciate it if you could follow them to the Guest House downtown."

After Blackwell assured him he would, Sam walked to his SUV and surveyed the surrounding area. Nothing looked out of place, but then nothing had looked out of place at the Selbys.

52

Emma took a ragged breath and hugged her arms to her waist as she stared out her living room window into the waning sunlight. The images of Mr. Selby and his daughter lying in pools of blood haunted her. Why were they shot? Did their digging into Mary Jo's case trigger the shootings?

Suddenly cognizant that she was a perfect target, Emma backed away from the window and pulled the curtains. The clock over her fireplace chimed five times. She should be getting dressed for her dinner with Corey. Even though she'd told Sam keeping the date would be better than dwelling on the shootings, maybe she should cancel it. She took out her phone and scrolled to Corey's number. When he answered, she said, "I hate to cancel on you this late, but I'm just not up to going out to eat."

"What's wrong?" he asked. "Are you ill?"

The concern in his voice almost undid her. "Not exactly. It's . . . just been a horrible day." And even worse for the Selbys.

"That's all the more reason to go out with me. I promise to take your mind off all your troubles."

Emma found herself weakening. She really didn't want to be by herself right now, and Sam was busy. If she kept the dinner date, she could at least learn more about the person who didn't want the Mount Locust project to go forward.

"Pretty please?" he said.

His entreaty almost brought a smile to her lips. "If we can make it an early night," she said.

"I promise to have you home by eight. How's that?"

"Sounds good."

In her bedroom, Emma searched for something to wear to the Guest House. Something that was easy to get into. She found a pair of black slacks and a silk shirt the color of emeralds. Buttoning the shirt almost proved too much, but she finally wrestled the buttons into their holes and then slipped her size sixes into a pair of Jimmy Choos.

Like the outfit she'd worn Saturday night, the clothes had been Christmas presents from her mother, who never quit trying to improve Emma's wardrobe. It crossed her mind that if it weren't for her mom, she would have very few nice outfits. Had she even properly thanked her for the gifts? Emma found her phone and dialed her mother.

"Is something wrong?" her mom asked instead of saying hello.

She really needed to call her mom more often. "Nothing's wrong. I just wanted to thank you for the outfits you bought me this Christmas. And the shoes."

"Oh."

She needed to thank her mother more often too. Then maybe she wouldn't sound so surprised.

"I'm glad you like them, but what's the occasion? Hot date?"

"It is a date, but don't sound so hopeful. It's only business."

"What kind of business meeting would call for Jimmy Choos? And besides that, how do you expect to ever get married if you don't start dating again? You've barely gone out with anyone since you broke up with Trey last year, and I'd really like to have grandchildren before I'm too old to enjoy them."

"That'll never happen." Where was her black satin clutch?

"What? That I won't be too old or you're not getting married?"

The memory of Sam's kiss sent her heart rate spiraling. "Relationships never work out for me."

"They would if you worked at it instead of giving up."

You're a fine one to talk. Emma bit the words back even though her mom had been the one who walked away from the marriage, not her dad.

"Who is this meeting with?"

Emma checked the back of her closet door where her other handbags were and found the purse she was looking for. "I'm not sure you know Corey Chandler, but he's the one who invited me to dinner to discuss a business matter."

"Did you say Corey Chandler? The attorney? He asked you out?"

"Yes." The total surprise in her mother's voice again rubbed Emma like a cactus. Maybe she should've let her mom know that she did date sometimes. "You know Corey?"

"Yes. I met him when he was with Cooper, Rossetti, and Thompson here in Jackson. He's extremely bright, except for the fact that he set up practice in Natchez. The Jackson law firm was about to make him a partner."

"I'll ask him why he gave up a lucrative practice to move to Natchez," Emma said. She transferred her driver's license and keys from her backpack to the small purse and then decided to throw in a tube of lip gloss.

"Don't you dare. That would make you appear nosy."

"Yes, ma'am." She was trying not to laugh.

"Wait, I remember now. Corey interned with Wendall Peterson, and he lured Corey down there three years ago with an offer of a partnership."

Emma had forgotten those particulars. "Didn't Wendall up and die less than a year later with a heart attack?"

"Yes, and Corey inherited the practice. I understand he's doing quite well for himself there."

"Well, we're just friends," she said.

"What better way to start a relationship."

Her mother was terrible. A call beeped in on Emma's phone,

and she glanced at the ID. Corey. “Gotta go, my ‘date’ is here,” she said.

“Don’t joke,” her mom said. “And tell him I said hello.”

“Yes, ma’am.” Emma switched the calls. “Hello?”

“Good evening. I’m out front and wanted to let you know I’ll be at your door in less than a minute.”

“You don’t have to come up the stairs, I’ll come down.”

“Never. Besides, I’m already here,” he said as the doorbell rang.

It was a good time to try out the doorbell camera Sam had installed, and she switched over to the camera app on her phone. The image of Corey at her door, adjusting his tie, appeared in real time. She quickly opened the door. “Come in.”

Wow. He looked good. Instead of his normal navy suit, he’d dressed down in black chinos and a cashmere sweater over a button-down shirt. Heat crept into her face when she realized he’d caught her admiring him. “Coming upstairs really wasn’t necessary.”

“But it was,” he said as he stepped past her. “And your front door shouldn’t have been unlocked.”

“Five minutes more and it would have been locked,” she said.

“Good.” Corey glanced around the room. “I love these old houses, and when one is turned into apartments, I’m always interested in seeing how it turned out.”

Her cell phone rang, and she glanced at the caller ID. Sam. “I need to take this,” she said. “Look around.”

As he walked around her living room, she turned away from him and pressed the answer button. “Do you have any news on the Selbys?”

“There’s been no change in either of their conditions,” he said. “The doctors said the next twenty-four hours will be critical.”

“I hope they make it. Thanks for letting me know.”

“You sound . . . odd. Is someone with you?”

“Yes. We’ll talk tomorrow.”

“Wait. I wanted to let you know that I decided to enter the

information from Mary Jo's case into ViCAP. I'll let you know if I get a hit."

ViCAP? The acronym sounded familiar, but she couldn't place what it was. "What is that?"

"Violent Criminal Apprehension Program."

She remembered now. She'd heard it mentioned on a reality police show recently. The detective had used the program to discover if there were any crimes similar to the one he was working on. "Let me know what you find out."

"Look . . . I don't think you should go out with Chandler," he said, his voice gruff.

"Too late." Thank goodness she wasn't on speaker. Talking about Corey while he stood nearby was getting sticky. "Thanks again for calling."

"Just be careful tonight."

"I will." She felt like making a face at the phone. Sam was persistent if nothing else.

"Call me if you feel the least bit uncomfortable, and I'll come get you. I won't be far from the Guest House."

"There won't be any need for that." This was getting ridiculous, and if she didn't know better, she'd think he was jealous. "Goodbye."

His answering goodbye was almost a growl. She slipped her phone in the black satin clutch and turned to Corey. "What do you think?"

"You look nice. Really nice."

Her face heated again. "I was talking about the apartment."

"Oh. I like what they did. Whoever made the renovation maintained the integrity of the house."

"I think so too. You seem to know a lot about carpentry."

"It's one of my hobbies," he said.

"That's interesting," she said, adding the information to her knowledge of the attorney. "And by the way, you look nice too. I don't think I've ever seen you without a tie."

He touched his collar. "I suppose you haven't, but maybe we can remedy that. Shall we go? Our reservation is for six fifteen . . ."

She locked the door behind them, then followed him down the steps.

"How much longer will you have to wear the brace?" he asked.

"A couple more weeks."

"I'm sure it's a terrible inconvenience."

"You don't know the half of it," she said with a laugh. "Especially during the dig last week."

"Did you tell me you finished the excavation for the sheriff?"

Emma's breath hitched. She didn't want to discuss Ryan with Corey. "If not, I'm telling you now. There won't be any more digging at the slave cemetery."

"Good. My client will be very happy to hear that."

By the end of the evening, maybe she would have the name of that client. She allowed Corey to escort her to a white Lexus and open the passenger door for her. "Is the car new?" Emma asked as she slid across the pristine white leather seat.

"No. Three years old," he said. "I bought it right after I arrived in Natchez."

"How do you keep it so new-looking?" she asked once he was in the driver's seat.

"I have a pickup I use for dirty work." He pushed the start button and pulled away from the curb.

Emma tried to picture him in a pickup. Corey Chandler just didn't seem the type. "I gather it isn't a monster truck."

He laughed. "You are delightful. No, it's a late-model four-wheel drive." Then he turned somber. "I want you to understand I wasn't listening to your phone conversation, but I got the feeling you'd gotten bad news."

She'd tried to keep her voice down, but the apartment wasn't that big. "I have a couple of friends in the hospital, and I'd hoped to hear they were better."

"They're not?"

"No. Still critical." Emma didn't want to get into particulars. She held the armrest as he made a sharp turn and drove toward the downtown area.

"I'm sorry."

"Thank you. Oh, my mom said to tell you hello."

He stopped for a traffic light, and Emma sensed Corey looking at her and turned toward him.

"Your mother remembers me?"

"Yes, and she spoke highly of you."

53

Sam had arrived back at Emma's apartment building with the two license plate readers in time to see Corey Chandler's white Lexus pull away from the curb. With darkness closing in, he'd been tempted to wait until morning to install the cameras, but he was here and he had a good hanging lantern he could use. By the time he'd installed and synced them, it was almost seven.

Sam's stomach growled. Emma's sandwich hadn't stuck with him, and he was tempted to drop by the Guest House and grab a bite before he entered the data into the programs. But if Emma happened to see him, she would assume he was jealous. And he wasn't. Sam simply didn't trust the attorney.

Instead he drove to his sister's house and was glad to see Jenny's car wasn't parked out front. He might as well enter the data into RISS and ViCAP from the house. He set his computer on the bar and noticed Jenny had cooked, and whatever it was smelled delicious. While the computer booted up, he peeked inside the pots on the stove. Green beans, a roast, and potatoes. She hadn't mentioned company was coming. He was tempted to fix himself a plate, but she may not have expected him to eat, and so he settled for another sandwich and took it to his room. He'd just finished it when the front door opened.

"We're home," Jenny called.

"I'm in my room."

A minute later his sister knocked softly. "I didn't think you'd be back so early."

Jace pushed past her. "You should've been at practice! I made two goals."

"Son, don't bother your uncle. He's busy," she said.

"I'm not busy yet." Sam snapped his laptop closed and shifted his full attention to Jace. "Say practice was good?"

The boy nodded. "Coach is letting me start tomorrow's game." He turned to his mother, who was chewing on her thumbnail. "I'm hungry."

"Well, we can't eat until Granna gets here. Did you wash your hands after you got home?" His nephew looked down at his hands and shook his head. "Go and wash. Now." Jenny pointed toward the bathroom.

"Aww, I wanted to tell Sam about the game and—"

"Now, young man." She looked up but avoided Sam's eyes. "Flu is raging in this town."

He could tell something was bothering Jenny other than her son's hands. After he left, Sam said, "Mom's coming for dinner? Something special going on I don't know about?"

"Uh . . . no." Jenny took a deep breath. "Dad's coming too."

Sam stared at her. "Did you say . . ."

She lifted her chin. "Yes, that's exactly what I said. Dad's coming with Mom." She checked her watch. "And they'll be here in ten minutes. I almost didn't tell you because I really wish you would talk to him . . ."

Sam's jaw went rigid, and he pressed his lips in a thin line. "How can you—"

"But if you can't be civil, I'd rather you leave."

"That's exactly what I'll do." He grabbed his computer bag and slid the laptop inside. She followed him to the front door. "I don't get it," he said. "After the way he beat Mom down emotionally, cheated on her . . . the way he's been all his life, how can you just act like nothing's wrong?"

"He's changed, Sam. You'd see that if you would talk to him."

He jutted his jaw. "I can't believe you've fallen for his con."

"I can't believe you won't even hear him out."

For an answer, Sam slammed the door behind him and hopped in his SUV. He spun out of the drive, headed to the Port Gibson District Headquarters. When he reached the Trace, he reminded himself to slow down to the fifty-mile-an-hour speed limit.

He didn't understand how Jenny could betray him like this. And his mother. How could she take Martin Ryker back again? He tried to block images of being whipped with a leather belt, but they surfaced anyway, morphing into the times when his father's words hurt worse than the belt.

No! He would not give his father power over him. Sam forced his grip on the steering wheel to loosen and focused on the narrow two-lane road. Thoughts of his dad crept in, and his hands tightened on the wheel again.

Whatever is true, whatever is . . . Not now. He blocked the words from the verse in Philippians his mom had made him memorize as a kid. Sam wanted to think about the wrongs his dad had done. It kept the anger fresh.

He braked as his headlights caught a deer on the side of the road. The magnificent buck turned his antlered head toward him, then raised his white tail and jumped away from the road. He released the breath trapped in his chest. *Whatever is pure, whatever is lovely . . . think on those things . . .*

Was it possible his dad had changed? Even if he had, after what he'd done to Sam . . . his father didn't deserve forgiveness.

Forgive us our trespasses as we forgive those who trespass against us.

More of his mom's influence. And what about Emma? He wanted her to forgive him . . . He brushed the thoughts away and focused on watching for deer.

Before long, he pulled into the Port Gibson office and parked under the outside light beside Clayton's SUV. He grabbed his computer and hurried inside the low building, where his field ranger sat at one of the two desks that were in the larger room. "No lingering effects from Friday night?" Sam asked.

Clayton shook his head. "No. After whatever was in the coffee wore off, I was good. Did you get the report back on what was in it?"

"Clonazepam. It's used for seizures and sometimes anxiety." Something Sam could use about now. "Too much and it'll knock you out."

"I'm assuming too much can kill you as well."

"Right." Sam sat at the empty desk and booted up his computer.

"Need anything before I hit the Trace? Brooke made coffee first thing this morning, so I'm pretty sure it's strong."

"I'll pass," Sam said with a laugh. After Clayton left, he connected to the internet and pulled up the RISS portal and logged in. He would try the regional program first, and if he didn't get a hit there, he'd log into ViCAP, which was an FBI program that covered the whole United States. He had most of the information entered when the door opened and Brooke entered the office. She laid her flat hat on the desk Clayton had vacated.

"Many speeders out there today?" Sam asked. It was hard for drivers to adhere to the fifty-mile-an-hour speed.

"A few. Mostly doing fifty-five. Since I was feeling magnanimous today," she said, looking at her engagement ring, "I handed out a couple of warnings. Did you find someone to shadow Emma?"

"I did." Sam leaned closer to his laptop. "Looks like I got a hit," he said.

"On what?"

As he opened the file, Sam told her about the shootings and about Mary Jo receiving daisies from an unknown person. "I uploaded all the information into RISS."

"And the database returned more murders similar to Mary Jo's?"

He scanned over the file. "Looks like it. Let me print this out."

54

Emma had never eaten at the Guest House. They'd parked on the street and walked through a small French Quarter courtyard with a fountain that would be wonderful to dine in during the spring and autumn. A little chilly for tonight, though. A hostess showed them to a table inside, and Corey held her chair out for her.

"Thank you," she said as he scooted her closer. "I love this place. It's so cozy."

"Maybe we can come back one evening when it's not business related."

Smile. Emma didn't want to get the evening off to a wrong start, and she forced her lips upward in what she hoped didn't look like a grimace. Sam was right about Corey being interested in her.

"What would you like to drink?" he asked as their waitress approached.

Emma looked up. Amy was stitched over her pocket. "Is the coffee good here, Amy?"

"It's very good—the best in town, if you ask me," she said with a smile.

That's what everyone said. "I'll try it and let you know."

"And I'll have iced tea," Corey said. After Amy brought their drink orders and Emma had sipped her coffee, he asked, "How is it?"

"It's good—strong without being bitter."

"I'll remember that." He opened his menu and then peered at her over the top. "Do you see anything special you'd like to order?"

She hadn't even looked at her menu and picked it up, perusing it. She'd heard the Mediterranean food was fabulous here. "The chicken kebob looks good," she said.

"Do you like salmon?"

While the prices were moderate, the salmon was the costliest item on the menu, and she never ordered expensive food. "I think I'll go with the chicken."

"But do you like salmon?"

"Well, sure, but—"

"Then salmon it will be. Now for your sides?"

"No. I'm not in the mood for salmon." She was tired of men telling her what to do.

"But it's so good for you," he said. "And a green salad with feta and the vegetables would go well with it."

"I eat healthy every day of my life. Tonight, I want to splurge." She glanced at the menu once more. Was he insisting because the salmon was costlier? Was he trying to impress her? If so, she could fix that.

"How about I order the steak and the sides you chose, except leave off the feta," Emma said, closing her menu. She glanced up to find him studying her, like he'd never really seen her before. "What are you having?"

"I think I'll splurge with you," he said with a smile. Corey motioned for the waitress, and she hurried over. When he finished ordering for them both, she said, "I'll be right back with your salads."

"You surprised me a little," he said as soft music played in the background. "I don't often see that side of you."

She almost said "get used to it," but instead she allowed a tiny smile to surface. "I just hated to see you waste your money."

"That was very thoughtful of you," Corey said.

His words were warm, but the slight twitch of his right eye as he unwrapped the napkin around his knife and fork told a different story. Mr. Corey Chandler wasn't accustomed to women not falling right in line with what he wanted.

"Do we want to get business out of the way while we wait for our food?"

"Sure. Maybe we can start with why your client doesn't want the project to start."

"Why don't we start with why you want to do it? I understand from your supervisor the project is your idea."

Corey had been asking around about her. "My reasons are twofold. I want to document the lives of the people who lived in the cabins. And as for the slave cemetery, I think it's important to give dignity to those buried there. They didn't have it when they were alive, but if there's any way possible, they'll have it now." Emma sat back in the chair, warming under his intense scrutiny. "And now I'll get off my soapbox."

"I will give you this—you're very passionate about the project."

"Oh yes."

"Why?" he asked. "Most people are motivated by more than ideals. What's in this for you?"

She blinked. Did she dare tell him one reason was that it would open the door to a promotion and her dream job? Emma lifted her chin. There was nothing wrong with having ambition. "I want to be a National Park Service historian, and competition for those positions is fierce."

Corey smiled. "You would make a good one."

"Does that mean you'll put in a good word for me with your client?"

His blue eyes twinkled. "Yes, and I'll see what I can do to smooth the way for you."

"Who is this client?" Emma knew he wouldn't tell her, but she couldn't keep from asking.

He lifted an eyebrow. “You know I’m not at liberty to give you that information.”

“At least tell me why he doesn’t want the project done.”

The waitress picked that moment to bring their salads, and Corey smiled at her. “Thank you, Amy.”

Emma dipped a piece of lettuce in her raspberry vinaigrette. She was getting pretty good eating with her left hand because she hadn’t given up, and she was not giving up now either. “Is it because I’m not a person of color?”

He coughed and patted his chest. “Sorry. I swallowed wrong.”

“Was it something I said?”

“You are very direct,” he said. “Why is it so important to know who my client is?”

She laid her fork down. “If someone opposed something you very much wanted to do, wouldn’t you want to know about the opposition?”

Corey leaned against the back of the chair. “I suppose. Tell you what, I’ll talk with my client, and perhaps I can make him see that you would be the best person to conduct this project.”

“Would you really?” When he slowly nodded, a smile spread across her face. “Thank you!”

Talk dwindled to almost nothing until they were almost finished with their salads. “So, where did you go to law school?” she asked.

“The University of Mississippi Law School.”

“Ole Miss? Really? What years?”

When he told her, she tilted her head. “I think Trey Carter and Gordon Cole attended Ole Miss then. Did you know them?”

“Not then, but I’ve met them since I moved to Natchez. I didn’t know Trey went to law school.”

“He wanted to be a lawyer, but his dad, Sheriff Carter, had other ideas. Trey ended up with a degree in law enforcement and went to work for his dad as a deputy, and now he’s Nate’s chief deputy.”

Corey tilted his head. "How about you? Where did you go to college?"

"Mississippi State University. I just completed my master's in American history."

"I'm impressed," he said. "How did you find the time?"

"I did most of it online, except when I defended my thesis," she said. "And I think I'm qualified to complete the project at Mount Locust."

"I would say you are. What if I took part in the project? Maybe as an advisor? I'm certain my client would drop their objections if you agreed."

Before she could answer, their main course arrived. "This looks good," she said, avoiding his question. If the client wanted someone of color to oversee the project, Corey didn't fit the bill any better than she did. She paused with her fork in midair. Unless there was no client.

Corey looked up from his food. "What?"

Heat rose on her face. Why did these thoughts pop into her head?

He laid his fork down and then checked the front of his shirt. "Did I spill something?" When she shook her head, he asked, "Then why are you looking at me like that?"

"Why would your client accept you and not me to work on the project?"

"He doesn't know you, but he does know and trust me."

She could see his point, but that didn't mean she had to like it. "With my credentials—"

He stopped her. "I will assure him you will do the job better than anyone else. Satisfied?"

"Yes, and thank you." Sometimes being straightforward worked.

He picked up his fork again. "What did you discover in that hole at Mount Locust?"

55

While the file printed, Sam dialed the number the hospital had given him for the ICU nurses' station. Both Mr. Selby and his daughter were still hanging on and still critical. He disconnected and texted the information to Emma before he relayed the news to Brooke.

"I hope they make it. Emma must be pretty shook up over it," she said and walked to the kitchen.

"She is. I'm going back by her apartment when I leave here." There was a case of water in the corner, and Sam grabbed a bottle, uncapping it.

Brooke came back with a cup of coffee. "So, how is it going between you two?"

He almost spat the water out. "What do you mean?" he said when he quit coughing.

"Anyone can see you two belong together. Never knew why you broke up in the first place," she said. "I take that back. Emma has trouble giving relationships time to gel."

"Why do you think that is?" Sam asked. Maybe if he knew why, he could reduce the fallout when he told her his secret.

Brooke pressed her lips together. "That's something you two should talk about . . . not me and you."

"You're right," he admitted. "But if you have any suggestions . . ."

She thought a minute. "If you hit a rough spot, make Emma talk about her feelings. Don't let her cut and run."

The printer shut off, and Sam retrieved a stack of sheets from the tray. In the query, his parameters had included murders with couples as victims and where the female received flowers from an unknown subject. It appeared that four fell within that framework. He would spread his search nationwide after he looked over this report, if he thought it was warranted.

After scanning the pages, he set aside two of the cases. In one, the murderer was caught prior to Mary Jo's death. In the second case, the flowers the victim received had been roses. Neither of them felt right for a connection to Mary Jo, but he may have found the connection he was looking for in the other two cases.

He made notes on a yellow legal pad as he read the reports. The first murder occurred just outside of Oxford, Mississippi, two years after Mary Jo's death. The man's body was found by hunters. He was shot in the back, just like Sandra Wyatt. The woman was found a couple of days later in a wooded area within half a mile of the man, and the coroner put her death at a day later than the man's. Cause of death was listed as blunt force trauma. She held a crushed daisy in her hand. A family member had told police she'd received a bouquet of daisies just days before she was murdered. The police were never able to discover who had sent the flowers or who committed the murders.

Sam stared at the report, and then he handed the file to Brooke. "Read this and tell me what you think."

He read the next file, writing more notes. This murder had taken place four years ago, and like the other case, the man was murdered first and then the woman, with their bodies found within a mile of each other in a heavily wooded area near Raymond, Mississippi, a small town in Hinds County south of Jackson. Again, the man had been shot and the woman had blunt force trauma. She had received daisies only days before her death.

While no daisies were found at the murder scene, two days after her funeral, a bouquet showed up on her grave.

Sam handed Brooke the second case and then leaned back in his chair as he read the witness reports. In both cases, it appeared the woman had been stalked. "What do you think?" he asked as Brooke laid the second file on the desk.

"Looks like the women were the target of the same stalker." She chewed her bottom lip. "There are four years between these two murders, with the first one occurring two years after Mary Jo and Ryan were killed—if Ryan was killed the same night. I think they were his first kills, then these."

"But why kill the man?"

"They were always first, so to clear the way for the stalker?"

"Could be," he said. "Have you ever heard of erotomania?"

"No. What is it?"

"It's when someone believes another person is in love with them despite clear evidence to the contrary. A couple of famous cases involved Jodie Foster and her stalker, John Hinckley, and then there was Peggy Ray, who stalked David Letterman."

"Yeah, I remember the Hinckley case. He shot a president, trying to impress Foster." She tapped the files. "You think that might be what happened here?"

He sighed. "Possibly. These cases aren't a perfect fit, but I think I'll see what else I can learn about them."

"But if someone was in love with Emma, why would they shoot at her? Twice?"

Sam thought a minute. "We may be dealing with two different shooters. At Mount Locust, what if the killer had come back to remove Ryan's body, and he was just trying to scare her away?"

"But why hadn't he moved it before now?"

"I doubt he would ever have moved the body if the cemetery hadn't been set up to be mapped again," Sam said, trying to think like the killer. "He knew once Ryan's body was identified, Mary Jo's case would be reopened."

"Okay, that explains that shooting, but not the one at Emma's apartment."

He tapped the files. "Maybe this shooter was trying to get rid of me. If I hadn't stooped to get her keys, I would be, if not dead, badly wounded."

Sam checked for the names of the investigating officers. Eric Lane was a detective with the Hinds County Sheriff's Department in Jackson, and Doug Marsh was with the Lafayette Sheriff's Department in Oxford. He looked up the sheriffs' phone numbers in both cities. Neither detective was on duty, but dispatch in Jackson gave him the investigator's cell phone number. He dialed, and when Eric Lane answered, they made arrangements to meet the next morning at nine thirty. Before he disconnected, he asked Lane if he'd ever encountered a case involving erotomania. The detective hadn't, but said he would research it before Sam arrived.

Sam left word for the detective in Oxford to call him, along with a request that he research erotomania. His gut told him these two cases were connected to Mary Jo's case and therefore Emma.

Brooke stood. "I'm headed home." At the door she turned and looked at him. "The person who dug up Ryan's body knew how to operate a backhoe. Have you checked with Guy Armstrong about employees who worked in maintenance ten years ago? If the person who killed them worked for the park service, they would have been familiar with the backhoe . . . they might even know how to start the machine without a key."

Sam gave her a thumbs-up. "Good thinking."

When she left, he looked up Armstrong's phone number and dialed. After Sam identified himself, he said, "Can you get me a list of employees from ten years ago? And how many of them are current maintenance employees?"

"Can I get back to you tomorrow?" Armstrong said. "I'll have to research that."

"Sure."

"Do you just want the names of permanent workers?"

"What do you mean?"

"Well, we had and still have a lot of seasonal employees," the manager said. "Workers like Trey Carter. Every summer when he was in college, he worked for me. I can probably name a couple more if I think about it."

"Yeah, I'd like a list of the seasonal workers as well." Sam stared at the files on the desk. "Did Trey ever operate the backhoe?"

"Yeah. And he was a good worker. I really hoped he'd stay on, but his daddy wanted him in the sheriff's department. Anyway, I'll get you a list of names tomorrow."

Sam hung up and tented his fingers. So, Trey Carter was working as a park service maintenance employee ten years ago.

56

Sam gathered the files scattered across the desk and slid them into an envelope. He'd tried to reach Trey, but he didn't answer. After he tried again, Sam dialed Nate's number.

"Rawlings," the sheriff answered.

"Ryker here. I'm trying to reach Trey, but he's not answering."

"He took a few days off to go deer hunting before the season ends," Nate said. "Whatcha need?"

"Did you know he worked for the park service ten years ago as a seasonal maintenance worker?"

"No. Are you saying he might be involved in Mary Jo's and Ryan's deaths?"

"Not yet, but according to the maintenance director, Trey worked for him most summers during his college years, operating a backhoe. I want to talk to him." Vehicle lights flashed across the window. "Do you know where he is?"

"He's at his cabin. I've been there, but it's been a while. I'll get the directions and call you back."

"Good deal." After exchanging a few more words, Sam hung up and walked to the door. He frowned. Was that a motor running? Maybe Clayton had returned from his rounds. When he opened the door, a tan Civic that looked a lot like his sister's car idled in the parking lot. What was she doing here? If there was an emergency, she would have called. It was too dark to see who was driving, and he rested his hand on his gun as he approached the car. The window lowered, and Sam stepped back when he recognized his father behind the wheel.

"Hello, Sam."

"What do you want?" he asked through a rigid jaw.

"You won't come to me, so I thought I'd come to you," his father said, then he took a deep breath. "I want to apologize and ask your forgiveness."

"You've got to be kidding."

"I'm not." His dad's gaze skittered away, and neither of them spoke. He lifted his chin and looked Sam in the eye. "I was a terrible father, and I'm sorry for everything I ever did to you."

Sam narrowed his eyes. "Don't you think it's a little late for an apology?"

Even in the dim light from overhead, his father's face turned white. Or had it already been white?

"I don't blame you for being angry, son—"

"Don't call me that."

His dad dipped his head, and he pressed his lips together. "All right, but I wanted you to know I'm not the person I used to be."

He waited for his dad to continue, but the silence grew until it was broken by the haunting sound of an owl's hoot. Sam tapped the side of his leg. "Well, if there's nothing else, I need to be somewhere."

His dad's shoulders drooped. "Sure. I just wanted to try to make amends before . . ."

"There are some things in life you can't undo."

"I know. And I'll have to live with what I did to you and your mom the rest of my life. However long that will be. I thank God every day that she's forgiven me. I certainly don't deserve it." He cleared his throat. "And I wanted you to know how proud I am of you," he said, his voice breaking.

The words Sam had wanted to hear his entire childhood

threatened to buckle his legs. He stiffened his back and folded his arms across his chest. He was not forgiving his father. Not tonight. Not ever.

The older man sighed. "I just have one more thing to say, Samuel, and then I'll leave you alone. If you hold on to this hatred, it will destroy you."

With those words, he closed the window, and the car slowly rolled toward the Trace. Was it possible his father had changed? "*You'll never amount to anything.*" The memory of the words hardened his heart, and Sam turned and walked to his SUV.

He checked his watch. A little after eight. Emma probably wasn't home from her dinner with Corey Chandler, and Sam certainly didn't want to go to his sister's and face that inquisition. Why was his dad driving Jenny's car, anyway? If Sam were a betting man, he'd bet his dad lost his in a card game. Drinking and gambling had been his vices of choice.

When he parked in front of Emma's apartment, her lights were on. Sam climbed out of his SUV and used the key she'd given him to unlock the front door. Once inside, he hurried up the stairs and rang Emma's doorbell. Surprise showed on her face when she opened the door.

"Sam? I wasn't expecting you tonight." She stepped back. "Come on in."

"Are you busy?" he asked as he crossed the threshold into the entry hall.

"Just posting a few things on Facebook," she said.

"You seemed surprised when you opened the door," he said. "Didn't you check the camera app?"

"I did. I'm just surprised you came back. Would you like a cup of decaf?"

"Not tonight. I thought you might like to know what I found out from RISS." He couldn't keep from noticing she wore makeup and that she'd dressed up. For Corey? Not necessarily for him, but he had taken her to a nice restaurant, and it was only natural she'd dressed accordingly. Maybe it was time he asked her out to someplace special.

"Well?" She followed him into the living room. "What did you find out?"

Sam brought his attention back to the case. "Are you off tomorrow?"

She nodded.

"You want to drive up to Jackson in the morning?" He explained what he'd discovered. "I have a nine thirty appointment with the detective in charge of the investigation at the Hinds County Sheriff's Department."

"I'd love to." Then she eyed him suspiciously. "But I thought you were cutting me out of the investigation."

He didn't want to tell her he feared she might get into more trouble on her own than if she was with him. "You want to go or not?"

"Of course I do, but—"

"Okay!" He raised his hands. "If I'm not going to be in town, I like knowing you're safe."

Her eyes widened. "Oh. How about Oxford? Will we go there as well?"

"It depends on how much time it takes in Jackson. Oxford is not quite two hours from the capital, but it'd be a four-hour trip back."

"What time do you want to leave?"

"Seven thirty, quarter to eight?" His cell phone rang. Nate. "Ryker," he answered.

"I have the directions to Trey's cabin," Nate said. "I'm emailing them to you."

"Thanks. Which direction is it in?"

"It's thirty miles south of Natchez off 61, back in the boonies," Nate said. "You don't want to try to find it at night."

"Do you know how long he planned to be off?" Maybe he could wait until Trey returned to work.

"He said a few days."

"I'm going to Jackson tomorrow morning. If I get back in time, would you like to ride along to his cabin?"

"Probably a good idea. I've at least been there once."

Sam disconnected and turned to Emma. "Sorry."

"What was that about?"

"Trey. Did you know he worked for the park service maintenance crew during the summers when he was in college? And he operated the backhoes."

"You're kidding. That means he would be familiar with how they work. Have you asked him about it?"

"Not yet. He's off hunting, and that was Nate giving me directions to his cabin. I hope I have time to look him up tomorrow, which means we definitely won't be going to Oxford."

"You don't seriously think he killed Ryan and buried him at Mount Locust, do you?"

"Someone did."

"But that would mean he killed Mary Jo and these other cases you found as well. I just don't see Trey doing anything like that."

"You never completely know a person. He and Gordon and your brother were drinking that night, and they could've gotten into a fight after they left the tavern." His mother's ringtone sounded on his cell phone. "Hold on a minute. It's my mom." He punched the answer button. "Hello?"

"Sam, you have to come to the hospital."

His heart pounded in his chest. "What happened? Are you all right?"

"It's not me. It's your dad. He's had a heart attack."

57

As he listened to the live feed on his phone, he cleaned the .22 rifle and laid it next to the .22 semiautomatic pistol that had been his mother's gun.

The bug had proven to be invaluable. It kept him one step ahead of Ryker, but now another problem had cropped up. One he should have taken care of a long time ago. He picked up the pistol, aimed it at the door, and slowly squeezed the trigger.

Click.

He frowned. Ryker was going to talk with the investigators in Jackson and Oxford. Had he put the murders together? It didn't matter if he had. There was nothing linking him to the cases.

Both women had been just like his mother. He'd tried to tell them the men they were dating were no good, but just like his mother, they wouldn't listen. They kept taking the men back time after time. He hadn't meant to kill them. The men, yes, but not them.

Just like he would kill Ryker. And soon too.

Suddenly memories bombarded him, spiraling him down the rabbit hole. *He was a boy again, holding his mother's hand. She was acting strange, like she'd taken too many of her happy pills, and she smelled funny. A scent he now recognized as whiskey.*

They walked up the steps to the old house, and he was scared.

"Mama, I thought Daddy was at work."

"Hush, boy. We don't want him to hear us."

As quiet as mice, they crept inside. Voices. His daddy's and someone else's. A woman. Why did his mama have a gun?

"No!" That was his daddy yelling. The woman screamed.

Bang!

He pressed his hands against his ears and squeezed his eyes shut.

When he opened them, his daddy was leaning over his mama. "Why, Margaret? Why did you do it?"

He stared at the blood pooling around his mother's body. It was all his fault. He should have protected her. This would never again happen to someone he loved.

Static on the bug jerked him back to the present. It was time to take care of his new problem, one he hadn't anticipated. Why were people so greedy? If he paid him to keep his mouth shut, it would only be the beginning.

He glanced down at the directions he'd been given to bring the money. Only it wasn't money he was delivering and not at the appointed time. It would be done tonight, then he would be free to follow Ryker to Jackson. Maybe he would even have the opportunity to dispose of the ranger.

58

Sam had turned chalk white. "What's wrong?" Emma asked when he disconnected.

He tapped his phone against his hand. "It's . . . my father. He's had a heart attack, and Mom wants me to come to the hospital."

"I'll go with you. Give me a second to change into jeans." She hurried to the hall.

"I don't know that I'm going."

Emma stopped and turned around. "You have to. Your mother needs you. And Jenny. She needs you too."

Sam paced her living room floor. He stopped by the window. "What if I'm responsible for his heart attack?"

"That's crazy thinking," she said.

He pinched the bridge of his nose. "No, it isn't. He came by the Port Gibson office while I was there tonight. Wanted to apologize . . . asked for my forgiveness."

"And you didn't give it to him."

"I can't."

She took his hand. "No, Sam," she said gently. "It's not that you can't forgive him, it's that you won't."

His face hardened. "You don't understand." He shoved his hands in his pockets and turned and faced the window. "I have scars on my back where he whipped me with a leather belt until the blood ran down my legs. I was ten, and he was drunk and told me to get him another beer. I made the mistake of telling him he'd had enough."

Emma pressed her fingers to her mouth. She'd had no idea.

He turned to her. "Even as bad as the scars on my back are, the scars he created inside me after that are harder to bear. Mom threatened to have him arrested if he ever hit me again, and she made him go to rehab."

"So, it got better?"

He barely raised one shoulder. "He never hit me again, but he never lost an opportunity to tell me how worthless I was. I can't count the times he told me he wished I'd never been born, that he could've had a good life if it hadn't been for me."

She slipped her arms around his waist and pulled him close the way she would a child who was hurt. Slowly he relaxed, and she laid her head against his chest, hearing the thud of his heart. "I'm so sorry."

"It hardly seems fair that he lives his life the way he wants to, and at the end, it's all wiped away. He doesn't deserve it."

She searched for words to comfort him with, but the only ones that came to her were likely to anger Sam. "None of us deserve it."

Emma felt his breath still as her words brought a thick silence.

"Yeah, that's what my mom always says." He was silent for a minute, then he said, "Forgiveness should be true, from the heart. Not because it's what I'm supposed to do. I don't feel like forgiving him."

"Sometimes we do the right thing even when we don't feel like it," she said. "If you do, the feelings will follow. Eventually."

"Fake it until you make it?" His voice was laced with sarcasm.

"Something like that." She didn't seem to be getting through to him. "Maybe if you knew why he was like he was, it would help bring closure."

"I don't need closure. I just need everyone to get off my back about him."

"But he's not the only one affected. Your mom needs you right now, and you're not there. I think you should go to the hospital if for no other reason than to be with her. And your sister."

Sam stared at her, resistance stamped on his face, but there was something more, something she recognized. Guilt. That she knew well. "I'll go with you." She tugged him toward the door.

Surprisingly he followed. When she turned to lock her door, he said, "I'm just going to support Mom and Jenny. I'm not going in to see him."

"That's up to you, but if he dies before you work this out, you'll be the one left behind. What if down the road, you have regrets? Regrets you'll deal with the rest of your life." She knew how that felt, but could she tell Sam? "I . . ." She swallowed and began again. "I would give anything to tell Ryan I'm sorry for what I said to him the night he disappeared."

"What do you mean?"

"I've never told anyone. We were alone and Ryan was being Ryan. Mean drunk. I . . . told him I wished he'd leave and never come back. Those were the last words I ever spoke to him."

"Oh, Emma." He put his arms around her. "You didn't mean it, and he knew that."

"That's just it—I did mean it. I was so angry. He'd ruined our birthday—we'd had a good time until he kept drinking and got nasty." She looked up at him. "Now he's gone, and I can't take back the words. If you don't give your dad a chance, you'll never know what might be."

"I don't know—"

"Just promise me you'll think about it."

He stared at her for a long minute. "I'll think about it."

"Good."

Sam followed her to his SUV and opened the passenger door. By the time she had her seat belt fastened, he was getting in on the other side. Emma's apartment was only five minutes from the hospital, and they were soon walking through the doors of the emergency room waiting area, where they were told his dad had been transferred to the ICU.

They rode the elevator in silence, and after they stepped off, they followed the signs to the ICU waiting room. His mom, Rachel, stood when she saw Sam, and Emma followed as he went straight to her. Emma squeezed her hand when Rachel turned to her. "Thank you for coming."

She nodded and stepped back as Sam's sister leaned into his hug, totally ignoring Emma except for shooting a hard glare at her. She believed the woman truly hated her.

"How is he?" Emma asked Rachel.

"They're getting him ready for a heart cath," she replied. "His cardiologist believes he has a blockage in the main artery that's barely letting blood through."

"Are they going to do surgery?" Sam asked.

"The doctor hopes he can put a stent in the artery and not have to open him up, but if not, yes."

Sam nodded and turned to Jenny. "Where's Jace?"

"I dropped him off at a friend's house."

The Ryker name was called, and everyone turned toward the nurse who approached them. "Mrs. Ryker?"

Rachel nodded.

"He wants to see you before we take him to the cath lab," she said.

His mother turned to Sam. "Come with us. Please."

He stiffened and shook his head. "I . . . I can't."

Emma didn't know how he could turn down the pleading in his mother's eyes. Then his mother's shoulders dropped and she lifted her chin. "No. You're choosing not to go with us." Still holding her head high, she followed the nurse through the ICU doors.

"Come on, Sam," Jenny said. "It won't kill you, and it may save his life."

His head jerked back as though she'd slapped him. Emma touched his arm. "You don't have to say anything, but your presence might make a difference. Give him something to fight for."

She thought he was going to refuse, but just before the doors closed, Sam swallowed hard. "Hold the door," he said.

59

They stopped outside a room with a curtain pulled across the window. Sam's mother looked up at him. "Thanks, son. I know this is hard."

He pressed his lips together to keep from asking how she could be there. And why was she taking care of her ex-husband now after the way he'd treated her? While Sam had never seen his mother physically abused by his father, Sam had seen him ridicule her, and he knew for a fact he'd cheated on her.

When his mom discovered the lashes on Sam's back, she had kicked his dad out of the house until he got help with his anger issues and drinking problem. Then his old man had conned her into letting him come home after completing an alcohol rehab. She'd finally divorced him when she caught him cheating with a neighbor, but by that time Sam was out of the house. What in the world had he said to get back in her good graces?

Sam was drawn to the bed in spite of his resolve. The man lying in the bed was pasty with dark shadows under his eyes. *Broken* was the only word Sam could think of to describe how he looked. How much had he actually changed? *He apologized.* Sam had to admit the man he remembered never believed he'd done anything to apologize for.

His dad's eyes fluttered open, then widened, and became shiny.

"You came," he whispered.

Sam waited for the dig to come, words like *You must think you're going to get something out of this*. Or *What do you want?*

Instead his dad simply smiled. "Thank you."

Sam nodded curtly as his mother and sister crowded closer to the bed. "You're going to be fine," his mother said. "The doctor is very optimistic that he can patch you up."

"Yeah, Dad," Jenny said. "Just hang in there."

"You're a good woman, Rachel. You too, Jenny. I don't deserve you." His gaze never left Sam's face. "You either, son."

Sam couldn't keep from flinching, and pain crossed his father's eyes.

"Could you leave me and Sam alone a minute?" he asked.

Panic surged through him. He didn't want to be alone with this man. Sam may have already caused him to have one heart attack. Maybe what his dad said was true, and he couldn't do anything right.

"You sure?" his mother asked, looking from her husband to her son.

"If he'll stay . . ." His dad's voice trailed off.

"I'll stay." He had no choice. But it didn't mean Sam had to believe anything his father said.

"We'll be in the waiting room." The two women stepped outside the room.

When they were alone, his dad said, "I want to thank you for taking care of your mother when I let her down."

Sam wasn't expecting that. "I didn't have much choice." He cringed at the bitterness in his voice—exactly what he'd been afraid of. He tried again. "I hear you have a brokerage firm now."

"Yeah. I know you didn't have a choice." The monitor over his head beeped faster as his heart rate increased. "I was a miserable failure as a husband and a father. I want you to know I don't blame you for not forgiving me."

He stared at the man in the bed. *Sometimes we do the right thing even when we don't feel like it.* "How about we talk about this after your surgery? Who knows, maybe we can work something out."

His dad's eyes widened, then he blinked them furiously. "Thank you," he said, his voice cracking. "That's more than I ever hoped for."

It took all Sam had in him to not look away. "Why don't I get Mom and Jenny back in here before they come after you."

His dad gave him a thumbs-up.

Maybe he shouldn't have led his dad to believe they would talk later, but his conscience wouldn't let him do anything else. Anyone going into the cath lab and possibly surgery needed every advantage, and Sam wasn't going to be responsible for taking one away, especially since he might be the reason his dad was here. He pushed the button that opened the ICU doors, and his mother and sister stood waiting on the other side. "I told him I'd come get you."

"Thanks, son." His mother squeezed his arm. "And thank you for what you did."

"Don't," Sam said. "I—"

"No, don't say you didn't do anything. It took a big man to offer him hope."

A lump formed in his throat. "You better hurry if you want to see him before they come get him."

He turned to where Emma stood waiting. "How did it go?"

Sam blew out a breath. "I feel like a hypocrite." He scanned the room. "Do you see any place to get a cup of coffee?"

"Over in the corner."

He followed her to a small eating area and waited while an older woman poured her coffee. When she turned around, Emma's eyes widened.

"Ms. Carter, I hope nothing is seriously wrong with your family," she said. Then she turned to Sam. "This is Trey's aunt."

Her hands were full, so he simply nodded. "I'm Sam Ryker."

She returned his nod and then moved so they could pour their coffee. "TJ's here," the older woman said. "He fell at the assisted living place, and the nurse insisted that he get checked out."

"I hope he'll be okay," Emma said.

Sam shot her a curious look. He knew for a fact she couldn't stand the former sheriff. Maybe it was another one of those do-the-right-thing instances.

"He had a CAT scan and was transferred to ICU. They haven't told me anything other than he's dehydrated. I'm afraid they'll find a brain bleed." Her voice wavered. "But the assisted living center didn't send anyone to help me with him, and he's throwing one fit after another. I can't reach Trey at his cabin—there's absolutely no cell service out there. He's the only one who can handle his father other than the male nurses at the facility."

"I'm sorry," Emma said.

Tears filled the older woman's eyes. "My brother doesn't want to be here, and he's difficult on the best of days. Tonight he's ordering me to get him out of here, and then he tried to pull out his IV. They've tied his arms to the bed, and that's made him even worse."

Emma patted her shoulder. "Do you think it would help if Sam talked to him?"

She turned and stared at Sam. "Would you? He seems to respond better to men, plus you have on a uniform. He may respect that."

Sam took a step back. "I-I'm not sure what I can do . . ."

"Just tell him you know Trey, and that he sent word for him to behave."

How did he get himself into things like this . . . Emma. She was the one who volunteered him. He turned to her, and she was encouraging him with her eyes.

"I think you should talk to him," Emma said.

Finally he got it. This would be a chance to talk to the former sheriff. "Will they let me in to see him?"

"They should—it's still visiting time."

"What room?"

"The third one on the right after you go through the doors."

Once again, Sam walked through the ICU doors, this time pausing outside Carter's room. He wasn't certain how to question an Alzheimer's patient. He rapped on the door and didn't wait for an invitation to enter. A nurse stood by the bed, hanging a bag on the IV pole while she ignored the man's string of curses. She looked around.

"Can I help you?" she asked.

"The sheriff's sister sent me in here to talk to him."

"Are you his son, Trey?"

Sam shook his head. "A friend of Trey's." He stepped closer to the bed. The former sheriff had stopped his cursing and regarded Sam with wary eyes.

"Do I know you?" Carter growled.

"I'm Sam Ryker, the Natchez Trace chief law enforcement ranger," he said, using his I'm-in-charge-here voice.

Immediately the sheriff's demeanor changed. "How can I help you, officer?"

"I have a case I'd like your advice on," he said, "if the nurse will allow it."

"Whatever it takes to calm him down," she said, palming her hand as she walked to the door. "I'll be nearby if you need me."

"Just a minute," Carter said. "Untie my hands. I can't discuss a case all trussed up like this."

She wavered, and he let loose another string of words that burned Sam's ears. "How about I untie the one with the IV? And only if you promise not to pull it out."

Once he promised, she removed the restraint and then left them alone. Sam pulled up a chair near the bed and sat down, hoping to convey to Carter the impression they were equals. Carter tried to pull himself up. "Hold on, and I'll raise your bed," Sam said.

"Thank you," he said when Sam had elevated him to a sitting

position. "Now, this case you need help with, does it tie in to any of my recent cases?"

Carter thought he was still the sheriff. Maybe Sam could use that to his advantage. "No, it's an older case. But first, you have to promise to quit giving these nurses and your sister a fit. That's what Trey would tell you if he was here."

"Where is that pup? He ain't been worth a dime since his ma died." Carter narrowed his eyes. "He had no business letting them bring me here. Ain't nothin' wrong with me."

"You're dehydrated. As soon as they get fluids in you, you'll go home."

He tried to cross his arms, but the restraint on his right hand stopped him. "Well, why in tarnation didn't they tell me that?"

"That I can't say, but if you want to go home, do what they say and quit giving them trouble."

"Tell me about the case."

"It involves Ryan Winters and Mary Jo Selby."

The heart monitor briefly went crazy, then after an initial flurry of beats, it returned to its steady rhythm. "What about it?"

"Why is there no file on the case?"

Carter seemed to assess Sam. "You say you're a friend of Trey's?"

"I am. I was at the Hideaway with your son and Ryan Winters."

"Gordy was with you too."

Sam nodded. He didn't know how bad Carter's Alzheimer's was, but tonight his mind was clear. He hoped it held. "What do you know about that night?"

Carter didn't answer right away; instead he felt his pocket and cursed. "They took my cigarettes."

He gave the older man a minute, and when he didn't say anything, Sam asked, "What happened to the file on the Selby murder?"

"Should be there . . . unless Trey moved it. He's my chief deputy, you know."

"Yeah." He leaned forward, encouraging the former sheriff to continue.

Carter took a deep breath. "He didn't murder that girl."

Interesting way of answering, considering Sam hadn't asked if Trey had killed Mary Jo. "How about Ryan?"

"Him either."

"But Trey knows something about what happened?"

The former sheriff's eyes turned cagey. "I told my boy to keep his nose clean. I had an election that year and that girl's death cost me votes. If word had gotten out—"

Abruptly the monitor went crazy again with beeps and a buzzer sounding. Carter's face turned white, and he pressed his hand against his chest. The door flew open, and the nurse charged in. She motioned toward the door. "You're out of here."

Sam didn't move. He was so close to getting his answer.

She fisted her hands on her hips. "Now!"

He shot Carter a look of frustration. "Yes, ma'am. Can I come back when—"

"Absolutely not. You upset him, and I'm not allowing that to happen again."

60

While Sam was back with Sheriff Carter, Emma checked on George Selby and his daughter. There'd been no change—both were extremely critical. Her heart heavy, she walked to the magazine rack and looked for something to read. Their area of the waiting room had pretty well cleared out. Ms. Carter was in a corner recliner, and Rachel had gone to the restroom, leaving Emma and Jenny. Sam's sister paced near the phone as she waited for news from the doctor.

Emma looked up as Jenny stopped in front of her. "Where'd you say Sam went?"

"Sheriff Carter's sister asked him to try to calm her brother down." Emma tensed at the anger in Jenny's voice. "What do you have against me?"

Jenny stared at her. "You have to ask? You're leading my brother on."

"What are you talking about?"

"You're going to break his heart again, just like ten years ago."

Jenny's words stung. "No. I—"

"Yes, you will. I've watched you do it with every man you date. You date them a while, then you find something wrong with them and break it off."

Emma stiffened as heat blazed in her face. "I do not."

Jenny rattled off the names of four men, including Trey, that

Emma had dated. "You're telling me you didn't lead them on and then drop them when you got bored?"

"Those relationships just didn't work out," Emma protested. "It's different with your brother. I . . . I really care for him."

"You won't feel that way when you know the whole truth about that night. And then you'll break his heart all over again."

Lead settled in Emma's stomach. "What are you talking about?"

"Sam hasn't told you everything. He'd already left your brother at the Hideaway when I called him for help."

"What do you mean?"

"Just what I said—I know he told you he left Ryan to come help me, but Sam had left the Hideaway half an hour before I called him that night."

The words hit Emma like a shotgun blast.

"Jenny!" Sam strode toward them. "This is not your concern."

"It will be when she dumps you. I don't want to see you hurt again."

Emma turned to Sam. "You said you left to help her with a flat tire . . ." His face had turned as pale as the white wall behind him. "That's not true?"

"I did go help her, but . . ." His shoulders dropped, and he wouldn't meet her eyes. He sucked in a breath and expelled it. "Ryan and I had an argument in the parking lot. He swung and hit me in the jaw. I shoved him, he fell down, and then I walked away and got in my car. I was almost home when Jenny called. Then after Ryan went missing, you somehow got the idea I left *because* Jenny called, and I let you believe it. Not that we talked much after that."

The bottom fell out of her stomach, and she stumbled to a chair. All this time he'd let her believe a lie. "Why didn't you tell me before now?"

"I've tried," he said.

"Well, you didn't try hard enough." She backed away from him. "I'm leaving."

"You can't," he said. "You don't have transportation."

"I'll call an Uber." She turned and almost bumped into Sam's mom.

Rachel grabbed Emma to steady herself. "I heard what Jenny said. Don't leave."

She tried to break free. "I can't stay."

The hospital phone rang, and they all froze. Jenny snatched the receiver up and listened. "This is the Ryker family."

As she listened again, the air seemed to go out of her and she sank into the chair beside the phone. "Thank you," she said and looked up, her eyes shiny. "They were able to stent the blockage. The doctor will be out to talk to us shortly."

Emma was glad for them, but she had to get out of there. "I have to go."

"Please don't leave," Sam said. "You ran away ten years ago. Don't do it again."

She took a step back. Running was what she did best.

His chin jutted and he rested his hand on his gun. "I'll put you in protective custody if I have to."

"You wouldn't!"

Determination radiated off Sam like heat. "Someone tried to kill Mr. Selby and his daughter just this afternoon because of Mary Jo and Ryan's case. Any judge in Natchez will give me a protective order." His eyes pleaded with her to stay. "Your apartment is much more comfortable than the jail, and if you'll wait, I'll take you home in a few minutes."

There was no doubt in her mind that if she tried to leave, Sam would do what he threatened. The fight went out of her and she huffed a breath. "I'll stay, but I'm not talking to you."

Crossing her arms over her chest, Emma marched to another section of the waiting room and plopped into a vinyl chair. Once again, she felt like she'd been sucker punched, and nothing Sam said would change what he'd done. She grabbed a magazine and thumbed through it, not really seeing the pictures or articles.

"You ready?" Sam asked.

She hadn't seen him approach and just about jumped out of her skin. "Yes," she said stiffly.

Neither of them spoke on the elevator ride to the first floor. When the doors opened, she started out and Sam told her to hold the door open and wait. Once he'd checked out the lobby, he motioned her off. "Walk close to me," he said.

Either the words or the seriousness in his voice penetrated her wall of anger, and suddenly the distance to his SUV in the darkened parking lot seemed like a hundred miles. She swallowed hard and didn't pull away when he used his hand to guide her. Within minutes they pulled into the parking area behind Emma's apartment.

"I think this is the safest way in and out," he said.

She'd been surprised Sam hadn't tried to defend himself on the way home. "You're probably right."

He cleared his throat. "Thanks for making me go to the hospital tonight."

That was the last thing she'd expected him to say. "You're welcome, but I think you would have come to that decision without me."

"Maybe," he said. "Sit tight until I can come around."

Silly her, thinking he would just let her get out and walk up to the apartment by herself. "Sure."

He hovered close as they climbed the steps and she unlocked the back door. Once inside, he moved quickly through each room while she waited in the living room.

"All clear," he said when he finished.

"Thank you." She couldn't bring herself to look at him, staring at the floor instead.

"Do you have any coffee?"

She jerked her head up. "You're not leaving?"

"No. A good friend advised me earlier tonight not to let you cut and run, so we need to talk."

Had to have been Brooke. Emma walked to the kitchen on wooden legs to make a pot of coffee. “Decaf?”

“Leaded if you don’t mind.”

She waited while the coffee brewed, then took a cup to him on the sofa before returning for her own. She waited for him to speak, but the silence grew until she couldn’t stand it. “Did you learn anything from Sheriff Carter?”

“Not a lot.” He related what the former sheriff had said. “And then something happened to his heart, and the nurse ran me off.”

Emma processed the information Sam had shared. “Do you think Trey could have killed Mary Jo and Ryan?”

“I don’t know. I want to question him, but it’ll be after I question the detectives. Are you going with me?”

She hadn’t thought that far ahead. It would mean spending at least four hours alone with Sam . . .

“I shouldn’t have let you believe a lie about what happened with Ryan at the Hideaway. I wanted to tell you the truth a long time ago, but I truly was going to tell you tonight.”

It was easy enough to say that. “Why tonight?”

“You’re not going to believe this, but I decided to tell you when I was talking to my father.”

“What do you mean?”

“I realized if I couldn’t forgive him, then I couldn’t expect you to forgive me if I told you the truth. And I knew then I couldn’t go another day without telling you the truth.”

“You’ve forgiven your father?”

Sam nodded. “I’m still angry, but I don’t hate him any longer. Do I want to hang out with him? No, but a very wise person once told me if I do the right thing even when I don’t feel like it, the feelings will follow.”

Now he was using her own words against her. But not really. “Even if I forgive you, it doesn’t mean I’ll want to hang out with you.”

“I’ll take that.” A grin pulled at his lips. “But unless you want to hire a bodyguard, you'll be stuck with me until this case is over." Then he took a sip of his coffee. "And you do make good coffee, but I need to leave—we should be on the road by seven thirty in the morning."

When he walked to the front door, she said, "Did you forget which way we came in?"

"No. I want to walk the perimeter before I leave. Be sure and deadbolt the door behind me."

She followed him, but before she could close her door, the one at the end apartment opened, and Gordon Cole stepped into the hallway, followed by her neighbor, Taylor. He kissed her soundly and then turned around to leave. His eyes widened. "You two startled me," he said. "I didn't know anyone was within five miles of here."

That was obvious, and Emma hid a smile. Dr. Gordon Cole was totally smitten with her neighbor.

"Do you have a minute?" Sam asked. "I have a couple of questions I'd like to run by you."

Gordon frowned and checked his watch. "I can give you a few minutes. What kind of questions are you talking about?"

"I'd rather not say out here in the hall. Can you stop by Emma's a second?"

The doctor glanced back at Taylor and nodded. "See you tomorrow at eight?"

"Yes," Taylor said, "and be on time."

Emma followed the two men inside her apartment. She had no idea what Sam wanted to talk to Gordon about.

Gordon's smile faded. "What's this all about?"

"I was talking to Sheriff Carter tonight," Sam said, "and he made a remark that left me with more questions than answers."

"Oh? Why would you pay any attention to anything he said? The man has Alzheimer's."

"He seemed pretty clear tonight when he said Trey wasn't responsible for Mary Jo Selby's death."

Gordon stared at Sam, and his Adam's apple bobbed. Slowly he shook his head. "I can't help you there since I don't have a clue what he was talking about."

Emma didn't believe him. "Are you saying you don't remember anything?"

"That's exactly what I'm saying."

"Come on, Gordy," Sam said. "You left the Hideaway with Trey and Ryan the night Mary Jo died, and she was with you."

"That was a long time ago, and I was pretty out of it that night." He palmed his hands. "By the time we left the Hideaway, I was wasted."

"Where'd you go?" Sam asked.

"I don't know. I remember leaving the tavern and nothing else until Trey dropped me off at my folks' house. That's it." Gordon's face had turned pasty, and sweat beaded his upper lip. "Anything in between is gone, but why don't you ask Trey? He was the one who wasn't drinking much."

"I plan to." Sam's frustration spilled over into his voice. He took a card from his wallet and handed it to the doctor. "If you remember anything, give me a call."

"Of course, but I doubt anything more will come to me."

After he left, she looked at Sam. "Do you believe he doesn't remember anything?"

"No. He's hiding something, just like Sheriff Carter."

61

After a restless night, Sam crawled out of bed at six. He tried to avoid Jenny, who was already up and getting Jace ready for school. He was still angry at her for her outburst at the hospital.

Sam called the hospital to check on George Selby and his daughter and was told they were slightly improved but still critical. Then he texted his mom to check on her and received a message back that his dad was better and that he would go home today.

Home to the house they'd once shared until the divorce. Another text hit his phone, his mom asking when he would drop by the house. His finger hovered over the keys, and then he shoved his phone in his pocket. He wasn't ready for that. Sam had held on to his anger for so long it was hard to let it go. What if Emma had the same trouble forgiving him? He slipped his phone back out. *Soon*, he texted.

Jenny came into the kitchen while he was drinking his second cup of coffee. She poured herself a mug, and cupping it in her hands, she turned to him. "All right. I'm sorry for what I said to Emma last night."

"You should be. Why did you do that?"

She jutted her chin. "To show you Emma Winters would throw you under the bus the first chance she got."

He had to believe Emma would come around. "Did it ever occur to you I might be in love with her?"

"All the more reason for her to know before you invest any more of yourself in the relationship."

"Who made you God?"

"Look, I apologized. I don't want to see you hurt again."

"I'm a big boy now. I think I can take care of myself, and I'm not sure you should be handing out romantic advice, anyway." The flash of hurt in her face made him wish he could call the words back as soon as they left his mouth. "I'm sorry, Jenny. That wasn't fair."

"No, it wasn't."

"The thing is, it's like I've been hit by a two-ton truck. Emma is the only woman I've ever wanted to marry."

Jenny gaped as she stared at him. The words surprised even him.

"But don't you understand? That could never happen until she knew the truth about what happened between you and Ryan," she said. "Look, I did you a favor. If you two can overcome this, you may have a chance."

He glared at her. "Don't do me any more favors."

She glared back at him over her coffee. "Don't worry, I won't."

Running feet sounded down the hall. "Sam!" Jace cried as he bounded into the kitchen. "Can you take me to the soccer game this afternoon? And can I have pancakes for breakfast, Mom?"

Disappointment hit Sam hard. "I'm sorry, Jace, but I have business in Jackson today. I may not be back in town in time to take you." And if he was, he needed to look Trey Carter up.

The boy dropped his head. "But all the dads will be there, and if you don't go, I'll just have Mom."

"What am I?" his mom asked. "Chopped meat?"

"Aw, Mom, you know what I mean."

Sam glanced out the window. "It's raining—maybe the game will be canceled."

"It's supposed to quit by noon," Jenny said and pulled out the makings for pancakes. "Jace, you just have to accept that Sam is busy today. Maybe your grandfather can take you."

No way. "You know he's not physically able." Sam would just have to find a way to be back by three. There should be enough time after the game to find Trey. "I'll rearrange my schedule and pick Jace up after school."

"Are you sure?" Jenny asked as she mixed the batter.

"Yes." He ruffled Jace's hair.

"You don't mind if I come watch, do you?" Jenny asked.

"Of course not, Mom." The boy looked up at Sam. "You're the best uncle in the world."

"I don't know about that," Sam replied with a laugh.

"Jace, bring your homework so I can check it while you're eating," she said. After Jace left, Jenny poured a small circle of batter on the griddle. "How many pancakes do you want?"

"None, thank you. I plan to grab breakfast before the drive to Jackson," he said as Jace returned with his homework.

A few minutes later, Jenny put the stack of pancakes in front of her son. "Here you go." Then she turned to Sam. "Do you have time to look over his math while I look at his spelling homework?"

Sam hesitated, wanting to get on the road. But helping out with Jace was the main reason he'd returned to Natchez. He resisted checking his watch. "Sure. Hand it over here."

The boy was neater than Sam had ever been. "Looks good. You must like math."

"I do. Better than spelling."

Jenny handed his papers back. "And it shows. You've misspelled three words in your sentences."

"Where?"

"That's for you to find while I finish dressing."

Jace groaned. "Would you help me, Sam?"

"And no, your uncle can't help you," she called from the hallway.

"I'd like to, but you heard your mom. Besides, I have to leave."

"It'll be your fault if I get a bad grade."

The boy was a con, for sure. "No. It'll be your fault. You can find them."

A few minutes later, Sam dialed Emma's number as he backed out of the drive. "Would you like breakfast?" he asked when she answered.

"No, thanks. I've already eaten."

His stomach dipped at her cool tone. "I'll be there in a few minutes."

He stopped by McDonald's and picked up a sausage and egg biscuit and another cup of coffee and ate on the way. Emma was ready when he arrived, and they were soon on the Trace headed to Jackson, with the windshield wipers keeping a steady rhythm as they drove the deserted road. The atmosphere in the SUV was as gloomy as outside. He kept a check in his rearview mirror as the miles rolled off, occasionally catching sight of a pickup.

"My supervisor okayed me to work at Mount Locust tomorrow instead of Melrose," she said after miles of silence.

He remembered that Mount Locust was only open to the public Thursday through Sunday. "I should be free to take you there."

"If not, I can hitch a ride with Brooke." She turned to him. "What do you hope to learn from this detective we're going to see?"

"I'm not sure. Maybe find the connection to these murders and Mary Jo. And Ryan."

"It still doesn't feel real that Ryan is dead," she said. "In my mind it's like he'll come back to Natchez one day."

"I feel that way too."

"What do you think Sheriff Carter meant when he told you Trey didn't kill Mary Jo?"

"I don't know. That's what I plan to ask Trey this afternoon when we get back."

"We're not going on to Oxford?"

"Not today. I promised Jace I'd take him to his soccer game."

She shot him a questioning look.

"It's important. Besides, I thought I'd see if the Jackson investigator would take part in a conference call with the detective in Lafayette County. If we learn something we need to check out, we can do it tomorrow."

Once they hit the Jackson city limits, he concentrated on navigating the heavy traffic, barely arriving at the police department on time. He texted Detective Lane they had arrived, and the detective met them inside the front entrance. The lanky, midfifties detective had a couple of inches on Sam's six-one. His blond hair was parted low and combed over the top of his head, covering his baldness.

After the introductions were made, Lane led them to a small conference room. "Make yourselves at home. Can I get you something to drink?"

As he'd followed the detective, Sam had gotten a look at a pot of coffee that looked like tar. "Water will be fine." Emma echoed his reply.

"Probably a good idea," Lane said and chuckled. "I've pulled all the files and made copies for you, and I have contact information for the victims' families in case you want to interview them."

"You think they'll talk to us?" Emma asked.

"The Fisher family will—I hear from them on a regular basis wanting to know if any new information has surfaced. They want the killer found and punished."

"What suspects do you have?" Sam accepted the file from Lane.

"None. We know someone sent notes to Kimberly Fisher and figure it's the same person who gave her daisies, but we've been unable to discover who that person was."

"What kind of notes?" Sam asked.

"They're in the folder there."

Sam flipped through the folder until he came to an envelope. When he looked inside it, there were three notes, each of them with a drawing and message in printed text. One looked exactly like the card Emma had received with a dead rat on it. He held it up for her to see. "Look familiar?"

Emma's fingers shook when she reached for the note. "It's identical to the drawing I received."

"Do you know if these were mailed to her?" Sam asked. Emma's card had been slipped under her apartment door.

"There's no way to know. Her sister found the notes in Kimberly's home desk after her death."

"How about the daisies? Any clue who sent them?" Emma asked.

Lane shook his head. "The flowers weren't from a florist, so I couldn't trace them that way. Kimberly lived in a cul-de-sac but had no security camera and neither did her neighbors. Except for an eighty-year-old gentleman with cataracts, all her neighbors were at work. And she had no enemies.

"We thought we had a lead when her sister mentioned there was a man in her office building who advised her to drop her deadbeat boyfriend, but she didn't know his name, and our investigation didn't turn up this mysterious man—she was a receptionist for a billing company and a lot of people stopped by her desk."

"Where did she work?" Sam asked.

"In an office building not far from the medical center."

"How about the other offices?"

"Mostly companies that had a connection to the medical center, although there were a couple of law offices and accounting firms."

Emma tilted her head. "How about the boyfriend who was murdered?"

"He was another matter. A recovering alcoholic who had been abusive in the past. If she'd died first, he would have been our prime suspect. At one time they'd been engaged, but after he hit her in a drunken stupor, she ended the engagement. He promised to go to rehab and stay straight. They had recently gotten back together after he got out of rehab." Lane shook his head. "You've heard of the perfect murder? This was it."

"You know there's a similar crime up around Oxford?" Sam asked.

"Yes. I got in contact with the detective in charge after I entered the crime in RISS. Lieutenant Doug Marsh. The cases are practically identical. I talked to him this morning, and we set up a teleconference through my laptop for ten."

Good. Lane had anticipated Sam would want to talk to the Oxford detective. He checked his watch. Another thirty minutes. "Do you think he might be available now?"

"Let's see," Lane said.

A few minutes later the detective appeared on Lane's laptop. "Good mornin'," Marsh said, his Southern drawl more pronounced than Lane's. The Hinds County detective introduced Emma and Sam.

"Do you have a murder case that matches ours?" Marsh asked.

Sam turned the computer where he could see the detective better and Marsh could view him. He figured Marsh to be in his midforties. Since the detective sat in an office chair, Sam couldn't tell much about his size other than Marsh's broad shoulders filled the camera lens and his lean face led Sam to think the detective didn't spend a lot of time sitting around eating donuts. "From what I've read and heard about your case and Lane's, I believe they're connected to mine. Happened ten years ago, and I suspect it's our murderer's first kill."

"How come you're just now investigating?"

"It's complicated," Sam said. "Until recently, there was only one body, that of Mary Jo Selby. The sheriff at the time believed a man who went missing about the time of her death was her killer, and the case wasn't investigated thoroughly."

Lane leaned forward. "I haven't asked this previously, but what makes you think her murder is linked to our cases?"

"The daisies, and we believe the missing man was killed the same night. My victim received a bouquet of daisies not long before her death, and her sister couldn't remember much about the man who gave them to her. I'm just now investigating because the missing man's body was only recently found, giving me the opportunity to reopen the case. I'd already been looking for an excuse after I discovered the murder case file was missing."

"What does the current sheriff have to say about that?" Marsh asked.

"The sheriff who investigated the Selby murder has dementia, and the sheriff we have now just took office. He's still getting his boots on the ground."

"So not much help there," Marsh said.

"Right. The former sheriff's son was one of the last people to see the Selby girl alive, and I plan to question him later today."

"Any chance the man who went missing killed your victim?"

Emma leaned closer to the laptop. "No. We found where he was buried last week, and while I'm not a forensic anthropologist, I believe the body has been there since he went missing ten years ago. The site is within a few miles of where Mary Jo Selby died."

Sam pulled out the notes he'd made and laid out all the details of their case for the two men, beginning with discovering where Ryan's body had been buried and then removed. "We found his college ring and one bone, but it was enough to identify him."

Then he told them about the daisies Emma had received and the anonymous notes, how someone fired on them at her apartment, and then George Selby's and his daughter's shootings.

"It sounds like our killer is living in Natchez," Lane said.

Sam looked up from his notes. "That's my conclusion."

"What's the connection to Oxford and Jackson, though?" Marsh asked. "Do you have a suspect who has either lived in both places at the time of the murders or has relatives in the area?"

"I wish. I don't have any suspects at all," Sam said. "I want to question the former sheriff's son, but—"

"Wait a minute," Emma said. She looked over the notes Sam had taken, then turned to the laptop. "Both Trey Carter and Gordon Cole were in Oxford when your victim was murdered. They were at Ole Miss then."

"What?" Sam jerked his head toward her. "Are you sure?"

"Yes. They graduated in 2013, a year after Ryan would have graduated. And both had come home the weekend Mary Jo was killed to celebrate Ryan's twenty-first birthday. And mine," she added. Her eyes widened. "It just dawned on me that Gordon went to medical school in Jackson . . ."

"How about Trey? What did he do after graduation?"

Her face paled. "He attended the police academy in Jackson."

62

Emma couldn't believe it. Trey Carter a murderer? She shook her head to clear it. It wasn't possible that the man she'd dated for several months was a killer. That he'd killed his best friend . . .

He *was* controlling . . . but that didn't make him a murderer. "Trey and Gordon aren't the only men I know who lived in Oxford and Jackson at the time of the murder," she said. "Corey Chandler attended Ole Miss the same time they did, and then he practiced law in Jackson until three years ago."

"When did you learn that?" Sam asked.

"Last night." She added Corey's name to her notes and then marked through it. "But as far as we know, he wasn't in Natchez when Mary Jo and Ryan were killed. He would have been at Ole Miss then, so that basically eliminates him."

"We need to make sure he wasn't in Natchez ten years ago." Sam leaned toward the computer. "Did you two research erotomania?"

Both men nodded. Emma had skimmed over a few internet articles. "What I read," she said, "was that an erotomaniac's behavior could closely resemble that of a single-minded stalker, and like stalkers, they could even perceive themselves as being the 'savior' of the object of their attention."

"Yeah, I read that," Marsh said. "And all that love they have could turn to rage if they thought the object of their desire was never going to return their love."

Lane agreed. "I discussed this with my psychologist brother-in-law last night, and he said most people with this psychological disease are harmless, but not all. If there was an early childhood trauma, especially involving the man's mother, he could have developed that 'savior' complex involving the woman that he perceived was in love with him."

Emma propped her elbow on the table and rubbed her forehead. It was so hard to believe she could be the object of some man's obsession. She looked up and glanced at each man. "If some man believes I'm in love with him, wouldn't I know it?"

"I wish my brother-in-law were here. He could explain it better than me," Lane said. "Let's say a woman is being stalked by someone with erotomania. She has no idea the erotomaniac has feelings for her. He has delusions that she loves him, and that whoever is keeping her from him is a threat. He can even think she's sending him coded messages through social media." He paused and turned to Sam. "If you're dealing with an erotomaniac, both of you really need to be careful."

"You agree with me that I was the target Friday night?" Sam asked.

Both men nodded, and the thought made Emma sick. "Do the three of you agree that we now have three, maybe four people to interview—Trey, Gordon, Sheriff Carter, and maybe Corey?"

Sam frowned. "I agree those are people of interest for *me* to interview."

"I agree," Lane said. "You're a civilian and don't need to be involved."

"And be sure to take every precaution to keep yourself safe," Marsh chimed in.

"But it was my brother who was killed, and I was the one shot at. You're not locking me out."

"Emma," Sam said softly. "What if this man learned you're

working with me to try to put him in jail? He could very well turn on you and decide if he can't have you, no one can. I don't plan to tell your parents they've lost another child."

She hugged her arms to her waist. Her life was spiraling out of control, and there wasn't one thing she could do about it. "You'll keep me informed about what's going on, right?"

Her face grew hot under Sam's probing eyes. "Yes, but I want you to promise not to go anywhere alone and that you'll keep your door locked at all times."

"I'm already doing that. But how about you? He tried to kill you."

"Don't worry about me, I can take care of myself."

Sam's smile fell short of reassuring her. If they were right that the cases were connected, this man had already killed six people and wounded two others. She caught her breath. "I wonder how Mr. Selby and his daughter are?"

"Last I heard, they were still critical," Sam said.

"Could you call about them?" Emma desperately wanted them to survive the attack. And just as desperately she wanted to catch the man responsible.

Sam unhooked his cell phone from his belt and called the hospital. After he spoke a few words to someone, he said, "Thanks. If there's any change, could you let me know?" Then he turned to the others. "The daughter seems to be improving, but Mr. Selby is still critical."

Emma pressed her lips together and stared at her white knuckles as she gripped the table edge with her good hand. "We have to catch this man before he harms someone else," she said and raised her head. "If he wants me so badly, maybe we could use me as bait. Set up a scenario—"

"No!" Sam thundered. "You are not getting anywhere near this psycho."

"He's right," Lane said. "You could get hurt . . . or worse."

"But I can't live like this."

"We'll catch him," Sam promised. He turned to Marsh. "Send me a list of people you think I need to interview in Oxford." Then he turned to Lane. "I assume there's a list in the report you gave me, but is there anyone I can talk to while we're in Jackson?"

The Hinds County investigator glanced over his papers. "There's one. The victim's sister lives just off Highway 18. I'll give her a call and tell her to expect you . . . in what, the next hour?"

"That'll work."

Emma gathered her papers. Since Sam couldn't drop her off anywhere, at least she'd get to sit in on this interview.

63

With his other problem taken care of, he'd been free to follow Ryker and Emma from Natchez to the Hinds County Sheriff's Department, his frustration and anger growing with each mile. Ryker was forcing Emma to go with him, but the ranger would soon be out of the picture. If only he'd had some way of recording the meeting with the investigator.

Not to worry, though. Emma would fill him in. She looked out for him that way. Just last night when he looked at her Facebook posts, he saw her coded message to him, telling him to be careful, that Ryker would stop at nothing to get rid of him. Her last post had been worded to let him know she was deeply in love with him.

His breath stilled as Emma and the ranger exited the sheriff's department. He fell in behind them, keeping at least two cars back. When they reached the Natchez Trace, it would be harder to stay invisible. His anxiety grew when Ryker exited off I-20 onto Highway 18. *Where is he going?*

Raymond. His mouth dried. Kimberly Fisher's sister lived in Raymond. *Relax.* The sister knew nothing. He'd be okay.

Emma.

It was time. He would go ahead to Natchez and wait for her.

Sam turned off Highway 18 onto the county road where Kimberly Fisher's sister lived. He turned to Emma, who had been quiet after they left the Hinds County Sheriff's Department. "I hope you're not upset with me."

She sighed. "I'm not happy, but I don't want to be a liability. You are going to allow me to go in with you?"

He didn't want to leave her in the SUV, not after telling her she was in danger. "Yeah. Just this last time."

The GPS announced they'd arrived at their destination, and Sam parked behind a small sedan. The door to the brick, ranch-style house opened, and a woman who appeared to be in her forties stepped out onto the small porch. He grabbed the file Detective Lane had given him and climbed out of the SUV. Emma met him in the front yard, and they walked to the house together.

"Ranger Sam Ryker?" the woman asked.

"Yes, ma'am," he said. "And I assume you're Paula Johnston, Kimberly Fisher's sister?"

"Yes." She gave Emma a quizzical glance.

Sam introduced Emma. "We believe whoever murdered your sister killed Emma's brother."

Sympathy flooded Paula's face. "I'm so sorry, Ms. Winters."

"Call me Emma, please," she said. "And thank you. I still have trouble believing he's gone."

"Won't you come in?" They followed her inside, and she invited them to sit. "It's been four years, and sometimes, like Emma, I still find it hard to believe. How can I help you?"

"What can you remember about the men your sister dated?"

"That's just it—she didn't date anyone except Adam—that's the man who was killed—although I tried to get her to go out with other men. He was terrible to her. I still don't understand her fascination with him."

"Your statement in the report indicated Kimberly received daisies a few days before she died and then there was a bouquet at the funeral," Emma said. "Do you know who sent them?"

"We never learned who sent them. And they didn't come from any florists around here. Detective Lane checked all the florist shops in the area, and the few orders for bouquets of daisies weren't gerberas, the flowers Kimberly received."

Emma glanced at Sam. "Maybe this person grows his own."

He hadn't considered that. "How about friends? Was your sister close to anyone other than family?"

"Hardly. Adam had practically isolated Kimberly. If she'd ever married him, I probably would have completely lost touch with her." She rubbed the back of her neck. "Although there was this one person . . . he stopped by her desk sometimes, and I assumed he worked in the same building as Kimberly, but Detective Lane couldn't pinpoint who he was."

Sam flipped through the file Lane had given him. "Did she ever mention his name?"

"If she did, I don't remember." Paula stared down at her hands and the ring that she twisted. "You have to understand, our relationship was strained. Adam didn't like me because I tried to get Kimberly to break it off with him. The only time she ever called was when she kicked him out."

"It would really help if you could remember."

She raised her head, pain showing in her eyes. "I have mentally gone over every conversation I can remember. What I've told Detective Lane and you are things I've pulled out, but . . . her calls were always about Adam, and I sort of tuned her out after a bit."

"There was no one she was close to at her job?" Emma asked.

"No. Adam saw to that. Kimberly had a great job at the billing company. Management was really pleased with her work, wanted to move her up in the company. Just before she was murdered, they had moved her over to their offices in the medical center. She was so smart, there is no telling how far she could have gone." Paula shook her head. "Too bad her judgment in men wasn't better."

Sam shifted his attention to Emma. "Didn't you tell me Gordon was on staff at the medical center before he returned to Natchez?"

"Yeah. He's been back in Natchez a little over a year," she said.

He turned to Paula. "Is it possible the man who advised her to leave Adam was a doctor?"

She thought a minute. "I'm sorry, but I just can't remember. It's been over four years, and I never met the man."

"Do you recognize the name Gordon Cole?"

Paula frowned as she repeated the name. "It's somewhat familiar, but I'd hate to say yes and be wrong."

Sam understood. "What can you tell me about the notes your sister received with the drawings on them?"

"Not a lot."

"Do you know when she received them?" Sam asked.

"I found them after she died and figured they were threats from Adam."

Sam checked his watch. It was a little after one. If he was going to pick up Jace for his soccer game, they needed to leave. "Thank you for your help." He handed her a business card with his cell number on it. "If you think of anything or remember the name of the man who befriended Kimberly, give me a call."

As they hurried to his SUV, Sam turned up the collar of his jacket against the north wind. It had turned much colder while they were in the house, and like Jenny said it would, the rain had ended. As they pulled out of the drive, Emma said, "I can't believe we're considering Trey or Gordon as murderers. There has to be someone else."

Sam wasn't so sure. Emma hadn't seen the sordid underbelly of society like he had. "Did you recognize the handwriting on the cards?"

"They were printed, and while they look the same, it would be hard to know for sure. Maybe a handwriting expert could tell."

"I don't know," he said. "It's harder to analyze a hand-printed document because many of the distinguishing features that are in a cursive text aren't there." Sam tapped the steering wheel. "Let's figure this out. We know Gordon and Trey were in Natchez when Mary Jo was killed. How would we find out where Corey Chandler was?"

Emma was quiet a minute. "Wait—Mom said Corey interned for Wendall Peterson's law office at some point. Maybe it was then."

"How can we find out?"

"I doubt Mom will remember the year, but I know Wendall Peterson's administrative assistant. I have her number in my contacts. Melanie didn't stay on when Corey took over the office, but she'd been there forever. I'll call and ask." She checked her phone. "When I get reception."

"If Corey was in Natchez, that gives us three suspects for Mary Jo and Ryan's deaths."

"What if h-he wasn't killed the same night as Mary Jo?"

The hitch in Emma's voice caught his attention. This was hard for both of them. "You okay?"

Her eyes were wet when she raised her head. "Yeah."

Sam nodded at her notes. "Is anything making sense to you?"

"I see a pattern. Trey and Gordon were a year behind Ryan and me even though we were about the same age. Something about their birthdays made them start school late. For the murder that occurred in Oxford, they would have still been at Ole Miss." She leaned against the seat. "And Corey too—probably in law school."

"How about the Fisher-Clark murders in Raymond? Which of our suspects were in Jackson?"

She flipped through her notebook. "I made notes on that case too. Gordon was in Jackson at the medical center when Kimberly and Adam were killed. And according to my mom, Corey worked for a prestigious law firm there from his graduation from law school until three years ago when he relocated to Natchez. I'm not sure where their office is, but it could be by the medical center. Trey is the only one who probably wasn't living in Jackson at the time of their deaths—he would have already completed his law enforcement training at the academy."

"He would've been two hours away . . . unless he was in Jackson doing additional training. I need to check that out."

"What are your plans from here?" Emma asked.

He thought a minute. "Until I can put Corey in Natchez ten years ago, I think I'll stick with interviewing Trey and Gordon, starting with Trey—find out if he was in Jackson when Kimberly was murdered. He fits the profile best."

"Why him?"

"He has control issues—you said yourself he tried to change you and that's why you broke it off with him."

"It's just so hard to think of him that way," she said. "After Trey, I assume you'll talk to Gordy, I mean Gordon?"

"Yes. I'll save Corey for last. I may not even have to interview him."

She checked her phone again. "I have a couple of bars. Do you still want me to call Wendall Peterson's administrative assistant?"

"It won't hurt. There's a pullout just ahead. We'll stop there."

Emma gave a small gasp. "I need to charge my phone. Do you have a charger?"

"Should be one in the console. Oh, wait. I took it out. Do you want to use my phone?"

"She won't recognize your number. I think I have enough juice to call her."

At the pullout, Sam checked his phone. He had a call from Charlie Shaw. It must have come in while they were in a dead zone. He listened to the message while Emma scrolled to the administrative assistant's number and called.

"I'll put it on speaker when she answers," she said. But the call went to voicemail and Emma left a message detailing her reason for calling, telling her it was urgent that she talk to her. "Maybe she'll call back soon," Emma said as they pulled back onto the Trace.

He nodded. "The owner of the Hideaway left me a message, but the background noise was so loud, I couldn't understand him." Sam called the number back, and it went straight to voicemail. "I'll try again later and let you know what he says."

"You're going to be busy with Jace and then going to see Trey. Want me to call him?"

He hesitated. "If I don't reach him before I drive to Trey's cabin, you can. Nate says there's no service out there. But I figure I'll talk to him before that. I'll let you know," he said with a smile. The atmosphere inside the SUV was so different from earlier. "You're a good one to brainstorm with."

"Anytime."

He hesitated, hating to ruin the mood. "I know you're planning to go back to work at Mount Locust tomorrow, but is there any chance you could work at one of the other park locations so you'll be around people?"

"Because . . . ?"

"We're getting closer to discovering who the killer is, and it could get dicey. It's just too dangerous for you to hang out at Mount Locust alone."

65

Jace was the last kid in the car line when Sam pulled up to the school. Traffic had slowed them once they got to Natchez, and then he'd had Emma's apartment to check out. "Sorry, bud," he said when his nephew piled into the back seat.

"We're not late yet," Jace said, grinning.

The boy's excitement squeezed his heart. He hoped Jace would be okay when Sam had to leave early, but for the next hour, he would stand in as a dad for his nephew—Jace would not be the kid without one.

An hour later, Sam hugged his nephew. "Sorry I have to leave, but I have a case I'm working on."

"That's important too," Jace said. "You're the best!"

When some of the other dads had to leave as well, Sam didn't feel quite as bad. "I'll make it up to you."

Sam glanced in the rearview mirror as he drove away. Jace was still waving, and he turned his siren on for a second, knowing it would thrill the kid. A few minutes later, he texted Nate and asked if he still planned to go with him to interview Trey and received an affirmative. When he pulled into the sheriff's department, Nate met him out front.

"Have you heard from your chief deputy?" Sam asked.

"No. I even tried to raise him last night when they put his dad in ICU."

"I'm surprised he doesn't have his radio with him."

"When he goes to his cabin, it's because he wants to get away from everything," Nate said. "And no landline either since there's not another house within five miles of the place. He doesn't even have electricity, uses a generator."

Sam had never wanted to escape civilization that bad. "I guess if something was really important, someone would go and get him."

"Yeah. So far that hasn't happened." Nate tilted his head. "Do you really suspect him of killing Mary Jo and Ryan?"

"He's my best suspect."

As they drove, Sam asked if Nate had been able to interview either George Selby or his daughter.

"Not yet. The father is in a drug-induced coma, and Mrs. Wyatt's doctors have put a no-visitors order in place, but if she keeps improving, I hope to talk with her tomorrow."

A thought niggled at the back of Sam's mind. He groaned.

"What's wrong?"

"I was supposed to call Charlie Shaw at the Hideaway," Sam said. He glanced at his phone. One bar. Maybe . . . Nope, the call failed. He could usually send and receive texts with one bar, and handed his phone to Nate. "Text Emma and ask her to call Charlie Shaw. And text his number—it's in my recent calls. She'll know why."

Fifteen minutes later, they turned off a paved road onto a gravel one that turned to sand and finally a sand-dirt mixture. With overcast skies, it wouldn't be long before it was pitch black. "Looks like there have been a few trips in and out, but how does he get in here when it rains?"

"Four-wheeler, if it rains very much. I think he leaves his truck back where the road is gravel," Nate said.

The cabin was made of logs and much nicer than Sam had expected. He and Nate stepped out of the SUV. The sun had set and Sam shivered, zipping his jacket against the cold wind.

There were no lights on inside the cabin and no sign of Trey, other than his four-wheel-drive pickup parked beside the cabin. "I hope he's here," Sam said.

"He may be out hunting. If he is, he'll be back soon since it's getting dark." Nate walked up on the porch and rapped on the wooden door. "Trey, you here?"

No answer.

Sam scanned the area. The cabin and yard had that empty feel, like no one was home. "If the door's open, do you think he'd mind if we waited inside?"

"Naw." Nate tried the door, and it opened easily.

Thick curtains shuttered the windows, and the house was dark and cold. "Reckon we could start the generator?" Sam asked as they both used the flashlight app on their phones to illuminate the room.

Nate groaned. "Oh no!"

Sam followed Nate's light and froze. Trey lay face up on the floor with a dark circle on his chest. Sam reached him first. The dark circle was blood from a gunshot wound. He felt the deputy's wrist. "No pulse," he said. "And he's stiff."

Nate knelt beside Trey and shined a light in his eyes. "Probably happened in the last twenty-four hours. We need to make sure we don't destroy any evidence."

They carefully backtracked out of the house, and Nate used Sam's radio to call for the crime scene unit and the county coroner, then they waited in the SUV. Thoughts raced through Sam's mind. Why had Trey been killed? He wished they'd paid more attention to the car tracks in and out of the area. "Do you think there might be shoe prints on the floor? If Trey didn't use the cabin much, and he hadn't swept since he'd been here . . ."

When Nate didn't answer, Sam turned to him. The sheriff stared through the windshield, his face a stony mask. When he realized Sam had said something, he gave a slight shake of his head.

"Sorry," he said gruffly. "I didn't know Trey much outside of the job, and the election caused a few problems, but we'd put that behind us. He was a good man, and the department is going to miss him."

Sam nodded somberly. "It's always hard, losing someone you work with."

Nate took a deep breath. "Yeah. What were you saying?"

Sam repeated his question, and energy seemed to spark in Nate.

"You know, we can do a little preliminary work while we wait. You still have any of that gel lifter stuff in your SUV?"

"Yep, but before I get it out, let's see if there's anything to lift."

They climbed out of Sam's SUV, and Nate squared his shoulders. "We're going to get whoever did this."

Sam nodded his agreement. They started with the front porch, and after angling the lights on their cell phones almost level with the porch, footprints appeared. "Some of these are ours," Nate said. "But there are at least a couple of shoe prints different from either of our shoes. You have enough sheets to take several prints?"

"Yeah." Sam returned to his SUV for the tools he needed. They were able to get several clear prints that they could compare to Trey's shoes.

By the time they finished, the CSI team had arrived, followed by the coroner. Sam itched to call Emma and make sure she was all right. He checked his phone and groaned. The text asking her to call Shaw hadn't gone through.

66

Emma slouched on the sofa. While she'd been with Sam today, it'd been easy to forget that he'd lied to her about what happened the night Ryan was killed. Maybe not lied, but he'd let her believe a lie. Doubts filled her mind like rocks. Once again she was tempted to cut and run, but was that because that's what she always did in a relationship? Maybe it was time to grow up. Cut Sam some slack. She sighed. Was she being too hard on him? Ryan could be a jerk when he was drinking. *Could be?* More like always.

In her mind, she could see how Ryan and Sam's argument could've happened. It was probably even the same argument she'd had with Ryan earlier that night. After their mom and dad had left the restaurant, Ryan had been determined to stop off at the restaurant bar. An hour later, it was evident he'd been drinking before he even arrived at the restaurant. Three drinks didn't make a person as drunk as he was.

"Come on, Ryan, you've had enough," she said. "Let's go."

"Nope." He turned and ordered another whiskey sour. "Don't want to. But you can leave, Li'l Miss Perfect. Run home and tell Mama and Daddy your brother is getting drunk."

"That's enough," Sam said. "Let's go."

Ryan downed the drink and shuddered. "Okay. I wanna go to the Hideaway, anyway." He moved toward the door, his body very erect and walking very carefully and precisely. While Sam went to get his truck, she tried again to get him to go home, and he shoved her.

Emma whirled on him. "You know, you're always talking about taking off. I wish you'd just do it. No one wants to be around you. Life would be a lot easier if you were gone!" she hissed. "I wish—"

"What? That I wasn't your brother?" He swayed. "At least I'm my own person and don't pretend to be perfect."

Emma pushed the thoughts away. She couldn't change the past, but in her heart she knew if she could ask Ryan for forgiveness, he would give it to her.

A text dinged on her phone. Maybe it was Sam. She'd forgotten to charge the phone after he left, but it was plugged in now. She hurried to the kitchen counter and tapped the screen. Corey. Swallowing her disappointment, she read the text.

My client called. I know it's late, but can I stop by and share my good news with you?

Emma hesitated, glancing at her watch. How did it get to be nine thirty? Should she answer his text? He was on their suspect list, but Corey being the murderer seemed so farfetched. Instead of texting, she called him. "What's the good news?"

"My client is withdrawing his opposition," he said. "I'll tell you all about it over the coffee I've brought from the Guest House."

A load lifted from her shoulders. At least one thing was going right today. "Good." A beep sounded on her phone, and she glanced at it. Sam.

"I'm in front of your apartment," Corey said.

"Come on up. I'll press the button that unlocks the front door."

Emma would call Sam as soon as Corey left. When her doorbell rang, she checked the camera app. True to his word, Corey stood in the hallway with two cups in his hands.

She opened the door. "Did he really withdraw his opposition?"

"Yes indeed."

"Come on in," she said, stepping back to allow him room to get past her.

"I think this is still hot—I just got it and came straight here." He handed her a cup with the Guest House logo on it. "Can you manage it?"

"Sure." She took the cup and led the way into the living area. Corey took the sofa, and she settled in the chair across from him and flipped the top back on the cup.

"How did you convince him?" she asked and sipped the coffee. "Ooh, this is as good as I remembered."

"It is, isn't it," he said. "I just told him you would do a better job than anyone I knew of."

Her heart warmed toward Corey. "I appreciate your vote of confidence." She took another sip of the coffee. "I wonder if the Guest House would tell me what brand this is."

"I'm sure they would," he said. "What are your plans? When will you start the project?"

"Tomorrow. My supervisor has said I can work there instead of Melrose." Unless Sam insisted that she work somewhere else.

"Good." He looked around the apartment. "Is there any way I could look at what you have from the project in 2000? That would give me an idea of what you're going to do."

"Sure. It's in my backpack. Be right back." She walked to her bedroom and retrieved the report. It was such a relief to know she didn't have to jump through more hoops to conduct her project. Back in the living room, she spread out the report on the coffee table in front of the sofa. As they talked, it was obvious from his questions that Corey was interested in the project.

She didn't know how long they'd been discussing her plans when her cell phone rang. Her heart skipped when Melanie Ferguson showed up on caller ID. How was she going to get the information she needed with Corey sitting beside her? "I need to take this in private," she said, standing. "Be right back."

Whoa. Emma grabbed the doorframe in the hallway. She'd moved too fast and paused to get her balance before she slid the answer button. "Hello?"

"Emma, Melanie Ferguson returning your call. I know it's a little after ten, but I've been away from my phone, and your message sounded urgent."

"Thanks," she said and walked to her bedroom. "Do you remember the person I called about?" She didn't want to use Corey's name in case he could hear her.

"Yes. Corey Chandler interned for Wendall in 2011. He started in January. I remember because that's when I broke my leg."

The year Mary Jo and Ryan were murdered. "Are you sure?" Emma's head felt odd.

"Positive. He called me at home on several occasions for help finding files that Wendall wanted."

"How long did he intern?"

"Three months. He was leaving the week I returned to work."

Melanie sounded so far away. "Okay. Thanks." She disconnected and tried to get her bearings.

"Emma, is something wrong?"

Corey? She turned as darkness closed in on her.

67

The Rohypnol had taken effect.

Corey had waited until he knew Ryker wouldn't be coming back. Greg Hart, Emma's neighbor, had come and gone, the blonde at the end of the hall was away. Everything was working out perfectly.

He smiled. "We'll be together now. You don't have to be afraid of your feelings for me any longer."

He stood and walked to the bookcase, where he retrieved the bug. He didn't think it could be traced back to him, but there was no need to take a chance.

"I . . . I don't know what you're talking about." Emma rubbed her forehead. "I don't feel well," she said. "The room is spinning."

He furrowed his brow. "You look as though you're about to pass out," he said. "I'm going to take you somewhere safe."

"No." She shook her head as if to clear it. "Why are you here?" she asked.

"We'll talk about it later, after you're feeling better." He slipped her coat over her shoulders. "Don't want you to get cold, do we?"

A sudden urgency to get away from the apartment washed over him, and he hurried her down the stairs. She was compliant but getting sleepy as he guided her to his truck. He'd thought about collecting some of her clothes and makeup, but he wanted nothing from her former life at the cabin.

Once Corey had her seat belt fastened, he slipped her shoes off and hurried around to the other side of the club cab truck. Once he got out of town, he would put her in the back seat, where she could sleep.

Corey jerked his head in the direction of an approaching siren. His premonition had been right! He'd barely turned the corner when flashing blue lights pulled in front of Emma's apartment.

They would know in minutes she was gone. He'd have to take a roundabout way to the cabin and avoid any highways that might have a roadblock.

No matter. Excitement thrummed through his body. Emma was his now. All he had to do was get her to the cabin, where he would keep her locked up until she yielded to her love for him. He could see in her face she was still afraid of her feelings for him. Time would change that.

68

Sam hung around the cabin until the local funeral-director-slash-coroner was allowed to examine Trey's body. After his preliminary examination, he informed them Trey had died from a gunshot wound to the heart, and from his experience, he figured he'd been dead at least eighteen hours, maybe even twenty-four. The medical examiner in Jackson would pinpoint the exact time of death during the autopsy.

"If you don't need me any longer, I want to find Gordon Cole and talk to him," Sam said to the sheriff.

"Good idea," Nate said. "I'll catch a ride with one of my deputies."

"Do you know where Gordon lives?"

Nate rubbed his forehead. "Doc lives on Cole Road, but I'm not sure about Gordon. Let me ask around." He disappeared inside the house and reappeared a few minutes later with the doctor's address and cell phone number. "The coroner is old friends with him," Nate said. "You know how to get back to the main road, right?"

"Yeah. Stay on the dirt road until it intersects a gravel, then take a left."

Nate gave him a thumbs-up. "Call dispatch if you need anything, and they'll contact me on the radio."

As soon as Sam had cell coverage, he dialed Emma's number.

It went straight to voicemail. He checked the time. Eight thirty. He bet she forgot to charge her phone. As soon as he interviewed Gordon, he would drive to her apartment and make sure she was all right.

After he put Gordon's address into his GPS, he dialed the doctor's number and got an answering service. He left a request for the doctor to call him. Sam followed the directions from his navigation system and wasn't surprised when an hour later, the directions took him to a ritzy part of town and a house that sat on at least three acres of ground. A fence surrounded the property with a security gate at the entrance. Sam stared at the keypad, then redialed the doctor's cell phone. He was about to disconnect when the doctor answered. "This is Dr. Cole."

Sam identified himself. "I'd like to talk with you a few minutes."

"About . . . ?"

If he said Mary Jo Selby, he figured the doctor would find an excuse to not talk to him. "Trey Carter."

"What about Trey?" Gordon's voice was cautious.

"He's dead."

A sharp gasp sounded through the phone. "What? How?"

"That's what I'd like to discuss with you."

There was silence on the line, and then the front gate swung open and Sam drove through. Gordon met him at the front steps dressed in sweats and athletic shoes.

"Come inside," Gordon said. Sam followed him inside and down the hall to what looked like a TV room. "What happened to Trey? Was he killed in the line of duty?"

"No. Someone shot him at his cabin. Do you have any idea why?"

The doctor blanched. "I need a drink."

He walked to a bar on the far side of the room and poured a good two inches of amber liquid into a glass that he tossed down in one gulp. Judging from his reaction, Gordon hadn't known about Trey's death . . . or he was a good actor.

He turned to Sam. "Tell me what happened."

"Not much to tell, yet. Nate and I drove out to talk to Trey about Mary Jo Selby and Ryan Winters's deaths."

He swallowed hard. "Y-you found Ryan's body? Where?"

Sam watched his expression. "We found where he'd been buried."

Gordon leaned against the bar and closed his eyes.

"You want to tell me about it?"

"There's nothing to tell."

"Really? I think I'll go see what Sheriff Carter has to say when he discovers his son is dead."

"You can't pay any attention to that old man."

"He was pretty clear the other night when he told me Trey didn't murder Mary Jo. Was it you who killed her?"

"No!" His face flushed.

"Well . . . since Ryan is dead, and now Trey, that just leaves you . . ."

"None of us killed her! There was someone else there that night."

"Who?"

The doctor shook his head. "I don't know. But there had to have been because I didn't kill them and I never thought Trey did."

Sam tapped his hand on his leg. "Can you drive a backhoe?"

Confusion clouded his eyes, and then he turned and poured another drink, downing it as quickly as he had the other. A picture emerged in Sam's mind. No wonder it'd been hard to figure out. The shooting at Mount Locust was not connected to Emma's stalker. "You and Trey buried Ryan's body the night Mary Jo died . . . but why?"

Gordon wiped his mouth with the back of his hand. "You're crazy."

"I don't think so." Sam hesitated, pulling his thoughts together. "If you aren't the killer, then you're next."

"What?"

"Think about it. There were four of you at Loess Bluff that night. Mary Jo. Ryan. Trey. All dead. You're the only one left who knows what happened, except for Sheriff Carter, and I doubt the murderer is worried about him. But you, that's a different matter."

Gordon sat down hard in the chair beside the bar and stared at the floor. A grandfather clock in the corner ticked off minutes as Sam waited him out. After five minutes, the doctor's shoulders slumped and he exhaled hard.

"You want to tell me about it?" Sam asked.

"I don't remember everything," he said, his voice low. "I remember riding in the front seat, with Ryan and Mary Jo in the back. They were making out . . . we parked, must've been at Loess Bluff. Music. I remember hearing dance music. And Mary Jo laughing. Then Trey was shaking me, waking me up. He said Ryan and Mary Jo were dead, and he'd called his dad."

"Did Trey see who shot Ryan?"

"No. He said he'd left them to answer the call of nature. He heard the shots. When he got back to where Ryan was, he was dead and Mary Jo was gone. When Sheriff Carter got there, he reamed us both out good. Sobered me up." His voice trailed off. "I think I need another drink."

"No, you need to get this off your chest. Why did you bury Ryan and not Mary Jo?" When Gordon hesitated, Sam said, "If you didn't kill either one and you're worried about going to jail, pretty sure the statute of limitations has run out on obstruction of justice."

Gordon's face showed that was exactly what he was worried about. "It was all the sheriff's idea," he said. "He was afraid if word got out that Trey was even at the scene of Mary Jo's death, it would cost Carter the election. Her murder almost did.

"He planned it all. Trey knew how to get the keys to the backhoe, and we buried Ryan at Mount Locust because the backhoe was handy. When we went back for Mary Jo's body, the hunters had found her.

"While Sheriff Carter dealt with them, Trey drove Ryan's Mustang to Memphis and I followed in Trey's pickup. It didn't take long for the car to get stripped." He looked up. "Who do you think killed Trey?"

Before Sam could answer, his cell phone rang. Merit Health? "Excuse me," he said and swiped the answer button. "This is Ryker."

"Mr. Ryker, this is Sandra Wyatt's nurse at Merit Health. Ms. Wyatt is awake and very insistent about speaking to you."

"I'll be right there." Once the nurse gave him the room number, Sam hung up and eyed Gordon. "I have to leave, but before I go, do you remember who Mary Jo came to the Hideaway with that night?"

The doctor frowned. "I had forgotten she was with someone. I can't recall who it was, but maybe if I think about it . . ."

"I'll be in touch. But in the meantime, if I were you, I'd watch my back."

69

Nausea crept up into Emma's throat. She was going to be sick, but instinct told her not to move. Where was she? Lying on something, for sure. The smell of leather. She was in a car or, judging by the rough ride, more than likely a pickup. One with a back seat.

Emma tried to open her eyes, but her eyelids were so heavy. *Think.* She couldn't, no matter how hard she tried. It was like a fog bank had rolled into her head, one that only odors could penetrate.

Suddenly Emma realized she wasn't alone. Of course she wasn't—she was lying in the back seat of a vehicle. Why had it taken this long to realize that? Had she been drugged? That was the only answer. *Regroup. Take deep breaths and maybe the fog will lift.* At least the noisy tires covered her breathing as she sucked in air.

Her nose itched, and Emma scratched it. Her hands weren't bound! *Okay. Make a plan.* But first she had to figure out what was going on. What was the last thing she remembered? Sam. She'd been angry at him. But somehow, she didn't think she was now. Was he driving?

No. She didn't know how she knew it, but Sam wasn't anywhere near her, and whoever had put her in this truck was dangerous. Maybe she could talk to him, reason with him—how did she know it was a man? A shadowy memory surfaced. Corey.

It all came flooding back. He'd stopped by her apartment with coffee to celebrate something . . . then she got a phone call from Melanie. Her mouth got drier. Corey had been living and working in Natchez when Mary Jo was murdered.

Where was he taking her? Maybe she could talk to him. Get him to turn her loose. Uh. No. She had the advantage of surprise as long as he didn't know she was awake. Emma felt on the floorboard for any kind of weapon she could use when they stopped, and her fingers closed on a round piece of steel. Tire iron.

The truck slowed, and the melody of a song floated from the audio system. Whitney Houston singing, "*I will always love you.*"

70

Sam turned into the hospital on two wheels and parked next to the entrance. Instead of waiting for the elevator, he took the stairs two steps at a time. It was a little after ten, and family members who were staying the night in the waiting room were arranging for places to sleep. He crossed the room and was immediately buzzed inside the unit.

"Is Ms. Wyatt still awake?" Sam asked when he reached her room.

"She's in and out, but go on in. She's asked to see you as soon as you arrive."

Sam stepped inside the room. Sandra Wyatt lay hooked up to wires and tubes, but she turned toward him. "Good, you came. My dad . . . how . . ."

"I don't know. Earlier today I was told he was holding his own. I don't think there's been any change." He stepped closer to the bed. "How do you feel?"

"Like I've been shot." She managed a tiny smile below the nasal cannula. "Have you found the person responsible?"

He shook his head. "We're working on it. Sheriff Rawlings would be here, but he's tied up on another case tonight. He'll see you tomorrow," he said. "The nurse said you had something to tell me."

She gave him a small nod. "The man who gave Mary Jo the

flowers." She paused to breathe deeply. "Don't remember his name, but she said . . . he was going to be a lawyer."

Corey, maybe? "Did he live here in Natchez?"

"Don't know . . . wish I did . . . but that's all I remember."

Talking tired her, and he hated to ask more questions.

"Sorry it's not more. Just seemed important . . ."

"You said you met him once. Do you remember *anything* about his appearance?"

She closed her eyes and sucked oxygen through the cannula. Suddenly her eyes popped open. "His eyes. They were blue, but really pale . . ."

That fit Corey. His cell phone rang, and he silenced it but glanced at the ID. Chief Pete Nelson. "I'm leaving now. If you remember anything else, have your nurse call me. Doesn't matter what time it is." Sam squeezed her free hand. "We're going to get who did this to your family."

Sam waited until he was in the hallway before calling Nelson back. "You're up late," he said when the chief of police answered.

"Yeah. I had an officer on the night shift check the database for the license plate reader in front of Emma's apartment. The records show Dr. Gordon Cole's vehicle numerous times, but nothing compared to two vehicles registered to Corey Chandler. The last record showed he was at her apartment at nine thirty. When Emma didn't answer my call, we came immediately, lights blazing. She's not here, Sam."

"What? She has to be. Her truck is at Mount Locust."

"I'm inside her apartment now, and only her cat and phone are here."

"Corey must have her." The knowledge made him sick. "Do you know how long he was there?"

"No, but she answered a call on her phone at ten fifteen. We just missed them."

Where would he take her?" Nate said.

Sam looked up from the computer he'd brought upstairs to Emma's apartment. "I don't know. I don't find any records where he owns property in Adams County. Any hits on the BOLO?"

Nate had arrived not long after Sam, and he and the Natchez police chief had put out a Be-On-the-Look-out for Corey Chandler's pickup. The truck license plate had been the one that showed up the last time on the license plate reader.

"Except for the house on Mulholland Road, there's nothing in his name. Same for surrounding counties."

Pete looked over Sam's shoulder. "Do you think he might have used a holding company?"

Sam's heart sank. If he had, they might never find him.

"We need a real estate agent," Pete said. He was quiet a minute. "Your dad. When my folks were looking for a farm, they said he knew where every piece of property in the county was."

"Don't you know anyone else?"

"I've heard he knows every piece of property that's been bought or sold in the last five years," Nate said.

Time was ticking away. Was he going to let Corey Chandler kidnap Emma and get away with it because he was too proud to ask his father for help? Sam jerked his phone off his belt and dialed his mother's number. "Is D-Dad there?" he asked when she answered.

"Is something wrong?" she asked.

"Yes. Corey Chandler has kidnapped Emma."

"No! Why?"

"It's a long story. Is Dad there?" he repeated.

"What does Emma's kidnapping have to do with your dad?"

"Mom, just let me talk to him, please." Sam waited for his father to come to the phone. Every second that ticked off put Emma in more danger. What if he was wasting time?

"Sam, your mom told me what's going on. What can I do?"

The concern in his dad's voice almost undid him. "Corey Chandler has to know roadblocks would be set up when we discovered he kidnapped Emma, so I figure he's taking her somewhere near here until things calm down and he can smuggle her out. I've looked online, but I can't find where he owns any property. I . . ." He took a deep breath. "I thought you might know somewhere else to look."

"Let me think," his dad said. "Hold on a second." Sam heard him ask for his computer, then he came back on the line. "Corey Chandler. That name is familiar . . ."

Keystrokes sounded through the phone. "Yes . . . I thought so."

"What did you find?" Sam asked.

"He's handled the deed for several pieces of property here in Adams County and over in Jefferson County. Here—I found it. He bought it through a holding company," he said. "Three thousand acres of timberland bordering Adams and Jefferson Counties. It's along the Mississippi, so if he's running, he could be planning a boat trip."

"How do I get to it?" Sam asked.

"I showed him the property, so I can show you the way."

"Just give me the directions or an address."

"Directions? Impossible. There are too many twists and turns. And there is no address. I know a shortcut, so I'm afraid it's me or nothing."

"I'll be there in ten minutes."

72

The pickup bounced over the ruts, jarring Emma's head. They had stopped somewhere, and she'd dozed off again. Now it seemed as though she'd been riding forever. She had thought once or twice about hitting Corey over the head with the tire iron, but if she raised up, he would see her. No. She had the element of surprise and would wait until they stopped. He didn't know she had the weapon.

She'd never hit anyone in her life. Her mind still felt fuzzy, but maybe she could talk him into releasing her.

"Why are you doing this?"

"I wondered when you would say something."

He'd known she was awake. "You didn't answer my question."

The pickup slowed to a standstill.

"Why are you stopping?"

"To let you sit in the front seat," he said. "That way we can talk. I've been waiting for this day for so long."

The truck stopped, and Corey climbed out. This was her one chance. With the tire iron gripped in her left hand, she sat up and took in her surroundings. It was so dark, she could only see the trees caught in the truck's headlights.

A second later he opened her door. Emma jumped at him with a scream and swung the tire iron. It connected, and the thud of the tire iron breaking bone sickened her. Corey roared and grabbed his shoulder.

No! He was supposed to be knocked out. She planted her hands on his chest and shoved him, and then took off running. Pain stabbed her bare feet. *My shoes!* He'd taken off her shoes. Ignoring the pain, she ran the way they'd come.

Darkness surrounded her. She could barely make out the road until lights flashed behind her. Somehow he'd turned around and was coming after her. Gritting her teeth, she jumped the ditch that ran along the road and struck out through the woods.

73

Which way here?" Sam asked when they came to a crossroads in the middle of a wilderness. It seemed like they'd been driving for hours, but it'd probably been only forty-five minutes. True to his word, his dad had shown them a shortcut, saving precious time.

"Take a left," his dad said.

"People actually live out here?" Pete said from the back seat.

"Not many," Nate replied. "And the few who live here like living off the grid. I've worked for the sheriff's department for fifteen years, and I can't remember ever being called to this area."

"You say his name isn't on the deed for this land?" Sam asked. He looked in his rearview mirror to make sure Nate's deputies were behind him.

Beside him, his father shook his head. "He said he represented a holding company."

If it hadn't been for his dad, Sam doubted they would have ever found the property.

"There!" his dad said when the SUV headlights picked up a side road. "Turn there."

The road wasn't much bigger than a path. Certainly not big enough for two cars if they met someone. They rounded a curve and Sam slammed on the brakes. They'd almost plowed into a pickup truck.

74

Corey's shoulder throbbed. He couldn't believe Emma was like the others. Where was she? He'd grabbed the nightscope he kept in his truck and lifted it to his eyes, scanning the area. Nothing moved. He thought about attaching a thermal scope, but the woods were too thick.

A north wind blew, chilling him. Emma didn't have on a coat, so she would probably move soon. And when she did, he'd have her.

Emma braced against the tree with the tire iron still in her left hand. She'd run until she could run no more. Her feet hurt. And she was cold. She edged around the tree. Corey was to her left and down from her. He had a gun, maybe even a nightscope. That's the only way he could have tracked her. If he did and she moved, he would see her. How did he move through the woods so silently? She peeked again.

He was gone. Her heart leaped into her throat. Where was he? If she threw the tire iron and then ran in the opposite direction, she would have nothing to protect herself with. If she could just find something, a branch, anything.

Emma knelt and ran her hand over the ground. Her fingers closed in on something smooth and hard. A rock. Using the sharp end of the tire iron, she dug around it and tried to pry it loose.

Once she had it loose, she transferred the rod to her weaker hand. Which way to throw the rock? She had no idea where she was or how to get back to the main road.

Doing something was better than waiting for him to find her, and she drew the rock back to throw it.

"Drop it."

Her heart almost stopped. He stood not ten yards away.

"Emma!" The shout came in the opposite direction from Corey.

That was Sam's voice! She jerked her head toward the voice. "He has a gun!"

Had Sam heard her?

Corey's hand closed on her shoulder. He held a pistol to her head. "You will never get away from me. Now drop the tire iron!"

She dropped it but still held the rock in her good hand. "Why, Corey?"

"You're mine. If I can't have you, no one can. But right now, you're my insurance. Now walk."

He pushed her toward a clearing. When she stumbled, he jerked her up and she swung the rock, hitting his head. Corey went to his knees, and she took off running again, this time toward the voices. "Sam! Where are you?"

Corey grabbed her ankle, bringing her down. Seconds later he stood over her. "Do that again and I'll kill you. Now get up."

Corey used a scope to scan the area. "This way."

They walked, getting farther and farther away from the voices, until they came to a road. "To the left," he said.

At least walking was easier here. "Where are we going?"

"You don't need to know."

She could barely get her breath, but Corey wasn't even breathing hard. Why hadn't Sam found her? Emma tried to slow down, but Corey nudged her with the barrel of his gun. After they'd walked for what seemed like miles, a cabin came into view. Who would build a home in the middle of this wilderness? She heard water lapping against land. The Mississippi River?

"Too bad you didn't want me. This could have been yours."

"Are we stopping here?"

"You ask too many questions." He turned and cocked his head toward the path they'd just taken. "Where did they go?" he murmured.

"Why did you kill my brother?"

"He was going to hurt Mary Jo. I couldn't let him do that."

"But then you killed her."

He shook his head. "That was an accident. She ran from me. Slipped and fell into the ravine. When I reached her, she was already dead."

"Those other women didn't run from you."

"Shut up!" He jerked her by the arm. "Come on."

"Where are we going?"

"Away from here." He flashed the beam toward a path and half dragged her to wooden steps that led down to the river, where a boat was tied to a dock.

No. She wasn't getting on that boat . . . Halfway down the steps, she stumbled, and when he reached for her, she grabbed his hand and jerked him off balance. He fell past her, flailing in the air as he grabbed for the handrails.

Emma bolted up the steps. Suddenly a bullet whizzed past her. She was a sitting duck on the stairs. Ducking under the rail, she jumped, grabbing anything she could to keep from tumbling down the side of the cliff.

Everything she caught only slowed her descent until she lay sprawled next to the water. Suddenly Corey stood over her with the pistol aimed at her head. "I don't know why you had to fight me."

He raised his arm. Emma closed her eyes.

A shot rang out. Then another.

She opened her eyes. Corey lay sprawled at her feet, and someone was running toward her.

"Emma! Are you all right?"

"Sam?" She'd barely raised up when he scooped her up in his arms. Behind him was Nate and . . . was that Sam's father? "How did you find me?"

"My dad. He remembered the boat dock, and we took a chance that's where Corey was headed. I was so afraid we wouldn't make it in time."

He set her on the bottom of the steps, and she glanced toward where Corey lay. Nate knelt beside him. Sam gasped and she brought her attention back to him.

"Your feet are bleeding. Where are your shoes?"

Emma had been so scared she'd forgotten all about her feet. "He took them. Thought it would keep me from running."

Sam smoothed her hair back. His brown eyes held hers captive. "He didn't know you very well, did he?" His lips claimed hers. When he released her, he said, "I'm never letting you go again."

She laid her head on his chest. "Good. 'Cause I'm not letting you go either."

75

THREE WEEKS LATER

Emma climbed out of Sam's SUV at the Natchez City Cemetery and glanced toward where they'd buried Ryan. Gordon, hoping to mitigate some of the trouble he faced for interfering with an investigation, had shown them where he'd helped Trey bury her brother's skeletal remains at his cabin. She was thankful they hadn't dumped them in the river.

Sam waited at his SUV while Emma walked up the hill to Ryan's grave. She'd come to the cemetery today to say her good-byes and knelt in front of his headstone. Gordon had confessed that Sheriff Carter had orchestrated the whole sad affair when Trey called him, panicking because Mary Jo and Ryan were dead.

She traced his name with her finger. Ryan Thomas Winters. Ten years of looking for Ryan, and he was so close all that time.

"I'm sorry I didn't go with you that night and that I was so angry with you," Emma said softly. She rocked back on her feet while a mockingbird sang in the tree shading the grave. "When we were little, you were the best brother ever. I wish things had been different."

Things like his addictions. She'd finally come to let go of the guilt from the words she'd hurled at him the night of their birthday. But she also accepted that Ryan alone was responsible for his choices. "I miss you like crazy," she said. "And I love you . . ."

Emma stood and stared at the tombstone another minute and then turned toward Sam's SUV. An older black gentleman waited near it and was talking with Sam.

The stranger removed his hat as she approached. "Miss Winters?"

"Yes?"

"I'm Herbert Perryman. The volunteer at Mount Locust said I'd find you here. Could I have a word with you?"

She glanced at Sam.

"I think you'll be interested to hear what he has to say, and I'll be right over there," Sam said, pointing where she'd just come from.

Emma turned her attention to the older man with a gentle smile. "What do you want to talk about?"

"It's about the slave cemetery at Mount Locust and the cabins," he said, his words slow. "I was Corey Chandler's client."

She stared at him. Emma had decided there never had been a client. "The one who was trying to stop the project?"

"Yes." He twisted the hat in his hands.

"Why?"

"When I was young . . . well, even before I was born, things that got done to black folks got covered up by white folks, and . . ." He stopped to take a breath. "I just want to make sure the truth is told about how the slave conditions were here at Mount Locust."

"You think I'll slant my findings in favor of the owners of Mount Locust?"

"I did." He studied her, his rheumy eyes watering. "But after I read about what happened to you and your folks and your brother, I decided you would be fair. I'm here today because I want to apologize for any problems I might have caused you."

"Thank you, and I promise you, Mr. Perryman, my findings will reflect whatever is here, good or bad." She stared at the ground for a minute. *Perryman*. It all fell into place, and Emma lifted her head. "You're a direct descendant of one of the families buried here."

He nodded. "My great-great-grandfather."

She tilted her head. "How would you like to help me on the project?"

His eyes widened. "Really?"

"Really. You could help document what we find. How the slaves lived, what they ate, everything."

"I'd like that mighty fine, Miss Winters. Mighty fine."

She offered her hand, and he shook it. "I'll start the project in three weeks. And call me Emma."

"I'll be there."

He turned and slowly walked to his car.

Emma walked back to Sam, who drew her into his arms. "Are you ready for next week?"

She nodded and then lifted her head. His dark brown eyes captured hers. "Are you?"

"Let me think . . . I have the ring, the pastor lined up, and the honeymoon planned. Yeah, I'd say I'm ready, unless you want to elope tonight."

Her lips quirked in a smile. "As wonderful as that sounds, our parents would kill us."

"And my sister too." He checked his watch. "Isn't that shower she's throwing for us in half an hour?"

She gasped. "We better hurry."

Sam opened her door, but before she slid across the seat, Emma turned once more toward Ryan's grave. She would miss her brother, but she finally had peace.

LOVED THIS BOOK?

Read On for Chapter One of the
Next Thrilling Book in This Series!

COMING SOON

Come on! It was almost midnight, and the light in Cora Chamberlain's bedroom blazed like a neon sign.

He ground his teeth as rain poured from the skies, running off his black slicker.

Tornado watches had been issued for the area, and while those were as common as thunderstorms around Natchez in the springtime, he never remembered a June tornado. Still, it'd be his luck for a tornado to hit the town tonight. Especially since nothing else had gone right, starting with the phone call an hour ago from Miss Cora that had him standing in a copse of woods outside her antebellum home.

"You'll never believe it, but I discovered more journals—three to be exact!" Even at ninety-two, Miss Cora's reedy voice had not lost its haughty, imperious tone. "I now have proof that my grandfather Chamberlain was innocent of murder. Do you know what this means, Sonny?"

No one called him by his boyhood nickname except the aging spinster. "Of course I do," he said. "You'll be able to clear his name."

"Yes! My father's greatest wish was to restore his grandfather's reputation," she said. "I do wish I knew where I put that first journal. Then I would have the complete set to publish."

"That was unfortunate, but maybe one day you'll find it." Not happening. Not when it was in his possession.

"Well, you'll never believe who actually killed Zachariah Elliott, but I think I'll make you wait until tomorrow to find out," she said.

It wasn't the identity of the real killer that had him waiting for her bedroom light to go out. He'd always heard that the devil was in the details, and it was the details surrounding the murder over 150 years ago that promised to increase his bank account.

Miss Cora had promised not to tell anyone that she'd found the journals, a promise not that hard to extract since it was after ten o'clock when she phoned him. Anyone else she might tell was already in bed asleep. Except for Ainsley Beaumont, but Miss Cora was old school. If she told you something, you could take it to the bank.

When he asked where she'd found them, she'd babbled some nonsense about showing him tomorrow. Well, he wasn't waiting for tomorrow.

He rubbed his hand over his eyes, wiping away the rain. There was no way she would let him take these three journals home to read, not after she'd *misplaced* the first one. It had taken him a while to convince her that she hadn't given it to him.

The corner light on the first floor dimmed to black. Hopefully a sign things were turning around. He'd give her thirty minutes to fall sound asleep before he entered through the cellar and crept up the secret passageway that opened into the library on the first floor. It was where he should find the journals since the library was where Cora was writing the book that would clear her grandfather's name.

The woman was remarkable to navigate computers the way she did at ninety-two. Too bad she had to die. But it shouldn't be too hard to make it look as though she'd died of natural causes in her sleep. A pillow should do the trick.

A sudden pop of lightning was followed almost instantly with thunder that shook the ground. He looked up as more lightning revealed a thick wall-cloud. He didn't have time for violent weather tonight.

However, maybe the noise of the storm would hide his breaking and entering, and he wouldn't have to wait thirty minutes. He slipped away from the woods and dashed to the cellar steps at the back of the two-story house and descended to the doorway.

When another bolt of lightning lit up the sky, he used a branch that had fallen from the nearby Magnolia tree and broke the glass pane above the handle just as the follow-up clap of thunder shook the windows.

Once he unlatched the door and was inside the cellar, he eased behind the stairs and stood still, letting rain run off his slicker and listening for any sign he'd been heard. When no telltale footsteps sounded, he used the flashlight on his phone to illuminate the wall and find the small hole in the second panel of wood.

Once he triggered the latch, the door swung open noiselessly, and he quietly climbed the steep stairs. At the top, he unlatched the sliding door and pushed it to the side and stepped into the library. He'd found the secret stairway as a young boy, and as far as he knew, no one else was aware of it.

Once again, he stood perfectly still while the storm raged outside. So far no tornado sirens sounded. When he was certain Cora hadn't heard him, he flicked on the light from his phone again and scanned the room, stopping at her desk.

He frowned. Where were the journals? They should have been if not on the cherry desk beside Miss Cora's laptop, then on the table beside it. Sweat beaded his face. He had to find them. If he didn't, and she published them, he would lose his advantage . . . and five grand a month.

A thorough search revealed no journals. Could she have taken them to her bedroom? What if she had referenced them on her computer? He stood behind the desk and booted up her email, relaxing after he found nothing pertaining to the journals in her sent box.

"You! What are you doing in my house?"

He whirled around. Miss Cora stood in the doorway, looking like an avenging angel with her white robe cinched around her and her finger pointed straight at him. "Sonny?"

"Where are they?" He took a menacing step toward her. "The journals. What have you done with them?"

She turned her head slightly toward the bedroom. He'd been right. She'd taken them to her bedroom. He rushed past her, knocking the old woman down. He ignored the resounding crack her head made when it hit the floor. On her bed, he found one journal on the table beside her bed. *Where are the others?*

He quickly returned to the library and shook her. "Where are they?" he demanded, then frowned. Her face was the color of ashes. He felt her wrist. No! She couldn't be dead. Not until she told him where the other two journals were. Maybe in a safe somewhere?

He froze at the sound of a door opening.

"Cora! Wake up! There's a tornado coming!"

Rose, Cora's sister.

"Where are you?" Her voice, so like her sister's, rose to a high pitch. "We have to get in the cellar!"

Maybe he should kill her too. No. The police would assume Cora fell and hit her head, causing a brain bleed, but two deaths would cause suspicion.

He would find a way to return and tear the house apart if need be to find those other journals. He could not take a chance on anyone else finding them.

"Cora! Where are you?"

"You check her bedroom, and I'll check the library."

He didn't recognize the new voice, but there was no time to think about that. The door had barely closed behind him in the secret passageway when the woman with the voice he didn't recognize cried, "Oh no! Grandmother, quick! The library. Cora may have had a stroke!"

It could be no one other than Ainsley Beaumont.

Seconds later he heard her say, "Siri, call 911!"

ACKNOWLEDGMENTS

As always, to Jesus who gives me the words.

To my family and friends who believe in me and encourage me every day, thank you.

To my editors, Lonnie Hull DuPont and Kristin Kornoelje, thank you for making my stories so much better.

To the art, editorial, marketing, and sales teams at Revell—Michele Misiak, Karen Steele, Erin Bartels—thank you for your hard work. You are the best!

To Julie Gwinn, thank you for your direction and for working so tirelessly with me and for being my friend.

To the rangers who have patiently answered my questions, thank you! Any mistakes I make are totally on me.

To my readers . . . you are awesome! Thank you for reading my books.

Patricia Bradley is the author of three series—the Logan Point series (*Shadows of the Past*, *A Promise to Protect*, *Gone Without a Trace*, and *Silence in the Dark*), the Memphis Cold Case novels (*Justice Delayed*, *Justice Buried*, *Justice Betrayed*, and *Justice Delivered*), and the Natchez Trace Park Rangers series (*Standoff* and *Obsession*). Bradley is the winner of an Inspirational Readers Choice Award and a Carol finalist. She is cofounder of Aiming for Healthy Families, Inc., and she is a member of American Christian Fiction Writers and Sisters in Crime. Bradley makes her home in Mississippi with her two fur-babies, Suzy and Tux. Learn more at www.ptbradley.com.

Also by
PATRICIA BRADLEY . . .

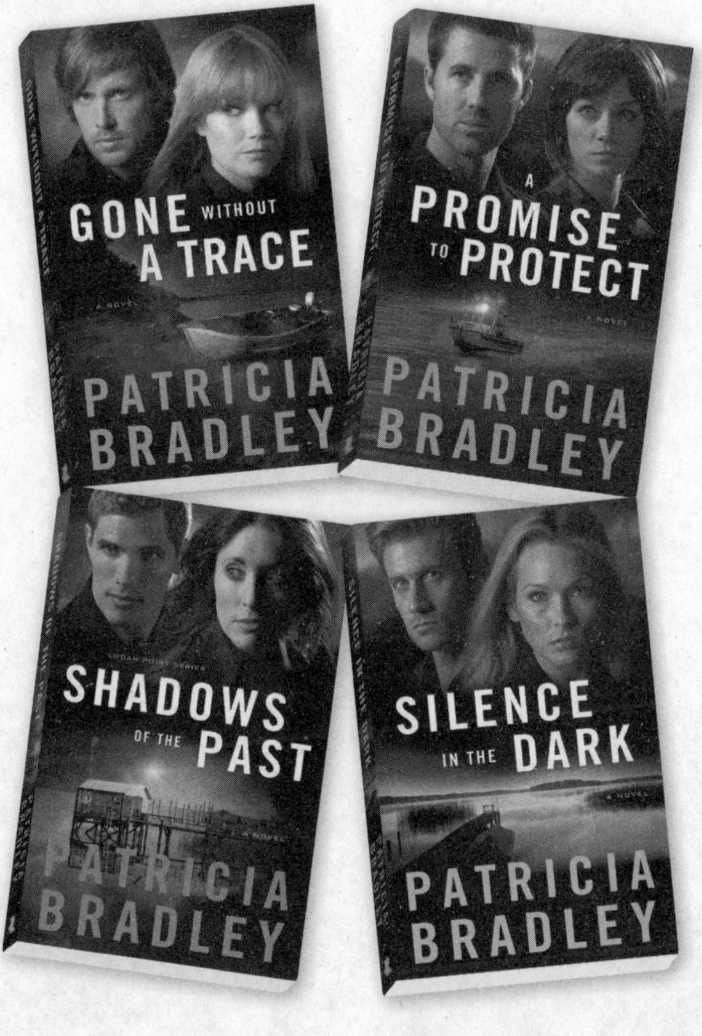

Revell
a division of Baker Publishing Group
www.RevellBooks.com

Available wherever books and ebooks are sold.

Meet

Patricia BRADLEY

www.ptbradley.com

 PTBradley1

 Patricia Bradley Author